claiming pretty

LOVELY BROKEN DOLL
book three

USA TODAY BESTSELLING AUTHOR
SIENNA BLAKE

CLAIMING PRETTY

LOVELY BROKEN DOLL
BOOK THREE

SIENNA BLAKE

Love doesn't just promise forever. It builds it—brick by brick.

Here's to the ones who love us despite our broken pieces. The ones who don't let go.
And the ones who love us <u>more</u>.

Please consider your mental health before deciding to read this novel.

THE WARDEN

I followed Ava into my father's secret Blackthorn laboratory, my nerves stretched taut, every instinct on edge as I braced for whatever secrets this place held.

The sconces flickered to life, their faint yellow glow barely cutting through the heavy shadows that clung to the room. The air was dense, choking, thick with the sharp tang of chemicals mingled with a sickly-sweet musk I knew too well.

Ava was ahead of me, but she was just out of reach, her shoulders tense as she moved silently between the workbenches.

Her silence was heavier than the room itself.

But I could tell she could feel my presence behind her, just like I *felt* her all around me—on my lips, in my arms, around my cock, the memory of her all-consuming heat lingering like an ache.

Ava's guilt radiated so strongly from her it felt like it

seeped into my bones. She was already pulling away, turning into a ghost before my eyes.

A kiss had turned into sex. No therapy to mask it, no punishment to justify it. Just raw, unfiltered need.

She'd kissed me.

She'd *begged* me to fuck her.

No matter how much guilt clouded her eyes now, no matter how much she tried to pretend it didn't happen, I knew it meant something.

Ava *felt* something for me.

Maybe it wasn't the same as what she felt for Ciaran. Her heart still ached for my brother.

And she still hated me. How could she not?

After everything I'd put her through, everything I'd done in the name of saving her.

But something had shifted. There was a crack in the wall she kept between us, and I could feel it.

There was *something* there between us now, buried beneath her anger and the hatred. A thread, fragile but real, connecting us.

Something that was *ours*.

And that was a start.

A spark was all it took to envelop a forest with wildfire. There was a spark between Ava and me. All I had to do was fan it.

I wouldn't give up now. I couldn't.

I'd sacrificed too much, risked too much, to lose her now. Even if it meant I had to break my own brother's heart.

I tried to steel myself against the flood of guilt that threatened to drag me under every time I thought about hurting Ciaran—and how I'd have to destroy him to have her.

My own flesh and blood. My brother. My twin. My mirror. The other half of me.

But she was more important than *anything*.

No matter how far I had to go, no matter what lines I had to cross, I'd make her see that she was mine.

I clenched my fists, forcing the guilt down, burying it deep where it couldn't reach me. This wasn't a battle I'd lose. Not to Ciaran. He'd crossed that line first.

He'd sworn to protect her, to keep her safe—but never to touch her.

She was mine. She'd always been mine.

But he'd stolen her anyway, justifying it because he thought I was dead.

Could I really blame him?

I watched Ava as she moved gracefully through the laboratory, her steps light, almost floating, like she was dancing between the shadows.

Her delicate fingers trailed along the shelves, brushing over the dark bottles haphazardly stacked there, her touch reverent and curious.

Her hair fell over those sharp, intelligent eyes, veiling them just enough to make me crave their full focus, as she tilted her head to read the peeling labels written in Latin, her plump lips moving silently around the ingredients, her mouth forming shapes I couldn't look away from.

Was it any wonder he'd fallen for her?

All you had to do was watch her *be.*

Her movements were like music, fluid and captivating,

while her very presence was a song that lodged itself in your soul, demanding you listen.

Ava didn't just exist; she *commanded* attention, effortlessly, unknowingly, like gravity itself bent toward her.

And I couldn't blame Ciaran for wanting her. But I wouldn't forgive him for taking what was mine.

A surge of aching, broken need almost overwhelmed me as I fell in love with her all over again.

I never stopped. Not since the day I watched her step out of the car and lift her face to stare at Blackthorn Hall.

"Ava…" I murmured, reaching for her, my hand brushing against her arm.

Her eyes lifted to meet mine, and in them, I saw everything—desire, conflict, and a guilt so deep that almost made me look away. Almost.

She pulled back, her movement sharp, as if my touch had burned her.

The sting of rejection hit me harder than I wanted to admit, a twisting ache in my chest.

Rising fears clawed at the edges of my thoughts—had I gone too fast? Misread her? By reaching for her, had I only pushed her further away?

The thought settled like ice in my stomach. *I was losing her.* Again.

She cleared her throat. "There's got to be something here… answers."

Her shoulders tensed as she avoided my gaze, feigning interest in the rows of journals stacked on the heavy mahogany desk at the far end of the lab.

I wanted to speak, to pull her back from whatever edge

she was teetering on, but every step I took closer to her, she seemed to pull farther away.

I clenched my jaw, letting my eyes scan the room as I wrestled with my tangled emotions, layering them with ice until I felt calm once again.

On the rows of cluttered workbenches stretched out before me were glass beakers and vials, some filled with strange, dusty substances, others stained with the remnants of experiments long evaporated, crowded every surface. The hollow clink of glass echoed faintly as my sleeve brushed against a bench, the sound sharp enough to make me flinch.

"This…" Ava's voice broke the brittle silence. "I've seen this before."

I followed her to the desk, my pulse quickening.

Her gaze was locked on a journal, her hand brushing over the crest embossed on the worn cover, snakes twisted in a circular Celtic knot.

"Dr. Vale," she murmured, her voice distant. "He had this emblem engraved on his signet ring."

A chill ran down my spine as the pieces began to fall into place. "You're sure?"

She nodded, her throat bobbing as she swallowed hard.

"And… and Mr. Byrne," she continued, her voice shaking now. "Liath's father—he had a ring on his finger, just like this. The same crest."

I stared over her shoulder as she opened the journal to the first page.

My chest tightened. I knew that handwriting.

It belonged to my father.

A familiar chill slithered down my spine, but my blood

turned to ice when my eyes landed on a single name etched onto the page.

Mona.

My mother.

Ava gasped softly, her fingers clutching the edges of the journal as she quickly closed it. "Ty... you shouldn't see this."

Her voice was careful, like she thought I might shatter if I looked too closely.

But I already knew. The weight of the journal, the name, the handwriting—it all fell into place like a grim puzzle. A sick, dreadful certainty settled in my gut.

This was it. The journal my father had kept for his "research." The one he used to document every monstrous experiment he'd done to my mother.

The world tilted for a moment, rage rising like bile in my throat. I clenched my fists, swallowing hard against the storm brewing inside me.

"Let me see it," I demanded, my voice sharper than I intended.

Ava turned to face me, concern etched into her features. "Ty, no. This... this isn't something you want to read."

"I don't *want* to read it," I said, my voice cracking under the weight of my emotions. "I *need* to."

She hesitated, her brow furrowing as if she was searching for the right words to protect me from myself.

"The truth will set you free?" she murmured, trying to comfort me.

I shook my head, the bitterness seeping into my voice. "No. But lies will imprison you."

Ava studied me for a long moment before letting out a quiet sigh.

Slowly, deliberately, she placed the journal down on the table between us. Her hands lingered on the cover for a moment, reluctant to open it again.

I didn't wait. My hands closed over hers, her warm touch grounding me, and together we opened the journal.

Whatever was inside, whatever horrors awaited, we would face them together.

I could barely focus on the words as Ava slowly turned the pages, everything becoming a blur.

But the journal entries seemed to be broken up with strange chapter headings—*Silver Moth, The Raven, The Dark Queen.*

What the hell did they mean?

"Oh my God, Ty," Ava said as she stopped at an entry.

Midnight's Daughter.

I leaned closer, my gaze dropping to the worn page. The ink was faded in places, but my father's precise, clinical handwriting stood out in stark contrast.

"Look." Her finger hovered over the list of "ingredients" halfway down the page, pointing it out like it held the key to something she couldn't yet say aloud.

My eyes narrowed as I scanned the words.

Curare.

Lycorine.

Scopolamine.

My stomach twisted when I realized what I was reading.

"This…" My voice faltered. "This is a recipe."

Those headings, those strange entries… were drug concoctions born from his experiments.

I shuddered, thinking of how much my mother must have endured at the hands of a madman.

"A recipe for the memory suppressors," she finished, her tone brittle but steady. "The ones my therapist gave to me. And to Liath."

Her words hit me like a blow, sharp and unforgiving.

I swallowed hard, the sharp tang of chemicals in the air suddenly unbearable.

"I began to suspect my father was involved in something… dark," I admitted, my jaw tightening. "But this…"

This was more sickening than I could have ever imagined in my vilest nightmare.

Ava nodded, flipping the page.

"And this," she said, her voice dropping. "This is how to distill oleander into a tasteless, odorless, but lethal tea."

The air froze around me, her words striking a chord so deep it felt like a knife in my chest as I stared at the formula on the page.

"The tea that killed your mother," Ava whispered, almost to herself.

My hands curled into fists, nails biting into my palms as rage flared, hot and all-consuming.

If my father weren't already rotting in the ground, I'd have gladly sent him there again.

Without thinking, I snatched another journal off the desk, needing to do something, anything to keep from shattering. The pages fell open to what looked like a diary filled with cryptic entries and symbols I didn't understand.

Codewords, riddled with meaning that eluded me.

But a single word drew into frightening focus—*Sochai*.

Irish for *Society*.

My fingers trembled as I flipped through the journal, each entry a fresh wave of frustration.

"Are you okay?" Ava's voice was soft, her touch light as her fingers brushed my arm.

I froze, her concern cutting through the anger, but I couldn't let it take hold. Couldn't let it pull me from the edge I was balancing on.

I won't be okay. Not until this is over. Not until Ava is mine.

"We have to go back to Darkmoor," I said, meeting her eyes, the truth settling like a stone between us. "We have to end this."

The words carried more than a plan; they carried a promise—a vow. No more running, no more hiding in the shadows.

This time, it would end, one way or another.

"But first..." Reaching into my pocket, I pulled out the vial I'd been carrying, holding it up between us. The liquid inside glinted faintly in the dim light. A promise and a threat.

This wasn't over—not by a long shot.

"...time for your final session."

AVA

T he vial felt heavy in my hand, far heavier than it should have, the liquid inside catching the faint light of the laboratory sconces.

I hesitated as I stared at Ty.

His eyes, sharp and unreadable, locked on mine, and I felt the weight of the moment pressing down on me like a suffocating shroud.

"No sex," I said, my voice wavering despite my attempt to sound firm.

He tilted his head, his expression unreadable, but I could see the way my words settled on him, like he was turning them over, weighing them. His silence stretched, thick and heavy.

I shifted under his gaze, feeling exposed.

"You didn't protest last time," he said finally, a smirk tugging at his lips. "In fact, you *liked* it. More than liked it. You *begged* for it."

Shame slammed into me, hot and suffocating, a flush rising to my cheeks. The memory clawed its way to the surface, my desperate plea barely out of my lips before his cock thrust into me, the way I had let him consume me, the way I pulled him in closer despite everything. Despite the guilt.

Despite Ciaran.

"No sex," I repeated, forcing the words past the constriction in my throat, refusing to meet his eyes. My voice cracked, betraying the storm churning inside me.

Ty's gaze didn't waver, piercing and unrelenting, as if he could see every thought, every conflicted emotion that I was desperately trying to bury.

After what felt like an eternity, he nodded slowly. "As you wish."

Relief barely had a chance to settle in before he stepped closer, so close I could feel the warmth radiating from him, his lips hovering just inches from mine. My breath hitched, my chest tightening as my heart thundered in betrayal of my resolve.

"But mark my words, hummingbird," he murmured, his voice low, a dark promise that sent a shiver racing down my spine, "before this is over, you'll be begging me to fuck you again."

I sucked in a sharp breath, my gaze helplessly drawn to his mouth. The pull was magnetic, instinctive, and my traitorous body leaned forward before I could stop myself, desire twisting inside me, sharp and unforgiving.

I tore my gaze away, stumbling back like his presence had burned me.

"I-I won't," I stammered, though the words felt weak, hollow, even to me.

He didn't answer, but his smirk said everything he didn't need to, cutting through me like a blade.

My hands trembled as I brought the vial to my mouth, the glass pressing against my lips like ice.

I tipped it back, the liquid sliding down my throat with a strange mix of sweetness and sharp medicinal bitterness, like strawberries tinged with steel.

My last session.

I would uncover the truth, even though every nerve in my body screamed that I didn't want to know. Not really.

But there was no turning back now.

My stomach twisted, nerves and dread tangling into a knot that wouldn't loosen.

I'm going to remember what I did. The thought echoed, sharp and relentless.

But it wasn't just the threat of buried memories that had me on edge.

Ty stood nearby, orbiting me, his presence electric, magnetic. Every step closer, every lean in, every casual touch sent shivers down my spine, the kind that weren't entirely from fear. His nearness was edged in guilt now, a guilt I felt every time our eyes met.

I don't want him.

I repeated this to myself like a mantra, over and over, trying to smother the ache in my chest, the warmth that crept through me every time he was near.

It's just the adrenaline. Leftover panic from almost dying at the farmhouse. The memory of fear, the rush of relief, all tangled together in a way my mind couldn't separate.

I'd read about trauma bonds somewhere, how near-death experiences could flood your body with endorphins, tricking your brain into craving comfort, connection. Lust.

That had to be it—just my shattered psyche playing cruel tricks on me.

And then there was Stockholm Syndrome. I'd read about that too. How captives could confuse dependence and fear for something else, something softer, something that felt like care. Like love.

That's all this was. A trick of biology. A cocktail of chemicals in my traumatized brain, twisting reality until I couldn't tell the difference between gratitude and longing. Between survival and desire.

It wasn't real.

But when the paralytic took hold of me and Ty pulled me into his arms, holding me close, my body betrayed me, my skin burning where his hands pressed against me.

He laid me out gently on the hard surface of the workbench, the chill seeping through my clothes as the drug took over, locking me in place.

The smell of the lab filled my senses, sharp and chemical, mingling with that all-too-familiar musk of the drug.

It was suffocating.

But then a breeze swept in through the door Ty had left open, soft and unexpected, carrying with it the earthy scent of the greenhouse beyond.

And then I felt him—Ty's lips trailing along my neck, slow and deliberate, down my body. Each kiss left damp patches on my skin that cooled in the breeze, sending shivers racing down my spine.

His touch was gentle as he pulled off my dress, his

fingers gliding over my skin with a tenderness that felt so at odds with the storm of guilt raging inside me.

I hated myself for how much I craved his touch.

This is the last time. The final session. The final excuse.

After tonight, there'd be no more reason for Ty to be this close, to touch me like this. No more twisted therapy to blur the lines I kept trying to draw between us.

After this, I'd go back to Ciaran. Back to the one I loved.

But the thought felt hollow, an ache settling in my chest at the realization.

I shouldn't feel this way—not about Ty, not when every touch sent warmth rushing through me, a warmth I had no right to feel.

I shouldn't be sad that this was the last time.

I shouldn't want him to keep touching me, shouldn't want his nearness to last a little longer.

What's wrong with me?

Ciaran would hate me if he knew. It would break him to see what I felt—to see me like this, letting Ty so close, feeling *this* for his brother. He'd look at me with those intense eyes, full of betrayal, full of heartbreak, and I wouldn't even be able to blame him.

I'm betraying him. I'm betraying him right now.

My throat tightened as Ty's tongue brushed over my pussy, his growl vibrating through me.

"Fuuuuuck, your scent… your smell… everything about you intoxicates me."

My body begged for more, even as my mind screamed to pull away.

I wanted to hate him for making me feel like this. For making me weak.

But the truth was, I hated myself more. Hated myself for the excuses I kept trying to make—that this was just the therapy, just the leftover tension from the paralytic, just my body reacting to his touch, to his tongue, nothing more.

But that wasn't true, and I knew it.

I hated that I wanted this. That I wanted *him.* Hated that I wasn't strong enough to stop it, to shove these feelings back down where they belonged.

I was supposed to love Ciaran. I *did* love him. So why did I crave Ty's mouth, his tongue, his *cock*? Why did he… consume me?

It wasn't just guilt eating at me. It was anger—at myself, at Ty, at his fucked-up way of saving me. Anger that Ty made me feel anything at all.

Anger that I wanted more than just his lapping tongue— I wanted him to pin me down and fuck me, to take me, to ruin me.

Even now, knowing it was wrong, knowing it would hurt Ciaran if he ever found out.

But deeper than the anger, deeper than the guilt, there was a grief I couldn't ignore.

This was the last time I'd get to feel Ty like this. The last time I'd let myself have this moment, however fleeting, however stolen.

The last time he'd worship me, touch me, *see* me.

After this, I'd have to bury it all. Pretend none of it ever happened. Pretend I hadn't betrayed Ciaran.

And yet… I knew this wouldn't be the last time I thought about him.

Ty had burrowed under my skin in a way I couldn't undo, no matter how much I tried.

Waves of pleasure washed over me and I could feel the tension building inside me as Ty licked and sucked.

"Mine. All mine. Only mine. Only me," he muttered.

I fought against the wave of guilt and longing, but it didn't help. The feelings churned inside me, sharp and relentless, leaving me drowning in a storm of emotions I couldn't control.

Why can't I let him go?

As my head rolled to the side, my gaze fell upon the greenhouse through the open door. The oleander flowers swayed gently in the breeze, their delicate pink blooms almost taunting me.

And then the memory hit me—sharp, sudden, and undeniable.

I slipped through the greenhouse, the cool, damp air making me shiver, weaving between the tables laden with pots and tools.

The oleander stood tall, its pink blossoms swaying gently as if they were waiting for me.

A flower that could make someone sleep in small doses—and kill in larger ones. At the time, I hadn't understood why the professor had said this with such pride, but now the memory lingered, sharp and unrelenting.

Using the handkerchief, I reached out, wrapping my shaking fingers around the stem of a soft and fragile oleander flower and plucked it, the faint snap of the stem sounding louder than it should have in the stillness.

I quickly snatched another, then another.

I didn't understand why the professor did what he did last night, why his hands left bruises on my arms and thighs, why he... hurt me. Bile rose in my throat, bitter as poison.

But I knew I didn't want it to happen again.

My chest tightened, the thought pressing down on me like a weight.

If he's asleep, he can't hurt me again.

In the kitchen, my bare feet were silent against the cold floor.

My hand shook as I tossed the oleander flowers into the professor's favorite pot along with the professor's favorite tea, watching them float and settle in the boiling water, their poison steeping, growing darker with every passing second.

The sharp scent of the brew tickled my nose, metallic and faintly bitter, and my stomach twisted.

My hands hovered over the pot as doubt began to creep in. Is this enough to make him sleep? Or too much?

"What are you doing?"

A voice shattered the silence, and I jumped.

Ciaran stood in the doorway, his sharp eyes narrowing at me.

I gasped. How long had he been watching me? Did he know what I was doing?

Panic clawed at my chest. He'll tell. He'll get me in trouble.

"I..." My voice came out on a croak. I swallowed and tried again. "I was just making tea... for the professor."

His glare didn't falter. I had no idea if he knew what I had been trying to do.

Ciaran's gaze flicked past me to the teapot. His frown deepened as he walked toward it, his steps slow and deliberate, like a predator cornering its prey. "Brownnosing little Ava. Trying to become the professor's favorite, huh?"

I stepped in his path, my arms spreading out instinctively.

"Go away," I said.

He didn't stop. He shoved me aside with a hand on my shoulder, not hard, but enough to make me stumble back.

"It's not for you!" My voice cracked as I lunged forward, my hands fumbling for the teapot. "It's for the professor!"

Ciaran snatched the pot off the counter and held it high above my head.

"For the professor, is it?" he said, his tone dripping with fake sweetness. "A little bedtime brew?"

My breath caught in my throat. Did he know? Was he guessing? My stomach churned as his smirk twisted into something sharper.

Tears stung my eyes as I tried to grab it, jumping to reach it, but he was taller, stronger, and far more stubborn. "Give it back."

"What's wrong, Ava?" he asked, stepping closer, towering over me. "Don't want me to have a taste?"

"Don't drink it!" I cried, tugging at his arm, but he twisted away, keeping the teapot out of reach.

He shoved me back, hard enough to make me stumble into the counter, his voice low and menacing. "Get. Out."

I turned and fled the kitchen, my heart hammering as tears burned hot against my cheeks.

Oh God. What had I almost done?

I couldn't move as the paralytic held my body frozen, unable to cry out *stop* as Ty licked my soaked pussy while he pushed two fingers inside and curled them around.

I hurtled toward the edge, the rush of pleasure coursing through me as I fought against the paralytic's hold, torn between wanting more and desperately needing it to end.

The orgasm hit me hard, my whole body trembling as the pleasure crashed over me along with a dislodged memory, the last piece falling in place.

The moment I stepped into the sitting room, the world tilted beneath me, the floor dropping away as if I'd stepped into a void. A sharp gasp escaped my lips.

Ciaran stood there, looming over the professor's motionless body, his broad shoulders rigid with tension. Despite the tautness of his stance, his breaths were steady—controlled, deliberate. Too controlled.

My gaze fell to the figure sprawled on the floor, the professor's lifeless form unnaturally still.

I'd never seen human skin so pale before. It wasn't just bloodless—it was translucent, almost waxy.

The oriental rug beneath my feet muffled my steps as I tiptoed closer, each hesitant move adding to the oppressive silence.

My heart hammered against my ribs, yet it wasn't fear that twisted in my chest—not quite.

"Is he...?" I asked, my voice barely audible, the unspoken question choking me.

Was he asleep or...?

Ciaran's head turned to meet my gaze, his eyes unflinching, cold, and utterly unrepentant.

"He won't ever hurt you again," he said, his voice calm, almost detached.

There wasn't a shred of guilt in his tone. No apology. No hesitation. He didn't even flinch.

I swallowed hard, my throat dry, as a storm of emotions roared inside me, crashing and colliding.

Relief, disbelief, guilt—all tangled together so tightly I couldn't pull them apart.

"What's going on here?" Ty's voice rang out behind me, sharp and filled with tension, as he stepped into the room.

His gaze snapped to the professor's body and he froze, his expression darkening, his eyes wide with realization.

"Father's dead," Ciaran said flatly, his voice like a blade cutting through the air.

My gaze drew to the table where the teapot sat there, innocuous and still, its spout tilted slightly toward the edge of the tray.

My teapot.

My tea.

My knees buckled, and before I could hit the floor, Ty caught me, his strong arms wrapping around my trembling frame.

The truth slammed into me like a freight train.

"I did it," I whispered, my voice barely audible, yet it echoed in the room, undeniable and damning.

Ty's arms tightened around me, his body a shield against the chaos, but I couldn't stop the guilt from swallowing me whole.

My tea.

My plan.

My fault.

"I killed him."

I had killed my foster father.

Not Ciaran. He lied to me about killing his father to protect me from the truth.

Not Ty. Who took the blame and went to jail to protect me from the punishment.

Me.

THE SHADOW

I kneeled in front of my brother's grave and pressed the blade I'd named in his honor against my stomach, its cold steel biting into my skin.

I imagined Ty laughing from deep below the earth where he lay.

"Forgive me, Ty," I whispered to the wind as it whipped through the towering yew and cypress trees flanking the winding gravel paths of Glasnevin Cemetery, their gnarled branches entwined above to create shadowy arches.

Around me, Celtic crosses and ornate Victorian head-stones jutted from the earth, their once-crisp inscriptions eroded by the relentless touch of time, some markers leaning precariously, bowed under the weight of decades, their surfaces cloaked in moss and lichen.

The same way I was bowed over Ty's grave.

If I couldn't rest beside Ava, then I'd lie here, near my brother.

They were the only two people I loved. The only two who mattered.

"If she's gone, then..." My voice cracked, the words catching in my throat. "I don't want to live."

I sucked in a breath, trying to summon the courage to do what needed to be done. I closed my eyes, willing myself forward, the weight of everything pressing down on me like a storm I couldn't outrun. And I—

My phone buzzed.

The sound jolted me, breaking through the haze of despair.

My jaw clenched, irritation flaring at the interruption. *Of all the times—*

I closed my eyes tighter, gripping the knife harder, trying to block out the noise. I was so close. Just a breath away from ending this torment.

The phone buzzed again.

I growled under my breath, scowling as I dropped the knife with a soft thud onto the grass beside me.

My hand shot to my pocket, pulling out the phone with shaking fingers, ready to silence whatever had dared to intrude.

Then I saw it—the notification. And I froze.

Ava's name.

For a moment, I couldn't breathe, couldn't think, my mind racing to catch up.

The program I'd written, the one I'd set to bug Ebony's mansion phone, had just triggered.

An alert every time Ava's name was mentioned. My thumb hovered over the screen as my heart thundered in my chest.

I tapped it, activating the playback.

"Ebony? It's me. Ava."

Her voice. Her voice—so familiar, so real—stabbed into me like a knife, but not one of pain. Relief flooded through me, sharp and overwhelming, washing over the despair like a tide, leaving me breathless.

She was alive.

I let out a strangled gasp, my vision blurring as tears welled up. My chest shook, and I nearly started sobbing right there in the cold dirt beside Ty's grave.

Every ounce of the weight crushing me seconds ago evaporated, replaced by something I couldn't name. Relief. Hope. A sliver of salvation.

I clutched the phone tighter, my pulse thundering in my ears.

She was alive. And I wasn't going to let her slip away again.

My breath caught, the rush of relief faltering as a new, sharper fear clawed its way up my throat. *What if it's a trick? A trap?*

I stared at the phone in my hand, my heart pounding so loudly I could barely think.

The Society—they were clever, ruthless. What if they'd figured it out? What if they knew I was the one getting rid of their members? They could be threatening her, forcing her to say those words.

I glanced over to the dead Dr. Hickey lying nearby, eyes lifeless and mouth open in a final plea.

Dr. Vale.

Mr. Byrne, Liath's adopted father.

Mr. Heeley. Sarah's father.

And now Dr. Hickey. Keela's father.

Luring me out would be the perfect move.

My thumb hesitated over the screen, my pulse quickening. *It could be doctored. Her voice, her words—* I hit replay, needing to hear it again.

"Ebony? It's me. Ava."

I listened closely, analyzing every inflection, every breath.

I'd know Ava's voice anywhere. It haunted me in my sleep. It was *her*, raw and unpolished, the same tone she always used when she was trying to sound calm but wasn't.

Still, the knot of panic refused to loosen.

Ebony's voice, warm and familiar, broke through the static. *"Oh, my darling girl. It's been so long. I thought you were in Croatia for the rest of the holidays?"*

Croatia? That didn't make sense.

My brows furrowed as I leaned closer, straining to catch every word.

"Oh, yeah. Right." Ava's voice, quick and awkward, carried that telltale hesitation I knew too well. *"I thought I'd surprise everyone, caught an early flight home. Only, uh, my flight to Dublin got redirected... I'm stuck near Shannon Airport."*

My mind raced, caught between the flood of relief that she was alive and the gnawing doubt that something far more dangerous was going on.

Shannon? Why Shannon? That was on the literal other side of Ireland. And why the hesitation?

Ava was a terrible liar, but why would she lie to Ebony about where she'd been? Why wouldn't she tell Ebony the truth? Why not say she'd been kidnapped?

If anyone would believe her, it was Ebony. She was a surgeon; she'd had enough broken people on her table to know how dark this world could get.

Unless… Ava didn't want to scare her.

That sounded like Ava. Always trying to protect people, even when it was she who needed protecting. Always so damn stubborn, carrying the weight of the world on her shoulders, like she had something to prove.

But the thought didn't ease the knot in my stomach. If she was alive—and it really was her—then she was still in danger. Whatever lie she was spinning, it meant she didn't feel safe enough to tell the truth.

That was enough to make my blood run cold.

How the hell did she escape from the Society? The thought ricocheted through my mind, sharp and unrelenting.

Nobody escaped them. Not without help. Not without blood.

Was it even possible?

Ava wasn't weak, far from it, but the Society didn't let its prey go willingly. She couldn't have overpowered them, not on her own. So how? Who helped her? *Why* had they let her live?

The Society didn't leave loose ends.

If she'd escaped, they'd be hunting her. And if she hadn't escaped… I clenched my teeth as a cold knot of suspicion formed in my gut.

What if this wasn't an escape at all? What if they *let* her go? That thought twisted like a blade in my side.

The Society didn't take chances. If she was free, it was because they wanted her to be. They'd use her, turn her into a trap, a pawn in a game I wasn't even seeing yet.

I rubbed my temples, trying to think, to focus. If Ava had escaped, it wasn't a miracle—it was a move. A deliberate, calculated move. And I needed to figure out who had made it… before they used her to destroy us both.

"*Could you send someone to pick me up?*" Ava's voice wavered, just enough to set my nerves on edge.

"*Of course, Ava,*" Ebony replied, her voice softening, warm with relief. "*I've… I've missed you.*"

"*I've missed you too, Ebony,*" Ava said, and I could hear the crack of emotion in her tone, the kind of vulnerability she rarely let show.

My chest tightened, the weight of everything pressing in on me suddenly lighter, as if I could finally take a full breath.

Ava was alive. She was really alive.

The words replayed in my head, over and over, like a lifeline I hadn't realized I was gripping.

She was coming home.

And I would be there to meet her.

AVA

T he police officer loomed over me, his judgmental gaze flicking between me and the body on the floor. "What happened here?" he demanded.

I opened my mouth to answer, to confess, my body trembling with the weight of the truth. I took a step forward.

But Ty moved faster.

He stepped in front of me, his hand brushing mine for the briefest moment before shoving me behind him. He pushed me hard into Ciaran's arms, shielding me with his body.

"I did it," he said, his voice steady, unshaken. "I poisoned him."

"No!" The word tore out of me, raw and desperate. "Ty—"

"Quiet, Ava." He turned on me, his glare like a whip, sharp and commanding, forcing the protest to die on my tongue. Then his eyes shifted to Ciaran, whose face had gone ashen.

"Keep her calm," he snapped.

And then it hit me—what he was doing.

He was taking the blame.

"Ty, no!" I screamed again, my voice breaking, but it didn't matter.

29

Ciaran's hand clamped over my mouth, silencing me with a firm grip.

"Quiet, Ava," he hissed, his voice strained, his hold on me anything but steady.

My vision blurred as the officer snapped handcuffs onto Ty's wrists, securing them behind his back. The metallic click echoed like a death knell in the room. They began leading him away, the officer's grip firm and unyielding.

"No!" I struggled harder, my voice muffled against Ciaran's palm.

Ty twisted his head, his gaze locking on me for a fleeting second. "Wait," he said, his voice sharp and desperate. "I just need to talk to Ava—"

"No talking," the officer barked, shoving him toward the door.

Ty's body tensed, his shoulders pulling back in defiance, but another officer grabbed his other arm, hauling him forward like a caged animal.

I felt Ciaran falter behind me, his hold loosening just enough.

I slammed my elbow into his stomach with all the force I could muster. He let out a guttural groan, his grip releasing.

"Ava, no!" he gasped, but it was too late.

I bolted after Ty.

The rain hit me the moment I burst through the mansion's front doors, cold and slicing, soaking through my thin dress. Red and blue lights painted the sprawling lawn, illuminating the gravel drive and the blackthorn trees lining the estate. I felt like I was drowning in those lights, the colors spinning and blurring as my bare feet skidded against the wet gravel.

"Ty!" I screamed, my voice hoarse, almost swallowed by the storm.

Ciaran's strong arms wrapped tight around my shaking body, holding me back.

I saw Ty in handcuffs, fighting against the officers who were trying to drag him toward the police car.

Ty shouted at me, eyes wild like a trapped animal, but all I could hear was the roar of blood rushing in my ears.

The crack of the officer's knuckles against his cheekbone brought sound crashing back in.

I heard officers shouting and rain splattering. For a moment his head hung heavy between his shoulders, most of his weight supported by the men dragging him backward.

But as they opened the door to the police car to shove him in, he lifted his head and found me with his gaze.

His eye was already swollen from the knuckles of the police officer's brutal fist. But the pain etched across his face was deeper than the darkest bruise.

He screamed, "I love you more!"

"Wake up, Ava."

A soft nudge pulled me from the depths of sleep, and I blinked groggily, the world outside the car window a blur of dark shapes and scattered lights.

"We're almost there," Ty said, his voice low, smooth, and calm in the quiet hum of the car.

I sat up straighter, my heart stuttering in my chest as I looked out the window.

The familiarity hit me like a punch, sharp and disorienting.

The neat rows of grand old Victorian mansions stretched along either side of the street, set back from the road, their facades steeped in history, their wide, sweeping drives flanked by towering birch and oak trees, their heavy wrought-iron gates gleaming in the soft light of gas-style lanterns lining the cobblestone sidewalks.

My stomach twisted, nerves churning as I tried to process the flood of emotions rushing through me. Anticipation, dread, hope—it was all tangled together, suffocating.

It all looked exactly the same. Like nothing had changed in the three months since I was taken.

But *everything* had changed.

I was a murderer.

I had killed Ty's father—*Ciaran's* father.

I hadn't meant to. God only knows, I hadn't. I just wanted him to *stop*. The tea was supposed to make him sleepy, nothing more.

But I must have put in too many flowers. Too much oleander. Too much poison.

And Ciaran—poor, clueless Ciaran—had taken the tea to his father, unaware of the deadly concoction he was handing over. He didn't know he was delivering a death sentence.

But I did. *I did this.*

Did that make *me* a monster?

The question twisted in my mind, sharp and jagged. I hadn't planned to kill him. But when I'd thrown up that drugged hot chocolate, I had been too awake.

I had remembered.

And then he'd taken me to the hospital… left me alone for a week.

But then the bruises started again.

I had wanted him gone. Wanted the fear and bruises to end. Deep down, hadn't I known what I was doing? Hadn't I known that oleander wasn't just for sleep? Had I really miscalculated… or had some part of me wanted it to happen?

That night at Mr. Buckley's farmhouse still haunted me, but I felt no guilt killing the masked men who had come after me.

Self-defense felt… justified. They'd come for me, and I fought back.

I was a survivor. I did what I had to do that night to survive.

With the professor, it wasn't the same, was it?

They were faceless men.

But the professor was a father to two boys, a complicated man who was tough but who loved his sons fiercely.

I had options, didn't I? I could have gone to Ty. Told him everything. He would have listened, right?

The professor's voice crept into my thoughts, cutting through my attempt to rationalize. His low, menacing tone echoed in my head, sending a shiver down my spine.

"My sweet, sweet girl, this is our little secret. Besides, even if you told anyone, no one would believe you."

The memory tightened my chest, shame and fear swirling together in a nauseating cocktail. I'd been so sure back then that he was right. That if I tried to tell Ty, he wouldn't believe me.

The professor was *his* father, after all. A man Ty respected. Looked up to. Loved.

What if Ty turned on me? What if he sided with the professor and not me? What if telling him made everything worse?

I'd been on my own. No one to turn to, no one to trust.

But none of that erased the truth: the professor—Ty and

Ciaran's father, their only other family—was dead. *Because of me.*

Was that why Ty kept me locked up? Had he been subconsciously punishing me? Had he actually never forgiven me even though he said he did?

Ciaran only told me he'd killed the professor because he'd been masquerading as Ty. But did he know? Could he forgive me?

Could I forgive myself?

And then there was the nagging voice in the back of my mind, cruel and insistent. *He deserved it.*

The man I'd poisoned wasn't just a victim. He was a monster. He had hurt me, hurt others, twisted his power into something vile.

Didn't I do the world a favor? Didn't I save myself, save Ciaran, save countless others from his cruelty?

I shook my head, disgusted at the thought. That wasn't justice. That was murder. It didn't matter what he'd done. It didn't change the fact that his life ended at my hands. *What does that make me?*

I glanced over at Ty, seeking something—stability, reassurance, maybe even distraction—but the moment our eyes met, my breath hitched.

He was already looking at me, his gaze steady and intense, even as he drove slowly down the quiet street. No cars. No people. Just the two of us.

The weight of his stare made my chest tighten. Before I could look away, his hand slid over mine.

His touch was warm, grounding, but it only made the chaos inside me worse. He opened his mouth, like he was gearing up to say something—something important.

I couldn't handle it.

I tore my eyes away, yanking my hand out from under his.

The loss of contact was immediate, but I ignored the pang it brought, reaching for the radio and flicking it on in one jerky motion.

Anything to fill the silence, to avoid whatever he was about to say.

"Ava, you can't avoid talking to me forev—"

"Shh," I snapped, twisting the volume knob to drown him out. My stomach flipped as the announcer's voice cut through the tension.

"...Darkmoor student Marie McConnell, who went missing last week, has tragically been found dead. Preliminary reports from the coroner's office suggest she was poisoned by a drug derived from oleander..."

The words hit me like a blow, a cold shock spreading through my veins.

Oleander. My foster father's vile recipe. The Sochai.

This is the Society cleaning up.

My hands clenched into fists in my lap. My stomach churned, nausea rising as the weight of the truth pressed down on me.

If we didn't take them down, if we didn't stop them—*I'm next.*

I glanced at Ty again, but he kept his gaze locked on the road, his jaw tight, his hands gripping the wheel a little too hard.

He was thinking the same thing. I could feel it. The unspoken fear, the urgency crackling like static in the air.

The car slowed as we pulled up to the gates of my

mansion in Dublin, the wrought-iron looming dark and silent against the backdrop of the glowing city beyond.

I stared at it, my chest tightening further.

Home.

But the word didn't feel right anymore. I felt like an intruder, like somehow I didn't belong here anymore.

My gaze shifted to the mansion next door—the one Ciaran had been living in. Its windows were dark, the porch light extinguished, leaving it shrouded in shadows.

A pang of uncertainty gripped me. Was he still there? Had he waited for me, night after night, hoping I'd come back? Had he been looking for me? Or had he left, given up, moved on?

The thought twisted painfully in my chest, but deep down, I knew the truth.

Ciaran wouldn't stop looking for me. He couldn't. No matter how much time had passed, no matter what had changed, he would never give up on me.

He *loved* me.

Another wave of fear twisted in my stomach, tangling with the other emotions already flooding me.

How would Ciaran react to what happened over the summer? To what I'd done? To *me*? Would everything still feel the same between us, or had everything changed for him too?

The car rolled to a stop, and Ty turned to me, his smirk breaking the tension in a way that felt too easy, too deliberate.

"Welcome home, hummingbird."

The nickname made me blink, caught off guard.

"Why do you call me that?" I asked, my voice quieter than I intended.

His smirk deepened, his eyes glittering with a private meaning he didn't share. "Maybe one day I'll tell you," he said, his tone teasing, maddeningly cryptic.

Before I could press him, he leaned in. His hand found my chin, tilting my face toward his, and for a moment, all I could feel was his warmth, his presence enveloping me, consuming me.

My breath hitched, my lips parting instinctively as he drew closer, the world narrowing until it was just him.

Just Ty.

And as much as I told myself to stop him, as much as guilt and fear clawed at my chest, I couldn't move.

I didn't want to move.

THE WARDEN

"Welcome home, hummingbird," I said as I pulled the car to a stop in front of Ava's mansion. But the words felt hollow in my throat, a cover for the nerves clawing at my chest.

I hated this place—not the house itself, but what it stood for. What it had become.

My brother had stamped himself all over it, all over *her*. Ciaran had filled it with his memories, his presence, memories that I couldn't erase. A past I couldn't rewrite.

Ava's gaze shifted to me, her voice quiet but piercing as she asked, "Why do you call me that?"

Her question threw me. For a moment, the nerves receded, replaced by a flicker of hope.

She noticed. She noticed my nickname for her.

She might not want to talk about *us*—about what happened between us at Blackthorn Hall—but she cared enough to ask about my nickname's meaning. That had to mean something, didn't it?

Maybe I was delusional, but I couldn't help it. She

wouldn't have asked if she didn't care, if there wasn't a part of her—no matter how small—still tethered to me.

Still mine.

"Maybe one day I'll tell you," I said, letting the words hang between us like a promise.

I leaned in, closing the space between us, drawn to her like gravity itself demanded it.

The air shifted, charged and heavy. Her lips parted slightly, her pupils dilating just enough for me to notice. It was instinctive, unconscious—her body betraying the pull she felt even if her mind was fighting it.

Her lips were soft and inviting, parting on a soft gasp, and for a heartbeat, I forgot everything else as I closed the distance.

She didn't pull back. She didn't turn away.

Her breath hitched, her gaze locked on mine, beckoning me closer.

Her hand pressed against my chest, firm enough to stop me. It hit me harder than any shove could have.

She pulled back, and her gaze dropped, avoiding mine.

"I'm sorry," she whispered, the words laced with something I couldn't place. Guilt? Regret? Pain? "But I'm *with* Ciaran. I… love him."

It was like a knife to the soul, ripping me open, but I didn't flinch. Not outwardly. I couldn't show her how much her words destroyed me.

Her eyes were clouded, her expression unreadable. "You and I… we're just friends. Best friends. It was just… therapy. And now it's over."

I felt the lie in every word she spoke.

Therapy?

Friends?

No. That wasn't what we were. It had never been that simple. The way she'd submitted to me, touched me, *clung* to me—it wasn't clinical. It wasn't just recovery.

She felt it too, the pull between us. She might not be ready to admit it, but I knew.

I stayed silent, my hands tightening on the steering wheel.

She didn't want me to call her out. Not yet. She needed to believe her lie for now, to convince herself she was doing the right thing.

The memory of Ciaran's promise came rushing back, unbidden, sharp and taunting.

"Ty," he hissed, his voice going in and out on the crackling line, "it shouldn't be you in prison."

I'd closed my eyes and pressed my forehead against the hard metal edge of the phone box.

Ciaran sounded on the edge of a breakdown, his emotions always so volatile. "I'll tell the cops that—"

"You'll not say a fucking word," I snarled, gripping the phone so hard the ancient plastic cracked.

There was silence on my brother's end.

I tried to breathe evenly, aware of the officer watching my rounded back. I couldn't lose control like that again. In this cursed place, it could prove fatal.

I needed to ensure that my brother didn't do anything stupid. So I had been forced to call Ciaran instead of who I really wanted to speak to: Ava.

I missed out on my last chance to speak with her. To tell her goodbye. To tell her I loved her.

I knew it would haunt me for years to come, but I was always the one who had to do the hard things. Make the sacrifices. Be the fucking "good guy."

But it would be worth it if she was safe and protected.

"Listen, Ci." It was a struggle to speak as the emotions choked me. "You are going to let me take the blame for Ava or—"

"Ty—"

"Or..." I hissed, "you'll join our father. Do you understand me, brother?"

He was silent, my threat hanging over us.

Maybe he was stunned. Maybe he didn't recognize this version of me—cold, unyielding, capable of saying something so dark. But he needed to understand. There was nothing I wouldn't do for Ava.

Nothing.

Besides, this was my *fault.*

I couldn't believe it when Ava told me she'd killed our father.

"I killed him." The words had shattered something inside me, left me grappling with the truth of what she'd done and why.

And when our butler had entered the room to find his master dead and raced for the phone, Ava ran out into the garden.

I had tried to go after her. But Ciaran held me back.

And then he had told me.

Our father's twisted, sick little secret. A truth he'd only just uncovered himself, but one I should have known all along. One I should have seen.

The revelation had stunned me into silence, a heavy, suffo-cating silence that felt like it would bury me alive.

My father had been hurting Ava. He'd been drugging her—and hurting her.

My Ava.

And I—I hadn't been there to stop it.

The guilt clawed at my chest, relentless and cruel. I should have known. I should have known.

But I was too fucking busy with the debate team, science club, the fucking fencing team.

I should have been home instead. Protecting Ava. Instead of sneaking into her bedroom at night after I got home. Offering her stolen comfort for her nightmares when I should have been stopping her nightmare all along.

I should have been there to protect her. To shield her from the monster in our house.

If I'd known, I would have killed our father myself.

But I hadn't.

And because of that, Ava had been forced to act. To brew that tea, to poison. She'd had to deal with it herself because I hadn't been there for her when it mattered most.

It was my fault. And so now I would pay.

With a sigh, I closed my eyes.

But now with me in prison—with me carrying out my penance —I couldn't protect her. The thought of Ava out there, vulnerable, without me to shield her—it was unbearable.

I didn't beg, least of all beg my brother, for anything. But for Ava I would.

"I know you don't like her," I said, forcing my voice to remain steady. "But please, for me, Ci, promise me you'll look out for her."

"Ty!"

"Please," I begged, cutting his protests off, my voice raw. "She's got no one else. You don't have to talk to her or even let her know you're watching over her. Just... please, until they release me, you have to protect her... for me."

He was silent for a moment, too long, and I felt something sharp twist in my chest.

"Okay."

Relief flooded me, but it wasn't enough. Not yet.

"But swear," I said, my voice cracking, "swear you won't touch her."

Ciaran's voice was a mere whisper. "I promise I will never touch her. She's yours, Ty."

Ciaran had kept one promise.

And broken the other.

He hadn't just protected her—he'd taken her. Stolen the one thing I couldn't bear to lose.

In the car Ava turned away, her fingers reaching for the door handle. She was slipping through my fingers again, and I hated how helpless I felt. How powerless.

But I wasn't done. Not yet. Ava could lie to herself, to me, even to Ciaran. But she couldn't lie to her heart.

I wouldn't give up. Not until she was mine again.

As Ava moved to step out of the car, my hand shot out, wrapping around her arm, stopping her.

Her eyes widened, startled, but I held firm.

"You've always belonged to me," I said, my voice low and unyielding. "And I will prove it to you."

Her expression faltered for just a moment—just long enough for me to catch the flicker of guilt in her eyes. But then she drew in a breath, steadying herself, and when she spoke, her voice was soft but unwavering.

"Maybe if I had fallen for you first," she said quietly, the words landing like a blow, "things would be different. But… it's always been him."

For a second, I couldn't breathe. Her words hit harder than I thought anything could. Harder than all the abuse I suffered in prison. Harder than learning my own flesh and blood had been abusing her.

It's always been him.

The truth of it slammed into me, dragging me into the past, to the moment everything shifted. I remembered the change in her, the way she began to look at Ciaran differently. Like she saw something in him she couldn't find in me.

I remembered the day I climbed into our treehouse to find it empty of her, her scent of jasmine a ghost in the air, and to spot her out the window riding away on the back of *his* motorbike.

I never found out what had happened between them, but now I knew for sure.

Somehow, some way, Ava had fallen for Ciaran.

I had lost her five years ago.

And it seemed I was doomed to keep losing her over and over again.

The McKinsey mansion was unnervingly quiet, like a stage waiting for its actors to take their marks. It was the kind of silence that wrapped around you, pressing in, making every creak of the floorboards feel louder than it should.

I leaned against the doorframe of Ava's bedroom, watching her pace.

She was nervous—flustered even. She kept glancing at herself in the mirror, brushing her hair back into place, her hands fidgeting with invisible wrinkles in her clothes.

I didn't have to guess why.

She wanted to see *him*. Wanted to greet Ciaran alone, to reunite with him.

The thought twisted in my chest like a knife, jealousy threatening to rise. But I forced it down, hardening myself against it. I'd learned how to bury those emotions. I'd had to.

Ava wasn't mine anymore. Not yet.

"I'll be fine," she shot back, trying to push me out of the doorway.

I didn't budge.

"What if the Society's men show up?" I argued.

She rolled her eyes and reached down beside her bed to pull out a small bat. She held it up with a smirk, the wooden handle snug in her grip.

"You taught me to defend myself, remember?" she said, her nervous tension giving way to her usual fire. "Let them come. We'll follow their rolling heads straight back to whoever sent them."

Her confidence was almost enough to make me smile. Almost.

"Cute," I said, my tone sharper than I intended. "But I'm still not leaving you alone."

She opened her mouth, probably to argue—when I heard it.

A sound. Faint, deliberate. Someone was here.

I shushed her, my ears straining against the oppressive quiet. Another noise followed, soft and careful, coming from the balcony.

My muscles coiled, every nerve on high alert.

"Stay back," I said under my breath as I slipped into the shadows of her room.

Ava ignored me, of course. She turned toward the balcony, gripping the bat tightly, her jaw set.

The lock jiggled, the faint metallic rattle sending a ripple of tension through the air.

Then the handle began to turn.

From my place in the dark, I braced to strike.

Ava raised the bat, her knuckles white against the polished wood.

The door opened, and a tall dark figure stepped through.

Ciaran.

Ava's reaction was instant and visceral. She froze, her eyes widening as if she couldn't believe what she was seeing.

The bat clattered to the floor, forgotten.

Her entire face lit up, love and relief flooding her expression in a way that hit me like a punch to the gut.

Ciaran crossed the room in two quick strides, grabbing her and pulling her into his arms.

"Ava," he breathed, his voice raw with emotion. "Is it really you?"

And then he kissed her, his arms crushing her to him as his mouth *claimed* her.

I couldn't look away, no matter how much I wanted to. I watched as her body softened against his, her frame molding to his as if it belonged there, their lips moving together like they'd done this a hundred times before—like she was *his*.

The faintest sound escaped her, a breathless, almost inaudible sigh, and it was like a knife to my chest.

My world narrowed to that single moment, every other sound and sensation fading into the background. Jealousy flared hot and sharp, but deeper than that was the ache—the unrelenting, bitter fear that she would never kiss *me* like that.

I cleared my throat, stepping out of the shadows.

Ava jerked back, her eyes wide as she turned toward me, as if she only just fucking remembered I was here.

Ciaran reacted just as quickly, pulling a knife from his belt and spinning to face me, his stance defensive and ready.

For a moment, I stared at him, at the mirror image of my own face. My twin. My family. My rival.

"Hello, brother," I said, letting a faint smirk curve my lips. "Did you miss me?"

THE SHADOW

"Hello, brother. Did you miss me?"

My feet felt rooted to the floor, my body frozen as I stared across Ava's bedroom, my eyes locked on a ghost.

For a moment, my mind refused to believe what it was seeing.

Ty.

He stood there, leaning casually against the wall like a shadow brought to life.

The same face I'd spent years trying to forget. The same face I saw every time I looked in the mirror. My brother. My *dead* brother.

I blinked hard, my breath catching in my chest.

This wasn't real. It couldn't be.

Ty died in prison months ago. I dropped black roses onto his casket in the ground. I broke down over his fucking grave, and I'd buried the grief deep enough to forget how raw it used to feel.

Had I hit my head? Had Ava's return—her kiss—overwhelmed me so much that my brain had finally cracked? Was I hallucinating him because of the guilt gnawing away at me since the day I broke my promise?

"I promise I will never touch her. She's yours, Ty."

I shot a glance back at Ava, desperate for confirmation, for proof that this wasn't some cruel hallucination conjured by my unraveling mind. That she could see him too. That I wasn't losing my grip on reality.

"He's alive," she said softly, her lips curving into an uncertain smile.

Alive.

The word echoed in my head, ricocheting like a bullet, but it only made the room feel like it was spinning faster.

I turned back to Ty, my chest tight, my pulse erratic. The sight of him, solid and standing there, did nothing to slow the storm in my mind.

"You're alive," I whispered, my voice hoarse, disbelieving. The words felt heavy, foreign, like they didn't belong in my mouth.

Relief slammed into me like a freight train, so powerful it almost brought me to my knees. He was alive. My brother was alive. My twin. My blood. The part of me I thought I'd lost forever.

I took him in, piece by piece, the sheer brutality of his presence cutting through the room like a blade. His figure was harder, sharper, every line of his body carved with purpose.

The coldness in his glare was unrelenting, a stark contrast to the brother I once knew.

Black tattoos snaked across his forearms, dark and menacing, each one an unspoken story I didn't recognize.

The boy I had grown up with was gone, replaced by a man I didn't know—a stranger wearing my brother's face.

"I'm alive," he repeated, his voice low and bitter, as his lips curled into a humorless smirk. "Disappointed?"

Guilt slammed into me like a fist to the gut.

He was alive.

And I'd betrayed him in every way that mattered.

The memory of Ava's lips on mine hit me like a slap, her warmth still lingering, her love etched into every fiber of my being.

My chest tightened as the truth threatened to choke me.

I had broken my promise. I hadn't just touched her. I'd taken her, fallen in love with her, stolen her.

I couldn't even deny it. I had kissed Ava like she was mine right in front of him.

And now Ty stood here, watching me like he knew every shameful thought running through my head.

"What is happening?" I demanded, my tone sharper than I intended as my confusion and panic bubbled to the surface. My head was spinning, and I couldn't put the pieces together fast enough.

I turned to Ava, my gaze hard, desperate. "Where the hell have you been? I thought *you* were dead."

She opened her mouth, but no words came out, her expression caught between guilt and something unreadable.

I swung back to Ty, unable to keep still, unable to think straight.

"And you…" I jabbed a finger toward him, anger and disbelief warring in my chest. "You're supposed to be dead, *too*! What the fuck is going on?"

Ty's smirk faded, his expression darkening, and the weight of his stare made my stomach twist.

I shook my head, trying to make sense of it all, but the answers felt just out of reach, taunting me.

Everything I thought I knew, everything I thought was certain, was unraveling before my eyes.

And the worst part? I wasn't sure I wanted to know the truth.

"Ava, darling." Ty's voice cut through the tension like a blade, calm but sharp enough to draw blood. "Perhaps *you* want to tell him."

Darling?

"Don't call me that," she snapped. Her glare could have melted stone, but Ty didn't even flinch.

She turned to me, her expression shifting, her shoulders tightening as if bracing for impact.

"Ciaran," she said carefully, her voice laced with something that set every nerve in me on edge. "Maybe you should sit down."

My anger flared, hot and uncontrollable, rising like a tidal wave.

"I don't need to sit down," I growled, my voice cutting through the air. "I need someone to tell me what the fuck is going on. Right. Now."

She flinched, just barely, but I caught it. I saw the way her gaze darted away, guilt flashing in her eyes like a warning siren.

The sight of it sent a fresh wave of panic crashing through me, icy and suffocating.

What the hell was she guilty about?

My stomach churned, my fists clenching as my thoughts raced.

Fear slammed into me, sharp and unrelenting. Why had she come back with *him*? Why was my dead brother standing here, alive and looking far too calm, as if he'd been waiting for this moment all along?

And most of all—what did that guilt in her eyes mean? What had she done?

"Well," Ava began, her voice quiet but steady, as if bracing herself for the explosion she knew was coming, "Ty... saved me before Cormac could hand me over to the Society."

My glare snapped to her, my anger boiling over before I could stop it.

"That was three fucking months ago," I spat, my voice rising with every word. "No word. No call. *Nothing.* I thought you were being tortured in a goddamn basement. I thought you were *dead*."

The last word came out louder than I intended, echoing in the room like a gunshot.

Ava shuffled awkwardly, her gaze dropping to the floor, her discomfort painfully obvious.

"I'm sorry," she said, barely above a whisper. "Ty wouldn't let me..."

She trailed off, but she didn't need to finish. The unspoken truth hit me like a hammer to the chest.

Ty kept her from me.

I turned my fury on him, my jaw tightening as the realization crystallized.

"What did you do with her?" I growled, stepping

forward, my fists clenched at my sides. "Where did you take her?"

Ty stood his ground, unbothered by the heat of my rage, his voice calm, almost detached. "I was helping her face her demons."

"You *what?*" I roared, closing the space between us, my face inches from his.

"I took her back to Blackthorn," he said evenly, meeting my gaze without a flicker of hesitation. "I took her *home.*"

The words slammed into me like a truck, leaving me reeling. My mind raced, piecing together the implications of what he'd just said.

Ava remembered. *She knew.*

I spun around, the room tilting beneath me as the weight of it all crashed over me.

I was stunned speechless as my gaze landed on her, her expression a mixture of hurt, guilt, and something I couldn't quite place.

She knew. She knew the lies I'd told her. The things I'd let her believe. The truths I'd buried to protect her.

"Ava..." Her name came out a whisper, an apology already forming on my lips as I stepped toward her, my chest tightening at the pain in her eyes. "Ava, please... we need to talk."

Behind me, Ty chuckled, the sound low and sharp. "Don't let me stop you."

I ignored him. He didn't matter right now. Nothing did except her.

The weight of her gaze was crushing, and all I could think about was explaining, begging for forgiveness if that's what it took.

I'm sorry. I was only trying to protect you.

I took another step toward her, my hand reaching out as if I could erase the hurt with a single touch, but before I could speak, the sound of the front door opening and closing cut through the air.

The click of heels on the stairs followed, precise and deliberate, and then Ebony's voice, expectant but laced with worry, a sharp contrast to the charged atmosphere in the room.

"Ava?"

Ava turned toward the sound, her expression flickering with relief and something else—something I couldn't name.

She must have called Ebony to let her know she was back.

But I wasn't ready for interruptions. Not now, not when everything was unraveling.

"Wait—Ava," I said again, desperate to keep her attention, to say what I needed to say before she could turn away. Before I lost her completely.

"Just a minute, Ebony," Ava called out, her voice steady, too steady. "I'm in the bathroom."

Then she turned to Ty. *To Ty.* Not to me. Her gaze was sharp, her voice low and urgent. "Get him out of here."

The words hit me like a slap, a cold wave crashing over the fire of my anger. *Get him out of here.* Like they were a team. Like they were against me.

Ty didn't hesitate. He grabbed the collar of my shirt, his grip firm and unyielding. Before I could process it, he was dragging me toward the balcony door.

"What the fuck—?" I started to fight him, shoving back against his grip, my fists ready to fly.

But Ty leaned in close, his voice cutting through my fury like steel. "Don't be a fucking eejit. Not here."

His tone was sharp and urgent—a warning.

A crack of logic seeped into my desperation, cooling the reckless edge of my anger.

He was right. Not here. Not now.

We couldn't let Ebony—or her damn bodyguards—catch us here.

I clenched my fists, every muscle in my body screaming for a fight, but I forced myself to nod.

Relief flashed across Ty's face for a brief moment before he pushed the balcony door open, the cool night air rushing in like a slap. He nudged me forward.

I slipped out onto Ava's dark balcony, the faint scent of ivy and damp stone wrapping around us.

Behind me, Ebony's voice drifted through the quiet night, elated and warm. "Ava! My goodness. My driver said you weren't at the Sheraton. What happened to you?"

The stone balustrade was slick under my palm as Ty and I climbed over it, the ivy tangled and twisting, threatening to snag on every step.

My breath came fast and sharp, my pulse pounding in my ears as I led him through the shadows and through a rusted side gate onto the property next door.

And then suddenly I was alone with my *dead* brother.

Ty stared at the front door of the mansion next to Ava's —the one I'd been calling home for the last few months—his eyes lingering on the intricate wrought-iron fixtures, his hands shoved casually into his pockets, like he hadn't just upended my entire world.

"So," he said, his tone infuriatingly casual, "are you going to invite me in?"

I stared at my twin, my mind still trying to process that he was standing there in front of me on the front lawn under the dim moonlight.

You're alive. You're really alive.

Relief crashed over me like a tidal wave, overwhelming and unexpected.

For a moment, the miracle of having him returned to me hit me, and all I wanted was to wrap his arms around him to make sure he was real.

"Fuck, Ty… I…" I began, my voice breaking.

A flicker of emotion crossed his face—something raw, unguarded. For just a second, I saw the Ty I remembered, the boy I grew up with.

"I… missed you too," he said, his voice softer than I expected.

I remembered how I'd watched from afar as his wooden coffin was lowered into the ground, only a priest standing over him, unable to believe that he was gone. I'd stood over his grave, the rain soaking through my clothes, the weight of grief crushing me, feeling like a part of *me* had died.

I'd stared at the gravestone, my vision blurred by tears I couldn't hold back, my knees buckling as I finally let myself break. I'd whispered apologies to the cold, unyielding ground, begged for forgiveness for not being there, for letting him die alone in a prison.

The pain of losing him had carved itself into my chest, a hollow ache I'd thought would never heal.

Now I wondered who had been in his coffin instead,

who I had mourned. And whether my brother had been watching *me* break down over his grave.

My fist connected with his jaw, the impact reverberating up my arm.

"You let me think you were dead!" I roared, the betrayal boiling over, spilling out of me.

He staggered back, his eyes flashing with surprise.

I swung again, and though Ty managed to block the next blow, I felt the heat of my anger driving me forward, unstoppable. "Do you have any idea what that did to me?"

Ty raised his hands, defending himself, but his voice remained maddeningly calm.

"It was unfortunate," he said, sidestepping another punch. "But necessary for my escape from prison. Don't take it so personally."

"Personally?" I laughed bitterly, the sound ripping from my throat. "You could have told me after you escaped. Instead, you let me believe it for months. *Months*, Ty!"

The pieces started to fall into place, the truth settling in my gut like a stone.

He hadn't told me because he hadn't wanted me to know. He hadn't wanted me to suspect that *he* had taken Ava.

This whole time I'd been hunting down the Sochai, and my own fucking brother had her.

Ty and I circled each other on the damp grass, the moonlight casting a ghostly sheen over his face, making his cold eyes seem almost lifeless. Every muscle in my body coiled tight, my breaths shallow as I waited for the right moment to strike.

"You had Ava for *months*," I growled, my voice low,

dangerous. "You could have told me. I was losing my fucking mind thinking she was *dead*."

Ty didn't flinch, his calm demeanor infuriatingly unshaken. "I couldn't let you know I had her. You would have interfered with my plans."

Plans? My stomach twisted at the word. What plans? *What the hell had he been doing with her for months?*

"What did you do to her?" I demanded, my voice rising, the venom in my tone undeniable.

His jaw tightened, his composure beginning to fracture. For a split second, something flickered in his eyes—something too fleeting to name.

"I made her face her past," he said, each word cold and unrepentant.

"You *what?*" The words ripped from my throat, pure fury taking hold.

I lunged at him, my anger exploding into motion, the sheer force of it sending us both crashing to the ground.

We rolled, the damp earth clinging to our clothes, the world narrowing to the sound of labored breaths and the sharp crack of fists meeting flesh. Every blow carried the weight of years—grief, betrayal, anger—all of it boiling over into this moment.

"I made her stronger," he said, his voice edged with accusation. "Something you didn't have the guts to do."

"You asshole," I roared, pinning him beneath me, my hands fisting the collar of his shirt. "You hurt her."

My elbow dug into his ribs, and he hissed in pain, but his knee came up sharply, narrowly missing my stomach.

"I *saved* her," he spat out as he tried to shove me off him. "And I *will* take her back."

"She loves *me!*" I shouted, desperation mingling with my anger.

He shifted his weight suddenly, twisting his hips, and the next thing I knew, I was on my back, the breath knocked out of me.

Ty pinned me, his forearm pressing against my throat just enough to keep me down.

"Only because you broke your promise," Ty hissed, his words cutting deeper than any punch.

Guilt surged through me, relentless and brutal. He was right. I'd sworn to him that I wouldn't touch her.

And I'd broken that promise in every way imaginable. The weight of my betrayal twisted inside me, throwing off my focus.

Ty's next hit connected with my jaw, sharp and brutal.

"You don't deserve her," he spat, his eyes blazing as he hit me again. And again.

I lifted my arms over my face to defend myself, absorbing the blows. But my guilt slowed my defenses, weakening my arms as I felt the weight of everything I'd done.

"She was always mine," Ty said, his voice like a final verdict, each word dripping with conviction.

Rage flared hot inside me, chasing away the guilt. I snarled, twisting beneath him, using the momentum to roll us again. I clawed for leverage, finally managing to get on top.

"That's not your choice," I snarled. "That's *hers.*"

With one final shove, we tumbled apart, collapsing onto the wet grass, bruised and bloodied, both too exhausted to move.

The silence stretched between us, broken only by our ragged breaths.

I glanced over at him, my twin, the brother I barely recognized anymore with motives I couldn't read, couldn't trust. His face was smeared with dirt, a thin trickle of blood running from his split lip.

The calculated calm in his expression unnerved me, setting my nerves on edge.

What was his endgame? Ava? Revenge? Or something I couldn't see coming?

"She's chosen," I said, my voice low, bitter. "She chose *me*."

Ty chuckled, a hollow sound that made my stomach twist. "Are you sure about that, brother?"

His words lingered, filling the quiet with doubt I couldn't shake.

My mind flashed to Ava—to the way she had looked at him, the guilt in her eyes, the shift in her that I couldn't ignore. My chest tightened, the fear like a blade twisting deep.

Did she love me enough? Would I end up being the one she wanted?

Ty pushed himself to his feet with a deliberate, almost casual ease, then extended a hand to me.

I grasped his hand, letting him haul me up.

"This isn't over," he said, his voice calm, yet laced with a quiet menace that made my jaw clench. "I'll keep fighting for her."

"And I'll do whatever it takes to keep her," I shot back, my voice hard as steel, every word a challenge.

"Then may the best brother win."

AVA

"It's not a competition," I called weakly after Ty and Ciaran as they wedged themselves in the doorway of my new dorm, each one stubbornly trying to exit first.

Their shoulders collided, and the resulting glare-off would have been comical if it wasn't so exhausting. They broke free, nearly taking the doorframe with them, and thundered down the narrow staircase toward the moving van parked below.

I sighed and sank back against the mattress of my four-poster bed, staring up at the soaring cathedral ceilings.

The top "attic" level of Rochester House, one of Dark-moor's oldest residence halls, exuded a gothic charm that bordered on the eerie.

The slanted walls seemed to lean inward, creating a sense of intimacy—or perhaps quiet foreboding. Exposed wooden beams crossed the ceilings like the skeleton of the ancient structure, their dark grain polished smooth by time.

Dormer windows punctuated the walls, their glass panes warped slightly from age, letting in faint streams of afternoon light that dappled the wooden floors with a muted glow.

This top level contained three small bedrooms, each with its own quirks—crooked ceilings, uneven floors, and odd corners that seemed to belong to another time.

A shared living space sat at the center, where mismatched furniture and faded rugs gave the impression that generations of students had made their mark.

The kitchen, though compact, had a vintage charm with its antique fixtures and a window overlooking the sprawling campus grounds.

The bathroom was tucked away at the end of the hall, its claw-foot tub and tarnished mirror adding to the Victorian aesthetic.

It was beautiful in its imperfections, hauntingly lovely, and undeniably *Darkmoor*.

We'd all agreed that staying at the McKinsey manor was too dangerous now. The Society undoubtedly knew I was back, and the mansion was practically a beacon for trouble.

Moving into Darkmoor's dorms, especially as the new school year started tomorrow, seemed like the best option.

The twins, however, had turned my relocation into a testosterone-filled competition.

I wanted to help. I really did. But the thought of navigating those creaking, narrow stairs alongside two competitive forces of nature was a recipe for getting crushed.

Besides, every time I so much as moved to help, they would scowl and shove me back, ordering me not to lift a finger.

It was the only thing they seemed to agree on.

"This needs to go by the window," Ciaran said after they'd returned, his voice as cool and steady as ever, holding one side of my beloved leather tufted chair.

Ty, gripping the other side, yanked it sharply in the opposite direction, toward the cozy reading alcove where I'd placed the vintage lamp I found last summer with Lisa.

"Ava likes to study at night," he shot back. "You'd know that if you'd spent any *real* time with her."

They glared at each other, their tension crackling like electricity in the air. The chair wobbled dangerously between them, its weight amplifying the silent battle of wills.

Physically, they were identical. If not for Ty's haunting illustrative black tattoos ghosting down his arms and Ciaran's more traditional sleeve, it would have been impossible to tell them apart.

But their energies couldn't have been more different.

Ty was composed, like the calm before a storm—cold, unflinching, and deliberate.

Ciaran, on the other hand, was wild, his emotions always on display. He was a storm that never let up, raw and rabid, a heartbeat away from losing control.

"Just put it there," I said, pointing at a random stretch of slanted wall, halfway between the window and the lamp.

That location made absolutely no sense, but it was the quickest way to stop them from tearing the chair—and each other—apart.

At first, their bickering had been amusing.

It wasn't every day two ridiculously gorgeous twins fought over who got to haul your antique makeup vanity up four flights of ancient stairs. They clashed over everything, from my chair to my books to which box should be unpacked first.

But now? Now the tension between them felt like a ticking time bomb, and I wasn't sure I could defuse it.

But it wasn't just today. I'd noticed the bruises on their knuckles, the split lips they tried to hide.

Something had happened the night Ebony interrupted our reunion. I'd demanded answers, but neither of them had offered a single word.

Whatever was festering between them, they'd silently agreed to keep me out of it. But I wasn't naïve enough to think their restraint would last forever.

"You two are going to kill each other over a chair," I said, trying to sound exasperated, though my voice came out softer than I intended. "That's not important. Put it wherever you want."

They both glanced at me, their identical gazes softening briefly before snapping back to each other like magnets drawn to opposite poles.

It wasn't about the chair. It was never about the chair.

And no matter how much I wished they would stop fighting, I knew this wasn't a battle I could mediate.

Ciaran smirked, giving one last tug toward the alcove. Ty's jaw tightened, his knuckles whitening around the leather. The chair wobbled again, and I sighed, falling back against the mattress.

This was going to be a long semester.

"Hello?"

The familiar voice of my best friend, Lisa, echoed through the apartment.

My heart leaped into my throat. I shot up from the bed and bolted to the living room, my bare feet skidding slightly on the wooden floor.

Standing there, framed by the doorway, was Lisa—radiant and effortlessly put together as always. She wore a flowy summer dress with puffy sleeves that gave her an almost ethereal glow, her arms loaded with a precarious stack of folders.

Fuck, I missed her.

Without thinking, I ran straight for her.

Lisa's folders tumbled to the floor as we collided, throwing our arms around each other in a crushing hug that nearly took the breath out of me.

"Bish, where the hell have you been?" she hissed in my ear, her voice low and sharp with worry. "And don't give me any of that shite about sailing around the Mediterranean."

Her words hit me like a gut punch, squeezing my chest until it ached.

Lisa *knew*. She had known, somehow, that something was wrong. She'd seen through Ty's carefully curated faceless posts about my glamorous summer trip.

And the thought of her worrying—of her pacing, overthinking, trying to call me and getting no real answers—it hurt in a way I wasn't prepared for.

I pulled back slightly, my hands still gripping her shoulders.

Her eyes searched mine, her worry and frustration written all over her face.

"I'll explain everything, I promise, but later," I said, my voice tight, barely steady. It was the best I could offer her right now.

Lisa didn't look convinced. Her eyes narrowed, her lips pressing into a hard line like she was gearing up to demand answers. But before she could speak, her gaze shifted to something—or *someones*—over my shoulder.

Her mouth fell open in surprise.

"Holy shit," she whispered, her voice a mix of awe and disbelief. "There's two of them."

Ciaran appeared at my side, his grin devilish as ever.

"You must be Lisa," he said smoothly, his tone dripping with honeyed charm. "Ava's told me so much about you."

Ty stepped in on my other side, his arms crossed and his expression dark.

"Who are *you*?" he asked, his voice sharp and suspicious.

I smacked his arm lightly, shooting him a glare. "Down, boy. She's my bestie. We can trust her."

Ty didn't look convinced, his icy eyes flicking over Lisa like she was a potential threat.

Meanwhile, Lisa stood frozen, her gaze darting between the twins with wide eyes, her mouth agape. She seemed too awestruck to be insulted.

Pointing a tentative finger at Ciaran, she said, "So, if you're Ty, then—"

"He's *not* Ty," Ty snapped, his voice cutting through the moment like a whip.

Compared to Ciaran's warm, playful tone, Ty's words hit like a splash of cold water to the face.

Lisa's eyes darted between me and Ciaran, her expression morphing from awe to bewilderment.

"So you must be... Ciaran?" she said hesitantly, almost like she wasn't sure if naming him aloud would make him more real.

Ciaran wiggled his fingers at her playfully. "Present."

"Wait." I frowned, turning to Lisa. "How do you know Ciaran's name?"

Lisa's confidence wavered, and she bent down to gather the folders she'd dropped earlier, avoiding my gaze.

"Lisa," I said sternly, my voice low as I folded my arms.

Clearing her throat and blushing faintly, Lisa gave me a sheepish look. "Well, um, apart from coming here to see you... I also came to do new student orientation."

I tilted my head, still not understanding. "And?"

Lisa fidgeted with the packets, her fingers clumsy with nervous energy.

She hesitated, as if afraid to deliver the blow. "Meet your new roommates."

My brain stalled. "What?"

I turned sharply, my fists clenching at my sides, as my gaze snapped from the twins to the two spare bedrooms flanking mine.

Ciaran looked smug, grinning like a kid who'd just pulled off the prank of the century.

Ty, on the other hand, stood firm, his intense stare daring me to challenge him.

"*What*?!" I shouted louder this time, the word echoing through the penthouse.

Lisa glanced between the three of us and nodded. "Yup. They both are."

"What?" Ciaran barked at Ty, his tone sharp with annoyance. "*You're* living here too?"

Ty raised an eyebrow, crossing his arms over his chest.

"I could ask you the same thing," he said coolly, his voice edged with challenge.

"How?" I demanded Ciaran, my voice rising with frustration.

Ciaran slung an arm casually over my shoulders, his smile widening.

"You're lucky to have an incredibly talented *boyfriend*," he said with exaggerated pride. "I hacked the Darkmoor system, enrolled in their very selective journalism program, and assigned myself to the room next to yours."

I blinked at him, stunned but not entirely surprised. "Of course you did."

Turning to Ty, I glared. "And *you*?"

He shrugged. "I found some dirt on the administrator."

I threw my hands in the air, exasperated beyond belief. "You two are *impossible*."

Ty's gaze burned into mine, steady and unyielding. "I'm not letting you out of my sight."

Before I could snap back, Ciaran pulled me tighter against his side, pressing a kiss to the top of my head. "*I* am not letting her out of *my* sight."

Shaking off his arm, I slipped out of his grasp, marching across the room toward Lisa. I grabbed her arm in one hand and the folders in the other, dragging her toward my bedroom.

"Go *orient* yourselves," I growled, chucking the folders at the twins before slamming the door shut in their faces and turning the lock.

Lisa's wide eyes were still brimming with disbelief.

"Ava," she said slowly, "what the hell is going on?"

Lisa sat on my mattress, her flowy dress crumpling beneath her as she crossed her legs, her sharp eyes already scanning my face for answers.

Taking a deep breath, I brought her up to speed on everything—everything I'd pieced together about Liath and the other missing girls we'd been investigating last term.

The connection to a shadowy secret organization. The systematic abuse they orchestrated. The horrifying lengths they went to, to silence their victims and cover their tracks.

I told Lisa everything—all the harrowing details I'd uncovered—except for the one truth I couldn't bear to say aloud: that *I* was one of the orphaned girls they'd used.

Lisa was the closest thing I had to family outside of Ciaran and Ty, the one person who had always been my anchor.

But the thought of her knowing—of her piecing together the full extent of my past—made my stomach twist painfully. I couldn't bear to see pity in her eyes, those deep, understanding wells of empathy that had always been her strength.

I didn't want her to look at me differently. I didn't want to become a victim in her eyes, someone fragile, someone broken.

So I kept that piece of myself locked away, even from her.

"They drugged their victims—their *adopted daughters*—to stop them from remembering what happened to them," I explained, my voice tight with anger. "Including Liath."

Lisa's mouth tightened, and I could see the storm building behind her eyes.

"Liath's father…" she began, her voice faltering. "It's all over the news. Someone sent video evidence to the media—proof that he was the one abusing her."

A chill ran through me. "What?" My voice came out barely above a whisper.

Lisa nodded, her expression a mix of fury and disbelief. "He disappeared right after the story broke. No one's seen him since."

I felt a strange flicker of relief at the news. It was wrong, maybe, but knowing Liath's abuser had been outed—and knowing he was gone—gave me a grim sense of justice.

And yet, deep down, I had a sinking feeling that his disappearance wasn't a coincidence. Ciaran's name whispered in the back of my mind.

That sounds like something he'd do.

I swallowed hard, forcing myself to focus. "Dr. Vale was working with them to cover it up, giving the girls memory suppressors and convincing them they were crazy."

Lisa gasped, her expression darkening further.

"His house burned down," she said, her voice soft but heavy with meaning. "They found his body in the basement. Burned beyond recognition."

The room seemed to tilt, and my stomach churned. I knew instantly who was behind that. *Ciaran.*

A bitter lump rose in my throat, but I pushed it down. I couldn't let Lisa see how deep this ran, how far I'd been dragged into the darkness surrounding these men. I nodded mutely, biting the inside of my cheek to keep from saying too much.

"And Cormac?" Lisa continued, her gaze cutting into me. "He's missing too."

My blood turned cold, and an image flashed unbidden in my mind: Ty, his face blank and unflinching as he slashed Cormac's throat. The memory made me feel sick, and it took everything I had not to flinch.

"I—I didn't know that," I lied, my voice barely steady. The words tasted bitter on my tongue, but I couldn't tell her the truth. Not about Ty. Not about what happened that night.

It wasn't that I didn't trust Lisa. I did. With my life.

But trusting her and protecting her were two very different things.

And if Lisa knew too much—if she got caught in the crosshairs of everything that was happening—she would become a target. Just like I had.

When I finished talking, a heavy silence settled over the room, broken only by the muffled sound of arguing from outside the door.

"They're still going at it," Lisa said, rolling her eyes toward the door. She jumped up and pressed her ear to it, her face scrunching in concentration. "Arguing... about you."

I let out a tired sigh and sank back against the mattress. Of course they were.

Lisa raised a perfectly arched eyebrow as she flopped back beside me, her red hair spilling over the pillow. "If you're having kinky three-way sex with those two dark gods," she said with absolute seriousness, "and you don't give me every explicit detail, you're dead to me, bish."

Before I could protest, she jabbed a finger into my side boob, hard enough to make me wince. "Do you hear me?"

"No three ways," I groaned, shoving her hand away. "I'm *with* Ciaran."

Lisa blinked in surprise, then tilted her head. "I thought you were with Ty?"

"I was never with—" I started, but the words died as memories surged forward unbidden.

Ty's tongue tracing every inch of my skin, the heat of his mouth, the way his cock felt splitting me open.

My thighs clenched involuntarily, and my face flamed as I tucked a damp strand of hair behind my ear.

"I was never *in a relationship* with Ty," I said, my voice quieter.

Lisa narrowed her eyes, studying me with a blunt judgmental look that only a best friend could get away with.

"You know he's in love with you, right?" she said.

I flushed harder.

"He loves me like a friend," I lied, my voice cracking under the weight of the words. "He's my childhood best friend."

Lisa snorted, loud and disbelieving. "Girl, have you seen the way he looks at you? Like you hung the moon and stars. Like no other woman even exists. His body turns toward you as you move around the room. Even when you're not paying attention."

My chest tightened. Lisa's words struck deeper than I wanted to admit.

"I don't want to hurt either of them," I said softly, almost to myself.

"You're going to hurt one of them the second you choose," Lisa said, her voice gentler now. "That's how this works."

"I *have* chosen," I said, the words coming out more defensive than I meant. "I chose Ciaran."

Lisa raised an eyebrow, her silence stretching until it felt like she could see straight through me. "Have you, though? Really?"

"Yes," I insisted, forcing myself to meet her gaze.

My heart echoed the truth in my words, but deep in my soul, a tiny traitorous seed of doubt sprouted.

"Well…" Lisa sighed, leaning back against the pillows. "If those secret society bastards don't kill you for threatening to expose their asses, I can tell you this much; walking around with those two is going to do it. The girls on campus would gladly dig out your windpipe with their Louboutins just to get close to either of them."

I barely heard her. Something had distracted me—a distant noise I wasn't even fully conscious of registering until it sharpened into focus.

Lisa smacked my arm. "Bish, are you even listening to me?"

"Shhh," I hissed, grabbing her wrist before she could hit me again. "Listen."

I strained, trying to make sense of what had drawn my attention, but the room was filled with nothing but the muffled sound of Ty and Ciaran's arguing outside, the creak of the old house settling beneath us, and the faint noise of students returning to campus.

"Sorry," I mumbled, shaking my head. "I must be getting para—"

The balcony door rattled, the faint scrape of movement shattering the illusion of safety. My breath caught as my eyes darted toward the curtains.

Beyond them, I saw the shadow of a figure, crouched low, their dark clothing blending with the dusk as they bent over the lock.

Someone was trying to break in.

THE SHADOW

As soon as the door to Ava's bedroom closed behind her and Lisa, I turned to Ty, my fists already clenched at my sides.

The bastard leaned casually against the wall, arms crossed, his expression maddeningly composed. He didn't even have the decency to look guilty.

"So, you manipulated your way in here without telling me," I said, my voice sharp with anger.

Ty arched an eyebrow, his calm demeanor like a splash of ice water against my fire. "I could say the same about you, brother. Hacking the system? Very subtle."

"More subtle than *blackmail*. Besides, I'm her *boyfriend*," I snapped, taking a step forward. "You have no right to be here."

His lips curled into a faint smirk, and he tilted his head, regarding me like I was something small and amusing. "What Ava and I have is bigger than something labeled as juvenile as *boyfriend*."

"You're delusional," I said, my voice low and sharp as

Ty's presence grated against every nerve I had. "And you have ten seconds to get out."

Ty didn't even look at me. Instead, he crossed the room with maddening calm, his eyes scanning the front door. He tested the handle, the lock, and gave it a jiggle, his lips tightening in thought.

"We need a better lock," he muttered, almost to himself. "This one's flimsy. Probably wouldn't hold up to a strong kick."

I stared at him, my fists clenched, heat rising in my chest. "I'm serious, Ty. Get the fuck out."

"I'm not going anywhere," he said smoothly, his tone dismissive as he moved to the window. He tugged at the latch, checking its sturdiness. "Ava needs me."

"She doesn't need you," I growled, my voice rising with frustration. "I'm protecting her. And when she comes to her fucking senses from whatever brainwashing bullshite you've fed her, I'm taking her away from here, just like we planned."

Ty turned, one brow arched as if amused by my outburst. "You're not taking Ava anywhere. But *you* feel free to turn tail and run."

His words felt like a slap, and anger bubbled to the surface, hot and uncontrollable.

I followed him to the window, practically breathing down his neck. "I'm going to protect her from the Sochai, from her past, and especially from *you*."

He didn't flinch, didn't even meet my glare as he peered out the glass, his gaze sweeping over the grounds. "The windows are too exposed. We'll need bars here. Something discreet but strong."

"Are you even listening to me?" I snapped, my voice cracking with fury. "You're going to get her killed."

Ty turned his head slightly, his expression calm but his eyes sharp. "Ava doesn't need protection. Ava is a strong woman who needs someone to fight alongside her."

"Are you fucking crazy?" I spat. "You're going to encourage her delusional and frankly suicidal idea of taking down the Sochai?"

"Yes," he said simply, moving past me and heading for the next window. He opened it, glanced outside, and frowned. "And if you knew what she's capable of, you wouldn't be treating her like a helpless child."

"You're going to get her killed!" I shouted, the weight of his indifference pressing down on my chest like a vise.

He finally turned to face me fully, his voice cold and deliberate. "You don't know her anymore, Ciaran. She's outgrown you."

"Ava loves me," I roared, my hands itching to throw a punch, to knock that smug look off his face. "She chose *me*."

Ty's eyes narrowed, his glare sharper now, cutting straight through me. "Did she? Or are you clinging to a version of her that doesn't exist anymore?"

"She's the same Ava," I said, though the words felt hollow, even to me. "And she doesn't need you confusing her."

"I'm showing her who she is," he said, his voice low and measured, like he was talking to a child. "Who she can be. *You* are the one holding her back."

"What did you do to her?" I demanded, my voice shaking with anger. "What happened at Blackthorn?"

His lips quirked into a humorless smile. "Don't ask questions you don't want the answer to, brother."

My stomach twisted, the weight of his words settling like a stone. My voice dropped, quieter but no less dangerous. "Did you touch her? Kiss her? Did you fuck her, Ty?"

He stepped closer, his smirk fading, replaced by something darker, heavier. "That's between Ava and me."

My vision tunneled, the heat of jealousy and betrayal surging in my veins.

Ty stood there, infuriatingly calm, like this was all some game to him. Like my entire fucking world wasn't unraveling because of him.

I didn't think I could ever hurt my brother. Not really. But right now, murder sounded pretty good.

My hand dropped instinctively to the knife hidden at my thigh, my fingers curling tightly around the handle, the skin over my knuckles tightening as the rage simmered, threatening to boil over.

"If you don't—"

A bloodcurdling scream tore through the apartment, sharp and panicked, freezing the threat in my throat.

Ava.

I was already moving toward the door. My pulse pounded in my ears, her scream reverberating in my chest like a physical blow.

"Ava!" I shouted, my voice raw with fear.

Ty bolted for her bedroom, too, his cold composure cracking.

We both slammed into the doorframe at the same time, our shoulders colliding. Ty shoved me back with surprising force, his eyes wild, and I clawed at him, trying to push past.

"Get the fuck out of my way!" I snarled, the desperation in my voice betraying me.

"She's *mine* to protect!" he snapped back, his usually calm voice edged with something raw, almost feral.

The door wouldn't budge. Locked.

Both of us kicked out at the same time. The wood splintered around the lock, and the door flew open.

Inside the bedroom, the scene was chaos. A flurry of movement confused me at first—Ava and a masked man were fighting.

The intruder caught Ava's punch, twisting her arm, and Lisa screamed. But Ava didn't freeze.

Instead, she used his grip against him, twisting into him and jabbing her elbow brutally into his throat.

Where the fuck had she learned that?

Ty.

"Hey!" I yelled at the soon-to-be-dead man. "Touch her and die."

The masked man shoved Ava to the floor before bolting for the open balcony door. In one swift motion, he climbed over the balustrade, vanishing into the night, leaving nothing behind but the acrid smell of cigarette smoke.

"Coward," Ty spat, moving to the balcony in pursuit while I ran to Ava, sprawled on the floor, her chest heaving.

I wrapped my arms around her, lifting her gently onto the bed.

"Are you okay?" I asked, my voice shaking with the effort to steady it.

"I'm fine," Ava replied, her voice shaky but resolute.

Lisa, her face pale and stricken, tried to cut the tension with a weak laugh. "Since when did you become a ninja?"

Ava managed a small, tight smile, but it didn't reach her eyes.

Lisa was shaking so hard, she had to sit down on the corner of the bed.

"He's gone," Ty announced from the balcony, his voice cutting through the room like a blade. "Ran into the woods."

I brushed Ava's hair from her face, checking her arms for bruises, running my hands over limbs I'd already confirmed unbroken. The fear in me refused to let go.

"Are you hurting anywhere?" I asked. "Where did he hit you? Are you in shock?"

"She said she's fine," Ty snapped, his tone colder than the cool dusk air drifting in from the open balcony door.

Ava's eyes darted to him, something unspoken passing between them. Her breathing slowed, but I could see the weight of what just happened settling over her like a heavy cloak.

"Describe him," Ty said, his voice sharper now, commanding.

I shot him a glare over my shoulder.

"He was wearing a mask," I said darkly. "What's to describe?"

"I wasn't talking to you, Ci," Ty replied, his focus locked entirely on Ava.

Ava hesitated, her eyes shifting nervously between us. The air was taut with tension, like a bowstring ready to snap.

"Eye color," Ty pressed. "Height, build, race, facial hair, distinguishing features, disfigurements, tattoos, odor."

"Stop harassing her!" I snapped, the rage in my chest igniting again. "That was a hired fucking goon. Even if we could identify him, he won't know anything about the Sochai."

"She's not weak," Ty said, ignoring me, his focus on Ava unwavering. "Ava?"

Ava's lips trembled, tears welling in her eyes. "I-I…" she stammered, her voice breaking.

"Tell me what you remember," Ty repeated, softer this time, but no less firm.

I clenched my fists, ready to break his fucking face, but then Ava spoke.

"Above average build," she said, her voice low but steady. "Attacked with his left hand. Light-brown eyes. He wore a balaclava—cheap material, probably polyester. He smelled strongly of cigarette smoke. Something heavy like Marlboros or JPs."

She slumped after that, her strength depleted, the light in her eyes dimming as exhaustion took over.

Ty's lips twitched, just barely, his voice almost gentle as he said, "Good girl."

She shivered at the words, and my glare burned holes into him.

Lisa's mouth hung open, shock written all over her face as she glanced between the three of us, muttering, "What the actual fuck…"

Ty turned to me, his cold gaze cutting through the silence. "We need to talk."

"I'm not leaving her," I shot back, tightening my protective hold on Ava.

Ava's hand rested on my arm, her touch grounding me even as my blood still boiled.

"I'm fine, Scáth," she said softly, her voice a mixture of reassurance and exhaustion.

I hesitated, the need to stay warring with her quiet plea for space.

Ty didn't wait for my decision, heading for the door.

Gritting my teeth, I released Ava and followed him into the living room, leaving Lisa to sit with her.

Ty turned to face me, his expression as unreadable as ever.

"Until this is over, we're going to have to put our... differences aside," he said, his voice calm but firm. "For Ava."

I nodded stiffly, the tension between us still thick. "She isn't ever to be left alone."

"That we can agree upon," Ty said, extending his hand. "So... truce."

I stared at his hand, then grabbed it in mine, squeezing harder than necessary.

Ty didn't flinch, his grip matching mine, a silent reminder of the underlying tension in our so-called truce.

"Truce." I narrowed my eyes at my brother—my twin, ultimately, my *rival*. "For now."

AVA

I sat on the edge of the bed, my pulse still pounding from the fight, my muscles taut with leftover adrenaline. Every nerve in my body was alive, heightened, making me hyper-aware of everything—the cool draft from the open balcony door, the faint scent of cigarette smoke lingering in the air, and the sound of Ciaran's approaching footsteps.

He stepped into my bedroom and my breath hitched. His broad shoulders filled the doorway, his shirt stretched across the muscles of his chest, and his blazing icy-blue eyes locked on mine.

The storm of emotions in them—relief, worry, anger, love—made my stomach flip.

He was a force, raw and unrelenting, and just looking at him made my skin heat and my heart race. *Need* crackled under my skin.

We hadn't had a chance to be alone together since I got back. Right now, that was all I needed.

Lisa, bless her intuitive soul, seemed to catch on in the

way only a best friend could. With a flick of her eyes between us, she stood, smoothing down her dress.

"Running interference," she whispered to me. "Stat."

Before Ty could follow Ciaran into my room, she grabbed his arm, stopping him in his tracks.

"Time for new student orientation, Tynan," she said, her tone firm but light. "Let's go."

Ty didn't budge. His piercing gaze stayed on me, sharp and unreadable, lingering in a way that made my chest tighten.

I could hear Lisa muttering something to him, but his focus didn't waver.

"I'm not leaving," he said.

"Hey, bubby, read the fucking room," Lisa said, her voice carrying just enough sass to make Ty's jaw tick. "Those two lovebirds need to reconnect. And I don't think you want to be here to hear it. Or, you know… *see* it, considering her door won't close anymore."

"It's okay, Mhaor," I said, holding Ty's gaze, hoping he'd understand.

For a single moment, his mask slipped. The pain in his eyes flitted across his face, raw and unguarded, cutting into me as sharply as a blade.

The ache in my chest deepened, guilt twisting around my ribs like a vise.

I hated hurting him. But there was no undoing the knot of feelings inside me, no untangling the threads that bound me to Ciaran.

Ty's expression hardened again, and without a word, he turned and walked out.

"Darkmoor is actually a really cool old place." Lisa's

voice carried as she followed him down the hall. "We even have a legit passagetomb on the grounds aligned with the winter solstice or winter *grianstad* if you're up on your Irish."

The sound of their footsteps faded, leaving me alone with Ciaran.

My heart thudded in my chest as I looked up at him.

Ciaran stood there, his chest heaving, his fists clenched at his sides, like he was trying to keep himself from unraveling. But the fury in his icy-blue eyes betrayed him. It was raw, uncontained, and aimed squarely at me.

The room felt heavier, quieter, the tension between us thick and buzzing. For a moment, neither of us spoke, the silence stretching as the weight of everything unsaid pressed down on us.

"I thought you were dead," he growled, his voice breaking on the words, the edges rough with emotion. His hands flinched as if he ached to reach out for me.

"I know," I whispered as I stood facing him, my throat tightening. "I'm sorry. It wasn't my choice."

"Months, Ava. You were gone for *months*." His face twisted, his voice rising, the volume a whip crack against the silence.

God, I wanted to touch him, to pull him into my arms, to feel the safety of his warmth, his strength.

But hesitation held me back.

I saw the way Ciaran looked at me as I fought off the masked man—stunned, as if he didn't know me anymore. As if the girl he loved had been replaced by someone sharper, harder, someone he didn't quite recognize.

Had I changed too much for him to still love me? Had Ty

infiltrated my soul so deeply that the connection Ciaran and I once shared was beyond saving?

My throat tightened. What if I was no longer the Ava that Scáth loved? What if I had become someone he couldn't love anymore?

Because despite everything—the doubts, the guilt, the fear—I still loved him.

Even if I didn't deserve him anymore, even if we couldn't go back to how it was.

He was my Scáth, my shadow, my everything. And in this moment, that love felt like it might tear me apart.

I took a step toward him. "I was fighting to get back to you every day, I swear."

His eyes narrowed, disbelief flashing across his face. "Were you? 'Cause you and Ty look pretty fucking friendly now."

The accusation hit me like a slap, and guilt lanced through me, sharp and immediate.

But then came the anger—anger that he didn't believe me, that he didn't understand.

But before I could yell back, something shifted in his features, something that cracked his anger wide open and laid his pain bare.

"Is he..." His voice was raw, fractured, as if the words themselves were breaking him apart. "Is he the one you want now?"

It struck me like a dagger to the chest, stealing my breath.

The agony in his eyes, the vulnerability he was trying so hard to hide—it unraveled me.

I closed the distance between us, my hands reaching for him, all hesitation blown to dust.

"I love *you*, Scáth." My voice shook, but my words were certain, unyielding. "I'm yours."

Something broke in him at my words. He pulled me to him, crushing me to him like he was afraid I'd disappear again. His lips crashed against mine with a desperation that stole my breath.

I kissed him back just as fiercely, my fingers digging into his clothes, trying to tear them off, trying to strip away every last thing left between us.

It wasn't gentle. It wasn't sweet. It was fire and fury, a battle of need and raw emotion.

We fell onto the bed, pushing and pulling at each other as we fought to strip each other down, both of us trying to claim the other.

Our naked bodies collided, and the tension was electric, dark and all-consuming. Every nerve in my body was alive, buzzing with an intensity that made me feel like I might come apart at the seams.

The guilt, the confusion, the lingering feelings for Ty— they all slipped away and the world narrowed to just us.

This raw, electric naked connection. This dark bond.

Ciaran's lips only left mine to kiss down my neck to my breasts. He sucked at my nipples, the need tightening inside me to almost desperation, making me claw at his back with my nails.

"I painted this town red trying to get you back," he rasped as he ran his fingers along my soaked slit, teasing my entrance.

I let out a cry and rocked my hips to him, begging for

more. I was already too far gone. I didn't need foreplay. I needed *him*. Inside me. Now.

I stroked his cock, reveling in the weight of it, the thickness and heat.

"You killed Dr. Vale," I whispered as I positioned him at my entrance.

"Yes," he said, thrusting into me without hesitation, filling me, consuming me—taking up all the space in my heart once more.

We both groaned against each other's mouths.

Fuck. My body and my heart felt like they were on the verge of exploding, every feeling—relief, pain, love, desperate need—hitting me all at once.

"And Liath's father," I said on a choke as my emotions threatened to overcome me.

He grabbed my chin, forcing me to look right into his eyes as he thrust into me again. "Yes."

Tears pricked at the corners of my eyes, but I didn't look away.

This man, my Scáth, had left a trail of blood and destruction in his wake for me. And yet, as wrong as it was, I couldn't stop the surge of love that filled my chest.

This felt right. He felt right.

"And the other missing girls… you made their fathers disappear," I said on a moan as I wrapped my legs around his waist to pull him in deeper.

"Yes," he said again, each word punctuated with a thrust, his voice a brutal blend of pride and pain. "Yes. Yes. Yes."

I crushed my lips against his, my hands tangling in his hair as his grip on my hip tightened and he fucked me like I was his lifeline, like he couldn't breathe without me.

"Fuck," he growled, "I missed your tight little cunt. The way you grip me."

"Please," I whispered, my hips pushing back against him becoming frantic as my thighs trembled. "I'm so close."

He held himself over me with one hand, wrapping his other around my throat, firmly but not enough to cut off my oxygen. Not enough for what I needed.

He slowed his thrusts so he could hold me on the edge. "Say my fucking name."

"Scáth."

"My *name*, Ava."

"Ciaran."

"Fuck, yes." His fingers tightened, my head spinning as the edges of my vision whitened. "You are *mine*. Say it."

His thrusts became more forceful, driving deeper with each movement and the pressure inside me built to near bursting.

"Yes," I gasped, my voice strained against his grip. "I'm *yours*."

My admission, my words, were my undoing.

My pussy clenched around him and wave after wave of pleasure crashed over me as I screamed.

Scáth groaned, his hips stuttering as he followed me over the edge.

I felt the warmth of his release inside me, his body shuddering between my legs.

For a long moment, we stayed in that position, both of us panting and trembling with the aftershocks of our climax.

Slowly, Scáth released his grip on my throat and pulled away. He returned with a damp cloth.

I studied the way his messy hair fell over his eyes, catching in his long dark lashes. The way his forearm muscles flexed as he tenderly cleaned me up.

God, he was so beautiful it made my chest ache.

He tossed the cloth into my wash basket and slid his body beside me before pulling me against his chest. He pressed a gentle kiss to my forehead, a stark contrast to his aggression before.

"I've missed you," he murmured against my skin, his breath hot and damp. "Every second that he kept you from me, I *ached* for you."

I turned my head, seeking his lips with mine.

The kiss was slow and deep as the memory of the moment I fell for him echoed in my mind.

"One day... in my future house... I want a strawberry patch."

"What else do you want?"

"I want a big library with a view of the sea," I said before I could stop myself. "It will be filled with light. The shelves will be the color of driftwood and the couches the color of sea glass. And the books will be faded from the sun with pages bent and yellowed from long days on the beach."

My knees trembled against Ciaran's legs and my heart pounded painfully in my chest. I felt like I was getting more drunk instead of less.

"Each room will be light and airy and have blue drapes the color of... of cornflowers. And our—my—bedroom will have a peaked ceiling and overlook the sea. There'll be an antique writing desk beside a sunny window. And a large comfortable bed piled high with the softest pillows."

The corners of his wet lips curled up and my veins went cold with fear.

If he laughed at me, I would die.

"Would you have a porch... where we could drink tea?" he asked.

"Yes, a large wraparound porch," I whispered.

I didn't tell him that there had always been a boy on my porch, too. Always in the shadows. Always just a silhouette. I didn't let myself paint him in.

Until now.

Ciaran's face moved dangerously close to mine.

I gripped the kitchen counter more tightly.

"What about a forest nearby so I could chase you through it?" he asked.

Goosebumps erupted along my arms.

Pine drifted in through my nostrils even through the thick fragrance of the drying herbs. Pine and salt water. Rich earth and Ciaran's musk.

"Yes," I said, hypnotized by his eyes. "Pines, I think."

"Pines," he echoed.

"And the house shouldn't be too big," I said, breathing a little too quickly, "so that we can always find each other without having to yell."

"Unless I'm up on the small rooftop terrace with the telescope."

Ciaran smiled, and for a moment, it transformed him. It softened the hard edges of his face, a rare warmth breaking through his usual cruel mask.

"But we should always go together to count the stars," I said.

"Yes," he whispered. "I promise to never look at the stars without you."

Was it foolish to hope that Scáth and I could have our happily ever after? That the chaos and pain could somehow lead us here, to this fragile moment of peace?

"I missed you too," I whispered.

As I rested against him, feeling the steady rhythm of his heartbeat beneath my cheek, a quiet certainty settled in my chest.

I'd made the right choice. Choosing Ciaran felt right—it felt like coming home.

But even as that love anchored me, a shadow lingered in the unspoken spaces between us.

There was so much left unsaid—things I didn't have the courage to ask, truths he hadn't yet offered, questions that burned on my tongue.

They hovered like ghosts, threatening the fragile foundation we were trying to build.

For now, I held on to him, praying this moment could last just a little longer.

It didn't, though.

"Come with me," he said softly, his voice low and coaxing, like he was trying to pull me back into something familiar, something safe. "We'll leave tonight. Start over somewhere far away from all this."

I wanted to melt into his words, let them sweep me away into a dream of freedom.

But I couldn't.

"I can't." My voice came out barely above a whisper. "Too much has changed, Ciaran."

He stiffened, his fingers that had been tracing my bare shoulder froze. "This is because of Ty, isn't it?"

"It's not about Ty," I said, shaking my head against his chest. "*I've* changed."

His gaze sharpened, cutting into me like a blade, and the

muscles under his jaw twitched. "What happened when Ty had you?"

Guilt coiled in my stomach, sharp and bitter, as memories clawed their way to the surface.

The heat of Ty's body pressed against mine as he adjusted my fighting stance, his hands firm on my body, his instructions growling in my ear, igniting a power deep inside me.

The vulnerable look in his eyes when he told me about how he'd gotten the scar on his top lip, how my fingers had trembled as I traced it, and before I could think, I had leaned in and sucked it into my mouth, as if my lips could wash away the pain.

And eyes, fierce and unrelenting, locked with mine as I slid the knife into the masked man's chest, no words, only a shared understanding intimate in a way I couldn't explain.

I swallowed hard, my throat tight as I forced the memories back. How could I tell Ciaran any of this? How could I explain that my time with Ty hadn't just broken me, but it'd started rebuilding me, too.

My throat tightened, and I dropped my gaze, unable to hold his.

"It doesn't matter anymore," I said, the words tumbling out too fast, too shaky. "It's over."

"Then send him away," Ciaran said, his voice hardening, suspicion flashing in his icy gaze. "He'll only leave if you tell him to."

"Ty was my best friend. *Is* my best friend." I met Ciaran's gaze, willing him to understand. "I can't send him away. We need his help to take down the Society."

Ciaran's jaw tightened, his voice low and sharp, each word clipped. "That plan is suicide, Ava."

I pushed up from the bed, from him, the sudden movement breaking the fragile moment between us. My hands shook as I snatched my top from the floor, pulling it over my head. "Don't you believe in us? In *me?*"

Ciaran climbed out of bed, reaching for me. His voice softened, losing its edge. "Of course, I do—"

I whirled on him before he could finish, my frustration bubbling over. "*Ty* believes in me."

The second the words left my mouth, I regretted them. I saw the flicker of pain in his eyes, the way his hands dropped to his sides as if I'd struck him. It was a low blow, and we both knew it.

I took a steadying breath, my voice softer now, as I finished pulling on the rest of my clothes.

"Ciaran… I thought we could run, but now I know the truth. We can't. There's nowhere we could go that the Society won't find us. And even if they don't… I can't live with myself knowing I ran away."

His shoulders slumped, and the anger in his gaze dimmed, replaced by something raw and aching.

"I'm just scared about losing you," he admitted, his voice barely audible.

"I know," I said, stepping closer, my hand brushing against his arm. "I'm scared too. But we're stronger together. The three of us."

He stiffened at that, his jaw clenching.

"Fine," he said after a long pause. "He can stay for now. But only because I know he's the only other person on this fucking planet who would protect you like I would."

I pulled my hair up into a messy bun on my head, watching him in the mirror.

God, only three months ago all I knew was Scáth. There had been no Ciaran… no mirror image, no twin to complicate things.

"Why did you pretend to be Ty?" I asked him.

He didn't reply, his jaw tightening, but I saw the flicker of guilt in his eyes.

"Ciaran, please," I whispered, my voice softer now. "We can't have secrets from each other. Not us. They'll tear us apart if we do."

He turned me to face him, his fingers gently pushing a fallen strand of hair over my ear as he stared at me. His gaze traced every feature of my face as though committing me to memory. His eyes searched mine, and for a moment, I thought he might deflect again.

"Just give me a minute more," he whispered. "I want to see you… one last time before I tell you why I lied."

"I won't look at you any differently," I promised, my voice steady, though my heart was pounding.

"The truth is… I was ashamed," Ciaran admitted, his voice low and raw, holding my gaze, though I could see the effort it took not to turn away. "Ashamed of how I'd treated you. Ashamed I had let Ty be the one to go to prison. Ashamed that I had blamed *you* when you were being abused by my own damn father."

My chest tightened at his words, but I didn't speak, letting him say what he needed to.

"I was a fucking *idiot*," he continued, his voice cracking. "To think you were complicit."

Pain etched itself into every line of his face, and I

reached up, brushing my fingertips lightly against his cheek. His gaze was raw and vulnerable, and I felt my heart break for him all over again.

"I didn't want you to think of me as the boy who tormented you," he said, his voice barely audible. "I wanted to be the boy who always loved you."

My throat tightened as tears burned at the edges of my vision. "He might have loved me first," I whispered, my voice shaking with emotion. "But I loved *you* first."

His eyes widened slightly, the weight of my words sinking in. "So you remember…?"

"Yes," I said, nodding. "I remember everything. You don't have to hide anything from me anymore."

His gaze searched mine, hesitant and unsure. "What do you remember?"

I took a deep breath, forcing myself to stay strong, to sound like the survivor I had become. "I remember the professor… used to drug me with my hot chocolate. And when I was under, he abused me."

Ciaran flinched, his eyes clouding with anger and pain, but he stayed silent, letting me continue.

"One night, I got sick. I threw up my hot chocolate. And when he tried to touch me, I fought back."

Ciaran nodded slowly, his hand brushing against my arm in a gesture of silent support.

"I remember that night too," he said, his voice thick with emotion. "Watching… when you said no. That's when I realized…"

He trailed off, his eyes closing briefly as he grappled with the memory.

I reached for his hand, lacing my fingers through his, giving him the strength as I took strength from him.

"He forced an abortion on me. And then… and then I killed him," I said, my voice steady but hollow. "I put oleander in his tea. And… And Ty took the blame."

Ciaran's gaze bored into me, searching my face as if peeling back layers. "Is that it?"

I frowned, confusion twisting through me. "What else is there?"

He let out a sigh, heavy and full of something unspoken, his shoulders dropping under the weight of it. "There's one more thing I need to admit. Something you don't know…"

My heart stilled, the tension in the room tightening like a noose. I froze, unable to speak, barely able to breathe.

His next words sliced through the silence like a blade.

"You didn't kill him… *I* did."

THE SHADOW

I paused in the doorway, my eyes narrowing as I took in Ava standing by the kitchen counter, her back to me, her long dark hair tumbling down her back in tantalizing waves, waves I wanted to touch to see if it was as soft as it looked.

Her hands shook as she worked, her shoulders tense like she was bracing for a blow. The sharp, bitter scent of tea and something else—something metallic—reached me.

"What are you doing?" I asked, my voice cutting through the stillness.

She jumped, spinning around, her eyes wide with panic. Her hands were trembling, and I noticed the teapot on the counter, the faint wisp of steam curling in the air. Her lips parted, but no words came out.

"I..." she stammered, her voice barely above a whisper. "I was just making tea... for the professor."

My gaze slid past her to the pot. Something wasn't right. My instincts were screaming at me.

Her nervousness, the way she kept glancing at the teapot, the way she stood like she was ready to bolt.

My chest tightened.

I stepped toward her, my movements slow and deliberate, as if I were approaching a skittish animal.

"Brownnosing little Ava," I said, my voice dripping with mockery. "Trying to become the professor's favorite, huh?"

"Go away," she snapped.

I didn't stop. I reached out, my hand landing on her shoulder, and shoved her gently aside.

She stumbled, her small frame unable to resist me.

"It's not for you!" she cried, lunging toward the pot, her voice cracking. "It's for the professor!"

I grabbed the teapot before she could reach it, lifting it high above my head.

Her small hands clawed at the air, trying to grab it, but I was taller, stronger, her desperation fueling my suspicion.

"For the professor, is it?" I taunted, my smirk twisting into something sharper. "A little bedtime brew?"

Her breath hitched, and tears filled her eyes.

"Give it back!" she pleaded, her voice breaking.

"What's wrong, Ava?" I asked, my tone mocking as I stepped closer, towering over her. "Don't want me to have a taste?"

"Don't drink it!" she shouted, lunging again, but I twisted away, keeping the pot out of reach. Her panic confirmed everything.

She'd done something to the tea.

"Get. Out," I growled, my voice low and dangerous.

Tears streaming down her face, she turned and fled, her footsteps echoing in the hallway until they disappeared entirely.

I set the teapot down on the counter and removed the lid. The bitter scent of the brew wafted up, sharper now.

Along with black tea leaves, pink petals floated on the surface, soft and delicate, belying their deadly nature.

Oleander.

My chest tightened, a mix of rage and guilt clawing at my insides.

Ava had done this. Ava, who never stepped out of line, who endured in silence, had reached her breaking point.

She was trying to poison my father.

I counted the flowers, my heart thudding with every petal. But she'd miscalculated. This wasn't enough to kill him—just enough to put him to sleep.

My throat tightened.

This just confirmed it. She hadn't wanted his attention. She hadn't wanted any of it.

And I hadn't protected her. I hadn't been there to shield her from him, to save her from feeling like she had to do this herself.

My gaze swept across the counter, landing on a handkerchief haphazardly tossed aside.

A pale-pink petal peeked out from beneath it, its presence like a whisper of her hesitation.

I pulled back the cloth, revealing more flowers—more deadly oleander—enough to finish what she started.

I grabbed the handkerchief, scooping the remaining flowers into my palm, and threw them into the pot. They swirled in the boiling water, their color leaching into the tea, deepening its poison.

Could I really kill him? My father?

The thought twisted inside me like a knife. My feet moved, carrying me forward, but my chest felt like it was being crushed.

My father had always been cold, a man of discipline and control, his affection doled out like rare coins, if at all. He cared more for his work, his endless experiments, and his precious plants than he ever did for Ty or me. When my mother—our soft, kind, loving mother—died, he hadn't even cried. Not at the funeral. Not in the days after. He'd gone back to the greenhouse, back to his vials and his notebooks, as if nothing had changed.

And yet...

He was still my father.

I clenched my jaw, the teapot handle cold and unforgiving in my grip. Memories flickered in my mind, half-formed and sharp-edged.

My father teaching me to tie a tie for the first time, his hands precise but detached. His stern voice guiding Ty and me through fencing stances in the garden. The pride in his eyes—faint but real—when I'd managed to memorize the Latin names, both genus and species, for all the different kinds of lilies that he grew.

There was a time I'd wanted his approval more than anything. A time long before Ma died, when I believed if I worked harder, performed better, maybe he'd look at me like I mattered.

But I'd learned, far too late, that no amount of effort would earn what he simply didn't have to give.

And then Ava.

My grip tightened on the teapot lid in my hand.

He'd stripped away her innocence, her trust, her safety—all for what? Power? Pleasure? Control?

A part of me screamed that he didn't deserve the title of "father." He'd desecrated it with his actions.

But another part—a quieter, stubborn part—whispered that no matter what he'd done, he was still the man who had brought me into this world. The man whose blood ran through my veins.

Could I live with myself if I did this?

And yet, could I live with myself if I didn't?

Ava's face flashed before me—her trembling hands as she brewed the tea, the haunted look in her eyes when she'd fled the kitchen, the fear she tried so hard to hide.

She'd been forced to act because I hadn't been there for her. Because I had failed to protect her.

My father was a monster, but Ava wasn't. And I wouldn't let her become one.

This was the only way.

My hands shook, but my resolve was steady as I turned and carried the teapot out of the kitchen. It felt heavier than it should, like it carried not just the tea but the burden of what I was about to do.

He would never hurt her again.

Not after tonight.

I would carry this stain on my soul so she didn't have to.

I'd become a monster... for her.

I exhaled slowly, the confession leaving me raw, like an open wound exposed to the cold.

For a long moment, I couldn't bring myself to look at Ava, sitting next to me on the bed, our legs stretched out in front of us.

My eyes stayed fixed on my hands in my lap, fingers knotted together like they could somehow tether me to the present, keep me from unraveling completely.

Would she see me as a monster now? Would she hate me for what I'd done? For the punishment I let Ty take for me? For everything I didn't tell her?

Finally, I forced myself to look up, bracing for disgust, for judgment, for the slightest flicker of rejection in her eyes.

But what I found wasn't anger or revulsion. It was love—

pure, unwavering love that etched itself into every line of her beautiful face.

It gutted me.

"Why didn't you tell me this before?" she asked, her voice soft but tinged with something I couldn't quite place —hurt, maybe. Sadness.

A bitter laugh escaped me as I leaned my head back against the headboard, the weight of it all pressing down on my chest.

"I wanted to," I admitted, the words dragging out of me like stones. "But Ty… he fucking confessed out of nowhere. Then he made me promise not to tell anyone it wasn't him."

Her brows furrowed, her hand finding mine, her touch grounding me in ways I didn't deserve.

"Ty wasn't just protecting me," she whispered.

"No." I shook my head, the guilt clawing at my insides. "He wasn't. He was protecting *me*, too."

He'd taken *my* place in that hellhole. Without hesitation. Without a second thought.

"It should've been me," I went on, the words spilling out of me now, unstoppable. "He shouldered what I did. What I should have been punished for. And I let him. I fucking let him."

"You didn't let him," she said softly, her voice steady in a way I didn't deserve. "Ty doesn't *let* anyone do anything. You know that."

I laughed bitterly because she was right.

Ty had always been like that—unyielding, immovable, the only constant in a world that had always felt like it was falling apart.

Still, it didn't change the fact that I'd let him go to prison for something I'd done. That I'd let him carry a burden that was mine to bear.

Her hand moved to my face, her fingers brushing against my cheek. When I finally met her gaze, I saw strength there —quiet, fierce strength—and it made my chest ache.

"You did what you did to protect me," she said, her voice so soft it felt like a balm against the rawness inside me. "And Ty did what he did to protect both of us. That doesn't make you a monster, Ciaran. It makes you human."

Her words should have lifted the weight on my chest, but they only made me feel it more acutely.

I leaned into her touch, closing my eyes and breathing her in, trying to anchor myself in her warmth.

"I'm so tired of secrets," I whispered, my voice breaking.

"Then let's not keep any more," she said, her voice like a promise. "Not from each other. No matter what."

I nodded, pressing my forehead against hers, her warmth seeping into me. For the first time in years, I felt a flicker of something I hadn't dared to believe in for so long.

Hope.

Ava let out a slow sigh, her gaze dropping to the space between us. "Then I need to tell you what happened at Blackthorn..."

My chest tightened, that fragile hope crushing under the weight of dread. "Okay..."

Her hands twisted in her lap, and she hesitated, visibly gathering the courage to speak.

"Ty... he took me through a kind of therapy." Her voice was barely above a whisper when she finally spoke. "A... sexual form of therapy."

Her words hung in the air, sharp and heavy, cutting

straight through me, her admission reverberating in my head like the tolling of a funeral bell.

A *sexual* form of therapy.

My mind couldn't wrap around the implication, couldn't believe what she was saying.

"He touched you?" My voice came out low, sharp, dangerous. I searched her face for a denial, for anything that would contradict the images searing through my brain.

Her expression gave her away, a flicker of guilt, of shame. I didn't need her to say it.

Ty had done *more* than just touch her.

The realization hit me like a fist to the chest. Fury surged, burning hot and uncontrollable, and before I knew it, I was off the bed, my body moving on pure instinct.

I didn't care that I was barefoot, shirtless, just wearing my gray sweatpants.

I didn't care about anything except hunting down Ty and making him pay.

Ava blocked my path. "Scáth, wait!"

"Ava, move," I growled, my voice like gravel, raw and rough.

Her hands pressed against my chest, trying to hold me back. "Please," she said. "It was… just tough love. It didn't *mean* anything."

Didn't mean anything? My head spun. My chest heaved as I tried to rein in the rage clawing at my insides.

"Step aside, Ava," I repeated, my tone harder, colder this time.

"Promise me you won't hurt him."

"Can't. Promise. That." My words were ground out between clenched teeth.

Her expression shifted in an instant, her anger flaring to match mine.

"Ty has suffered enough," she shot back, her voice rising. "He has paid enough."

"He hasn't paid for *this*."

"Do you know what your brother went through in prison?" she said, her voice breaking. "He was just a boy, Ciaran. A boy in a cage with men. With monsters. Do you know what they *did* to him?"

Her words landed like a punch to my gut, knocking the wind out of me. My blood ran cold, the fury draining from my body, leaving behind a hollow, twisting ache.

I didn't know. I hadn't let myself imagine it.

Until now.

Ty had suffered for me. He'd gone to prison for a crime I committed. And while he was locked up, enduring God knows what, I'd been free. Free to live, to breathe, to seduce Ava. The girl he'd always loved.

My shoulders sagged under the weight of her words. My legs gave out, and I sank onto the bed. The rage that had burned so brightly just moments ago was replaced with something far worse—guilt.

I buried my face in my hands, disgusted with myself.

"I'm a shit brother," I muttered, the truth tasting bitter on my tongue.

Ava kneeled in front of me, her hands on my knees.

"Ciaran," she said softly. "You have to forgive him. Please… for me?"

Maybe I could forgive Ty for his… *sexual* therapy, if it helped Ava.

I lifted my head to meet her gaze, her plea slicing through me.

"Did it help you?" I said, my voice barely above a whisper.

"Yes," she said without hesitation. "He only did what he did because he was trying to save me. And he did. He *saved* me, Ciaran. I remember what your father did to me, and I'm still standing. I remember the pain, and I'm still smiling. I remember the darkness, and my heart is still filled with love."

Her words should have been a balm, but they only cut deeper. She was alive, whole, because of *Ty*.

The way she said his name. The light in her eyes when she spoke of him. It was like a blade twisting in my chest.

Ty had burrowed his way under her skin. He owned a piece of her now, a piece I wasn't sure I'd ever get back.

My fear was a living thing, coiling in my gut.

Ty wouldn't stop. I knew my brother. He wouldn't stop until he reclaimed her completely.

AVA

If it had been for anything less important, I would have asked Ciaran to stay. Begged him to stay.

I wanted him here, for our first night in the dorms. It should have been another moment for us—a chance to keep reconnecting, rebuilding *us*.

Instead, it was just Ty and me.

And that made me nervous.

Stupid. It wasn't as if Ty and I hadn't spent the entire summer together, trapped in Blackthorn Hall, bound by dark secrets and pain.

He was my best friend, had been since childhood. A part of me still clung to that—clung to him.

Maybe that was the problem. Because deep down, I knew exactly why I didn't want to be alone with Ty.

The part of me that clung to him wasn't innocent.

It wasn't the part that remembered childhood laughter or the warmth of his presence when I felt small and scared.

It was the part of me that remembered what happened between us in Blackthorn, the intimacy we'd shared, the way he'd let me see him. All of him. The way he peeled back his icy armor and let me touch the cracks underneath.

And the way he'd touched me, the way he'd licked my pussy, and the way he thrust his cock inside me and fucked me.

I still felt that pull, the ache in my chest when his walls dropped, the heat when his hand brushed mine. It terrified me, how much my body still reacted to him, even now. Even after everything.

That was why I didn't want to be alone with him.

Because a part of me *wanted* to be.

I pushed open my bedroom door, which wouldn't shut properly anymore, and found Ty sitting on the armchair he'd positioned to face my door. He'd been waiting for me and he wasn't even hiding that fact.

My breath caught as his gaze locked on mine, amusement flickering across his face.

"Hello, hummingbird."

Even though he was across the room, his voice felt like a whisper against my ear, soft and intimate, sending shivers skittering down my spine.

I flushed, heat pooling under my skin in a way I didn't want to think about.

"Don't call me that," I said quickly, too quickly.

He tilted his head, the corner of his mouth curving. "Why not?"

Why not? A good question—one I didn't have an answer for. It wasn't the nickname itself. It was the way it felt when he said it, like a thread pulling taut between us, something I wasn't ready to confront.

It felt too… personal. Too close.

Ty shouldn't be giving me nicknames. And I still didn't even know what it meant.

A part of me wanted to turn around and retreat back into my room, to yank the sheets over my head and pretend this wasn't happening.

But I knew better. If I showed him even a crack in my resolve, he'd burrow right in.

I squared my shoulders, determined to act like nothing had happened between us, like we were just friends. Because we were. We *were.*

I'd chosen Ciaran.

"Just… don't," I said, my voice sharper than I intended.

Ty didn't flinch. He remained in his armchair, one ankle casually crossed over his knee, wearing only a pair of black sweatpants. His muscled, tattooed arms crossed over his chest in a posture that was somehow both relaxed and predatory.

My eyes flicked to the tattoos and scars woven into his skin, like pieces of a dark story that only I knew how to read.

To the raven perched across his chest, wings outstretched across his collarbones as though ready to take flight. Its mechanical heart exposed, gears and cogs spilling out as if being torn apart.

To the broken hourglass with bloodred sand pouring out down his ribs, twisted branches and roots snaking through the cracks as if trying to hold it together.

And the cracked human skull across his stomach, nestled among thorny vines and black roses, with a flickering light glowing from within its hollowed eye socket.

Heat rushed to my cheeks before I could stop it.

"Can you put a shirt on or something?" I blurted, stomping toward the living room lamp to switch it on, doing everything I could to avoid staring.

"I'm perfectly comfortable," he replied, his tone a slow drawl. "Are you saying *you're* not?"

"No," I muttered, fumbling with the lamp. The soft amber light filled the room, but I instantly regretted turning it on. It illuminated too much—his piercing gaze, the smirk playing on his lips, the tension humming between us.

I quickly turned away, moving to switch on another light as if I were busying myself, but my heart hammered too loudly in my chest to ignore.

"Are you avoiding me?" Ty asked, his voice cutting through the silence.

"Of course not," I said, too defensive, too fast. "*I* am a student, you know? I actually have to *study*."

"I've been studying too," Ty replied, his voice low and smooth.

There was something in his tone that made me pause, the hair on the back of my neck rising.

When I turned, he was suddenly closer—*too close.*

I hadn't heard him move.

My breath hitched as I realized how near he was, the heat of his body brushing against mine. My chest grazed his, and I was painfully aware of how sensitive my skin felt, how my nipples tightened at the contact. Mortified, I fought the urge to step back—or worse, lean in.

Ty's eyes dragged over me, slow and deliberate, leaving trails of fire in their wake.

I tried to hide the shudder that rippled through me, but his smirk told me I'd failed.

"I'm going to make dinner," I said, forcing myself to break the spell, shouldering past him before I did something I'd regret. "If you want to help."

"I'm an excellent cook," Ty said, his voice darkening as he added, "as you already know."

I remembered holding back moans of pleasure as I ate yet another perfectly cooked meal under his watchful eye.

I remembered him feeding me when I was tied up and blindfolded before he fucked my mouth with his fingers.

I remembered that disastrous dinner when I'd tried to stab him and he'd done God knows what to my body when I was under.

I shoved the chaotic swirl of thoughts away, forcing myself into motion. Pots and pans clanged as I grabbed them blindly from the cabinets and tossed them onto the stove with more force than necessary.

"Did you know it was Ciaran who killed your father?" The words tumbled out before I could stop them, raw and jagged, my head still spinning from his confession.

Ty appeared beside me, silent as a shadow. His hand brushed my wrist, steadying my fumbling attempts to light the gas stove.

The brief contact sent a jolt through me, and I stepped back to the kitchen island, pressing my palms into the cool surface to ground myself.

"He finally told you, huh?" Ty said, his tone infuriatingly calm as he twisted the knob and ignited the burner in one fluid motion. "He finished what you couldn't."

I closed my eyes, breathing deeply, trying to steady my racing heart.

In the darkness behind my lids, I could hear him moving

—gathering ingredients from the fridge, the soft scrape of a cutting board being pulled from a cabinet, the metallic clink of a knife. Every sound was deliberate, controlled.

Peeking out through narrowed eyes, I watched him moving with feline grace, every motion fluid, like a predator biding its time. The play of muscles under his skin of his back, scarred and tattooed, was mesmerizing.

The sleeping reaper and the dark-haired girl leaning in to kiss him.

And farther down to the ghostly wolf that slunk around his lower back, its body half-faded into smoke.

And on the back of one sleeve was a ship trapped inside a glass bottle, the movement of his arm muscles making the flames that engulfed the ship look alive.

Before I knew it, my feet had carried me closer to him, his presence drawing me in like a magnet, even though my mind screamed at me to stay away.

"I went to jail thinking I was taking the fall for you," Ty said, his voice quiet but cutting as he set the cutting board down beside me. His knife flashed in the soft kitchen light, his movements precise. "Ci admitted later that he knew the amount of oleander you'd added wasn't enough. He added the lethal dose."

My fingers curled around the edge of the counter. His words sank in like cold iron. For all Ty's beauty, his ruthless, calculating core was never far beneath the surface.

I watched his hands work the knife, the blade moving so expertly over the garlic and onions it was almost hypnotic.

"But you stayed in jail for him?" My voice was barely above a whisper. "All those years?"

His scars caught the light as I scanned his body, the

marks of battles I hadn't been there to see. I ached to reach out and trace them, to piece together the pain they represented, but I kept my hands tight at my sides.

"Of course," Ty said simply, the knife pausing mid-cut. "He's my brother."

There was no emotion in his tone, no passion. Just a cold, matter-of-fact truth. But something flickered across his face—a crack in his armor, fleeting and almost imperceptible.

I knew their relationship was complicated. Actually, complicated didn't even scratch the surface.

But I also knew Ty *loved* Ciaran.

A pang of guilt twisted inside me. I thought it might have been easier if they hated each other—if the love they shared hadn't made the rivalry between them even more excruciating. It wouldn't be *me* tearing them apart.

They'd both already destroyed pieces of themselves for me. Ty had given up years of his life in prison. Ciaran had taken their father's life for me. How much more could I ask of them? How much more could I take?

"Do you want to wash the tomatoes?" Ty asked, pulling me from my thoughts.

I nodded weakly, the sound of running water filling the silence. I reached for the basket he'd brought earlier from the market.

Behind me, the hiss of onions hitting hot oil made me jump. I was too aware of his presence, the way the heat from the stove seemed to mix with the heat radiating off his body.

A tomato slipped from my hands and rolled into the sink.

Ty reached around me, his fingers brushing mine as he plucked it up. The deliberate graze of his skin against mine sent a shiver straight through me.

"Here," he murmured, his hands closing loosely over mine. The water cascaded between our fingers, warm and intimate.

My breath hitched as the closeness became almost unbearable.

"Why do you call me hummingbird?" I asked, the question tumbling out before I could stop it.

"You're smart. Why do you think?" His voice was low, teasing.

I should have turned away, pulled back. Instead, my nipples tightened from his nearness, and I hated the way my body betrayed me.

"Hummingbirds are small and weak," I said, the words tumbling out in frustration.

Ty froze behind me. In one swift motion, his hands gripped my hips and spun me to face him, pinning me between his body and the counter.

"Hummingbirds might be small," he said, his voice a low growl, "but they're fierce and protective. They're one of the few animals who are bigger on the inside than out… like you."

Oh.

His gaze burned into mine. "There's nothing weak about you, Ava. I don't know who gave you that idea."

The intensity of his words left me breathless, my heart pounding as his grip on me lingered. My resolve wavered, dangerously close to crumbling.

No. You chose Scáth.

I cleared my throat and stepped out of Ty's grasp before I could do something irreparably stupid.

He let me go, but the heat of him lingered on my skin, crawling under my defenses.

I busied myself by roughly chopping the tomatoes before throwing them into the fragrant mix of onion and garlic sizzling in olive oil.

The kitchen filled with the warm, rich aroma, a scent that should have comforted me but only added to the stifling tension.

As I stirred the sauce, willing my hands to stop trembling, Ty moved beside me.

He reached across to fill the pot with water, his body pressing against the side of mine with casual inevitability. He didn't move away immediately, his presence suffocating in a way that left me weak.

My resolve faltered, my grip on the spoon tightening as if it could anchor me.

Finally, he stepped aside, and I let out a breath I hadn't realized I was holding.

Ty set the pot on the burner, his tattooed forearms flexing as he adjusted the heat. The intricate black ink that covered his skin seemed alive under the flickering light, his scars weaving through the designs like threads of pain.

I tore my gaze away, forcing myself to focus on stirring the sauce as the tomatoes broke down.

He reached past me to grab the salt from the shelf above and brushed his arm across my breast. The contact was brief, casual, but it sent a jolt of need through me.

My breath hitched, and my fingers slipped on the

wooden spoon, and it bounced off the side of the pan and clattered to the floor, splattering red sauce everywhere.

Shit.

"You okay?" he asked, his voice low, smooth, as he leaned over my shoulder for the paper towels. His breath tickled my ear, and I froze, my pulse racing.

"Grand," I said, my voice higher than usual. I cleared my throat and tried again. "Just grand."

Ty dropped to a crouch behind me.

I froze, my grip tightening on the edge of the counter. I felt his breath ghost over the backs of my thighs, warm and deliberate. My knees threatened to buckle.

"You've made a mess, hummingbird," he murmured, his tone low, almost teasing.

He dabbed at the red streaks on the floor and the counter, his shoulder brushing against the backs of my legs, his movements slow, precise—calculated.

I sucked in a shaky breath, trying to keep my focus anywhere but on him. On the heat of his body so close to mine.

On the way he nudged my legs apart as he reached between them to supposedly mop up another spot of sauce.

The air felt charged, thick with something unspoken. My hands trembled where they gripped the counter, my breath coming in short, uneven bursts.

Finally, Ty straightened, the paper towels streaked red in his hand. He tossed them into the trash and turned back to me, his expression calm, as though nothing had happened.

"All cleaned up," he said smoothly, his gaze steady on mine.

I nodded, unable to trust my voice, and turned back to the stove, my cheeks burning as I snatched another spoon.

But even as I tried to focus on stirring the sauce, my legs still tingled where he'd touched them, and my heart wouldn't stop racing.

I hated the way I wanted him even when I didn't want to want him.

My mind screamed at me, reminding me of Ciaran, of the love we shared, of the promises I'd made.

But my body… my body was caught in Ty's orbit, pulled toward him against my will.

This was dangerous. Ty was dangerous. And yet I couldn't bring myself to walk away.

My heart raced, my resolve weakening with every second spent in his presence.

You're with Ciaran, I reminded myself again, clinging to the thought like a lifeline. *You love Ciaran.*

"Relax," Ty said, his fingers massaging my shoulders, his tone laced with amusement. "You're acting like I bite."

"You don't?" I shot back, trying to sound casual, trying to play off the heat coursing through me.

"Only if you ask nicely," he replied in my ear, his smirk audible in his voice.

"I'm *with* Ciaran!" I snapped and stepped aside so his hands slid off me.

His gaze never wavered, his dark, penetrating eyes assessing me in that maddening way that made me want to shove him away or pull him closer.

"For now," he said simply, his tone cool, but the words landed like a challenge.

I bristled, the steam from the stove dampening my

already overheated neck. "It's always a game with you, isn't it?"

His expression didn't soften, his lips didn't quirk into that cocky grin. Instead, his voice was low, steady. "I like winning."

I shook my head, my resolve crumbling under his intensity. "You can't win if I don't play."

He stepped closer, his body an inferno against mine. The stove's warmth paled in comparison to the fire licking through me as his breath fanned my cheeks.

"Don't forget, Ava," he whispered, his voice dangerous. "We were children together. I know you *love* to play."

I slid out of his reach and walked to the other side of the kitchen, rummaging around in a drawer for something to do.

But as we continued to cook, Ty moved around me, adding the bucatini to the boiling salted water, adding fresh herbs to the sauce, grating aged parmesan into a small bowl. His body kept brushing against mine, his scent—musk and sandalwood—filling my nose until he was all that I could smell.

I tried to tell myself that I was just imagining his nearness, just imagining that his casual touches were just accidents.

Ty leaned closer again, stretching for a wooden spoon near me. This time, there was no mistaking the hardness of his cock pressing into my lower back.

Heat flushed through me, and I snapped.

"Stop it," I hissed, crossing my arms as I turned to face him.

"Stop what?" he asked, feigning innocence, his calm expression betrayed by the glint of mischief in his eyes.

Asshole. He knew exactly what he was doing.

"Stop… *that*." I waved a hand vaguely in his direction, trying to encompass the infuriating combination of his dark smile, his wandering hands, and how inappropriately close his half-naked body was—*goddamn*, what a body.

His smirk deepened, sharp enough to cut.

"Well, if I'm going to be blamed for something," he said, voice low and dangerous, "I might as well make it count."

Before I could respond, he closed the space between us and crushed his lips to mine.

His hands gripped the back of my neck, firm but not painful, while his mouth was the opposite—soft, warm, intoxicating.

My resolve crumbled before I could stop it, my body betraying me as I melted into him.

Just for a moment.

Then reality slammed back into me.

I shoved him hard, staggering him back just enough to dart for the nearest weapon—a wooden spoon. It wasn't much, but it would have to do.

I pointed it at him like a sword, glaring. "Do that again, and I swear I'll shove you off the balcony."

For a moment, I thought the threat might actually land.

To my surprise, Ty didn't step closer. Instead, he turned and walked to the open balcony door, letting the soft evening breeze tousle his hair.

"What are you doing?" I demanded, spoon still raised.

He leaned out, glancing down.

"Checking to see how far I'd fall." He pulled his head

back inside. His strides were fast, deliberate, as he closed the distance between us again. "I'd probably die. But…"

Before I could react, he snatched the wooden spoon from my grip and tossed it across the room. "Worth it."

His hands seized my head, fingers tangling in my hair as his lips crashed into mine again.

This kiss wasn't soft—it was demanding, insistent, full of heat and illicit need.

His tongue pushed into my mouth, and his hands anchored me, pulling me closer as though he couldn't stand the idea of space between us.

His determination, his cold fury, it shattered my resolve, all my thoughts.

And this time, fighting him felt like the furthest thing from my mind.

The front door handle jangled, breaking the spell. Ty whipped his head around, his predatory focus shifting to the noise.

I slipped away from him, breaking free and rubbing my mouth with the back of my hand just as the door swung open and Ciaran stepped in.

Ciaran, dressed in a navy IT guy's uniform, closed the door behind him and paused. His sharp eyes flicked between me and Ty, lingering just a moment too long. Suspicion darkened his features, his jaw tightening as if he were trying to piece together a puzzle.

"What's this doing here?" Ciaran asked, snatching something off the floor and holding it up.

The wooden spoon.

Fuck.

A wave of guilt and shame crashed over me, sharp and unforgiving. That stupid, innocuous piece of kitchenware had become the symbol of something I couldn't take back—our forbidden kiss.

I hadn't started it.

But I had *wanted* it. I'd been *about* to kiss Ty back, caught in the moment, before Ciaran had interrupted us.

The air in the room grew heavier, thick with unspoken tension. Ciaran's gaze lingered on me, unreadable, and my stomach churned as the silence stretched taut, threatening to snap.

I crossed the kitchen quickly, a bright, forced smile on my lips as I snatched the wooden spoon out of his hand and wrapped my arms around him.

"Scáth. Hi," I said, my voice a little too breathy, too eager.

His hand came up to cup the back of my neck, his fingers threading possessively into my hair. His lips crashed into mine, the kiss deliberate and claiming.

The force of it stole my breath, and I melted against him, my heart racing for reasons that had nothing to do with passion and everything to do with fear.

Fear that this display—this obvious declaration—would hurt Ty.

But Ciaran didn't let me go. His grip was firm, almost defiant, as though he wanted to prove a point.

To Ty.

To me.

To anyone who might dare to question that I was *his*.

I kissed him back, pouring everything I could into the moment, trying to drown out the unease rising in my chest.

His touch was familiar, grounding, and I wanted to lose myself in it. In him. In us.

But the thought of Ty standing mere feet away made it impossible to sink fully into the moment.

Ciaran pulled back just enough to brush his lips over my ear, his voice low and possessive. "Missed you."

My breath hitched, and I nodded against him, unwilling to look over my shoulder at Ty.

"Missed you too," I whispered, even as Ty's gaze burned across the back of my neck.

Ciaran's gaze flicked briefly over my shoulder before returning to mine, his expression softening just slightly. But his body remained tense, his arm still wrapped protectively around my waist as though he were daring Ty to challenge his claim.

I knew what this was. A declaration of war. Not with me, but over me.

Even as I leaned into him, I couldn't ignore the knot of guilt tightening in my stomach. I'd made my choice, but I couldn't deny the ache that came with the thought of hurting Ty, the man who had bared his soul to save me.

The man who, despite my best efforts, still held a piece of my heart.

Ty slammed the bowls onto the low table in the living room with more force than necessary, the sound rattling through the tense air. His expression was tight, his anger barely contained as he barked, "Dinner is served."

I glanced at him, catching the way his jaw ticked, but before I could say anything, Ciaran cut in smoothly, taking control as always. "We can watch the footage while we eat."

Without waiting for a response, Ciaran moved to his fancy wall-mounted TV—the one he wouldn't let anyone else touch—and he plugged in a small USB drive.

He made a point of sitting down between Ty and me. He pulled me into his side, his entire leg firmly against mine as he settled in, his body language radiating possession.

Ty's eyes flicked toward the movement, his mouth tightening, but he said nothing as he sat stiffly on the other side of the couch, his bowl untouched.

I shifted forward, holding my own bowl in my lap as the security footage began to play.

The screen flickered with grainy black-and-white video of The Vault's dimly lit gothic dungeon-like interior, the bar where Liath was last seen.

My earlier swirl of conflicting emotions dulled, replaced by a sharp focus as I spotted Liath weaving through the dark tables dripping with ruby candles to the dark wood bar.

My heart tightened. This was the last that anyone saw her alive.

Liath sat at one of the high red velvet stools and ordered a drink from the guy behind the counter—I recognized him as the bartender I talked to when I went asking questions about Liath.

She seemed shaken. And she kept glancing around.

I remembered the voice message she left me that evening.

"I'm being followed. He's stalking me. Ava!"

I tried to take a bite of the pasta, the rich aroma of garlic and herbs filling the room, but I could barely taste it. My stomach churned with unease, my appetite disappearing entirely as I leaned forward, my eyes scanning every corner of the screen.

Then something caught my attention.

"There!" I said sharply, my voice cutting through the quiet. "Pause it."

Ciaran reached for the remote, pausing the footage just as I directed. I pointed toward the edge of the screen, my pulse spiking as I spotted him.

A man.

"He's watching her. Look at him. He's not just looking— he's studying her."

He was standing partially hidden in the shadows, his gaze fixed on Liath. He didn't move, didn't interact with anyone around him. His attention was solely on her, his posture unnervingly still.

The way he stared at Liath, as though she were the only person in the room, sent a chill down my spine.

Ciaran leaned in, his arm brushing against mine as he studied the screen. "Who the fuck is that?"

I squinted but I couldn't make out his features from this angle.

"Can you get a better shot of his face?" Ty said.

Ciaran picked up the remote and flicked across what appeared to be several camera angles.

He landed on one from a different side of the bar, facing the man.

Something tickled my memory. I grabbed Ciaran's knee. "Can you zoom in?"

With a press of a button, he did, the man's face filling up the TV.

He was handsome, perhaps in his mid-thirties, with sharp cheekbones and an unsettling intensity in his expression.

I gasped.

"France!" I yelled out and was met with blank stares from both brothers.

God, it was unnerving to have them both sitting side by side and looking at me with the same expression.

I explained, my words tumbling out in a rush. "I was with Liath and the girls in the south of France at this sailing thing. This guy was staring at her all night at this club we went to. We were trying to get her to go talk to him 'cause he was cute. But..."

My words faltered, the memory of our last holiday together flooding my mind like a cruel specter.

It had been the last time I saw Liath.

My gaze locked on the man's face frozen on the screen, and a shiver coursed down my spine.

"I swear that's him," I whispered, my voice barely audible over the tension in the room.

Images of that holiday flashed through my mind—laughing with Liath, teasing her about her obsessed crush. We'd joked about him, made light of the way he seemed to linger just out of reach, his attention glued to her.

But it hadn't been funny. Not really.

The icy realization hit me like a blow to the chest. He hadn't been a crush—he'd been stalking her. Watching her every move. He'd followed her to France and then back to Dublin; there was the fucking proof.

He had been stalking her for months and she hadn't known it. Not until it was too late.

He had taken her.

My stomach twisted violently, the weight of guilt crushing down on me as I stared at the screen.

If only I'd known.

If I'd looked closer, paid more attention, I could have stopped it. I could have done something.

I turned to Ciaran. "Can you run his face through, I don't know, facial recognition or something? Find out who he is?"

Ciaran frowned, leaning closer to the screen. His jaw

tightened, the hard lines of his face softening just slightly as he glanced at me.

"I can try," he said, his voice low, almost apologetic. "But don't get your hopes up. The image is super pixilated."

"Chances are," Ty added, "even if we could get a name, he's likely a Sochai henchman and knows nothing."

"We have to try, though," I said quietly, glancing back to the dark man on the screen. "We have no other leads."

Ciaran let out a sharp yelp, startling me so much that I almost dropped my fork. Before I could ask, he bolted out of the living room and disappeared down the hallway into his bedroom.

"What the hell?" I muttered, glancing over at Ty.

For once, his usual unreadable mask was replaced with genuine confusion, his dark brows furrowing as he followed the sound of Ciaran rummaging around.

Ty shrugged.

Ciaran reappeared moments later, waving a manila folder in the air like a trophy. His chest was rising and falling like he'd run a mile, but the grin on his face was boyish, triumphant.

"I can't believe I forgot I had this," he said, his voice tinged with exhilaration.

I frowned, a mix of curiosity and apprehension settling in my chest as I stared at the folder. "What is it?"

He threw it onto the low coffee table in front of me and gestured dramatically. "Go on. Open it."

The buzz of anticipation in his voice was infectious, but it didn't do much to settle the nerves twisting in my stomach. I set my food aside and flipped the folder open.

The world narrowed, the edges of my vision dimming as my focus locked on the papers inside.

My adoption papers.

The papers he'd stolen from me at the library.

The room felt too quiet as I scanned the documents, an unsteady feeling settling in my stomach.

Two sets of adoptions, one from when I'd been adopted by the Donahues and another from when Ebony had taken me in.

My eyes landed on two names that had haunted me in my dreams. My real parents.

Johnny and Molly Carey.

My vision blurred as tears welled up, the letters on the page smudging together. My chest ached, emotions crashing over me in a wave too powerful to fight. I barely had any memories of them, so it felt silly to cry over people I never really knew.

A hand touched my arm, warm and steady. Ty had shifted closer without me noticing, his face soft with concern.

"Are you okay?" His voice was low, almost gentle, the way it had been back at Blackthorn.

"Get your hand *off* my girlfriend," Ciaran snapped, his icy glare directed straight at Ty.

The tension in the room thickened in an instant.

Ty didn't flinch, didn't even acknowledge the venom in Ciaran's voice. He kept his gaze on me, his hand steady. "Settle down, asshole. This isn't about you. Ava?"

I gently pulled my arm free, the movement deliberate, and I wiped the tears from my eyes. The last thing we needed was a full-on brawl in our living room.

"I'm grand," I lied, the words shaky. "Just… I'm grand."

I took a steadying breath and forced my attention back to the papers, ignoring the palpable animosity radiating between the two brothers.

But my focus quickly shifted as my eyes landed on something else. A name that was all too familiar.

The Hallowstone Adoption Agency.

They had been the same adoption agency who brokered Liath's adoption to the Byrnes. The same adoption agency who brokered the deals for the other missing girls. The other *daughters*.

My breath hitched. The weight of the discovery settled heavily in my chest.

"That's the same agency," I said, my voice almost inaudible. "They placed Liath. And the other girls. They're working for the Society."

My words broke the icy standoff between Ty and Ciaran. Both of them turned their attention fully to me, their expressions shifting—Ciaran's to calculation, Ty's to something more unreadable.

"We have to get into their records," I continued, sitting up straighter. "Find out who owns it."

Ciaran rubbed his hands together, his confidence returning in full force. "That's where your genius boyfriend comes in. Sit back and watch the master at work."

He sat down next to me but didn't stop there—he pulled me onto his lap, making a point to wrap an arm firmly around my waist.

I let out an annoyed yelp, fully aware of his intentions. "Scáth, surely this isn't comfortable."

His grip tightened slightly, and he smirked against my ear. "You're my good luck charm, baby."

He set a keyboard on my lap and began typing, his arms caging me in as he used the TV as a monitor.

The warmth of his body against mine should have been comforting, but I was hyper-aware of Ty sitting next to us on the couch, his stare boring into me.

Minutes ticked by, Ciaran's fingers flying across the keys, his focus unbroken, then he let out a humph.

"What?" I straightened. "What does *humph* mean?"

"As far as I can tell, they're a nonprofit owned by a private company," he said, his voice tight with concentration. "Ownership records aren't public."

His fingers resumed their tapping, but I could feel the tension mounting in his shoulders.

I shifted in his lap, trying to get comfortable.

"You shouldn't keep doing that," he warned, his voice low.

"Doing wha—?" And then I felt it.

His cock hardening against my ass.

Oh.

My cheeks flamed hot, and I stilled immediately. "Sorry."

Ty leaned back on the couch, his arms crossing over his wide chest. "Should I give you two the room?"

"No," I said.

"Yes," Ciaran said at the same time.

Several tense minutes passed before Ciaran cursed under his breath, his hands falling away from the keyboard.

"I can't get into their servers," he admitted. "They must be offline and on-site."

"What does that mean?" I asked, trying to keep the disappointment from showing in my voice.

"It means," Ty said, "if we want to find out who owns Hallowstone… we've got to break in."

AVA

"Relax, hummingbird," Ty murmured, his voice low and teasing as we reached the front steps of the Hallowstone agency. His arm slung possessively around my shoulders, making me shiver. "You're supposed to look like you love me."

The problem was, I wasn't sure I was faking it.

Ciaran hadn't wanted me to do this.

Neither had I.

But we didn't have any other choice. Ciaran was the only one who could hack into the files, and someone had to distract the director so he could get into her office.

That someone was me and Ty, pretending to be a happy, hopeful couple looking to adopt.

The Hallowstone agency loomed before us, a relic of Victorian grandeur, its facade imposing, constructed of dark stone that seemed to absorb the weak sunlight filtering through the overcast sky. Ivy crept along the weathered brick, its tendrils clawing at the tall, arched windows framed by black wrought-iron grilles.

A steep, gabled roof crowned the building, its slate shingles faded and cracked with age. A pair of stone gargoyles perched at either side of the entrance, their grotesque faces twisted in eternal sneers as if daring us to step closer.

Ty helped me up the creaky steps to the porch, framed by ornate, gothic columns, their intricate carvings depicting thorny roses and skeletal branches that twisted together like a macabre tapestry.

The brass doorbell gleamed against the agency's dark, weathered door, a sharp contrast to the gothic decay around it.

I reached for it, but Ty's hand darted out, gently gripping my wrist and stopping me in my tracks.

"Hold on," he said softly, his tone unusually tentative.

I frowned, my hand hovering midair. "What is it?"

Ty slipped his free hand into his pocket and pulled out a small velvet box.

My breath hitched, my pulse racing as the weight of the moment sank in.

"Almost forgot this," he murmured, flicking it open with a smooth, practiced motion.

Inside was an antique engagement ring, the kind of thing that seemed too perfect to exist outside of dreams.

A massive marquise-cut diamond gleamed in the faint light, surrounded by delicate clusters of smaller stones that caught every hint of sunlight.

It was stunning. Unique and timeless. Exactly what I would have picked out for myself.

My throat tightened, and when I tried to speak, only a string of stammered sounds came out.

Ty chuckled, a rare sound that sent an unwelcome

warmth curling through me. He plucked the ring from its velvet nest.

His usual stoic mask was gone, replaced with something achingly raw. His cheeks flushed pink, and his lips curled in a smile so tender it felt like a punch to my chest.

I hadn't even realized I'd lifted my hand until I felt the cool weight of the ring sliding over my finger. I tilted my hand, the diamond catching the dull afternoon light, and my heart slammed against my ribs.

For a fleeting moment, I let myself imagine what it would be like to have a normal life. To be a woman who said yes to an uncomplicated proposal from an uncomplicated man. Who cried with joy and never from the memories of her buried darkness. Who imagined a simple forever with someone who didn't carry a soul full of scars.

My fingers pressed to my lips as I whispered, "It's beautiful."

"You deserve nothing less," Ty replied, his voice low, his words reverent.

I tore my gaze from the ring and looked up at him, but the lightness of his earlier smile had vanished, replaced with that intensity I could never escape.

My breath faltered under his stare, and I searched for something—anything—to break the spell.

"It looks real," I blurted out.

"It is," he said simply.

I blinked, thrown. "You stole someone's ring?"

His laugh was quiet, almost indulgent. "I bought it."

"When?" I demanded, incredulous. "When exactly did you have time to go ring shopping since last night when we made our plans?"

He took my hands in his, his fingers warm and steady against my trembling ones.

"Ava," he began softly, his voice thick with something unspoken. "I bought it years ago."

The air seemed to still around us, and my heart tripped over itself. "What?"

Ty's thumb traced slow, deliberate circles over the back of my hand.

"For you," he said, his words weighted with emotion. "I bought it for you."

My knees threatened to give out, but his grip kept me tethered.

"For me?" I whispered, the question barely audible.

He nodded, his jaw tightening like he was trying to hold himself together.

"Before I went to jail," he admitted, shrugging like it was nothing.

But it wasn't nothing.

It was everything.

My heart swelled, caught somewhere between aching and breaking. The memories hit me like a tidal wave—of him chasing me through rose gardens at Blackthorn Hall, of laughter and stolen glances.

All that time, he'd been carrying this secret. Carrying this ring.

He'd never seen me as just a friend.

I'd always been *his*.

The overwhelming wave of emotion swept me forward before I could think. Rising on my tiptoes, my lips searched for his. I didn't hesitate, didn't stop to consider the consequences.

But before our lips could meet, before I could fall into oblivion, before I could choose between damnation and redemption, the door opened beside us.

I rocked back onto my kitten heels and Ty cleared his throat.

A woman in a well-fitted pencil skirt tapped a pack of cigarettes into her palm before noticing us. "Oh. Excuse me."

She checked her wristwatch.

She had clearly been hoping to slip in a smoke break that we ruined.

She gave us a smile and held open the door for us.

"You must be Mr. Donahue," she said to Ty.

He inclined his head in assent and then gestured to me.

"May I introduce Mrs. Donahue," he said, interlocking his hand into the one on which I wore his ring. "My *wife*."

I should have hated the way my heart trilled.

My wife.

It should have felt wrong—unnatural, a lie we'd crafted to infiltrate this place.

But the truth was, I didn't hate it. Not even a little.

"...and finally, this is where we host our monthly family engagement events," the director said, her smile practiced but proud as she led us into a small ballroom that reminded me of the one in Blackthorn with its soaring ceilings adorned in intricate plasterwork and a massive crystal chandelier casting shimmering light over the polished parquet floors.

I nodded along, doing my best to appear like the devoted wife I was pretending to be.

This isn't real.

I told myself over and over.

But the words felt hollow, empty, as Ty's fingers, firm on the small of my back, sent waves of heat through me that were anything but pretend.

"Can you imagine, my love," Ty said as he pulled me closer, his arm wrapping snugly around my waist. "Us here, dancing, with our little girl or boy clinging to your dress."

My heart clenched, a sharp, unexpected pain slicing through me as the fantasy took root before I could stop it. I saw it so clearly—the grandeur of the ballroom alive with music, a child's laughter echoing as little hands clung to the hem of my dress.

It was a perfect, impossible dream, one that didn't belong to me. Not with Ty.

I shoved it away, hard, burying it before it could sink its claws in too deeply.

This wasn't real. It couldn't be.

I tried to laugh it off, forcing a smile even as the ache in my chest lingered like a stubborn bruise.

But Ty's firm muscular body, flush against mine, burned through the fabric of my dress, his touch maddeningly possessive as he stared down at me.

I felt the weight of his gaze, heavy and unrelenting, and I knew exactly what he intended. The line he meant to cross. The line he—*we*—both swore to Ciaran we wouldn't.

"Just... promise me you won't kiss her."

But God help me, I didn't move. I couldn't.

My breath caught as Ty leaned in, his lips brushing softly against mine.

I tore my lips away, guilt churning in my stomach, hot and suffocating.

I was betraying Scáth. I was betraying him by feeling this much. By letting my heart stutter every time Ty whispered "my wife" or brushed his lips against mine with a tenderness that didn't feel fake.

I hated that part of me wanted to believe it. That part of me didn't want to stop pretending.

And maybe that was the worst of it—knowing that deep down, I wasn't sure if I could even call this pretending anymore. Not when Ty looked at me like that. Like I was his whole world. Like I'd always been his.

"This must be such an emotional journey for the two of you," the director said, her tone empathetic. "Finding the right fit, building your family…"

"Our road has been challenging and painful," Ty said, his voice carrying a weight that went beyond the ruse. "And for a while, I thought she was going to choose someone else… But I vowed to her I wouldn't stop until she realized she was *mine*."

I swallowed hard, my pulse hammering against my ribs.

The director made a soft, approving sound, clearly charmed by Ty's devotion.

This wasn't just a game to him. And that scared me more than I cared to admit.

I had to put a stop to this. I had to remind him that I *wasn't* his and never would be.

I forced myself to meet Ty's gaze even though it felt like stepping into a fire. I reached out to rest my hand lightly on his arm, the gesture warm and affectionate—perfect for the ruse.

"True, it hasn't been easy," I said, my voice steady but laced with a pointed edge meant for him alone. "But I've always believed in staying true to my promises. To my heart. Even if it lies in the *shadows*."

If Ty felt threatened by my words, he didn't show it. The resolute stubbornness remained on his face.

"Promises are funny things, aren't they?" he said, his tone smooth but layered with meaning, his gaze never leaving mine. "Sometimes we make them to feel safe. Because we *think* they're right."

His hand brushed against mine, casual to an onlooker, but deliberate enough that I felt the heat of his touch like a brand.

"It's always been easy for you to hide from yourself, hummingbird. But I'll always lead you back to the truth. No matter how painful it is."

My breath hitched, the double meaning in his words slicing through the careful resolve I was trying to maintain.

The director might have thought we were speaking about family, about our fake courtship, but Ty's intensity told me exactly what he meant: I was lying to myself. About him. About us. And he wouldn't let me run from it.

The director cleared her throat and fanned herself. "My goodness, you two. It's clear how intensely you feel for each other."

I forced a laugh, swallowing the knot in my throat as I took a small step to the side.

Ty didn't let me go far. His fingers trailed down my back

before settling on the small of it, a reminder that he was still in control of this performance.

Even though it wasn't really just a performance for him.

My heart pounded as I avoided his gaze, my eyes darting to the clock on the wall.

Ciaran had to be almost finished. He had to be.

Ty's boldness was spiraling, and I wasn't sure how much longer I could keep ignoring how it affected me.

The director held out her hand to escort us out. "There will be plenty more time for any other questions you may have."

Ty held out his hand for me and I took it.

Before I could stop myself, I imagined that we lived in a different life. We would go out to lunch in the city. He would buy an expensive bottle of champagne to toast the start of our journey toward adopting a baby.

Our baby.

As we climbed into bed that night, the only thing on our minds would be what to call her. Or him. We'd shed a tear because we both were thinking Mona for a girl, after his mother.

A sadness settled in my stomach, because I knew it was not a life made for me.

Not with my past.

Not with the Sochai still out there taking girls, using girls.

Not with a good man's heart in my hands.

I walked with Ty out into the hallway, my head spinning.

The director thanked us warmly, her smile practiced and full of hope as she wished us luck on our "journey to parenthood."

But I couldn't summon even the pretense of a smile because my attention had been snagged elsewhere.

At the end of the hallway, a figure was retreating from the door of the director's office, moving too quietly, too deliberately. The black hood masked most of his face, but not enough to hide the flash of icy-blue eyes that burned with a familiar madness as they glared at where Ty held my hand.

Ciaran.

My stomach plummeted, fear gripping me like a vise.

Ty was still shaking the director's hand, his polite mask firmly in place, but the moment she turned toward her office, everything would fall apart.

She would see Ciaran. And then what? She'd scream. Call the police.

Perhaps even the Sochai. We'd *all* be caught.

I moved before my thoughts caught up, desperation guiding me.

"Oh, Ty," I said. "I think we've found our perfect agency!"

Ty barely had time to react as I flung myself into his arms, wrapping my hands around his neck and pulling his lips down to meet mine.

At first his mouth was stiff, unyielding against mine. He froze, likely shocked at my sudden initiative—and maybe even at the blatant betrayal of the promise I had made to his brother.

But then he melted into me, his arms tightening around my waist, pulling me flush against his chest.

His tongue swept across my bottom lip, coaxing a gasp from me, and I let him in, the taste of him overwhelming me, consuming me. The kiss deepened with a heat and intensity that stole the breath from my lungs.

A shiver of guilt rippled through me as somewhere in the back of my mind, alarms blared that Ciaran was watching, screaming that this was wrong.

That I wasn't Ty's. That I didn't belong to him.

But the kiss didn't feel wrong. It felt like fire. Like home. Like everything I'd tried so hard to suppress, clawing its way to the surface with an undeniable ferocity.

My heart swelled to the point of bursting, as though a dam deep within me had finally shattered, unleashing a flood of emotions I'd fought desperately to keep at bay. Like the buried memories I'd tried so hard to forget, they surged to the surface, refusing to be silenced.

There was no more denying it and there was no more *wanting* to deny it.

I still loved Ciaran. I always would.

But I had fallen for Ty, too.

Hiding in the empty office, I pressed my back against the cold wall and tried to steady my breathing. The faulty window latch had been a lucky find—one I planned to exploit—but for now, it was all about waiting for the right moment.

Waiting. And listening. Every sound outside in the reception area carried into this small room, clear as a goddamn bell.

"Welcome, Mr. and Mrs. Donahue. Please, come in," the receptionist said, her voice polite and warm.

The sharp click of Ava's heels echoed on the marble floor, a sound that sent a pang through me.

I could almost picture her walking in, poised and perfect, her hand lightly brushing Ty's arm as they kept up their ruse.

And then Ty's voice cut through, smooth and dripping with something I couldn't quite place. "Every time someone calls you 'Mrs. Donahue,' I keep expecting to be awakened from this dream. But you are my wife, aren't you? You are *mine*."

The words landed like a punch to my chest.

It wasn't just the words themselves—Ty's tone held a lightness, an unguarded warmth I hadn't heard from him in years. It was as if, for once, there was a beating heart beneath all that cold, calculated steel.

I fucking hated it.

Ava's laugh followed, soft and sweet like it was meant to taunt me.

The receptionist gushed, her cooing voice like nails on a chalkboard. "Oh, you two are just the cutest! I'll let the director know you've arrived. Coffee or tea for either of you?"

I held my breath, straining to hear their answers.

"My wife takes milk and two sugars in her coffee," Ty said, his voice steady and sure.

I froze, my blood turning to ice. *Is that true?*

I didn't know.

Ava and I had never actually spent a morning lingering over breakfast together.

"And my husband prefers his coffee black. Like his heart," Ava quipped, and the soft laughter that followed felt like a dagger between my ribs.

They knew these small, intimate details about each other. The kind you didn't learn in passing. The kind you learned by spending days—weeks—together.

My stomach churned. Of course they knew. They'd spent an entire summer side by side. Eating together. Talking. *Living.*

The realization slammed into me, hollowing out my chest.

Ty knew Ava in ways I didn't. In ways I hadn't allowed myself to.

Because I'd spent our childhood being her bully, being cruel to her and pushing her away.

And as adults, I'd spent most of my time with her lurking in the shadows, watching her from a distance. Hiding who I really was.

But Ty? He'd been right there. With her. Every damn day. Then. And now.

He knew her. Really knew her.

Jealousy clawed its way up my throat, hot and suffocating, but I shoved it down. There wasn't time to dwell. The clicking of heels and the steady thud of dress shoes signaled the director's arrival, her cheery voice cutting through the air.

"Mr. and Mrs. Donahue! It's so lovely to meet you. Please, follow me."

Focus. Ty and Ava had done their part. And if I didn't want their playacting the happy fucking couple to be for nothing, I had to do mine.

I peeked out of the office room, my pulse thundering in my ears.

On one end of the elegant hallway was the director's polished cherry wood door. At the other end stood Ava and Ty, the perfect picture of a beautiful couple.

The director extended a hand, her smile practiced and professional, but my focus zeroed in on *them*.

Ty's arm was draped around Ava's shoulders, possessive

and protective, and every fiber of my being screamed to rip it off her. Smash my fist into his smug, laughing face.

But we all had our roles to play.

They're pretending. At least *Ava* was pretending.

But then she glanced up at him, her smile radiant, as if the world began and ended with him. The way she leaned into him, relaxed and trusting, gutted me.

That wasn't fake. That wasn't for show.

A sharp, bitter pain stabbed through my chest, but I didn't have time to wallow in it. The director led Ty and Ava down the hallway, their laughter floating back to me like an echo of everything I was losing.

As soon as the hallway cleared, I slipped out, moving fast but silent. I darted into the director's office and moved behind the oversized mid-century desk. A sleek new computer sat there, powered on and ready for me.

I shoved a USB drive into the port, my movements efficient, but my thoughts chaotic.

The files began copying, the slow progress bar ticking forward, and I tried to focus.

My eyes kept darting to the closed door, my ears straining for footsteps, but all I could see—*all I could feel*— was Ava's smile as she looked at *him*.

Bright. Genuine. The kind of smile that used to belong to me.

My fingers curled into fists at my sides.

I could still hear her laugh, light and musical, and the easy confidence in her tone when she rattled off Ty's coffee order.

My stomach churned as jealousy clawed at me. Where

was Ty touching her now? Her hand? The small of her back? Her face?

I'd made them promise they wouldn't kiss, but they'd have to touch. Hold hands. Lean into each other. Pretend to be madly in love.

What if it wasn't all pretend?

I gritted my teeth and shoved the thought down.

Enough.

The files finished copying, the drive glowing briefly as it ejected.

I grabbed it, my heart hammering, and slipped it into my pocket. Time to get the hell out of this place and end my brother's little fantasy of playing house with my girl.

But my anger had made me sloppy.

I was halfway out the office door when I saw them.

Ava and Ty, standing just down the hall. Ava looked radiant under the soft light, her hand in Ty's, her face bright with her practiced smile.

A hollow ache flared in my chest at how effortlessly they played the part of a couple.

Then I spotted the director standing with them, her back to me, and I froze, every muscle locked.

All it would take was one look. One casual glance over her shoulder, and the director would see me standing there, caught red-handed.

I was so screwed.

Ava's eyes locked with mine, wide with panic.

In the very next breath, she turned to Ty with a honeyed smile and cooed, "Oh, Ty, I think we've found our perfect agency!"

Then her arms wrapped around his neck.

My breath caught, and I froze in place, rooted to the spot as her lips pressed against his.

The kiss wasn't fleeting. It wasn't a brush of lips for the sake of appearances. It was deliberate. Real.

Icy betrayal gripped me, spreading like poison through my veins. *She swore.* The one promise I'd demanded from both of them.

No kissing.

No crossing that line. And now here they were, breaking it right in front of me.

The sight of Ty's arms tightening around her waist, pulling her against him, was a knife to the gut.

My rational mind tried to speak through the chaos. *She's doing this to protect you. To keep the director from turning around and spotting you.*

But the jealousy, the fury, burned hotter than reason.

Ty didn't just go along with it—he leaned into it, deepened it. His hand slid possessively to the small of her back, anchoring her to him like he had every right.

Bastard.

My fists curled at my sides, my nails digging into my palms as I fought the urge to storm down the hall, rip her from his arms, and remind them both exactly who Ava belonged to.

But I couldn't—wouldn't—ruin everything. Not when the stakes were so high.

I forced my gaze away, the image of them searing into my mind like a brand, and I moved swiftly down the hall.

The kiss gave me the distraction I needed, the director's attention firmly occupied, but every step felt like dragging my feet through molten lead. My chest ached, each breath sharper than the last.

Reaching the room I'd scouted earlier, I slipped inside, the cool air from the partially open window cutting through the heat in my veins.

I climbed out through the window, the scent of damp earth and distant rain filling my nose, my heart still pounding as my feet hit the gravel outside. But it wasn't the fear of being caught that consumed me—it was the sight of Ava in Ty's arms, her lips on his.

She'd done it to protect me. I knew that. But knowing didn't erase the way her kiss lingered in my mind, how Ty's hands on her made my blood boil.

The line had been crossed, and my blood burned with a fury I could barely contain. I didn't know who I was angrier at—Ty or Ava.

Ty? I expected it from him. Of course, I did. I knew he'd use the married couple ruse as an excuse to push boundaries, to test how far he could go.

I couldn't even blame him, not entirely. If our roles were reversed, if it were me pretending Ava was mine, I'd do the same damn thing without hesitation.

But Ava? I trusted her. I believed her. When she kissed me and whispered, *"Scáth, my kisses and my heart are only for you,"* I'd let myself hope that it was true.

That it would always be true. That no matter how close Ty got to her, no matter how much he tempted her, she'd keep him at arm's length.

Now, that trust felt cracked. Fragile. The way she'd leaned into him, the softness in her expression—it wasn't just acting.

I got into my sleek black sedan, and before I could question my actions, I drove off without waiting for them. I didn't know where I was going. I just knew that if I saw them right now, I'd probably kill them both.

As the Dublin streets blurred past my window, fear twisted in my gut, sharp and suffocating.

Had something shifted between them? Had that kiss, however much of a performance she might claim it was, awakened something between them that I couldn't stop?

The thought was like poison, spreading through my veins.

I'm losing her.

AVA

Two days. Two fucking days since we infiltrated the adoption agency, and Ciaran was still gone. Still not answering his phone.

I at least knew he was alive. My messages had all been read, the small "seen" indicator glaring back at me like a taunt. But no response. Nothing.

The professor's voice filled the Nevermore lecture hall, sharp and deliberate, cutting through the air as he launched into the intricacies of Investigative Journalism and Ethical Boundaries.

I sat in one of the back rows of the vintage wooden desks. The ornate gothic chandeliers above cast a warm glow over the lecture hall, their intricate ironwork dripping with tiny lights.

My gaze wandered past the charcoal walls to the tall arched windows overlooking the green.

Last term, I'd looked out those same windows and spotted my stalker against that giant oak—Scáth.

Or at least, I'd *thought* it was him.

The memory of that moment felt sharp and raw now, like a wound I'd only half acknowledged.

I yearned to see my Scáth there again, his figure blending into the shadows, watching me with those piercing blue eyes.

I wanted to explain. To tell him the kiss at the agency had been nothing. A ruse. A way to save him from being seen.

But even as the thought crossed my mind, something deep inside me whispered a bitter truth: the kiss hadn't entirely been a lie.

But Scáth wasn't there now.

I remembered how I'd thought Scáth had left me when Lisa and I were in Paris, only to discover he'd been there all along, hidden completely out of sight. Was he doing the same now? Watching from the shadows, just beyond reach?

A nudge broke my thoughts. Lisa, sitting to my left, leaned in, her long red hair falling over her face, her nose wrinkling. "Is *he* actually studying journalism now?"

I followed her pointed glance.

To my right, Ty sat with one hand poised over his notebook, taking meticulous notes, and the other absently twirling a strand of my hair around his finger. He didn't even look at me as he did it, so casual it was maddening.

My lips pressed into a thin line as I caught a group of girls sitting a few rows ahead. They weren't exactly subtle, their stares darting from Ty to me, their jealousy so palpable it felt like another presence in the room.

"If he's going to follow me to every single one of my classes," I murmured to Lisa, my voice heavy with sarcasm, "the least he can do is take notes for me."

Lisa straightened. "Can he take notes for me, too?"

I leaned toward Ty, lowering my voice. "Can you make sure Lisa gets a copy of my notes, too?"

Ty finally looked up from his notebook, the faintest smile playing at the corners of his mouth. "For you, anything."

He punctuated the statement by tapping the tip of my nose with his finger.

I leaned back quickly, a flush creeping over my cheeks. I tried to mask it by turning my attention to my notebook, but my thoughts betrayed me.

It had been… nice. Too nice. Having Ty by my side all day, every day, since Ciaran disappeared.

And the last two nights… they were a mirror of how it used to be when we were younger.

Drowsy, half-asleep, I felt the familiar dip of my mattress and the warmth of Ty settling in beside me. Even in the haze of near-dreaming, I knew it was him.

A small shiver ran down my spine as his breath brushed against my hair, and his scent, that familiar sandalwood and musk, wrapped around me like a cocoon.

"If he finds you here, you'll get into trouble," I mumbled, my voice thick with sleep.

"Worth it," he murmured, his arm slipping around me, pulling me into his chest.

"Ty…" I protested again, even as I sank into the comfort of him. "He'll literally kill you."

He shrugged, his movement pulling me tighter against him. "I can take him."

It wasn't right. It wasn't fair. I had chosen Ciaran. I *loved* Ciaran. But he had just fucking *left* me.

And Ty wasn't making it easy to push him away. Not in the way he moved around me, anticipating what I needed with open doors or a fresh coffee, exactly the way I liked it, pushed into my hand.

He made me feel like I wasn't fighting this battle alone. Like I could rely on him for anything. Like he'd *always* be there.

Even now, as he sat beside me, his fingers brushing over the ends of my hair, he felt steady. Unyielding.

I forced my focus back to the lecture, but the weight of Ty's presence was impossible to ignore. And as much as I hated to admit it, I *liked* having him by my side.

The lecture hall door banged open with a thunderous crack, jolting everyone.

My heart leaped into my throat, and I turned sharply toward the noise.

There he was.

Ciaran stormed in, his eyes blazing, his jaw set like stone. Gasps and whispers erupted throughout the hall.

"Oh my God, there's *two* of them!" someone hissed, audible over the rising chatter.

Heat flooded my face as conflicting emotions swirled through me: relief at seeing him, guilt for the kiss with Ty, embarrassment at the scene he was causing, and something else—something primal—at how his presence commanded the entire room.

Ty visibly stiffened beside me. And I fought the urge to reach out and squeeze his knee in comfort.

Lisa elbowed me, her eyes wide as she glanced between Me, Ty, and Ciaran, her expression screaming, *What in the fucking fuck are you going to do?*

"Excuse me, sir," the professor said, his voice laced with irritation as he gestured toward the door. "This is a closed lecture."

Ciaran didn't even look at him.

"You're excused," he shot back, his tone dismissive, making the professor's face flush with indignation. Ciaran's gaze locked on mine, piercing through the distance between us. "I'm here for *her*."

The entire class collectively sucked in a breath, and I froze, mortified.

Crap.

"So sorry, Professor," I called as I grabbed my bag and stood. "I'll just…"

I muttered hasty apologies as I squeezed past whispering classmates. The soft hum of gossip followed me, buzzing in my ears. My face burned hotter with every step, their stares practically boring holes into me.

As I reached Ciaran at the doorway, half angry, half embarrassed, I hissed, "You have a set of stones on you, I'll give you that."

I pushed past him, determined to get outside before he said or did anything else that would make me want to curl up and die.

Ciaran stopped abruptly, holding out an arm like a barrier.

"Not you," he said coldly.

I turned, confused, and found Ty right behind me, his expression calm but his eyes dark and unyielding.

"Where she goes, I go," Ty said smoothly, shoving off Ciaran's hand as if it were nothing.

His voice carried across the room, and the students collectively gasped.

Ciaran's fists clenched at his sides, his face hardening. "You forget your place, brother."

Now Ciaran and Ty were locked in a silent standoff, their glares sharp enough to cut through steel. Their postures mirrored each other—broad shoulders squared, jaws clenched tight, fists curling and uncurling at their sides as if testing their restraint.

The air between them crackled with tension, and I swore they were one breath away from tearing into each other.

"Stop it, both of you," I hissed, stepping between them.

I turned to Ty, my voice sharp and commanding. "You. Stay."

His eyes flickered with something unreadable, but he took a step back, his hands raised in mock surrender.

Then I turned to Ciaran. My tone softened slightly, yet giving no room to argue. "You. Come."

Ciaran's fists relaxed at his sides, and with a curt nod, he stepped aside to hold the door open for me.

Before we could make it out, a guy sitting near the front broke the tension with a joking comment, loud enough for everyone to hear. "Are they like your dogs or something?"

Ty and Ciaran both whipped their heads toward him in unison, their teeth bared and *barked*.

Twin fucking growly woofs.

The room burst into laughter, but I groaned inwardly, pressing a hand to my forehead.

Lord help me.

"Come on." I grabbed Ciaran's arm and tugged him away. "We need to talk."

I stormed into our dorm apartment, the door slamming hard against the wall as my frustration boiled over. "Two days, Ciaran. Two days of silence!"

My voice cracked as I marched toward my bedroom, my chest tight with anger and hurt. "I didn't know where you were or if you were okay. You just fucked off and didn't even give me a chance to explain."

The door behind me slammed shut behind Ciaran, the force of it making me flinch.

"What was there to explain?" His voice was sharp, cutting, as he followed me through the apartment. "I saw enough."

I pushed open the broken door to my room, the creak of the damaged hinge grating on my nerves.

Of course, the door still wouldn't close properly. Thanks to the two of them.

I stepped inside, yanked my backpack off my shoulder, and tossed it onto my desk.

"You think you saw enough, but you didn't," I snapped, whirling around to face him, my chest heaving with emotion. "You're so quick to assume the worst."

"You were kissing him, Ava!" His voice rose, bristling with frustration. "You promised me—"

"To save you, you idiot!" I shot back, my voice shaking as my hands clenched into fists at my sides even as guilt threaded through me. "She was about to turn around and see you standing there!"

"And yet," he said, his tone dropping low, his jaw tightening, "it didn't look like saving me. It looked like…"

He stopped himself, his teeth clenching as if the words were too painful to say aloud.

"What?" I said, my voice hardening even as my chest ached. "It looked like what, Scáth? Say it, for fuck's sake."

He ran a hand through his hair, his pacing making the bedroom feel suffocating. "Like it wasn't the first time."

"Jesus Christ," I said, exhaling sharply as I turned back to my desk. My hands shook as I began pulling out my books, arranging them on the shelf to distract myself from the rawness of his accusation. "Whatever happened between me and Ty is…"

Over. I swallowed down that lie.

And tried again. "I chose you, Scáth. *You.*"

Suddenly, his hand was on my shoulder, spinning me around to face him.

His blue eyes burned with a mixture of pain and anger. "You have to send him away."

I flinched at the weight of his words, the finality in them.

Logic whispered that he was right. That sending Ty away would be the cleanest solution. No more temptation. No more… confusion.

And Ty would do it—if I asked. I knew that. He wasn't lying in the lecture hall when he said he'd do *anything* for me. If I begged him to leave, to do it for me, he'd go. And I'd never see him again.

But the thought of telling Ty that I never wanted to see him again—after all he'd done for me, after the sacrifices he made, after how he suffered so I could be free—it tore my soul into pieces. I'd no sooner send myself away.

"No," I said, voice firm. "Ty is staying. He's my best frie—"

"Your best friend doesn't *look* at you like that." Ciaran's voice rose, his frustration bubbling over. "He doesn't *touch* you like that."

"And boyfriends don't leave for two fucking days without saying a single word!" I shot back, my voice rising as my chest tightened with anger.

His silence was heavy, his jaw tightening as he wrestled with whatever storm raged inside him.

Finally, he spoke, his voice quieter but no less intense. "I left because seeing you with him… It broke me. And I didn't know how to put the pieces back together without… hurting someone."

"You mean hurting Ty," I said, my voice softening just enough to make my point clear.

He looked away, his anger dimming into something rawer, something heavier. "I needed time, Ava. To cool off. You don't know what it felt like to see you… him… *that.*"

"I get that you needed space, but you can't just *abandon* me without a word," I said, my voice cracking. "You need to *tell* me. God, send me a fucking text, leave a note on my bed, something, *anything* to let me know what's going on. If you keep pushing me away every time things get hard, you'll lose me, Scáth."

"I'm not pushing you away. I'm trying to hold on." Ciaran grabbed my arms, his hands clutching me so tightly it bordered on pain. "It's killing me, Ava, watching him try to take you."

"No one is taking me." I exhaled slowly, my anger morphing into need, though the hurt still lingered. "But you have to let me in. You have to *be* with me."

I studied my Scáth, his handsome features contorted with anger, his expression blazing with fire and wrath. But beneath the fury, I glimpsed something deeper—raw, unguarded pain, fragile and aching, hidden behind the storm.

In that moment, I realized Ty and Ciaran weren't so different after all. They both wore masks.

Ty's was made of ice, cold and impenetrable. Ciaran's was forged in flames. But beneath their masks, they were the same—fragile, wounded, and desperate to protect the parts of themselves they feared the world would destroy.

That *I* might destroy.

"I chose you," I said as I reached for him, my hands pulling at his shirt, trying to get at the smooth skin underneath.

With a snarl, Ciaran wrapped his hand around my throat, walking me back until I slammed into the wall.

"Tell me you don't feel anything for him," he hissed.

"I want you."

"You're going to leave me," Ciaran said with so much agony in his voice that my heart split right in two.

"I love *you.*"

His lips smashed against mine, his hands pulling my thighs around his waist, pressing my aching pussy against his hard cock.

I moaned with need mixed with anger and guilt, a heady poison.

Ciaran staggered as if drunk toward my bed, falling on me and knocking the air from my lungs.

"I love you," I said breathlessly when Ciaran pulled away from our kiss to pull my shirt roughly over my head.

"Little liar," he growled, fresh anger clouding his eyes and painting his cheeks a deep red.

He shoved me back to the bed, yanking my skirt and panties off, before diving onto me, preying on my nipples with his teeth, scraping and nipping violently. "Is he a better kisser than me? Huh?"

I reached for his pants, unzipping and kicking them off. I wrapped my hands around his hard cock and stroked him, spreading his pre-cum, my fists squeezing him with frustration.

"Does he touch you the way you like?" His hands were at my throat with the speed of a viper. Above me his eyes were blown out so wide they were almost consumed by black, by lust, by revenge. "Does he?"

Gasping for breath, I moved his cock to my entrance, desperate for him, for oblivion. "P-please…"

He choked me, cutting off my air as he slammed into me.

I cried out in pain, in pleasure, the feelings so intense, washing away all my thoughts, my confusion, my guilt. It was only his fingers around my throat that kept my scream from rattling the walls of my bedroom.

He began to fuck me, hard, bordering on violence, hurting me, punishing me.

I clawed at his back, digging my nails into his skin as I tried to keep up with the pace he set.

"Does he fuck you like I fuck you?"

His eyes were wild and uncontrolled, consumed by lust

and anger. Every thrust was forceful, his body slamming into mine with a fury that bordered on violence.

His fingers tightened around my throat, cutting off my air supply and making my vision darken at the edges.

But I didn't care. All I could focus on was the pleasure coursing through me, blurring the lines between pain and ecstasy.

My whole body erupted into goosebumps even as gray dots appeared on the high vaulted ceilings. I clenched around his cock as he battered me.

"Do you come just as hard for him?"

I pawed at his back, at the damp bedsheets beneath us.

A heady mix of sweat, adrenaline, and the musky scent of sex filled the air around us, overpowering and intoxicating.

"Fucking answer me," Ciaran growled, clenching my throat until I saw stars before he released me with a noise of disgust.

I let out a guttural cry, a mixture of pleasure, pain, and anger. Anger that he was still punishing me. Anger at myself for letting my feelings for Ty cloud me. Confuse me. Tempt me.

I shoved Ciaran off me and rolled on top of him, sinking back down onto him with a groan.

"I want you both," I hissed as I rode him, hard, unleashing my own fury, anger that he fucking *left*, rage that he just might not be everything I need. "Is that what you fucking want to hear? Huh?"

The bed creaked and groaned beneath us. The sound of skin slapping against skin echoed through the room, our grunts and moans mixing together.

"Fuck." He tugged at a fistful of my hair, making me bare the side of my neck to his teeth. He sucked and nipped, pleasure mixing with pain.

Nails and teeth and open palms. We were brutalizing one another. Our pants grew frantic as we desperately bucked against each other like we hated each other.

Ciaran groaned and the tortured words he forced between thrusts stung me like acid. "I'd hate you if I didn't love you so fucking much."

I kissed him and bit his top lip where Ty's scar would have been till I tasted blood.

"I hate that I love you so fucking much," I said, driving my hips back onto his cock harder and faster.

"Say it again," he said, nipping at my chin, my jaw, my throat.

"I love you," I repeated.

"Again."

"I fucking love you."

He grabbed my hips, pulling me down on his dick while bucking his own hips up.

Stars dazzled in front of my face, the whole bedroom fading into a haze.

I couldn't make out anything in the room with any clarity.

But I saw Ty.

Standing in the dark slit of the ajar bedroom door.

He was as sharply defined as a knife's edge.

I kept grinding onto Ciaran as I stared at Ty with a mix of fear and embarrassment and... most unwanted of all, arousal.

This wasn't an accident. Ty had returned so quietly that neither of us realized.

How long had he been watching us? Listening. Unflinching as I rode his brother's cock.

I should have screamed. Alerted Ciaran. Rushed over to slam the door, to bar it closed with a chair.

But the thrill of me watching Ty watching us, of the threat of Ciaran catching us, lashed down my spine. Sordid and dirty. Wrong but it felt so good at the same time.

In the end, I couldn't open my mouth to say a word even if I'd wanted to.

And I didn't want to.

My pussy ached, gushing all over Ciaran as he fucked me with his cock and Ty fucked me with his eyes. I felt the ghost of his hands on my breasts and I arched back, moaning.

I felt the muscles of my inner thighs twitching uncontrollably as Ty unzipped his pants and released his fully hard erection.

My nipples hardened to the point of agony over my voyeuristic crime.

But I couldn't look away.

Ty stroked himself with an infuriating ease. He didn't act like the criminal I felt I was. He was calm, sure, steady.

I took my pleasure like a thief. He took his like a god, like masturbating to the sight of me getting fucked by his twin was his birthright.

I dug my nails into Ciaran's shoulders and I moaned like a whore as the pressure in my lower belly reached its breaking point.

I shuddered and Ciaran groaned beneath me.

"That's it, baby," Ciaran said. "*Come.*"

I didn't care if I was going to burn for this. I needed it. I came with a throat-slicing scream and my back arched like I was possessed as waves of pleasure slammed through me.

I felt Ciaran come inside of me, hot jets of cum filling me as he shuddered beneath me.

I collapsed with a strangled moan against Ciaran's shoulder and he hugged me tight to his chest.

As I lay there, still reeling from the pain and pleasure, I looked back to the doorway.

"I love you," Ciaran whispered.

"I love you, too," I whispered back.

I watched Ty come over his hand in silence as he mouthed, *"I love you more."*

THE WARDEN

I fiddled with the bathroom lock, my fingers working on the picks with practiced ease, while my ears stayed tuned to any sound from the couch.

I could practically feel my brother's focused energy from here as he pawed through the files he'd stolen from Hallowstone Adoption Agency.

Any moment now, he could come stomping in, fists clenched, ready to catch me in the act.

Ava could keep pretending all she wanted—that Ciaran was the one for her, that he completed her, that he was enough.

She could fuck him and lie next to him all she wanted, but she was lying about how he satisfied her. How he made her whole.

But I knew better. I'd been studying her, learning her, becoming an expert in everything Ava McKinsey since the day we met. I knew her better than she knew herself, every flicker of emotion in her eyes, every catch in her voice.

She couldn't hide from me—not really.

Her connection with my brother might have been intense, but it was fragile. Thin and shallow, like the delicate crust of ice over a winter lake. One wrong move, and it would shatter.

I couldn't blame her for being with him. It was only natural, after all, for her to be drawn to the rush of a falling-star love—bright, breathtaking, but destined to burn out before it could leave a mark.

I had Eamon.

She could have Ciaran.

He would give her something I couldn't. Perspective. Contrast. The flare of kindling against the unrelenting fury of a wildfire.

Because that's what Ava and I were. Wildfire.

I remembered watching her last night, glorious as she rode him, her breasts gleaming with sweat, her mouth parted, but her eyes hungry and searching.

Ciaran had given her everything—his sweat, his tears, his anger, his lust, his heart, his cock, his lips, his every last ounce of will—and it hadn't been enough.

Ava searched out among the shadows for the missing piece and found it: *me*.

Need overwhelmed me and for a moment I had to lean my damp forehead against the wood of the door to catch my breath.

The stream of water in the shower stopped, the faint squeak of the handle twisting echoing in the otherwise silent room. I listened intently, hearing wet feet padding softly across the tiles, a towel pulled from the rack, followed by a quiet, almost contented sigh.

The lock slid open under my picks—a soft, inviting click

—and I seized the moment, slipping inside the bathroom.

Closing it silently behind me, I pressed my back against the wood, the oppressive humidity from the steam wrapping around me like a veil, thick with the scent of her jasmine shampoo.

My heartbeat thundered, but I forced myself to stay still, concealed by the fogged-up mirrors and the haze of heat.

Ava hadn't noticed me yet.

In front of the mirror, completely blurred by condensation, Ava tucked the towel around her chest, her hands tucking the edges into place.

Her hair, dark and glistening like raven feathers, clung to her shoulders, droplets trailing down her skin.

It was captivating. Hypnotizing. I was half convinced that if I reached out to grab a fistful of it, it would flutter against my fingers.

I stepped forward, deliberate and silent, moving through the steamy haze until I stood just behind her.

She still didn't sense me. Not yet. The old Ava would have. She would have felt me before I even breached the room.

She had grown careless. Soft. Too quick to unlearn the instincts I helped her hone at Blackthorn. Too coddled by my brother's suffocating protectiveness.

The thought simmered in my chest as I slipped my arms around her waist, pulling her back against me in one fluid motion.

She stiffened briefly, startled, but it didn't last. Her body softened almost immediately, melting into my embrace with a sigh that sent a rush of satisfaction through me.

Her hands found my wrists, clasping them tightly as if to

keep me close, and my lips curled into a slow, dangerous smile against the damp curve of her shoulder.

She gasped when I pressed my erection against her ass.

"Shhh," I whispered into her ear as I eased her towel open.

Her fingertips fluttered against my hand as if she considered stopping me, but the twitch of my cock made her murmur low in her throat and the towel fell to the floor with a dull flop.

Then she was naked and wet.

Her bare body was hot against mine, her pink nipples hard, her breasts already heaving as she rocked her ass against my cock.

Perhaps she thought I was Ciaran.

Or perhaps deep down she realized it was me and needed me anyway.

I'd only let her keep making excuses for so long.

But right now, I didn't care which twin she thought I was.

She was *mine*.

I palmed her breasts and she melted into my touch, head falling back to rest against my chest, lashes fluttering closed. Her hair soaked through my shirt and the fragrance of her jasmine shampoo filled my nostrils.

God, I wanted to drown in her, choke on all she had to give me with her thighs straddling my face.

Ava whimpered as I smoothed my palm over her soft belly and between her legs.

She used her fingers over mine to guide me toward her wet folds and I fought back a groan at the wetness of her.

The warmth of her.

I slid my fingers between her folds, relishing the slick heat.

Ava's breath hitched as I circled her clit with agonizing slowness. Her hips rocked against my hand, seeking more friction, more pressure.

I obliged, increasing my pace as I captured her earlobe between my teeth.

My free hand kneaded her breast, rolling the taut nipple between my fingers.

Ava's hushed moans filled the steamy air. Because *I* knew exactly how to touch her, how to coax those sweet sounds from her lips.

I dipped two fingers inside her, curling them to stroke that spot that made her legs tremble. Her inner walls clenched around me, hot and tight. I pumped my fingers in and out, building a steady rhythm as I rubbed circles on her clit with my thumb.

Ava's hips bucked against my hand, begging for more. I pressed my lips to her neck, tasting the lingering droplets of water on her skin. My teeth grazed her pulse point as I increased the pace of my fingers.

I'd stopped listening for Ciaran. He didn't exist in this moment. Nothing did except her beautiful body in my hands.

"Fuck," I murmured against her ear, "you feel so good, hummingbird."

Ava froze, her entire body going rigid even as I kept working her pussy. She whipped her head to mine over her shoulder, her eyes widening in shock as they met mine.

"Ty," she gasped, her voice barely above a whisper. "What the fuck?"

She pushed at my hands, but I ignored her weak protests because her pussy clenched my fingers as if refusing to let me go. I held her firmly against me. My fingers never stopped their relentless assault on her swollen cunt.

"Keep it down." He chuckled in my ear. "Or maybe you want my brother to come in and see you being finger-fucked raw by me?"

Wetness gushed from her, coating my hand, her body betraying her even as she tried to break free out of some misguided sense of loyalty.

"No," she whimpered, her voice cracking. "Ty, stop. We can't—"

But her protests were punctuated by breathy moans as her hips continued to rock against my hand.

I could feel the tremors building in her thighs, the way her inner walls fluttered around my fingers. She was close, teetering on the edge of coming.

"Fight it all you want," I growled, nipping and sucking at her neck, marking her. "But you love being pinned down by me and forced to come."

My other hand slipped up to her throat, not enough to choke her, but enough to remind her who was in control.

"The only choice you have, hummingbird," I said roughly, grinding my cock against her ass, "is whether you keep quiet so your little *boyfie* doesn't hear or you scream *my* fucking name."

Ava squeezed her eyes shut, tears leaking from the corners as she battled against the orgasm.

I felt the moment she gave in. The moment she embraced the inevitable.

"Fuck you," she whispered under her breath.

She bucked her hips wildly against my hand as I drove my fingers deeper, faster. I could feel her pussy clenching rhythmically, her climax building to a crescendo.

"Good girl," I purred, my lips brushing her ear. "Come for *me*, Ava."

A strangled cry escaped her throat as the dam finally broke. Her entire body shuddered violently, and I held her tightly against me as she came apart, my fingers drawing out every single last drop.

Ava's legs gave out, but I supported her weight easily, her pussy fluttering coming to a stop around my fingers, coating them in a fresh flood of her honey.

I slowly withdrew my hand, bringing my glistening fingers to my lips. The sweet musky taste of her exploded on my tongue as I licked them clean, my cock hardening to the point of pain as I savored every drop.

Ava sagged against me, her chest heaving as she struggled to catch her breath. I could feel the rapid pounding of her heart, the tremors still running through her body. Her skin was flushed, a rosy hue spreading down her neck and chest.

"Who's the better brother now?" I murmured, leaving one last love bite on her neck.

Ava's body went rigid, her muscles tensing beneath my touch. In a sudden burst of strength, she shoved me away, hard enough that I stumbled back a step.

Her eyes blazed with fury as she whirled to face me, her chest heaving with each ragged breath.

"Get out," she hissed, her voice low and dangerous. "Get the fuck out, Ty."

I smirked, reaching for her again, but she slapped my

hand away. The sharp crack echoed in the steamy bathroom.

"Don't touch me," Ava snarled, snatching her towel from the floor and wrapping it tightly around herself. Her knuckles were white as she clutched the fabric, as if it could shield her from what had just transpired.

I could see the war of emotions playing across her face—anger, shame, confusion, and beneath it all, a flicker of desire she couldn't quite extinguish.

I took a step closer, backing her against the sink.

"You don't mean that," I murmured, reaching out to brush a damp strand of hair from her face.

Ava flinched but didn't pull away.

"*You* leaned into my touch," I continued. "*You* tugged my hand to your pussy."

"I thought you were Ciaran." She glared at me. "My *boyfriend.*"

I snorted. "Ava, if you had a twin, I'd *never* confuse you. Even if I was fucking blind *and* deaf."

"You are insane," she hissed, tightening her towel around her.

I hummed under my breath as I adjusted the bulge in my pants. "Really? It wasn't your boyfriend whose eyes you couldn't tear away from when you were getting fucked."

"Fuck you," she said, her cheeks flaring red. "That didn't mean anything."

I shrugged. "Keep telling yourself that."

"Get *out.*" Ava turned toward the fogged-up mirror and snatched up her hairbrush and yanked it through her hair. When her towel slipped, she hurried to pull it back into place.

"It's not like I haven't seen it all," I said, leaning against the wall opposite her and crossing my arms over my chest. "Or had my fingers all over it, all in it."

Her hands flinched, but I kept going.

"My tongue knows every inch of you. I've licked you clean of anyone but me. I've come inside of you, Ava. Your mouth, your pussy, and your ass. I've possessed you, claimed you."

The hairbrush clattered to the counter and I wasn't sure whether she'd thrown it down in anger or whether it had slipped from her damp fingers at my words.

I was fine with either. I could *use* either; I could be her punching bag or I could be her forbidden fruit.

Ava snatched her bottle of lotion and began to rub it onto her arms, her movements sharp and jerky.

She glanced back at me over her bare shoulder. "How many times do I have to tell you that I'm with Ciaran?"

"Just once," I answered, "if you really meant it."

Ava laughed bitterly as she moved her hands to her shoulders. "I've told you *more* than once."

"I've not once believed you," I said in a low, dark voice.

Ava's hands froze around her neck, her back to me, the steamy mirror hiding her expression from me.

But I could imagine the fear which played like a shadow across her face. I knew without touching her that she'd broken out in a cold sweat. Increased pulse. Erratic. Uncontrollable. She knew I spoke the fucking truth.

She began to massage the lotion into her skin again. She wanted to continue to pretend.

I wouldn't allow that for much longer.

"You need to respect my decision," Ava said, lifting one

foot, then the other to the side of the bathtub so she could lotion her legs.

She did her best to speak evenly as she said, "Yes, we had a connection back at the mansion. But I was your *prisoner*. You were drugging me. You touched me for hours. Of course I came for you. Of course I felt… something. But I love him."

"You *feel* more than something for me, hummingbird," I said through gritted teeth, my voice rising.

Ava's eyes darted to the bathroom door, the thin barrier between us and Ciaran, then to mine in warning.

My cock responded to that look. I loved that fire. Her strength. Her sass.

She wasn't some helpless damsel waiting for rescue. She was a force to be reckoned with—a bad bitch who saved herself, who faced the darkness head-on and won. With me alongside her always, of course.

"Whatever existed at Blackthorn, it's over," Ava said, her voice steady as she rose to her feet, the towel clutched firmly around her.

I stepped in front of her, the sole of my boots brushing the outside of her bare toes, forcing her to face me. Her proximity was intoxicating, her scent of damp skin and faint jasmine invading me.

"Look into my eyes and tell me you don't feel anything for me," I said, my voice low and steady, though inside, I was anything but.

Ava swallowed hard, her throat working painfully. She lifted her chin, her gaze meeting mine with something that felt like courage battling guilt. Her hesitation was the crack in the dam I needed.

"Tell me you don't feel anything," I pressed, softer now, more insistent, "and I'll leave. I'll leave you alone… forever."

Her lips parted, and she swayed slightly on her feet, as if the weight of my words unsteadied her.

But she didn't move back. Didn't retreat. Ava never did. That was part of why I couldn't stay away.

She wavered on the precipice, and I leaned closer, relentless.

I never promised her comfort or sunshine and roses. But that's also not what Ava needed.

My love was consuming, raw, and unapologetically real. The kind of love that hurt but left her stronger, forged in its fire.

"I… I feel nothing," she said, her voice fragile, breaking like glass.

But her eyes betrayed her before the words had fully left her lips. They darted to my mouth, lingering there, her breath shallow and rapid.

"Liar," I murmured, leaning down, close enough to feel the heat of her exhale against my skin.

"I'm not… lying," she stammered, but her voice wavered, thin and uneven.

Her breaths came in small gasps, shallow and desperate, like she was trying to pull air from a vacuum. Her lips, slick and parted, quivered as I held her in my gaze.

"Let me prove it to you," I said, my voice barely more than a whisper before I closed the space between us.

The moment my lips claimed hers, a soft, startled sound escaped her throat.

She pressed her palms against my chest in a futile attempt to push me away, but her strength faltered almost instantly. She melted into me, her resistance crumbling as her hands slid upward, tangling in my hair, gripping my shoulders, pulling me closer as though she couldn't bear the space between us.

Her surrender was my victory, but it felt less like conquering and more like finding a missing piece of myself.

Ava wasn't just yielding; she was meeting me. Consuming me as I consumed her, the fire between us burning too bright to be ignored, too wild to be tamed, too deep to be put out.

I hummed against her lips. "This doesn't feel like *nothing*, hummingbird."

"Ava!" Ciaran's voice cut through the thick air, sharp and urgent. "I found something."

"Fuck." Ava shoved me back, her palms pressing against my chest with more force than I expected.

I let her push me, the steam billowing between us like a veil, but it couldn't hide the guilt etched across her face.

"Coming!" she yelled, her tone singsong, but when her glare snapped back to me, it was icy and cutting. "*Don't* do that again."

I tilted my head, a smirk tugging at my lips despite the heat of the moment. "Why? Afraid you can't say no?"

She let out a noise of pure frustration, a mix of anger and something else—something raw and unspoken.

Without another word, she shoulder-barged me, her wet skin brushing mine as she stormed past, the faint scent of her still clinging to the air, her towel clung precariously to her body.

I leaned against the counter, watching her go, the corner of my mouth curving further. Her retreat only left me hungrier, more determined. Whatever lines she thought existed between us had long since blurred.

But this wasn't over. Not by a long shot.

I let out a sigh, tamping down my desire and willing my erection to fade before following out after her.

I slipped out of the bathroom, my bare feet making no sound against the hardwood floor as I walked down the short hallway toward the living room. The muffled hum of Ciaran's computer monitor was the only thing I could hear —until I froze.

There she was. Ava. Sitting on his lap.

Ciaran lounged back on the couch like a king on his throne, one arm casually around her waist. His keyboard was tossed to the side, forgotten, and his other hand—fuck —his other hand was up her towel.

Ava giggled, a soft, breathless sound, and shoved at his hand, though not hard enough to make him stop. The sound cut into me, sharp and unforgiving, carving a hollow ache in my chest.

I would wait forever for Ava to realize she was mine, but watching her with my brother—with the *wrong* brother— was killing me.

Ciaran noticed me first, his sharp blue eyes narrowing.

"Where have you been?" he asked, his tone laced with suspicion.

I realized belatedly that my hair was still damp from the bathroom steam and there were wet patches from Ava's hair and body on my shirt.

"What have you got?" I said, ignoring his question and striding toward them like I didn't just have my hand right where his was not thirty seconds ago.

Ava shifted in his lap, her posture suddenly tense. Her cheeks flushed pink as she shoved at Ciaran's hand again, more forcefully this time.

He smirked, withdrawing his hand, but the smugness in his expression made my fists curl.

She slid off his lap, settling to his side so he could reclaim his keyboard. Her towel rode up slightly, exposing more of her creamy thigh than I could handle, and I felt the fire of jealousy burn hotter.

She avoided my gaze as I settled onto the couch beside her, deliberately brushing my shoulder against her damp one.

Her skin was warm from the shower, her scent sweet and intoxicating. And her nearness sent blood rushing to my dick again.

I brushed my finger along the side of her exposed thigh, out of Ciaran's line of sight.

She shot a glare at me, yanking her towel down her thigh and pulling it tighter around her as if it could shield her from the tension crackling between us.

I lifted an eyebrow and rubbed a finger along my pulse point.

Her cheeks flamed red and she pulled her hair down around her neck to cover the spot where I'd marked her with my teeth.

I smirked to myself, reveling in my brand on her.

My teeth marks on her skin.

My fingers coated in her juices.

Her pussy sated from my attention.

The voice inside my head was almost feral. *Mine*.

Ava was making me crazy, turning me into a gentleman

savage.

Ciaran seemed oblivious, his attention back on the screen as he clicked through files.

"Look what I found," he said, his tone triumphant.

For now, I shoved aside my wild thoughts.

Ava leaned forward, her interest piqued. "You found the owners of Hallowstone?"

"Not quite, but something else…" He pulled up a document on the screen, the bold header reading Donation Receipt.

The string of zeroes in the donation figure was staggering.

He clicked through to another receipt and then another. Each was nearly identical. Each bore the same donor name.

"The Darkmoor Alumni Association," I read.

Ava gasped, her hand flying to her mouth. "Ebony has a photo of the board on her study desk."

Her gaze darted between Ciaran and me, realization dawning in her wide eyes. Her voice wavered as she whispered, "Cormac's father, the dean, the police chief…"

Ciaran pulled up the alumni association's website. On the About page was a black-and-white photograph of the Board of Directors that matched Ava's memory.

There they were next to Ava's adopted mother, the three men in crisp suits, their smiles too knowing, too polished.

Cormac Foley Senior. Dean McCarthy. Commissioner O'Neill.

"One of them must be working for the Sochai," Ciaran said, his voice tight with certainty.

"Or," I said, as my stomach dropped into a pit, "*all* of them."

AVA

The moment I closed the front door of our dorm apartment, I felt a fleeting sense of triumph. Maybe—just maybe—I'd managed to sneak out without them noticing. That hope lasted all of five seconds.

When I started down the stairs, there they were, leaning casually against the wall on the landing below, arms crossed like they'd been waiting for me for hours.

Ty and Ciaran. My shadow and my warden. Matching smirks tugged at the corners of their lips, and for the first time in years, they looked exactly like twins.

"I told you she'd try to pull this," Ty said, his gaze raking over my outfit—an off-the-shoulder white top paired with a pink-and-gray plaid skirt. His eyes gleamed almost playfully. Almost.

"You would know," I muttered, clutching my books tighter and attempting to shoulder past him. But, of course, that didn't work.

Ciaran snagged my books from my hands with infuriating ease, holding them high above his head like we were kids again.

"Off to class so early, rabbit?" he teased, his voice laced with mock surprise.

"It's eight thirty," I grumbled, glaring up at him. "You're a night owl. Why are you even awake?"

Ciaran grinned lazily. "I'm *up* whenever you're around."

I rolled my eyes, but the smirk tugging at my lips betrayed me. With an elbow jab to his ribs, I snatched my books back.

His exaggerated wince made me hesitate, my irritation ebbing for just a second.

Sighing, I handed the books back to him.

His grin widened like a cat who'd just stolen cream.

"You're both not seriously planning to sit in on class with me, are you?" I asked as we descended the stairs.

Neither of them answered. Ty walked in front, Ciaran behind me, like they were trained for some sort of protective detail.

The idea seemed absurd—until we stepped outside, and they flanked me, Ty on my left, Ciaran on my right.

They moved seamlessly, too seamlessly, their eyes darting toward the towering oaks lining the path like they expected a sniper to jump out of the branches.

"There's no way this is going to work," I muttered, glancing between their ridiculously sculpted profiles.

"What do you mean?" Ciaran asked, feigning innocence.

I didn't even need to answer. A passing redheaded senior threw me the nastiest side-eye, her gaze flickering to the boys on either side of me like they were gods descended from Olympus and I was… me.

"That," I said, thumbing over my shoulder.

Ty and Ciaran exchanged a look above my head, something silent and conspiratorial that made me want to scream.

"We didn't see any threat," Ty said flatly.

"Threat?" I barked. "That wasn't a threat! That was toxic clique warfare."

Another group of girls on a nearby bench openly gawked at them before turning their sharp eyes to me. They whispered behind their hands as we passed them, their voices trailing after us. My back prickled as if they'd shot daggers at me with their stares.

"You didn't see that?" I demanded, waving a hand back toward them.

The twins traded glances again, shrugged in unison, and kept walking.

Lord help me. These men were clueless about the effect they had on the world around them.

"You're drawing too much attention," I hissed. "How am I supposed to sneak around campus and investigate the Darkmoor Alumni with two overgrown rottweilers at my shoulders?"

Ciaran grinned, a mischievous dimple appearing on his cheek, and I could practically hear the collective sigh of the girls on campus.

Ty, on the other hand, glared at anyone who dared look our way. His scowl didn't make him any less hot. If anything, it made him look even more attractive in that 'bad boy gonna eat you up and leave no crumbs' kinda way.

Lisa was right. "Under the radar" wasn't an option.

By the time we reached the quad, I could feel eyes

burning into me from every angle. The closer we got to the main college buildings, the louder the whispers grew.

"I can't be guarded by you two all the time," I argued. "We'll get nowhere."

"This very campus is involved with the Sochai who want you dead," Ty said, his head swiveling as though expecting an ambush.

I couldn't really argue with *that*.

"So we aren't leaving your side," Ciaran said as he slung an arm around my shoulders.

A nearby campus loudspeaker crackled to life.

"Ava McKinsey," came the tinny voice. "Ms. Ava McKinsey, please report immediately to the dean's office."

If the twins on either side of me hadn't already drawn enough attention, this announcement sealed the deal. The entire quad seemed to pause, heads turning, whispers surging like a wave.

I repressed a shiver as my mind flashed to the faces of the men we'd spent most of last night investigating: Cormac Foley Senior. Dean McCarthy. Commissioner O'Neill.

We couldn't find anything definitive to pin on them, not yet, but one of them—maybe all of them—had their fingers deep in the Sochai.

I glanced between my boys, suddenly glad for their overprotectiveness. But the knot in my stomach tightened. I couldn't bring them with me. Not to this.

I had to see the dean *alone*.

I was already on edge as I entered the dean's office, the smell of polished wood and old leather hitting me first.

The dean stood from behind his large mahogany desk.

"Ah, Ms. McKinsey. Thank you for coming so promptly," Dean McCarthy said, his smile warm and practiced as he gestured at the single chair facing his desk.

"Of course, Dean McCarthy." My voice was steady, but my pulse spiked as I walked farther into the room but chose not to sit. "Is there… a problem?"

The dean walked around the desk toward me. "We were just hoping to ask you a few questions."

My stomach tightened. "We?"

The door clicked shut behind me, the sound sharper than it should have been.

I forced myself not to react as Commissioner O'Neill casually leaned against the frame, his broad shoulders an impenetrable wall between me and the hallway.

It was a trap.

"You know Commissioner O'Neill, of course." The dean's tone was conversational, as though I'd bumped into him at a garden party.

"Hello, Chief." I forced a polite smile, even as my mind raced.

O'Neill didn't return the smile. His eyes felt invasive, like he was already peeling back my thoughts and inspecting them.

I held my ground, standing until the dean waved toward the chair, his hand brushing the porcelain teacup.

"Please, sit."

I hesitated but moved to the chair and lowered myself into it slowly.

To my horror, the dean dragged a chair over and placed it right next to mine, while the commissioner walked to my other side and turned to face me head-on, leaning against the edge of the desk like a chair.

The dean poured tea, placing a single cup in front of me.

"You're very kind, Dean," I said, matching his polite tone, even as my pulse raced.

He set the teapot down, pouring none for himself. None for O'Neill. Just me.

The steam curled toward my face as I lifted the cup and subtly sniffed the tea. Was that a medicinal note? Bitter, faint but unmistakable?

I only pretended to sip, letting the warmth brush my lips before setting the cup down in the saucer on my lap. My hands stayed steady, but my stomach churned.

"Are you here to update me on Liath's case?" I asked the commissioner, my tone light.

"Liath was deemed a runaway. Case closed, Ms. McKinsey. You know that." He chuckled, the sound dripping with condescension. "Unless you have any more disappearing evidence for me, Nancy Drew? Any more fanciful theories to entertain us with?"

I stiffened but forced a smile. "Then why am I here? Surely, the police commissioner has more pressing matters than entertaining a journalism student's 'fanciful theories' around a secret society conspiracy concerning her missing friend."

That landed. Both men stiffened, though the dean recovered faster, smiling faintly.

"I asked you here in a friendly environment," McCarthy said, his tone like a father lecturing a wayward child, "because the chief has some questions concerning Cormac Foley, your boyfriend—"

"Ex-boyfriend," I corrected sharply.

"Right," the dean said smoothly. "Ex-boyfriend, who disappeared last term."

I couldn't help myself. "Surely another runaway. Like Liath. Case closed, Commissioner."

O'Neill's jaw tightened, but his tone remained clipped. "Unlike Liath's case, Cormac's disappearance showed no signs of premeditated departure. He vanished into thin air. Coincidentally, after telling his father he was going to see… you."

My heart skipped. This had to be a ploy. I couldn't fall for it.

I kept my expression calm, even as my pulse raced. "He said that, did he? What day did he disappear again?"

"Are you saying Cormac didn't make it to your house at the end of last term?" Dean McCarthy's tone was almost idle, but his gaze was keen.

"That's what I'm saying," I replied evenly.

O'Neill leaned forward slightly, his weight shifting like a predator circling. "We know he was in your area, Ms. McKinsey. His phone pinged off a cell tower near your house."

"His phone pinged near my house?" I repeated with a hint of amusement in my tone. "Well, he wasn't the only one in my area, was he? Hundreds of people live nearby. Maybe he was visiting someone else. Or just passing through?"

"Not all of those people had an 'intimate' relationship with him," O'Neill said, his words cutting.

My fingers tightened around the teacup. But I forced my

face into a serene mask. "I don't know what else to tell you. I didn't see him."

McCarthy leaned forward, his smile disarmingly soft. "It's better to clear these things up early, Ms. McKinsey. Avoid misunderstandings."

"Were you angry after he broke up with you?" O'Neill pressed, his voice growing harder. "Wanted revenge? Pay back?"

"*I* broke up with him," I snapped, the words sharper than I intended.

O'Neill smiled faintly. "That's not what he told his father."

I set the teacup and saucer on the table deliberately, letting the silence stretch before speaking. "College boys aren't exactly known for being forthcoming with their parents. Especially boys with fragile egos and reputations to protect."

McCarthy's smile tightened. "You haven't touched your tea, Ms. McKinsey. It's Earl Grey. Your favorite."

My stomach twisted. I don't remember mentioning my tea preferences to anyone here. Was it a harmless coincidence—or proof that they'd been watching me? That they knew more about me than they let on?

"Where did you hear that?" I asked, my tone matching his fake politeness.

The dean waved a hand dismissively. "Goodness, I can't remember where I heard that little tidbit."

I smiled thinly. "It's lovely, but the taste is… strange. Perhaps the leaves have been left out too long. I notice neither of you are drinking the… tea."

The dean's smile faltered. O'Neill's stare intensified. I

knew that neither of them missed the hidden meaning in my response.

"So, am I right to believe," O'Neill pressed, "that you didn't see Cormac at all at the end of last term. Didn't… talk to him? Go anywhere with him, say, in his car?"

"I didn't," I said calmly. "I was probably already gone. On my sailing trip."

"Ah, yes," the dean said, his tone almost too casual. "Your summer trip around… Greece, was it? Croatia?"

The words were laced with the kind of false nonchalance that felt like a knife sliding between ribs. Another ploy to unnerve me, to remind me that they knew too much—more than they should.

I returned his smile. "I see you've been chatting with Ebony."

"She's very proud of you, my dear. She talks about you any chance she gets."

There it was—a flicker of something dark in his eyes, gone as quickly as it appeared.

My heart thundered in my chest. Was he threatening Ebony?

The thought sent ice through my veins. Nothing could happen to her—not because of me. I couldn't live with that weight.

I'd have to warn her somehow. But not directly. Ebony would never let it rest until she knew why I was so anxious. Maybe I could speak to her bodyguards instead, suggest they be extra vigilant. Yes, that might work. A quiet precaution to keep her safe.

O'Neill's voice cut in. "Who did you go on this trip with?"

"A friend."

"I need names and phone numbers," he said.

I frowned. "Why?"

"To check your alibi."

"Alibi?" I repeated, pretending to be confused. "I thought Cormac was only missing. Do you know something you're not telling me?"

"He was—*is*—still a missing persons case," the commissioner replied, but his little slip didn't go unnoticed by me.

He *knew* Cormac was dead.

He *knew* Cormac had been holding me hostage on behalf of the Sochai before he was killed.

But he couldn't reveal that he knew. Or he'd confirm his association with the Society I escaped from.

He continued. "But with these kinds of investigations, we have to consider all the possibilities."

I fixed my gaze on him, my pulse hammering in my ears. The veneer of professionalism he wore so tightly didn't fool me. Not anymore.

There was no way three missing girls—victims of the Sochai—had all been dismissed as "runaways" without the direct influence of someone at the very pinnacle of the Irish police force.

The realization sent a cold shiver down my spine. Commissioner O'Neill wasn't just complicit—he was orchestrating the cover-up.

And now, he was sitting across from me, daring me to slip, to give him the proof he needed to silence me, too.

The tension in the room spiked, heavy and oppressive. The faint hum of the overhead lights seemed louder now, the soft tick of the antique clock deafening.

Even the air itself felt charged, thick with unspoken threats and the weight of what wasn't being said.

My skin prickled, every nerve on high alert, as though the very room itself had turned against me.

The dean broke the silence, his voice growing soft, almost fatherly as he reached out to pat my knee. "You'd tell us if you knew anything, wouldn't you, Ms. McKinsey? We'd hate to see an innocent girl caught up in something way over her head."

I swallowed down the rising bile in my throat and smiled sweetly. "Of course. Cormac and I might not have been together anymore, but I'd hate to see him suffer anything he *didn't* deserve."

My gaze wandered over the desk, trying to look anywhere but at the piercing scrutiny of the men flanking me. I froze when my eyes landed on the penholder.

At first glance, it was an ordinary polished gold piece of office décor. But etched into its surface, small but unmistakable, was a Celtic knot made up of snakes—the crest of the Sochai.

Fuck. It wasn't just the commissioner. The dean was involved, too.

I was being interrogated by two members of the Society trying to kill me.

A chill ran down my spine and I fought to keep my expression neutral.

"Dean," I said, forcing my voice into a light, conversational tone, "that's a lovely penholder."

Dean McCarthy looked up, startled for just a fraction of a second before his practiced smile returned. "Oh, thank you, Ms. McKinsey."

I leaned forward slightly, resting my fingers on the edge of the desk as if inspecting it more closely.

"That crest in particular…" I trailed off, tilting my head. "It seems familiar. What does it mean?"

His hand darted out, as if out of instinct, to rotate the penholder so the crest faced away from me.

"This old thing?" He chuckled, his laugh sounding hollow. "I can't quite recall where I got it. Perhaps it was a gift."

A prickle of satisfaction coursed through me, though I kept my expression amused.

"There seems to be some holes in your memory, Dean," I said, my voice carrying an edge of mock sympathy. I leaned back in my chair.

"Perhaps Dr. Vale could prescribe you something to help with that. Oh, no, wait—" I paused, feigning sadness. "He was tragically killed, wasn't he? In that mysterious fire at the end of last term."

I knew from Ciaran that the Sochai had burned down Dr. Vale's house with his body in it to cover up the condemning evidence in Dr. Vale's basement.

I turned my attention to the commissioner, pretending casual curiosity but letting an edge of contempt enter my voice. "Do you have any leads on *that* case, perhaps?"

The tension in the room shifted, thickened. The chief's jaw tightened as his eyes bored into mine.

"Ms. McKinsey," Commissioner O'Neill said, his voice clipped, "I cannot comment on an ongoing investigation."

I leaned back slightly in my chair, letting a small, innocent smile play on my lips.

"Of course," I said, my tone light but my gaze unwavering. "It must be difficult, juggling so many open cases. Liath's disappearance, Cormac's, poor Dr. Vale…"

I let the names hang in the air like a challenge. "All happening so close together. Goodness, Commissioner, you must have your work cut out for you. I wouldn't dream of keeping you."

I stood, gathering my bag, and glanced toward the door. "If there's no more questions…?"

I moved toward the door, to the exit, to freedom.

"Ms. McKinsey," O'Neill called, his voice low, almost conversational, but the words carried a weight that stopped me in my tracks. "Don't leave town… again."

I looked back, keeping my expression calm and neutral, though my heart thudded painfully in my chest.

The dean and O'Neill exchanged a glance—one too quick for most to notice, but I caught it. They were playing their own game, and I'd just barely escaped.

Outside the office, I barely had a moment to exhale before a hand clamped down on my arm.

I jerked away instinctively, only to find myself face-to-face with Cormac Foley Senior.

AVA

"Ava," Cormac's father said, his grip still too firm to be polite, his touch making my skin crawl. "How lovely to see you again."

Cormac Senior was a sharper, older version of his terrible son.

His sandy hair had silvered at the temples but remained impeccably styled, every strand in place. His tailored navy suit hung perfectly on his tall, lean frame, paired with a pristine white pocket square—pressed and polished to perfection.

There was a quiet arrogance in the set of his jaw, but his eyes burned with something else entirely—anger, hatred, a promise of vengeance.

If he was part of the Sochai, too, then he knew I was involved in his son's—his only heir—death.

"Mr. Foley," I said, tugging my arm free as subtly as I could. "I'm so very sorry to hear about Cormac's... disappearance. I hope the police find him soon. If there's anything I can do..."

"Your concern is… touching, Ava," he said, his outwardly polite tone failing to mask the venom bubbling just beneath the surface. "Considering you were the last person to see him alive."

I didn't bother to mask my defiance. I met his stare head-on, my heart pounding but my expression unwavering.

"Why, Mr. Foley, don't talk like that," I said, my voice sweet but laced with barbs. "It's like you already know he's dead. And how could you know… right?"

His lips tightened, his polished exterior cracking for a fleeting moment. Fury flashed in his eyes, but then his gaze flicked toward the nearby receptionist. The mask slipped back into place, but I could see the cracks forming beneath.

"I will find out who took my boy from me," he said, his voice low and simmering with barely contained rage. "And I will make them pay."

My skin prickled, but I held my ground, refusing to let him see me falter. "I'm sure everyone involved will get exactly what they *deserve*."

His blue eyes, so like his son's yet so much colder, bored into me—a parting threat.

"Hopefully, he's just sailing around the Mediterranean, having the time of his life and forgot to charge his phone." I let out a patronizing laugh over my shoulder at him as I walked away. "Boys will be boys. You remember the Majorca incident last summer…"

His nostrils flared briefly, but he forced his lips into a tight smile. "Be careful, Ava."

I blinked up at him, pretending not to catch the menace beneath his words. "Excuse me?"

His voice was light, almost kind, but his gaze chilled me. "Well, you know… a good many students seem to be disappearing lately. I'd hate to see anything happen to *you*."

I forced myself to hold his gaze for a moment longer, letting my smile widen as though I hadn't noticed his threat.

I turned and walked away, my pulse hammering in my ears, his threat lingering behind me like a shadow, and I knew two things for sure.

They were onto me.

And this was far from over.

The lingering echo of Foley Senior's grip still burned on my arm, the veiled threats of the three powerful men—suspected Sochai members—clouding my thoughts all day like a mist.

Even now, as I walked through the Darkmoor campus library's history section, I couldn't shake the weight of their words—or the implication that I was already caught in their web.

The faint smell of aged paper and leather might have comforted me on another day. Tonight, it only reminded me of the old, suffocating power of the men who ruled this place.

Even the shadows between the towering shelves felt heavier, darker, as if I were walking into the mouth of a beast I'd never come out from.

My fingers brushed along the dusty spines of the library's ancient books, their titles barely visible in the dim light. But my focus kept slipping, wavering between the rows of forgotten histories and the heated argument brewing just behind me.

"It's simple," Ciaran said, his voice low and sharp. "We kill them. All three of them."

Ciaran's hands gripped my shoulders, his fingers digging in just enough to demand my full attention.

His blue eyes blazed, raw and untamed, as he leaned in closer. "They don't deserve to keep breathing after what they've done to you."

I froze under the intensity of his gaze, every nerve in my body pulling tight. The sheer force of his anger clashed with something deeper—something primal and protective that twisted my heart in ways I didn't want to admit.

He was wrong. Killing them wouldn't solve this. But the ferocity in his eyes, the unrelenting promise to keep me safe at any cost, sent a pang of love through me so sharp it almost drowned out my disagreement. Almost.

Before I could find the words to respond, Ty's voice cut through the moment, calm and calculated, the stark opposite of Ciaran's heat.

"It's not that simple, Ci," Ty said, his voice carrying a cold precision that made me shiver. "Just killing them doesn't solve the problem. It just makes more noise. And noise attracts attention we don't want."

The tension crackled between them, an invisible storm brewing in the air. Ciaran's glare snapped to Ty, his jaw tightening as if the mere act of restraint might shatter him.

I felt the moment splinter and took the opportunity to slip from Ciaran's grasp, my gaze focusing on a book title that made the hairs on the back of my neck prickle.

"Are you fucking serious?" Ciaran's voice rose, his frustration breaking past the tenuous restraint he'd managed to hold on to. "You'd rather sit on your fucking hands while they threaten Ava?"

Before I could answer—or before Ty could retort—the librarian's stern voice cut through the tension like a whip.

"Quiet. Or take this elsewhere," she said, her glare cutting over the top of her glasses as she peered at us from the end of the aisle.

I shot Ciaran a warning glare, gripping the edge of the nearest shelf to keep my growing frustration in check.

"Keep it down." My voice dropped to a harsh whisper. "Do you want everyone in Darkmoor to know what we're planning?"

Ty's voice cut through the tense silence like a blade. "I want them to suffer a slow, torturous, and excruciating death as much as you do," he said to Ciaran, his words measured but vibrating with barely restrained violence. "But we need to be smart about it."

I froze mid-reach, the weight of his words sinking into the tension thick between them.

Ty might not have been shouting like Ciaran, but the fury in his voice was no less terrifying. If anything, it was worse—controlled, deliberate, lethal.

Gripping the thick spine of *The Legacy of Darkmoor: Founders and Families*, I pulled the book from the shelf, its weight solid in my hands.

Without a word, I nudged them both toward a darker, quieter aisle away from the librarian's line of sight.

"He's right, Ciaran," I said, gripping the thick book

tighter, as if it could ground me in this storm of emotions. "We can't kill them yet. This kind of organization is like a hydra—cut off one head, and two more grow back in its place."

Ciaran's eyes snapped to mine, his expression darkening, but there was something else there—something raw, something vulnerable.

His jaw tightened, and for a fleeting moment, his anger gave way to something that cut deeper. *Why him, not me?* the look seemed to say, though he stayed silent.

"Right now," Ty said, his tone measured but no less intense, "we know—or at least suspect—that one or more of those three men are part of the Sochai. They are our only lead. Killing them would just destroy our only advantage."

I trailed my finger along the spines of the books as I scanned their titles.

"We need leverage," I said, half to myself, half to them, my voice low. "Information."

"Exactly," Ty said, stepping closer, his presence a steadying contrast to Ciaran's storm. "We need to find a weakness. An Achilles' heel. A linchpin."

He reached over and took the heavy book from my hands, his fingers brushing mine in a way that sent an unwelcome shiver down my spine.

His expression softened into something approving as he scanned the title before tucking the book under his arm. "Something that makes the whole organization crumble from the inside out."

Ciaran's eyes flicked between Ty and me, narrowing with suspicion. His jaw tightened, the tendons in his neck straining.

"Why are you taking his side over mine?" he asked, his voice sharp, edged with hurt he couldn't hide.

"This isn't about picking sides," I said firmly, pausing on another title: *Ireland's Elite: A Study of Power.*

"Really?" Ciaran shot back, his voice dropping to a dangerous whisper. "Because it sounds like you're both ganging up on me."

I yanked the thick book from the shelf and shoved it under my arm, my movements sharp from frustration.

"Because he's making sense," I snapped, glaring at him. "And you're letting your emotions control you."

He flinched at my words, but his expression hardened immediately, a storm brewing behind his eyes.

The sound of footsteps echoed faintly through the library, a group of students rounding the corner ahead. Their voices were low, punctuated by soft laughter and murmured conversation, but to me, it sounded deafening.

Cormac had been a student, just like any of them, yet he'd been working for the Sochai. The realization twisted in my gut—anyone here could be one of them. Every casual glance, every whispered conversation in the hall, every shadowed figure in the library stacks—suddenly, everyone was a suspect.

I froze, clutching the book tightly against my chest like a shield, my fingers digging into the spine of the book, the sharp edges biting into my palms.

Ty stiffened beside me, his posture shifting subtly. His sharp gaze followed the students, scanning their faces as though he could read their intentions with a glance.

He leaned slightly closer, his presence a silent reassurance even as my paranoia clawed at the edges of my mind.

Ciaran's hand brushed my arm, the brief contact pulling my attention back to him. His lips pressed into a thin line as his eyes darted toward the students. He was just as tense, just as wary.

"Come on," I muttered as I turned abruptly and ducked farther into the shadowy stacks, the boys flanking me like silent sentinels.

I lowered my voice even further. "We can't just run around spilling blood without knowing who'll replace them."

Ty took the second book from my hand and added it to the growing pile in his arms. "We need to think strategically. We're up against an organization older than any of us."

I reached for another book—*Shadows of Influence: Secret Societies in Ireland*—and flicked through its yellowed pages, frustration simmering just below the surface.

My anger shifted into something sharper, clearer, as determination tightened my grip on the book.

"This is bigger than all of us," I said, my voice quieter now but no less fierce. "And right now, we might be the only ones who even know the Sochai exists. We *have* to work together."

Ciaran's jaw remained tight. But I didn't miss the slight loosening of his fingers, the flicker of something behind his eyes—grudging respect, even if anger still held him hostage.

I slammed the book shut, the sound reverberating in the silence of the stacks and making both boys flinch. "If we don't figure out who the High Lord is—who's ultimately pulling the strings—we'll *never* stop them."

Ty reached out, pulling the book from my hand and

adding it to his pile without a word. "And if we don't stop them soon…"

"We won't live to try again," Ciaran finished for him.

"And…" I said, the weight of everything pressing down on me. "More girls will pay the price."

AVA

I'd walked into our dorm apartment later that night, yawning as I kicked off my shoes, Ciaran and Ty following behind me.

I heard Ty dumping the stack of books I'd checked out of the library on the dining room table with a thump.

As much as I wanted to start reading them, my eyes were glazing over.

"Good night," I mumbled, already aiming for my bedroom.

A firm hand wrapped around the back of my neck, stopping me mid-step.

The grip was familiar, commanding, and unmistakably Scáth.

"Where do you think you're going?" His voice was low, smooth, but it carried that edge of possessiveness that made my pulse spike.

"Um, bed?" My voice wavered as I turned to him, a little hopeful, a little unsure.

He smirked. "*My* bed."

My mouth opened, but no sound came out. I wasn't sure if it was his boldness or the way he said it—like it wasn't a question—that made a rush of adrenaline surge through me.

So much for sleep.

Over his shoulder, I caught a glimpse of Ty standing there in the living room, his jaw tight, his hand fisting the back of the couch.

For a fleeting moment, his mask slipped, and I saw it— the pain through the crack in the facade he tried so hard to keep in place.

Guilt weaved through me and I opened my mouth to tell Ciaran no, but then I clamped my mouth closed.

Screw Ty. I told him that Ciaran and I were together. Nobody forced him to live with us.

I tore my eyes away from Ty's, refusing to be guilted into feeling bad.

Scáth's grip didn't loosen as he guided me into his bedroom.

Ciaran's dorm bedroom was as chaotic as the man himself. The walls were a riot of pinned sketches, faded schematics, and scrawled notes layered haphazardly over dark damask wallpaper.

The room was dimly lit by antique lamps, their soft glow contrasting with the harsh blue light emanating from a laptop on his cluttered antique desk in one corner.

A battered leather chair sat in front of the desk, its surface cracked and well worn. The poster bed was unmade, the dark sheets spilling over the side, as though he'd kicked it down mid-battle during another restless night.

The faint scent of smoke and spice lingered in the room,

mingling with the sharp tang of whiskey from a decanter and used glass sitting on the mantle.

The door slammed shut behind me, the sound reverberating like a warning, and I flinched.

I turned toward him, but before I could scream, Scáth shoved me up against the wall, pressing a blade to my throat.

"Shhh…" he whispered, his voice soft, a total juxtaposition against the strength of his body pinning me. "If you fight me, I could cut you."

I froze. Fuck. Those words…

"If you fight me, I could cut you. You wouldn't want me to cut such a sensitive area, would you?"

I couldn't respond, my breath catching in my throat as memories flooded back. The cold press of metal against my skin, the exquisite tension between fear and desire.

"Remember?" he murmured, his lips brushing my cheekbone. "How you trembled under my blade?"

I nodded, unable to form words as heat pooled low in my belly. Having a cold sharp knife at my pulse point should have terrified me, but instead it sent jolts of electricity through my body, my skin tingling with anticipation, begging for his touch.

With agonizing slowness, Scáth began to trace the edge of the blade along my neck, following the curve down to my collarbone. The cool metal sent shivers across my skin, leaving goosebumps in its wake.

My breath came in short, ragged gasps as he dragged the knife lower, dancing it across my chest.

"So responsive," he purred, eyes dark with hunger. "I've missed this."

The tip of the blade caught on the neckline of my shirt. With a wicked grin, Scáth began to slice through the thin fabric, exposing my skin inch by torturous inch. The sound of tearing cloth filled the room as he cut a line straight down the center of my shirt.

"Don't move," he warned, voice husky. "We wouldn't want any… accidents."

I clung to the wall, my knees trembling, my nipples hardening as he cut away the remnants of my shirt and bra, the tatters sliding off my shoulders to the floor, leaving my breasts exposed and vulnerable.

His eyes raked over me, his gaze hungry and possessive.

"Beautiful," he murmured, trailing the flat of the blade down my sternum. "You have no idea how long I've wanted to have you under my blade again. No idea how much it turns me the fuck on."

My breath hitched as the knife dipped lower, tracing lazy circles around my navel, sending heat and wetness into my pussy. Every nerve ending in my body felt electrified, hyper-aware of the deadly instrument in his hand.

His eyes glinted with dark promise as he trailed the knife lower, catching the waistband of my skirt.

"You know, I don't much care for this skirt. Too fucking short. Exposing too much of what's mine. Especially to my greedy fucking brother."

He sliced through the fabric, the blade whispering against my skin as it cut a path down my thigh. The skirt fell to the floor, pooling at my feet.

"And these…"

His breath was hot against my neck as he pressed closer, the knife now tracing the lace edge of my panties. I shivered, torn between the urge to press into the blade and shrink away from it.

"These are in my way," he growled, hooking the tip under the delicate fabric. With a quick flick of his wrist, he shredded one side, then the other.

I gasped, flinching, waiting for the pain of him accidentally slicing me. But there was no pain. Just brutal need surging through me as my ruined panties fluttered to the floor, leaving me completely bare before him.

I felt desperately exposed, pinned between Scáth's hard body and the wall, completely naked while he remained fully clothed.

The cool air mixed with his hot breath caressed my heated skin, making me acutely aware of every inch of exposed flesh. Goosebumps raced across my skin, my nipples hardening into tight points.

And my pussy ached, soaking my thighs.

I stood there trembling, desperate, needy, while Scáth just trailed the flat of the blade lazily across my exposed skin, up my inner thighs and belly, across my breasts, circling my nipples.

"Scáth," I whispered. "Please…"

He smirked. "Please what, rabbit? Tell me what you want."

I swallowed hard, my throat dry, my heart racing, desire and fear mingling in a heady cocktail.

"I… I want…" The words caught in my throat. How could I admit to wanting this? To craving the danger, the thrill? How could I admit that I liked when he used his knife to make me come? That I wanted it again?

Scáth's eyes flashed with fire and he let out a growl.

"Say it," he commanded. "Tell me you want me to use the knife on you."

His eyes bored into mine, intense and unblinking.

I felt exposed, vulnerable—and not just because I was naked. It was like he could see right through me, past all my defenses, right into my dark little desires.

"I want…" I breathed, the admission sending a shiver down my spine. "I want… you to use the knife… on me."

"Use how?"

"I…"

"Say it. Claim it, rabbit. There's no need to be ashamed of what you crave."

"Fuck me with the knife handle," I blurted out, heat rising to my cheeks.

But there was no judgment on his face.

He smirked. "I have a better idea."

Oh. A dark thrill sent a shiver down my spine. What twisted things would my shadow do to me?

"Open your legs," Scáth commanded softly.

I hesitated, my legs trembling, momentarily unsure what I was signing up for.

His eyes burned into mine, dark and hungry.

"Open. Your. Legs," he repeated, each word deliberate and commanding as he pressed the sharp edge of the knife across a nipple, not enough to cut but enough to promise pain if I didn't comply.

Slowly, I parted my thighs, stepping my feet apart, exposing myself to him. The cool air caressed my swollen clit and folds, making me acutely aware of how wet I was. My heart pounded in my chest, a mix of anticipation and fear.

His gaze raked over me, his pupils widening with need.

"Don't move a fucking inch," he growled as he shifted aside.

His hand plunged downward, the blade flashing in the dim light.

My breath caught, heart stuttering as I waited for the sharp bite of steel against my most sensitive flesh. But the pain never came.

Instead, I felt the sudden vibration of the blade embedding itself into the wall between my legs, mere inches below my exposed pussy.

The knife quivered there, its polished hilt jutting out obscenely between my thighs.

His eyes gleamed with wicked satisfaction as he took in the sight before him, from my parted lips down to where the knife pinned me in place. "Now, show me how you ride that handle."

I stared at him, my breath coming in short gasps as I processed his command.

Slowly, hesitantly, with my fingertips on the wall beside me for balance, I lowered myself onto it.

The smooth, polished handle pressed against my swollen folds, sending a jolt of pleasure through me. I bit my lip, stifling a moan as I began to rock my hips, sliding my wet pussy along the length of the handle.

His eyes burned into me, dark with desire as he watched. "Good girl."

His fingers worked the buttons of his shirt open one by one, revealing tantalizing glimpses of smooth toned muscle and clean-lined tattoos beneath.

I watched, mesmerized, as he shrugged the shirt from

his broad shoulders. It fell to the floor, forgotten, as he moved to his belt. The soft clink of the buckle seemed impossibly loud in the tension-filled room.

My movements became more urgent, my hips rocking faster against the knife handle. The smooth, cool handle slid easily between my slick folds, sending waves of pleasure through my body with each stroke, the tension building low in my belly.

Scáth's eyes never left me as he finished undressing, his movements deliberate and unhurried. The contrast between his calm control and my desperate need only heightened my desperation.

He stroked his cock, already so hard, and I ached to have it inside me.

"That's it," he murmured, his voice low and husky. "Soak that handle for me."

I whimpered, my hips moving faster, my thighs trembling as I chased my release. The knife handle was dripping with my juices now, warmed from the heat of my body.

Just as I felt myself teetering on the edge of orgasm, he grabbed my hips and tugged me forward off the handle and toward him.

I let out a whimper as my orgasm fell away.

"Not yet, rabbit. You're going to choke on my cock first."

I went to drop to my knees, but he gripped my hips, stilling me, and shook his head. "Bend over from the hip and open that fucking mouth."

Shuddering with need, I bent forward from the waist, my legs still shaky from being so close to release.

I grabbed his hips to brace myself and tilted my head

back. The position left me feeling exposed and vulnerable, my wet pussy aching and empty.

Scáth's hand tangled in my hair as he guided my mouth to his cock.

I parted my lips obediently, my tongue darting out to wet them in anticipation.

The thick, blunt head pressed against my lips, hot and velvety smooth. I opened wider, letting him slide inside.

With a grunt, he thrust forward, burying himself to the hilt. I gagged as he hit the back of my throat, my eyes watering.

"Take it," he growled, holding me in place. "Take all of it and I'll let you come."

Tears pricked at the corners of my eyes as I struggled to breathe around his thick length. My hands gripped his hips tighter, nails digging into his skin.

"Relax," he commanded, his voice low and husky. "Breathe through your nose."

I forced myself to take slow, measured breaths through my nose, fighting against my body's instinct to panic. Gradually, my gag reflex eased, and I felt myself relax around him.

"Good girl," he purred, "Are you ready for your reward?"

Before I could react, he pushed me back, guiding me back onto the handle tip still jutting out from the wall.

"Let me see you fuck that handle while I fuck your mouth."

I groaned around his cock as I slid back onto the handle, letting it fill me up.

He hissed. "Fuck yes."

The handle wasn't as big as him, but it pushed in deep

and the little lip of the guard pressed against my clit when it was all the way in to the hilt.

Scáth began to thrust into my mouth, sliding me back and forth on the knife handle. The dual sensations overwhelmed me—the smooth handle inside my pussy, its lip pressing my clit, and his hot, thick cock stretching my lips and filling my mouth.

Scáth's grip tightened in my hair as he set a punishing pace, fucking my throat raw and me powerless to stop him, pinned between his cock and the handle on the wall.

Tears streamed down my cheeks as saliva leaked from my mouth and wetness gushed from my pussy, but I didn't want him to stop. The roughness, the way he used me, only made me want more.

"Look at you," he growled. "So fucking desperate. Riding that handle like the little knife slut you are."

His words sent a fresh wave of heat through me. I moaned around his cock, the vibrations making him hiss with pleasure.

My hips moved faster, grinding down hard on the handle. Each thrust pushed it deeper, the guard rubbing against my clit with delicious friction. The pressure was building again, coiling tight in my belly.

His thrusts became more erratic, his breathing ragged.

"Fuck, I'm close," he grunted. "You gonna come for me, rabbit? Gonna come all over that knife handle while I fill that pretty mouth?"

I moaned around his cock, begging him. The combination of his words, the relentless stimulation against my clit, and the utter fuckedupness of being spit-roasted by my boyfriend's cock and his knife handle pushed me over the edge.

My orgasm crashed over me, my pussy clenching rhythmically around the handle, my whole body shaking with the force of it. I cried out, the sound muffled by Scáth's cock.

He chuckled as he pulled me off the knife. "Change of plans. I'm going to fill this pussy—*my* pussy—while you suck your mess off my knife."

With a firm hand on my back, Scáth positioned me so I was face-to-face with the knife still embedded in the wall. The handle glistened in the dim light, slick with my arousal.

"Open," he commanded with a slap on my ass.

I whimpered as the delicious pain flared across my sensitive skin.

I parted my lips, my tongue darting out to taste myself on the smooth metal.

The flavor was sweet and musky, sending a fresh wave of heat through my body as I remembered how he made me suck up my juices off his fingers the very night he broke into my bedroom.

Slowly, I took the handle into my mouth, wrapping my lips around it as I had done with his cock moments before.

Behind me, I felt him grip my hips, his fingers digging into my flesh, the head of his cock pressing against my entrance, teasing me.

I whimpered around the knife handle, pushing back against him, silently begging him to fill me as need surged in me again.

With a low growl, he thrust into me, burying himself all the way in.

I gasped around the knife handle, my eyes rolling back at

the exquisite fullness. He was so much thicker than the handle, stretching me in ways that bordered on pain but felt so impossibly good.

"So tight, so wet for me."

He pulled back slowly, dragging against my sensitive walls, before slamming back in. The force of his thrust pushed me forward, driving the knife handle deeper into my mouth, making me choke on it.

Scáth set a punishing pace, each powerful thrust rocking me forward. The room filled with the obscene sounds of skin slapping against skin, my muffled moans, and his grunts of pleasure.

"Fuck," he hissed, his fingers digging into my hips. "I'm not going to last long."

He reached around me, his fingers finding my swollen clit. The sudden touch sent a jolt through me, making me gasp around the knife handle.

His fingers were rough and calloused, creating delicious friction as they circled my sensitive bud.

"Come for me again," he growled, his voice strained with the effort of holding back his own release. "I want to feel you strangle my cock with your cunt while you mouth-fuck that handle."

His fingers moved faster, applying just the right amount of pressure.

The overwhelming sensations of his thick cock stretching me and his skilled fingers on my clit quickly pushed me toward the edge.

My thighs began to tremble, my inner walls clenching around him.

My second orgasm crashed over me like a tidal wave, intense and all-consuming.

My vision blurred as pleasure surged through me, every nerve ending alight with sensation. I cried out around the knife handle, my body convulsing with the force of my orgasm.

Scáth groaned behind me, his hips stuttering as my inner walls clenched around him.

"Fuck, yes," he hissed, his fingers digging into my hips hard enough to bruise. "That's it. Milk my cock with that tight little cunt."

His cock seemed to swell impossibly larger inside me, stretching me to my limits. The overstimulation bordered on painful, but in the most exquisite way.

With a guttural groan, his hips jerked as he came, his cock pulsing inside me, flooding my insides. His fingers dug into my hips, holding me in place as he ground against me, prolonging his pleasure.

"Fuck," he growled, his voice raw and ragged. "Take it all, rabbit. Every last fucking drop."

I whimpered around the knife handle as he marked me as his from the inside out.

But as my pleasure haze began to fade, a terrible realization slammed into me, leaving me breathless.

God. We were so loud.

Ty would have heard it all.

Every moan, every cry, every dirty word must have echoed through the walls, slicing him like the knife I just came around.

A wave of guilt surged, threatening to pull me under,

and I had to fight it—clawing for air, for composure, for something to make it hurt less.

I didn't want to hurt him. I never did.

But it didn't matter what I wanted.

Somehow, I kept breaking him anyway, over and over just by loving his brother.

I fell asleep naked next to Scáth in his bed, still worrying about it.

And woke up when someone stuffed something into my mouth.

AVA

I gasped, but the sound barely escaped around the material shoved into my mouth.

I tasted my familiar musk and sweetness and knew this was the ruined panties that Scáth had cut off me earlier. What sick fuck—?

Before I could spit it out, a strip of tape was slapped roughly over my lips, sealing my scream in my throat.

My heart jackhammered as the weight of a body loomed over my naked body, a figure shrouded in shadows and a mask.

Scáth?

No... My head snapped to the side. Scáth was lying beside me, still and unresponsive.

Unmoving.

Fuck. This wasn't Scáth waking me for sex games. This was an intruder trying to take me. The Sochai had sent him.

Panic exploded in my chest, and I thrashed instinctively, my fists flying toward the intruder.

"Scáth!" I tried to scream, but his name came out as a muffled cry.

He didn't wake.

A jolt of terror shot through me, my body going cold even as I swung again, connecting with Scáth's arm. No reaction.

"Scáth!" I tried again, screaming against the gag, even as the intruder grabbed my wrists and taped them up in front of me, binding me with brutal efficiency.

"Shut up, Ava," he growled, his voice low and menacing. "He's not waking up anytime soon."

The words hit me like a punch to the gut. My mind reeled. Had he drugged Scáth? Or was Scáth *dead*? Did this bastard kill him?

No.

No.

And Ty. Oh God, Ty. Where was Ty?

I glanced to the door and screamed again, hoping, praying that Ty would hear me and come running.

But the door remained closed.

I struggled, trying to clear the fog of fear and think. Ty had taught me what to do in situations like this—how to fight, how to escape.

But my thoughts were a tangled mess, grief and terror crushing down on me until I could hardly breathe.

I kicked out wildly, managing to connect once with the intruder's side, but his weight bore down on me, pinning my legs. The tape came next, wrapping around my ankles in tight, unforgiving loops.

I screamed again, muffled and useless, as he manhandled me like I was nothing more than a rag doll. His strength was overwhelming, and no amount of twisting or writhing could shake him.

The world tilted as he hefted me over his shoulder, his muscled shoulder digging into my stomach. My vision swam, and my muffled cries turned desperate, frantic as he stole me from the apartment, jolting with every step down the stairs.

The dorm apartment was dark, eerily quiet, the stillness mocking my struggle. Where the fuck was everyone? Shouldn't there be students still up partying? Studying late?

Outside, the air was cold against my naked skin, but it did nothing to shock me back to reality. The only sound was his heavy boots against the pavement and my muffled sobs.

I screamed again, a pitiful, hollow sound against the gag, as he stopped beside a sleek black sedan. The soft *beep* of the car unlocking made my stomach drop.

The trunk popped open with a quiet hiss, and I renewed my fight, thrashing against him with everything I had left. My legs kicked uselessly, my taped wrists digging into my back, but he didn't even falter.

He shoved me into the trunk, the hard metal biting into my back as I hit it with a thud.

"Scream all you want, hummingbird. You're *mine*, now."

My muffled screams were drowned out by the sound of the lid slamming shut, locking me in darkness.

I don't know how long we rode in the car. It could have been two minutes. It could have been two hours.

Finally, the car rolled to a stop.

My ears strained as I heard the door open, gravel crunching beneath boots. The trunk popped open with a mechanical click, the sudden flood of light making me blink rapidly.

And there he was.

Those blue eyes stared down at me, glinting over the edge of his skeleton half-mask. The corners of his eyes crinkled, as if he were laughing at some private joke.

Ty.

Anger flared hot and wild in my chest. This time, I didn't just thrash—I *fought*.

My muffled screams tore from my throat as I cursed him through the gag, words twisted into incoherent mumbles, but the message was clear.

What the fuck was Ty doing?

What was this game he was playing?

He smirked, the kind of infuriating expression that only stoked my rage. With no effort at all, he grabbed me again, throwing me over his shoulder like I weighed nothing.

I slammed my fists into his back, over and over, but he didn't so much as flinch.

The world tilted as he carried me, the sound of gravel crunching giving way to the distinct *click* of his heels on polished marble, the blurred lines of ornate flooring passing under me.

I frowned. This flooring looked familiar. Where had he taken me?

Finally, he stopped, setting me down on my feet.

My legs wobbled beneath me, but before I could gather my balance, he spun me and pushed me back over something solid—angled.

The realization hit just as his hands worked quickly, efficiently. He hooked my bound wrists over something high above my head, forcing me to stretch out.

Rage and confusion warred within me, but beneath it all, an unwelcome heat began to build. My nipples tightened traitorously, sensitive peaks straining against the air as this position forced my back to arch, thrusting my breasts forward. I hated my body's response, hated how it betrayed me even as my mind reeled.

Ty stepped back, tilting his head like he was admiring his handiwork.

"What the fuck?" I tried to shout, but the gag muffled my words, reducing them to furious noise.

My breath hitched as my eyes darted around the room.

I knew this place.

The space was vast, almost cathedral-like, a few scattered wall sconces giving off a dim light. Overhead, the massive domed ceiling loomed, its metal beams curving into shadowed heights, the arched windows letting in fractured shards of moonlight across the walls.

Bookshelves lined the walls, crammed with ancient tomes and celestial charts, while the air was thick with the smell of aged paper, brass, and faint hints of dust. And a spiral staircase wound up to a shadowy platform above, disappearing into the darkness.

I was in the old Darkmoor observatory.

And I lay stretched out and naked on the monstrous telescope in the center.

I pulled at the bindings. But Ty had wrapped enough tape around them so that I couldn't tear them off.

Ty's eyes raked over my exposed body. His gaze wasn't cold like it usually was. It was wild and tormented with a touch of madness.

His glare burned into my skin, contrasting with the cold metal of the telescope pressed against my back.

"You only have yourself to blame for this, Ava," he said, his voice bitter and hateful.

He kneeled and sliced through the tape binding my ankles in one swift motion.

The moment I felt the tape fall away, I lashed out. My leg snapped up, aiming for his face, but Ty was faster. He caught my ankle mid-kick, his grip like iron. A low chuckle rumbled from his chest, the sound sending an unwelcome shiver down my spine.

"Nice try," he said, his hand like an iron band around my leg. "But I know all your moves. *I* taught them to you."

He yanked my leg to the side, stretching it out painfully wide.

I tried to twist away, but he held firm, cuffing my ankle out on the telescope mount. Panic surged through me anew.

Fuck. He'd set up handcuffs here already. He'd planned this. Of course, he planned it. It was Ty.

What else did he have planned?

I thrashed wildly, my free leg kicking out, but Ty grabbed that too and secured it to the other side, forcing my legs open wide so that I was fully exposed to him.

"Ty, goddammit…" I yelled around the panties stuffed into my mouth, trying to work my lips to get the tape off. "Let me go right now, asshole."

Ty stepped right up against me. "Bad girls don't get to make demands," he growled into my face. "Bad girls get punished."

Ty cupped my pussy with his hand, his fingers sliding between my folds, his touch rough and possessive. I tried to jerk away, but there was nowhere to go—the cuffs held me spread open and helpless.

"You're dripping all over my hand, hummingbird," he said on a growl, his voice dark with satisfaction. "Maybe I should change my punishment if you're enjoying this too much."

I shook my head frantically, denying his words even as heat pooled traitorously between my thighs. His fingers rubbed my clit, sending jolts of unwanted pleasure through me. I bit down on the gag, fighting the moan that tried to escape.

Ty leaned in close, his breath hot against my ear. "God, Ava, even when you're *with* him—fucking *him*—you're in *my* head. Under my skin. All the fucking time."

He pushed three fingers inside me and my eyes rolled back into my head at the way he filled me.

"You. You. You," he said with every hateful thrust into my pussy. "You've got me wrapped around your fucking fingers."

I fought against the rising tide of dark need, desperately trying to focus on my anger instead of the pleasure building low in my belly.

He pulled his fingers out and slapped my clit with his palm.

"You've got me in the palm of your fucking hand."

His hands went to his belt, unfastening it with quick,

precise movements. The sound of his zipper sliding down sent a shiver through me—part fear, part anticipation.

His cock sprang free. It jutted out proudly, thick and hard, the head already glistening with pre-cum.

I was stunned at the sight of him, looking obscene standing there in the middle of this beautiful old observatory with his button-up shirt, the sleeves rolled up, and dress pants, just his long thick cock hanging out.

Ty gripped himself, stroking his length as he looked at me, his eyes glittering with madness.

"You think you can let him fuck you, *loudly*, force me to listen to you screaming on his cock without making me lose my fucking mind. Huh?"

His gaze swept over my naked body as he stepped in close, my nipples tightening under his gaze, my pussy clenching around nothing.

"I'm going to punish you for making me so damn crazy."

He thrust into me without warning. Splitting me open. Filling me to fullness.

He didn't even wait for me to get used to his size as he began to thrust, fucking me hard like he was trying to hurt me.

Each thrust sent shock waves through my body, the telescope creaking behind me. His hands gripped my hips, fingers digging in hard enough to bruise as he used the leverage to pull me onto his cock again and again.

"This is what you wanted, isn't it?" he snarled, his voice rough with exertion and something darker echoing around the domed space. "To drive me fucking insane with jealousy? To push me *this close* to killing my own fucking brother? Huh?"

I shook my head frantically, trying to deny it even as my body betrayed me. My walls clenched around him, drawing him deeper with each punishing stroke. The friction was exquisite agony, pleasure and pain blurring together until I couldn't tell where one ended and the other began.

"It would have been so fucking easy, Ava. To slip twice the dose into his nightly whiskey so he'd *never* wake up. To *end* him."

I mumbled something around my gag as tears streamed down my face.

This was so wrong. So, so fucking wrong.

So why did I love it, want it, want more? Why did I crave this fucked-up shit?

"What was that?" Ty ripped the tape off my mouth.

I yelped at the sudden sting and spat out my panties.

"Fuck you, you sick fuck," I snarled at him, snapping my teeth as I tried to bite him, even as pleasure slammed through me.

"Your insults only make my dick harder." He leaned down and took a nipple into his mouth.

"Oh fuck." I arched into him, my hips bucking up to meet him, begging to be destroyed.

I came, hard.

My orgasm ripped through me, intense and almost painful in its force. I cried out, the sound echoing off the observatory's domed ceiling. My body clenched around Ty's cock, drawing him deeper as waves of pleasure crashed over me.

But Ty didn't stop. If anything, my climax only spurred him on. His thrusts became more frantic, more brutal. He grabbed my hair, yanking my head back as he pounded into me relentlessly.

"*My* pussy," he growled, his breath hot against my neck. "Mine. He might have claimed you first. But I will be your *last*."

I was overwhelmed, overstimulated, caught between wanting to push him away and pull him closer. My legs trembled in their restraints, and I could feel another orgasm building, impossibly soon after the first.

I came again.

I screamed as the second orgasm tore through me, even more intense than the first. My body convulsed, clenching around Ty's cock as he continued his relentless assault. It was almost too much to bear, bordering on pain.

Ty's rhythm faltered, his thrusts becoming erratic. With a guttural groan, he buried himself deep inside me, his cock pulsing as he came. I felt the heat of his release flooding me, marking me from the inside out.

For a moment, we stayed like that, both panting heavily. The air in the observatory felt thick, heavy with the scent of sex and sweat.

Ty pulled out slowly, and I whimpered at the loss. He stepped back, tucking himself away and fastening his pants.

I half hung from my arms, my shoulders screaming in protest, the ache sharp and unrelenting. My head lolled forward, mind too bleary to make sense of anything anymore, exhaustion draining my will to fight.

I barely registered Ty stepping toward me, his presence unmistakable even in my haze. His hands worked quickly, efficiently, removing the restraints with a precision that almost felt clinical.

The sudden release sent a jolt through my body, and before I could react, he caught me. Strong arms wrapped around my naked body, cradling me as though I were fragile, breakable.

I wanted to protest, to fight, but my limbs refused to cooperate.

Instead, I found myself being carried, Ty's grip steady and unyielding, his footsteps echoing in the vast room.

He laid me down on something soft—a blanket, warm and thick against the chill of the observatory. Something else he'd also planned.

I opened my mouth to say something, but the words died on my tongue as I glanced up, my breath catching.

Above us, the glass dome of the observatory stretched into infinity, revealing a night sky that took my breath away. The stars blazed against the inky blackness, a vast, shimmering canvas that made my chest ache with its beauty.

For a moment, it was as if the entire universe had been laid bare, infinite and overwhelming.

Ty lay down beside me, his arm pulling me close before I could muster the strength to push him away. His warmth seeped into me, his steady breaths unnervingly calm against the chaos still swirling in my chest.

He took my wrists gently, pressing soft kisses along the tender skin where the tape had been. The gesture was so at odds with the rage he just unleashed on me.

A sigh escaped me, long and shaky. The fatigue that clung to my body dulled the sharp edges of guilt already weaving its way into my mind.

For now, just for now, I let myself rest against him.

"Why did you bring me here?" I asked, the question slipping out before I could stop it.

"So we could look at the stars together," he said simply, as if it were the most obvious thing in the world.

I blinked, caught off guard. *Huh. That's... kind of sweet.*

"I still hate you," I muttered, though the bite in my words had long since softened.

His lips brushed against my hair. "I still love you more."

And as much as I wanted to push him away, to reject his words and everything they implied, I stared up at the stars instead, wondering if maybe—just maybe—he was telling the truth.

I woke to the soft dawn bleeding through the glass dome above, streaking the observatory in shades of gold and pink. For a fleeting moment, everything was calm. Peaceful. Ty's arms were wrapped around me, his steady breaths brushing against my hair.

And then it hit me.

Oh, God. We fell asleep here.

Panic gripped my chest, tightening like a vise. Ciaran. He was going to freak out when he woke up and I wasn't there next to him.

I shoved Ty's arm off me, scrambling upright.

"Ty," I hissed, shaking him. "Wake up!"

He groaned, rolling over with all the urgency of someone who had nothing to lose. "Mmm. Five more minutes, wifey."

"Five minutes? We don't *have* five minutes!" I snapped,

yanking the blanket out from under him and wrapping it around me. "Get up!"

He finally sat up, annoyingly calm as he stretched, like we had all the time in the world. "Relax, Ava. It's fine."

"It is *not* fine," I shot back, practically dragging him to his feet. "Get your ass moving before Ciaran wakes up and kills us both."

He grinned lazily, as if the idea of Ciaran's wrath amused him, but he didn't argue as I shoved him toward the door and out to the car.

The moment Ty pulled up to the dorm apartment, I didn't wait for him to fully stop.

I tumbled out of the car, barefoot and still wrapped in the blanket, and bolted for the stairs.

My heart pounded as I sprinted up, taking two steps at a time. I shoved open the apartment door, nearly tripping over myself in the process.

"Ava?" Ciaran's voice called from his bedroom, groggy but sharp with confusion.

My blood froze and I panicked, darting for the bathroom and slipping inside without being seen.

I flushed the toilet and turned on the taps, trying to make it sound convincing as I tried to calm my guilty heart.

I stepped out just as Ciaran banged open his bedroom door.

He was naked, his hair disheveled, his gaze narrowing on me as I tried to look as casual as possible.

"Morning," I said brightly, praying my voice didn't crack.

Ciaran's eyes dropped to the blanket wrapped around me, his frown deepening. Something in my stomach twisted.

Before I could say anything, the front door opened, and Ty strolled in, whistling like he hadn't just ruined my fucking life.

"What the fuck did you do to her?" Ciaran barked, his voice sharp enough to cut glass.

"Whoa." Ty held up his hands, feigning innocence. "Someone needs his morning coffee."

Ty pointed to Ciaran's naked body. "But first, pants?"

I silently panicked, my heart hammering against my ribs. If Ciaran had been on the verge of killing Ty last night, he'd definitely do it now if he found out that Ty had kidnapped me last night.

What he'd done to me.

And the fact that we fell asleep together afterward.

"Scáth," I said, stepping closer, trying to calm him. "Let's get you dressed before—"

He whirled on me, cutting me off with a pointed finger. "Where did you get that blanket?"

"What?" I blinked, startled.

I looked down at the blanket wrapped around me, really *looked* at it for the first time. It was navy blue, soft, with stars sewn into it like a night sky.

"I-I don't know," I stammered. "I just grabbed it on my way to the bathroom."

Ciaran's eyes burned into mine, disbelief etched into every line of his face. "That's Ty's. Our mother gave that to him."

The air left my lungs as the room suddenly felt too small.

Ciaran turned to Ty, fury sparking in his eyes. "Why is *my* girlfriend wearing *your* blanket over her naked body?"

Ty remained silent, the tension in the room pulling taut

like a wire about to snap.

Ciaran took a step toward him, then faltered, stumbling slightly. He must still be shaking off the drug Ty had given him last night.

I rushed to him, grabbing his arm to steady him and guiding him to sit on the couch.

"Sit," I murmured softly. "I'll get you some water."

Ty, infuriatingly unbothered as always, headed for the kitchen. "I'll start the coffee."

I kissed Ciaran's temple, whispering, "Just rest," before I made my way to the kitchen. The tension coiled in my chest like a spring as I filled a glass at the sink, Ty standing by my side near the kettle.

"Last night didn't happen," I whispered to him, my voice low but sharp.

Ty glanced at me, his expression unreadable. "It *did* happen. No matter how much you try to deny it."

A groan from the couch made us both glance over at Ciaran. He looked pale, his head in his hands.

I hated lying to Ciaran. *Hated* it. But the alternative was unbearable.

"Ty," I whispered. "If you tell him… he'll kill you."

Ty's mask slipped for a fraction of a second, the cold rage from last night glittering dangerously in his eyes. "Not if I kill him first."

The words hung in the air like a knife between us, sharp and heavy.

I swallowed hard, the tension between us thickening, suffocating. And for the first time, I let myself consider it— what if this was the only way it ended?

With one of them dead.

With an exhausted sigh, I tossed yet another useless library book onto the dining room table. It joined the clutter of laptops, newspapers, more books, and pizza boxes, each a monument to our increasingly desperate search.

The air smelled faintly of cold pizza and burned coffee, remnants of the time we'd spent chasing ghosts through dead-end leads.

Ty didn't tell Ciaran about the night at the observatory so things between Ciaran, Ty, and me settled into a weird kind of truce as we dug into researching the Sochai between classes.

"It's been weeks," I groaned, raking my hands through my hair. "And we still have nothing."

"These assholes created a system to legitimize and hide their twisted activities," Ty said from the chair beside me, his voice steady but simmering with quiet frustration. "They're experts at hiding. It's going to take time."

Ciaran, sitting on my other side, slammed his palms flat

against the table. "The bastards probably have high-level judges erasing public records, airline CEOs masking international travel, doctors forging documents—God knows what else."

He was right, of course. But David didn't need fucking constant reminding that he was up against Goliath.

I let out a sharp noise of frustration. "So what do we do now?"

Ciaran softened slightly, reaching for my hand and massaging the tension out of my palm, his touch grounding. "We'll figure it out."

At the same moment, Ty leaned closer, brushing a strand of hair behind my ear, his fingers lingering along the side of my neck.

A shiver went down my spine and a small, involuntary sigh escaped my lips.

The second it left me, I knew it was a mistake. Worse, I didn't even know which of their touches had caused it.

The apartment fell deadly silent, the cool breeze of fall cutting through the open windows doing nothing to cut through the thickened air that made it hard to breathe.

I didn't need to turn to know they had locked eyes. Each silently claimed my reaction as proof of his hold on me.

I gripped the edge of the table, willing the floor to swallow me. I didn't want it to be like this—caught between them, terrified of letting my feelings slip because of the small war it might set off. Always hurting one to please the other.

This wasn't just a rock and a hard place. This was two entire worlds, each with its own gravity, pulling me apart. And I knew it couldn't end anywhere but in destruction.

"There is one thing we haven't tried," Ty said, his voice low, too calm, that voice scaring me more than Ciaran's fiery outbursts ever could. "Ava, you've had more contact with the Sochai than you realize. At that clinic…"

The words impacted me like a blow to the gut. Flashes of that bright, sterile room threatened to drown me. The forced abortion. The cold hands. The suffocating helplessness. My vision blurred as the memory tried to claw its way to the surface, jagged and raw.

"I know it will be painful to go back… and I'm sorry." Ty reached into his pocket and pulled something out, setting it carefully on the table in front of me. "But maybe you might remember something more."

A glass vial, its delicate facets catching the dim light.

The sight of it sent a jolt of ice through my veins. My hand instinctively groped for Ciaran's, and my lower lip quivered despite my best efforts.

I had been strong enough to face my abuse. To fight back against the shadows that threatened to consume me. But *this* memory—it was the one that shattered me every time.

Could I do it? Could I let myself go back there? Could I willingly tear open that scar, relive that pain, for the greater good?

"What is that?" Ciaran asked sharply, his brows furrowing.

To him, it must have looked innocuous sitting there—a fancy bottle of perfume or a vial of face oil. But I knew better.

"It's a paralytic," Ty said matter-of-factly, his voice devoid of emotion. "And a mental disinhibitor."

Ciaran's face twisted with horror as his gaze snapped to me. "He made you take that?"

"Ava *chose* to take it at Blackthorn," Ty said, his tone clipped. "Just like it's *her* choice now."

Ciaran growled low in his throat, his fury barely contained.

I cupped his cheeks with my sweaty palms, trying to anchor him, but his wild eyes kept darting back to Ty.

"I know you wanted me to keep my memories buried," I said, desperation creeping into my voice. "But I needed to know, Scáth. I needed to face them."

Ciaran's voice cracked as he shrugged my hands off him. "So you chose poison over love? You chose *him* over *me*?"

"Yes," Ty said coldly.

"No!" I said at the same time. "I chose the truth!" I shouted, balling my hands into fists. "I chose *me*."

Ciaran was shaking with anger, his knee bouncing uncontrollably as he swore under his breath. "I won't let you get hurt ever again. I won't fucking allow it."

"She's strong enough now," Ty said, his words a calm provocation. "Thanks to me."

"After you brainwashed her and tortured her for months?" Ciaran roared, his chair scraping violently as he stood.

"Stop!" I shouted, but my voice was drowned out by the sound of his chair clattering to the floor.

Ty stood too, his movements measured. He pushed his chair back against the table with deliberate precision, his eyes cold as steel.

"You're a sick, sick fuck," Ciaran spat, his lips trembling

with rage as he unsheathed a knife, the sharp blade glinting with deadly promise.

"And you are a coward," Ty replied with cold fury and he pulled out his own lethal blade.

Both their eyes contained a murderous fury as they faced off, ignoring my screams for them to stop.

The tension that had been simmering between them since the moment Ty and I returned to Darkmoor ignited, crackling like a live wire finally overwhelmed by the current.

This was it—the storm breaking. They weren't just going to argue, weren't just going to throw words laced with venom or punch each other.

No, this time, they were going to cut each other into pieces.

Ciaran lunged, his blade slashing out, a raw, unrestrained force of anger, his movements wild but driven by pure emotion.

Ty leaped back smoothly, calculated in every motion, raising his weapon in front of him as he took a disciplined fighting stance, his sharp focus in stark contrast to Ciaran's explosive rage.

I stood helpless between them, knowing that once the first blood was drawn, there would be no stopping it.

They were going to kill each other.

Fuck. There was only one way to stop this.

I grabbed the vial from the table and yanked off the stopper as I stepped between them, wincing at the bitterness as I drank it down.

THE SHADOW

Ava tilted back the vial and swallowed down the bitter liquid. The paralytic. The disinhibitor. The poison.

My heart stopped.

"Ava!" I roared, the knife in my hand slipping from my fingers and clattering onto the floor with a hollow distant sound like in a dream.

I was across the room in an instant, grabbing her by the shoulders, crushing her against my chest as if I could will it back out of her.

"What have you done, baby? What have you done?" My voice cracked, the words spilling out before I could stop them. I gripped her tighter, like holding her could somehow undo the damage, erase what she'd just done to herself. To us.

"It's not too late," I told her desperately, my hands shaking as I cupped her face. "You can throw it up—"

"No, Scáth," she interrupted. "I want to do this. I *need* to."

Her eyes burned with conviction, and it killed me because I knew she wasn't going to back down.

Ty's voice cut through the haze. "If you love her, trust her."

I tore my gaze from Ava to him, and the rage that had been simmering in my chest boiled over.

"You." I let go of Ava to advance on him. "This is your fucking fault."

His expression stayed maddeningly calm, but I saw the tension in his jaw. "She made the decision, Ciaran."

"No," I hissed, my fists curling at my sides. "*You* made this happen. *You* planted the fucking idea in her head. Do you want her to suffer?"

"Of course I don't!" Ty snapped, finally losing that infuriating control. "It kills me to watch her in pain. But that's fucking life, Ci. You can't bubble wrap the ones you love from pain. You can only stand by them, support them, and honor them when they suffer."

I couldn't hear him anymore. Red clouded my vision as my arm lifted, ready to break his perfect, stoic face. But before I could swing, a sharp cry broke through the tension.

Ava.

We both turned as the empty vial slipped from her hand and hit the floor with a dull clatter and she began to fall.

Ty moved first, faster than I thought possible, catching her as her legs buckled.

I froze, guilt wrapping around my throat and choking me. I should have been the one to catch her.

Instead, I'd been too busy fighting with my brother to notice the woman I loved being pulled under.

Ty carried her effortlessly, like she weighed nothing, and

I followed uselessly as he brought her into her bedroom and laid her on the bed.

When I stepped beside him, he didn't look up at me. He didn't even acknowledge that I was there.

His whole attention was on arranging Ava's body.

He straightened her legs, adjusted her skirt over her thighs. He lay one arm at time at her sides and pushed her beautiful raven locks off her waxen face.

Ava, the woman I loved, was a prisoner in her own body, looking like a doll to be maneuvered this way and it made my stomach turn.

She began to whimper, her breath hitching, her eyes fluttering open and closed as though caught in a nightmare. Her chest rose and fell unevenly, her distress clear and growing.

"Fuck, Ty, make it stop," I begged, panic ripping through me. I'd never seen her like this before. Never seen her so fragile.

"I can't." Ty's face was calm but lined with something that looked suspiciously like pain. "She just has to get through it."

"That's bullshit!" I shouted, grabbing his arm and shaking him. "Fuck you, Ty. We need to help her. Do something."

His gaze turned sharp, meeting mine with an intensity that stopped me cold, his voice low and dangerous. "You want me to help her?"

"Yes!" I yelled back, desperation clawing at my chest.

Ty turned back to Ava, still fighting the demons of her past, locked away in her body. "You might not want to be here for this, *brother*."

Before I could ask why, Ty began to unbutton her top.

"Don't you fucking touch her," I snarled, wrenching Ty's hand away.

With a move I'd never seen before and with shocking speed, Ty twisted my wrist back, my bone a mere flick away from snapping.

I grabbed his wrist with my other hand in turn and we strained against each other, locked in an impasse.

His eyes were black coals ringed with a sliver of ice in the soft light of Ava's bedside lamp. "Do you want me to help her or not?"

I froze, every instinct in me screaming to keep fighting, to pull Ty away from her. To shove him against the wall and tell him to keep his fucking hands off her.

She was mine, damn it. Mine to hold, mine to comfort, mine to protect.

But as I stood there, torn between fury and helplessness, I knew that this was what they had done all summer.

Ty knew what to do, how to reach her, how to save her.

And that realization gutted me.

I hated that Ty knew how to bring her back. I hated that he understood her pain in ways I couldn't, that he was the one she needed in this moment, not me.

It felt like a betrayal, even though I knew it wasn't. Even though I knew this wasn't about me, it still pained me to give in.

Another muffled sob tore from Ava's lips and my chest constricted. The sound of her pain—it ripped me apart.

I couldn't take it anymore.

"Okay!" The word burst from me like an explosion, my

voice hoarse with frustration and defeat. "Help her. Do whate— just *help* her."

Ty didn't smirk, didn't gloat like I expected. He only nodded, his focus already back on Ava as if I hadn't been standing there about to rip him apart.

I felt like a fucking outsider in my own story, forced to watch as my brother—the twin I loved and hated in equal measure—was the one to save her.

A part of me wanted to close my eyes as Ty unbuttoned Ava's top and pushed it gently to the sides to reveal her bare chest. And yet I could not.

I couldn't ignore the way Ava shuddered beneath his touch, how her ragged breathing hitched when he murmured her name.

I didn't know whether it was for Ava's sake that I watched with rapt attention, to be there for her through this sadism. Or whether it was for mine.

Because as much as this whole fucked-up experiment revolted me, there was no denying Ava's incredible beauty in the soft lamplight.

Light glowed over her curves, her pink nipples straining, and my cock swelled in my pants.

I froze as Ty sat at her side and dipped his head toward her breasts.

"What the fuck are you doing?" I growled, my fists curling instinctively.

He ignored me as his lips ghosted over her skin, kissing, licking, tasting her. He circled one nipple with his tongue till it glistened wet in the lamplight while grazing his palm over the other.

"I'm here," he murmured to her, his voice soft, cooing, as

if I weren't even in the room. "It's me. It's only me."

Her breath hitched, her body arching slightly toward him, but her eyes were glassy, staring out into nothing.

I was struck with a horrifying realization: Ava wasn't here with us. She was back there, reliving her nightmares.

And Ty wasn't comforting her. He was grounding her. Pulling her back. Anchoring her to the present where she was safe and loved.

And I hated him for it—because it was working.

My heart rate quickened as Ty kissed down her stomach and along the waistband of her skirt.

My fingernails dug into the sides of my thighs as he pushed the hem of her skirt up her legs before licking a long, wet trail from Ava's knee all the way up her inner thigh.

Before I could protest, before I could even realize what the fuck was happening, Ty pulled aside her panties and buried his face in her pussy.

I stumbled back as my breath caught in my throat with such violence that it felt like I'd been punched in the windpipe.

It was like I was watching this behind glass, the only sound the crashing of my blood in my ears.

Ava lay like a doll as my brother defiled her.

This was how Ty had helped Ava resurface her lost memories, rolling her hard nipple beneath his thumb and forefinger, teasing her clit with his tongue, pushing his fingers into her wet pussy.

This was what he'd spent all those months doing over the summer.

I had been searching dark alleys, black snakelike rivers,

the nastiest corners of the internet for her.

Not even in my most twisted nightmares had I imagined *this*.

It was beyond fucked up, me watching my brother defiling my girlfriend's body as she lay paralyzed and trapped in her dark nightmares.

And yet a sick twisted surge of heat rushed through me, making my breathing quicken and my cock press painfully against my zipper.

As the air in the bedroom grew thicker and thicker and the sound of Ty's tongue moving over her pussy grew louder and louder, I found myself clutching to the bedpost to stop myself from tearing him off her and murdering him with my fists.

Ava's breaths grew shallow and heavy as moans squeezed from her heavy throat. Fuck. I knew that sound well.

Ava was close to coming.

No. That was *mine*. Her orgasms were *mine*.

I shoved Ty out of the way so suddenly he didn't have time to counter me. He landed with a thud on the ground.

I pulled her panties out the way, sucked her clit into my mouth, and plunged my fingers into her soaking pussy and curled them around, coaxing her over the edge.

Mine.

I felt her pussy ripple around my fingers, felt the warm gush of more wetness over my mouth, felt her shudder. The only sound she made was a heavy rush of air from her lungs and a muffled noise in her throat.

When her body stopped twitching, I carefully pulled my fingers from her, my gaze roaming over her, trying to gauge where she was in her head, trying to read her the way Ty seemed to read her.

A soft sigh escaped her lips, and her tense shoulders sank against the pillow. Relief washed over me. Whatever nightmare she'd been trapped in had finally released its grip on her.

Thank God.

But as her breathing evened out, the reality of what my own brother had just done to her hit me like a freight train.

The relief twisted into fury, my chest tightening as the anger surged hot and fast. I turned to Ty, who was calmly picking himself up from the floor, as if nothing had happened.

"Is that what you fucking did to her all summer?" I growled, my voice barely more than a rasp, low and dangerous.

He met my eyes with that maddening calm, his expression unreadable, the look that always made me feel like *I* was the one spiraling out of control.

"That was part of her therapy," he said evenly.

Part of her therapy? The words detonated in my mind.

Part of her therapy?

What the hell did that mean? There was *more*? He did *more* to her?

I stepped toward him, fists clenched, my pulse hammering in my ears. "What else, Ty? What the fuck else did you do to her?"

"Doctor-client privilege," the smug bastard said.

My hand instinctively reached for one of the other blades strapped to my body, fury coursing through me. "I'm going to—"

A choked sob escaped from Ava, slicing through my rage like a blade of its own. My attention snapped to her.

Her lashes fluttered, tears spilling down her cheeks in silent streams. Her hands jerked to her face as though trying to shield herself from the world, her body trembling.

The paralytic was wearing off. And whatever she had endured while she was under was still haunting her.

I was at her side in an instant, perching on the edge of the bed, my movements frantic but careful.

My hands moved over her body, searching for something—anything—I could fix. Some wound I could close, some break I could set. Anything tangible that I could make better.

But there was nothing. No visible wound to heal, no scar I could soothe.

"Shh," I murmured, the sound meant as much for me as for her, my voice wavering under the weight of my helplessness. "It's okay, rabbit. I've got you. I've got you."

Except I didn't. And it was killing me.

Ty reached for her, too, but I shoved him away before his hand could land.

"You've done enough," I snarled, my voice cracking under the weight of fear I couldn't suppress.

Ava cried softly.

I pressed my forehead to hers, needing the contact, needing to feel the heat of her skin and know she was still here.

I rocked her gently, my arms around her, though my own chest heaved with uneven breaths, my shirt clinging to my back with sweat.

The tension in me, the helpless rage—it coiled too tight, and I couldn't ignore how wrong it all felt, how wrong I felt.

"Shh, shh, shh," I whispered like a mantra, as if the words could drown out the storm inside us both.

"I saw something." Ava's voice cracked, a faint, haunted whisper cutting through the stifling silence.

"Quiet now," I said quickly, my lips brushing against her temple. "Don't speak."

"But—"

"You don't have to relive it." My words came in a rush, my mouth moving to hers, the kiss meant to silence her, to comfort her, to stop her from spiraling any further. "It's not too late. We can still run. We can leave it all behind. Just you and me, Ava. We can still—"

"No," she said, her voice firm despite her soft sobs.

"What do you remember?" Ty interrupted, his voice flat, almost clinical, as though the weight of what she'd done hadn't rattled him in the slightest.

I turned on him, fire blazing in my eyes. "You bastard. This is your fault. Can't you see she's suffering?"

Ava's voice broke through the rising tension. "I remember the hospital room... the overhead lights, so bright... the doctor's face covered with a mask."

I froze, my hands stilling against her shoulders as her words stabbed into me.

She was clawing through her memories, unearthing things I wanted to keep buried for her sake.

I hated this. Hated Ty for making her do it. Hated myself for being unable to stop her.

"What else?" Ty asked, leaning forward, relentless.

Her knuckles pressed against her eyes as she shook her

head. "Nothing. Just… I just want them to stop."

"Did you see any faces? Hear any names?" Ty pressed.

"Alright, that's enough," I barked, my voice shaking with barely contained rage as Ava shook her head, her tears starting again.

"Anything," Ty continued. "An eye color? A tattoo? A scar? A view from a window? A sign?"

"No!" Ava's voice rose into a cry, the sound tearing through me. "No, there's nothing else. Nothing—"

The air in the room grew heavy as her breath caught, and for a moment, she didn't speak, her body stilling against me.

I froze, and it appeared, so did Ty, one of us leaning in with hope, the other bracing for the worst.

"A sign," she whispered, her voice distant, her gaze unfocused.

Her fingers reached out, and mine instinctively brushed hers. I couldn't tell if she even knew it was me.

"Yes, a sign," she said, her voice growing stronger. "As I was being wheeled into the operating room…"

"Yes, Ava," Ty urged softly, his voice low and coaxing. "Good girl."

I clenched my jaw so hard it ached, but I didn't interrupt. My anger warred with something else—an unbearable fear that Ty might actually get her through this.

"The name," Ava murmured, her voice nearly drowned out by the frantic pounding of my heart. Her lips parted as if the words were too heavy to speak.

She blinked slowly, her eyes refocusing.

Then she said with a whisper that felt like thunder, "I saw the name of their clinic."

AVA

"How the fuck did this happen?" a gruffy older man's voice said. "I thought she was given the implant."

That voice. It was... familiar. But I couldn't place it.

"I'm sorry, a Thiarna Ard." High Lord. "I did not want to mar her lovely skin."

I recognized this second voice as... the professor.

He continued. "I used a contraceptive mixture that I—"

"You and your little concoctions," the first voice spat with disdain.

More harsh clattering of metal. Cold hands propped my bare feet up in strange braces, causing my nightgown to slip down my legs.

I wanted to cover myself up, but I couldn't move. I couldn't even cry out.

"You make sure she never remembers this, do you hear me?"

Someone leaned over me. A doctor wearing a surgical mask, the lights turning their features into a silhouette.

And then they were gone and I could hear whispers.

A loud crash made me jolt, like someone had thrown something across the room.

"You dare second-guess my command? You are my fucking heir. You will do as I say. Now... take care of it."

I stood between Ty and Ciaran, like matching stone sentinels, staring up at the charred remains of Ashcradle House, the hospital from my darkest memory.

Ashcradle House had once been located in one of the old Darkmoor campus buildings, supposedly abandoned during the Spanish flu. I remembered telling Lisa about it last term when we'd just found out that Liath had gone missing, but standing here now, it felt less like history and more like a nightmare come to life.

The collapsed outer wall exposed skeletal remnants of modern medical equipment. Hospital beds, their metal frames warped by fire, lay scattered amid the debris like corpses on a battlefield. The smell of smoke and ash lingered faintly in the cold night air, mixing with the damp scent of decay.

"They're always a step ahead," I whispered, anger and frustration tangling in my voice. "We're chasing our fucking tails."

The wind rustled through the towering bloodred oaks surrounding us, hissing like snakes in a pit. The trees swayed ominously against a starless sky, their twisted branches clawing at the void.

Ciaran reached for my hand as we stepped through the rubble, the crunch of charred wood and shattered glass beneath our boots the only sound breaking the heavy silence.

I frowned as I studied the hospital beds more closely.

Strange half-melted metal lumps were welded onto the frames—two near the waist, two at the foot.

Realization slammed into me like a freight train. *Clamps.* For wrists and ankles.

A memory tore through my mind with visceral clarity. Cold, unyielding metal snapping shut around my ankles. My legs forced apart. The sterile bite of disinfectant in the air, masking the scent of fear and blood.

My stomach turned violently. I stumbled back, tripping over the charcoaled remains of what used to be a chair.

Before I could hit the ground, Ciaran's arms were around me, pulling me flush against him.

"I'm sorry, Ava," he whispered, his voice thick with pain.

I looked at the surrounding ruin, the horror of what it had once been. Perhaps it was a blessing this place no longer stood, that it couldn't continue to exist as a factory for pain and violation.

But the knowledge of what had happened here—of what had happened to *me*—would never burn away with the ash.

"I can't take this anymore," I said, my voice breaking under the weight of my own anguish. Tears threatened to spill, but the scream clawing at my throat felt far more powerful. "How could human beings be so fucking *evil*?"

Ciaran's grip on me tightened. "We need to get you home," he said softly, as if I were made of glass.

"She's not a child who needs to be tucked in," Ty argued from behind me, his tone sharper than usual.

"Enough," I said, trying to steady myself, but neither of them listened.

Their bickering rose like a tide, grating on my raw nerves. Every word felt like a splinter under my skin. I turned, glaring at them as their voices overlapped, both trying to outshout the other.

Ciaran and Ty were supposed to be the answer. Together, we were supposed to take the Sochai down. But the only thing falling apart was *us*.

"*Enough, both of you*!" I screamed, cutting them off mid-sentence. My voice echoed through the ruins, fierce and unrelenting, the words tearing from me like a primal roar.

Both of them fell silent, staring at me.

My chest heaved with the effort of containing my fury, my fists vibrating at my sides.

I felt like I was standing on a knife's edge, every breath threatening to send me plummeting into chaos. My heart hammered painfully, caught between two opposing forces—two people who each held a piece of it.

"You have to stop doing this," I said, my voice cracking. "Both of you."

"Doing what?" Ciaran asked, his tone sharper than I'd expected.

"Fighting. Over me. Over everything. Like it's a competition. Like I'm a piece of fucking meat." I gripped the edge of the nearest crumbling wall, needing something solid to anchor myself. "It's *killing* me."

"That's rich," Ciaran said bitterly, his voice low. "You think this is easy for us? Watching you... wondering what you want, who you—"

"Who I *what*, Ciaran?" My voice rose, and I stepped toward him, heat flushing my skin. "You think this is easy for me? Being torn between two brothers that I—"

The words caught in my throat, snagged by the weight of what I was about to admit.

Ciaran's eyes widened, and Ty took a slow step forward, his gaze narrowing as if he knew what was coming.

I could feel the confession clawing its way out, impossible to keep locked away any longer. My fists clenched at my sides as I took a shaky breath.

"I—" My voice broke and I clutched at my heart. "I can't stop it, okay? I've tried. God, I've *tried*. But I can't, because—" My chest heaved, and the words finally spilled out, unrestrained and raw. "Because I love you both."

The weight in my chest lightened, but only for a moment. As soon as the words settled in the air between us, I regretted them.

Ciaran's face crumpled, like my words were a physical blow. His sapphire eyes burned with disbelief and something sharper—hurt. For a moment, he looked like he didn't know whether to run or fight, torn between his anger and his vulnerability.

"What?" he said, his voice cracking under the weight of the single word.

My stomach twisted painfully. "Ciaran—"

"No," he interrupted, shaking his head like he could shake the truth away. "No, you don't mean that. You *can't* mean that." His hands balled into fists at his sides, his knuckles whitening. "You love me, Ava. Not him. Not *him*."

"I'm sorry," I said, dragging a hand through my hair. My voice softened, guilt thickening every word. "I tried to stop it from happening, but I couldn't. I—"

My gaze fell on Ciaran as I spoke, my words for him. "I'm *sorry*."

I tried to reach for him, my hand hovering between us, but he flinched back like I'd burned him.

"You *have* to choose," he said, his voice dropping into something raw and guttural. His jaw clenched, and his gaze flicked to Ty, then back to me.

I shook my head, tears squeezing from my eyes as my heart shattered in my chest, my voice coming out as a broken whisper. "I'm sorry."

"Say it, Ava." Ciaran advanced on me as I cowered away from him. "Say you love *me* more."

"Ciaran, stop," Ty said, his voice calm but commanding, stepping forward to block his path.

"You did this!" Ciaran spat, rounding on him. "You fucking brainwashed her, corrupted her. You *stole* her from me, my own fucking *brother*."

"Stole her from you? *Stole her?*" Ty's fury hit me like a tidal wave, his usual calm shattering as his voice rose, full of raw, unleashed emotion. "You *promised* me you wouldn't touch her! You *promised* you'd keep your distance, but the second you thought I was dead, you pounced!"

My breath caught. Ty wasn't just angry; he was livid in a way I'd never seen before.

Ciaran's face twisted in anger, his shoulders tensing as he took a step toward his brother. "I was protecting her! Because you sure as hell weren't going to!"

"Because I was rotting away in jail for *you!*" Ty's voice roared, echoing off the night like thunder.

Ciaran stumbled back as if Ty had punched him, the color draining from his face.

Ty's eyes burned with a fury that scared me more than Ciaran's outbursts ever had as he advanced on his brother.

"You think you're angry because of me? Because of her?" Ty stabbed a finger into Ciaran's face. "You're angry because you preferred when she was helpless little Ava, and now you can't stand the fact that she's strong enough to make her own choices—even if it means not choosing *you.*"

The air between them crackled like a live wire.

I wanted to scream, to run, to pull them both back from the edge, but I was caught in the suffocating storm of their rage, my heart pounding painfully in my chest.

And I couldn't fucking take it anymore.

"Stop it! I hate you," I screamed at them. "I hate you both."

I turned and ran through the forest, branches whipping against my face and arms as I plunged deeper into the shadowy depths.

I had no idea where I was going. But I wouldn't stop. I couldn't stop.

The night air was thick with the scent of pine and damp earth, filling my lungs as I gasped for breath. My feet pounded against the uneven ground, roots and fallen branches threatening to trip me with every step.

Behind me, I could hear them. Ciaran and Ty, crashing through the undergrowth, their voices calling out my name.

The sound sent a shiver down my spine, a mixture of fear and a hot dark thrill.

Memories of them chasing me when we were younger flashed through me—*ready or not...*

It had been a game then, a fun pretty game, but this wasn't a game anymore, it was real. Terrifyingly real.

And it would end with someone's heart broken. Maybe I wasn't really running away from *them* as much as I was running away from *that.*

"Run, rabbit," Ciaran called from the distance, his tone a

mix of playfulness and menace that sent chills down my spine.

My heart pounded in my ears as I pushed harder, my legs aching as I leaped over fallen logs and ducked under low-hanging branches.

I tore past an overgrown mound tangled with morning glory, its delicate flowers gleaming pale in the moonlight—that must be the campus passagetomb Lisa was always going on about.

The thought was fleeting, gone almost as quickly as it came, drowned out by the crunch of leaves and twigs behind me, the sound of pursuit drawing closer.

Someone was right behind me. Getting closer. I could hear the sharp and precise breathing behind me, so close it felt like he was breathing down my neck, making my hairs stand on end.

Strong arms wrapped around me from behind, tackling me.

I screamed.

As we tumbled to the forest floor, he twisted mid-fall, pulling me on top of him so that his body absorbed the impact. The breath rushed from my lungs as we hit the ground hard, leaves and twigs crunching beneath us.

I could feel his heart hammering against my back as his hands grabbed me as if he couldn't get enough, my breasts, my hips, my thighs, igniting sparks beneath my skin.

"I told you," he hissed, his lips brushing my ear. "I'd always find you."

Ty.

I shivered, torn between the urge to fight and the need to melt into him. The little chirps and cracks of the forest faded away, leaving only the sound of our ragged breathing and the pounding of my heart in my ears.

Ty's hand pushed up my skirt, found the edge of my panties, and in one rough motion, he ripped them off.

I gasped as he rolled us over, pinning me beneath him on all fours. I heard his zipper go down.

"Wait," I breathed, but my body betrayed me, arching into his touch, shivering with need. "We shouldn't."

Ty's only response was a low growl as he thrust into me.

I gasped at the sudden fullness, my fingers digging into the earth beneath us. He set a punishing pace, each powerful thrust driving me forward.

The roughness of the forest floor scraped against my palms and knees, but the pain only heightened the pleasure. Leaves and twigs crunched beneath us as Ty pounded into me relentlessly.

The scent of pine and earth mingled with our sweat and sex, creating an intoxicating perfume, the cool night air on my flushed skin a stark contrast to the heat building within me.

Fuck, this was so wrong.

I bit my lip to stifle my cries, not wanting to alert Ciaran.

I couldn't stand to have my shadow find his brother—his rival—taking me, claiming me on the forest floor.

"Fuck," Ty hissed, "you feel like home."

Ty's words sent a shiver through me, igniting a fire that consumed all rational thought. His hands gripped my hips, pulling me back to meet each powerful thrust.

The surrounding forest faded away, replaced by a haze of pleasure so intense it threatened to overwhelm me.

My thoughts obliterated. All the guilt and heartbreak and angst dissolved under the waves of pleasure.

I couldn't help but moan, losing myself in the sensation of Ty filling me completely, stretching me to my limits, every nerve ending in my body singing in a dark trance.

I didn't hear the fast-approaching footsteps until it was too late.

AVA

I shouldn't have given in to Ty. But the way he claimed me—completely, utterly, without hesitation—shattered my defenses and swept away every rational thought.

And now, it was too late.

Ciaran had seen everything.

"You bastard." Ciaran's voice was a low, venomous growl as he emerged from between the trees.

Before I could react, he was on us, shoving Ty off me with enough force to send him stumbling back.

I let out a cry as Ty's cock was pulled from me.

"Stop!" I cried out, but my plea was drowned out by the sickening crunch of Ciaran's fist connecting with Ty's face.

The impact sent Ty reeling backward, his back slamming against a gnarled oak tree, a trickle of blood spilling from his split lip. His eyes, usually so calm and controlled, now blazed with a mix of pain and fury.

I scrambled to my feet, leaves and twigs clinging to my

skin, fear and the cool forest air raising goosebumps along my damp flesh.

My heart pounded so hard I could feel it in my throat, each beat a painful reminder of the chaos I'd unleashed.

To my surprise, Ciaran whirled and advanced on me.

Out of instinct I turned to run, my thighs slick with my wetness.

But I didn't get far.

Ciaran caught me, his strong arms clamping down on me. He whirled me to face him before slamming me against a tree trunk. "You make me fucking crazy."

He ripped my skirt off me before running his fingers through my wet, aching pussy.

I groaned, my head falling back against the rough bark of the tree.

"Hmmm," he growled, his fingers teasing along my slick folds, sending shivers of twisted pleasure through my body, "are you soaked for Ty or me? Or... both of us?"

"Both," I whimpered, unable to lie anymore. "I'm sorry."

A low growl rumbled in Ciaran's chest. His eyes, dark with desire and hate, locked on mine. In them, I saw a storm of emotions—anger, lust, possessiveness, and something deeper that made my heart ache.

He unzipped his pants and thrust into me, his cock filling me in one powerful thrust.

I cried out, my back arching against the rough bark of the tree.

His hands gripped my thighs, lifting me effortlessly. Instinctively, I wrapped my legs around his waist, drawing him deeper. The new angle sent sparks of electricity through my body, and I cried out, my fingers digging into his shoulders.

The scrape of wood against my skin sent shivers down my spine, pain and pleasure mingling in a heady rush.

For a fleeting moment, I wondered where Ty was. Was he close? Was he watching, the way he was watching when Ciaran fucked me the other night?

The thought sent a thrill of excitement through me, quickly drowned out by the overwhelming sensation of Ciaran moving inside me.

"I hate you, Ava," he hissed as he slammed into me. "I hate that I love you so much."

He fucked me like he hated me, like he was punishing me for loving his brother as well.

"God," I moaned, "you feel so good."

"Better than him?" he hissed, his hand coming around my throat, cutting off my air supply. "Tell me I fuck you better than him."

The world narrowed to a pinpoint, my senses heightening as blood roared in my ears.

"Tell me," Ciaran demanded, his hips never stopping their relentless rhythm. "Him or me?"

I gasped, struggling to form words as black spots danced at the edges of my vision, shivers of pleasure coursing through me, my nerves singing with a mixture of fear and dark pleasure.

Then, over his shoulder, I saw him.

Ty.

Standing in the shadows, his eyes blazing with a dark intensity that made my breath catch.

He stood there watching, stroking his cock, his gaze

locked on mine, his jaw clenching as his fingers tightened around his cock, the veins in his forearm standing out as he pumped himself in time with Ciaran's rhythm.

His chest heaved with each ragged breath, a thin sheen of sweat glistening on his skin.

His usual icy mask was cracked, a storm of emotions swirling underneath—desire, jealousy, and a hint of darkness as he waited for my response to Ciaran's devastating question.

Him or me?

Over Ciaran's shoulder, I reached out for Ty.

Ty swiftly moved toward us, not bothering to be silent anymore, his footfalls landing heavily on the dry forest floor. "Maybe you should learn to share, brother."

Ciaran's grip on me tightened as Ty approached. He growled, primal and possessive, his hips never faltering in their punishing rhythm.

I felt the vibration of his growl in my bones, low and feral, as Ty drew closer.

"Back off," Ciaran snarled over his shoulder, his voice rough and dangerous. His arm slid from my neck and shot out to shove Ty away.

Ty moved too quickly, his reflexes sharp. He sidestepped Ciaran's clumsy attempt with ease, his eyes blazing with a determined fury that unnerved me.

He didn't stop moving, circling us like a predator, his focus locked on me like I was his ultimate *prize*.

Ciaran's movements became erratic, torn between his desperate need to claim me and his instinct to fend off his brother. His thrusts grew wilder, more frenzied, as if he could somehow fuck Ty's very existence away.

I cried out, overwhelmed by the sensations coursing through my body, my head spinning at the raw primal masculine energy thickening the air. Their fight wasn't just for dominance; it was for *me*, and the intensity of their need set every cell in my body alight.

My body was on fire, my nerves buzzing with a desperate need for release.

I was so fucking close.

"Mine," Ciaran hissed as my pussy clenched around him.

But Ty, with the fluid grace of a predator, seized his opportunity.

In one swift motion, he hooked his arm around Ciaran's waist and wrenched him backward. The sudden movement sent us all tumbling to the forest floor in a tangle of limbs and leaves.

Ciaran's cock was pulled from my body, my body aching at the sudden cruel emptiness. I let out a whimper as my nearing orgasm began to fade.

Ty recovered first, grabbing me, lifting me by the hips back to all fours.

"Mine." He thrust back inside me from behind, his possessiveness making me cry out. "Come for *me*, Ava."

I was helpless as he held me down and fucked me in front of Ciaran, racing me back to the edge.

Ciaran scowled, his face contorting with anger as he scrambled toward us. He punched Ty, the sound of a fist on flesh echoing through the forest, and suddenly, I was empty again.

I whimpered, my body trembling as my release fell away.

"No, come for *me*." Ciaran yanked my hips toward him, my knees scraping the ground with a delicious flare of pain.

He filled me with one smooth motion, thrusting into me, reclaiming me.

I screamed with pleasure, with need and frustration as both boys fought over me, shoving and punching each other off me in an attempt to be the one to make me come.

I was filled and emptied and filled again until I could barely tell which cock was whose.

I was brought to the edge and pulled back, again and again.

Until I couldn't take it anymore.

I scrambled forward, pushing Ciaran onto his back and sliding my mouth down over his cock, pinning him down, taking control of him.

His groan of pleasure rumbled through me as I took him deep into my mouth.

His fingers tangled in my hair, guiding me as I worked him with my tongue. The taste of him, musky and primal, filled my senses.

I hollowed my cheeks, sucking hard as I bobbed my head, relishing the way his hips bucked involuntarily. But it worked. He forgot all about trying to fight Ty off me.

I lifted my ass high in the air, exposed and vulnerable, the air cool on my wet folds, making me shiver with need.

As I'd hoped, Ty strong hands gripped my hips as he thrust into me, filling me completely. I fell deeper onto Scáth's cock.

"Fuck," Ciaran cried out. "Again."

Everything else faded away as pleasure consumed me. As Ty's powerful thrusts drove me forward, pushing Ciaran's cock deeper into my throat with each movement.

I was overwhelmed by sensation, caught between them, filled completely from both ends.

Ciaran's fingers tightened in my hair as he fought to control himself. His hips jerked upward, driving himself deeper.

Behind me, Ty's pace grew frantic. His fingers dug into my hips hard enough to bruise as he pounded into me. Each thrust sent shock waves of pleasure through my body, pushing me closer and closer to the edge.

So close. So intense. The pressure in my body built up from everything.

"Fuck, Ava," Ciaran growled. "You're so tight."

"So wet for us," Ty added.

Their words sent a dark shiver down my spine.

The most intense wave of pleasure crashed over me as I was finally pushed over the edge. My pussy clenched around Ty's cock as I came hard, my vision going white, my screams muffled by Ciaran's cock in my mouth.

Ciaran groaned, his hips bucking wildly as my throat constricted around him. "Fuck, I'm gonna—"

His words cut off as he came, hot spurts of cum hitting the back of my throat. I swallowed greedily, drinking down every drop.

Behind me, Ty's rhythm faltered. With a guttural moan, he slammed into me one final time, burying himself to the hilt as he came. I could feel the warmth of his release flooding me.

For a moment, we stayed frozen like that—connected, panting, shaking in the aftermath. The forest was silent around us, as if holding its breath.

Slowly, carefully, Ty withdrew from me. Ciaran's softening cock slipped from my mouth as I collapsed onto the forest floor, my limbs like jelly. I whimpered at the loss of them, feeling suddenly empty.

Leaves and twigs clung to my sweat-slicked skin, dirt smeared my ripped top, and I could taste Ciaran on my tongue, feel Ty's cum trickling down my thighs. But for one blissful moment, I was satisfied and happy.

Reality hit me like a cold slap, snapping me out of the haze that had momentarily numbed everything else. The bliss faded, leaving a hollow ache in its wake, and guilt surged through me in a stomach-twisting wave.

I still had to choose.

The weight of it settled on my chest, heavy and suffocating. My gaze flicked between the two brothers lying on either side of me. Ciaran with my head on his thighs. Ty with my legs in his lap.

They were both disheveled and panting, their breaths uneven from the dark insanity that had just consumed us all. For the first time in what felt like hours, neither of them spoke.

The silence should have been a relief, but instead, it was deafening.

Ciaran's eyes burned with raw vulnerability as he brushed his fingers through my hair, his fierce possessiveness barely concealed beneath the surface. The way he looked at me was a plea, a demand, and a declaration all at once.

Ty rubbed circles on my thigh with his thumb, sending shivers up my spine. His gaze, steady and intense, felt no less powerful, no less desperate.

How could I ever choose between them?

The question clawed at my insides, leaving me feeling raw and exposed.

Choosing one of them would mean ripping the other apart, shattering what fragile threads were holding us all together. My heart, my mind, my body—every piece of me was tied to them both in different, irreconcilable ways.

I swallowed hard, the taste of ash in my throat, as the realization settled in. No matter what choice I made, we would all be destroyed.

In Ciaran's dorm bedroom, I'd expected to find him pacing his floor, but the room was empty.

My chest tightened as my gaze flicked to the open balcony door. A cool breeze fluttered through it, carrying with it the faint scent of smoke and pine.

I stepped out onto the balcony, my bare feet brushing against the cold tiles, and saw him on the roof, perched on the edge like a gargoyle, the wind ruffling his dark hair. My stomach twisted. He was too close to the edge, too still.

"Ciaran," I called softly. "What are you doing up there?"

"Go back inside."

The sharpness in his tone should have deterred me, but it didn't. If anything, it fueled my resolve.

I moved to the edge of the balcony, my fingers curling over the cold stone railing. "I'm coming up."

"Don't be stupid, Ava." He finally turned, his blue eyes blazing even in the dusk light. "You'll hurt yourself."

I rolled my eyes, planting my foot on the railing. "I'll be fine."

He cursed under his breath as I hoisted myself up with the strength I'd earned at Blackthorn, the training that had saved my life more than once. My muscles strained, but I made it up without faltering.

I crouched on the roof, steadying myself before moving toward him. His scowl deepened as I settled beside him, close but not touching.

"You're insane," he muttered, his bruised jaw tight.

"Maybe," I said. "But so are you."

For a long moment, neither of us spoke. The silence between us was heavy, oppressive, punctuated only by the faint rustle of the trees below.

He stared out over the campus, over the spires and stone towers that broke through the Darkmoor forest, his profile carved from stone, but his shoulders were tense, his hands, still dirty and grazed, clenched.

"What are you doing out here?" I finally asked.

He exhaled sharply, a bitter laugh escaping him. "Thinking."

"About?"

He turned to me then, his gaze raw, unguarded. "About how Ty's probably right."

I blinked. "Right about what?"

His lips twisted into a humorless smile. "That I'm not the best man for you."

The confession knocked the air from my lungs. "Scáth—"

"Exactly. I'm your *shadow*, Ava," he said. "Not the man who gets to keep you. Just the one who watches from the dark."

"That's not true," I said, my voice cracking. "You're—"

"Don't," he cut me off, his eyes searching mine. "Don't lie to make me feel better."

I looked away, my heart pounding.

"I'm not lying," I whispered. "I love you so much…"

His brows furrowed. "But?"

"But you terrify me," I admitted, my voice thick with emotion. "The way you love me. It's so intense, so… stifling. It feels like I'm choking and flying all at once."

He stared at me, the vulnerability in his expression cutting me to the bone.

"I'm sorry," he said quietly. "I just… I don't know how to love you any other way."

My chest tightened. "And that's the problem. I love you. But I've changed. And I love who I've become, who I'm becoming. I'm afraid of losing myself to you. Afraid that you can't love me if I'm not who you want me to be."

The silence stretched again, heavy with everything we weren't saying.

He reached for me, pulling me up and over his lap so I was straddling him.

Our foreheads pressed together as his fingers ran across my body from my neck, down my breasts, and then over my hips and legs.

Like he was trying to memorize the feel of me. One last time.

"I can't stick around if you choose him," he said finally, his voice breaking. "I can't watch you be with him."

"Ciaran…" My throat tightened as tears pricked my eyes, my fingers curling into his shirt. "I can't lose you."

"Then promise me," he said, his grip on my hips tightening as he pulled me closer, as his lips brushed against mine. "Promise me you'll choose me."

I hesitated, my heart splintering under the weight of his words. "I'm sorry. I can't promise anything—yet."

His jaw clenched, the hurt in his eyes nearly undoing me. "That's not good enough, Ava."

"I know," I whispered, tears slipping down my cheeks. "I know."

The minute I stepped into Ty's bedroom, his scent of sandalwood lingering in the air, I realized I'd never been in here before.

It was a reflection of him: masculine, orderly, and purposeful, with slate-gray walls and meticulously arranged furniture. The heavy oak desk held neatly stacked books and a closed laptop, while the bed, dressed in charcoal bedding, was made with military precision.

But the moment I caught sight of him sitting on the edge of his bed facing the full-length mirror, shirtless, bruised, and bleeding from a cut on the side of his forehead he was trying to clean, a first aid kit laid out beside him, my chest tightened.

"You're an eejit." I walked up to him and snatched the antiseptic pad from his hands. "Why didn't you ask for help?"

Ty gave me a wry smile, his lips quirking up even as he winced. "Guess I'm not great at that."

"Turn this way." Standing between his legs, I turned his

chin so I could see his wound properly, my hands steadier than I felt.

He hissed when I pressed the pad to his skin, his muscles tensing under my touch.

"Stay still," I muttered, dabbing at the wound with more care than I wanted to admit.

He chuckled softly, his breath fanning against my cheek. "So, you love me too, huh? It's not exactly how I planned for this to go."

I shot him a glare, but it lacked heat. "You can't plan what you're going to feel."

His grin faded, replaced by something quieter, heavier. "That's all I've ever done, Ava. Plan. Control. Achieve. But with you…"

I stilled, the antiseptic pad hovering over his skin. "With me, what?"

He reached up, his fingers brushing a stray strand of hair from my face. "I had a plan even with you, but now I know… I can't control what happens with us, can I?"

My throat tightened at the raw vulnerability in his voice. "Mhaor…"

"Don't," he said, his voice soft but firm. "Don't say anything just to make me feel better. I need you to be honest."

I swallowed hard, focusing on the wound again to avoid his piercing gaze.

"You make me feel safe," I admitted, my voice barely above a whisper. "You're my calm in the middle of the storm. But…"

I hesitated, unsure if I could say the next words aloud.

"But what?" he prompted gently.

"But I fell in love with him *first*," I said finally, the words cutting me as much as I feared they'd cut him.

He didn't react right away, his silence stretching between us as he wrapped his arms around my legs and tugged me against him.

I dropped the pad and brushed my hands through his hair still damp from the shower.

When he finally spoke, his voice was low, pained. "And that's something I can never change."

"I'm sorry," I said.

He exhaled sharply. "I know. I just wish I knew what made you fall for him all those years ago. Maybe I could have…"

The intensity of his stare was too much.

I tore my gaze away and fished the antique engagement ring out of my pocket, the large diamond catching the dim light of the room. My heart thudded uncomfortably as I held it out to him.

"Here," I said, keeping my voice steady. "This belongs to you."

Ty glanced at the ring in my palm, then at me. His expression didn't shift, unreadable as always.

But when he reached out, it wasn't to take the ring—it was to push my hand back toward me.

"Keep it," he said, his voice low but firm. "I bought it for you, anyway."

I blinked, momentarily thrown off-balance. My fingers closed reflexively around the ring as his hand lingered on mine for a moment too long. Warmth flooded my chest, and I hated the way it spread, unchecked and unwelcome.

"Ty," I started, shaking my head. "I can't—"

"Return it," he interrupted, cutting me off with a wry curve of his lips, "if you want me to propose to you for real."

I froze. His words hit me like a shot of adrenaline, lighting up every nerve.

My breath caught in my throat, and for a moment, I couldn't think past the implications.

He held my gaze, his eyes steady, waiting for a response I wasn't sure I could give.

"No pressure or anything," I muttered, shoving the ring back into my pocket. The small band might as well have been molten, searing through the fabric to brand my skin.

He chuckled, the sound low and rich.

"No pressure," he echoed, though the weight of his gaze said otherwise.

He pulled me down into his lap, cradling me the way he did that first time when he carried me to the nurse's office.

"But if I never get that ring back…" He hesitated, his jaw tightening. "I don't know if I can watch you love someone else. Even if it's him."

The confession shattered something inside me. My hands trembled as I clung to him with my arms around his neck.

His arm tightened around my back, steadying me as he kissed me.

I tasted the blood clinging to the cut on his lip, ran my tongue over his scar and felt him tremble underneath me.

"I'll fight for you, Ava," he said against my lips, his voice steady despite the emotion behind it. "But I won't trap you. You have to make the choice."

The weight of his words crushed me. I felt the tears welling up, but I refused to let them fall.

"And what if I can't?" I whispered.

He pulled back just enough to meet my gaze, his eyes dark and unreadable. "Then you'll destroy both of us."

The finality of his statement left me breathless. Guilt and heartbreak swirled in my chest, threatening to choke me.

I wanted to tell him it would be okay, that I'd figure it out. But as I sat there, tangled in his warmth and his pain, I wasn't sure I believed it.

The smell of rich tomato sauce and fresh basil filled the loft as I set a steaming pot of pasta down on the circular dining table set with plates, utensils, and glasses of water.

"Dinner's ready," I yelled, noting how ironic this little domestic scene appeared.

The brothers emerged from their rooms at the same time, their footsteps heavy on the wooden floor.

Ty's sharp blue eyes immediately locked on Ciaran, his lips pressing into a thin line.

Ciaran, ever the fire to Ty's ice, rolled his shoulders and set his jaw, shooting Ty a challenging glare. The air crackled between them.

"The first person to throw a punch goes to bed hungry," I said firmly, breaking the tension before it could boil over.

For a moment, they just stood there, glaring at each other, until I raised an eyebrow.

"Understood?" I warned.

They both muttered under their breath as they moved toward the table.

Ciaran dropped into the chair on my left while Ty took the seat to my right, neither of them sparing the other a glance.

I busied myself ladling pasta onto their plates, refusing to let their simmering resentment ruin the dinner I'd worked to make. The clink of the serving spoon against ceramic echoed awkwardly in the silence.

"If we're fighting each other," I said, my voice steady but heavy with meaning, "the Sochai wins."

Ciaran stabbed at his pasta, his shoulders tense. "Doesn't mean I have to like him."

Ty leaned back in his chair, folding his arms. "Trust me, the feeling's mutual."

I slammed my fork down onto the table, startling them both.

"Enough." My voice was sharp, leaving no room for argument. "You don't have to like each other, but you do have to work together. If you can't manage that, then we're all dead."

The weight of my words settled over them like a storm cloud.

Ciaran scowled at me. "You have to choose."

"I *will* choose," I said. "But not right now. Right now, we only have one goal…"

"Bringing down the Sochai," Ty said with a nod.

Ciaran let out a grudging grunt, pushing his food around his plate. "Fine."

I exhaled, letting a little of my frustration go. "Good. Now kiss and make up."

Neither of them moved.

I crossed my arms. "*Now*, boys."

Ty was the first to huff and he nodded, turning to Ciaran. "Ceasefire?"

Ciaran's jaw tightened, but after a beat, he nodded back. "Ceasefire. For now."

The tension between them didn't vanish entirely, but it lessened, shifting into something more focused.

"So…" I said as I twirled pasta onto my fork even though my hunger had vanished. "What do we do next?"

Ciaran was the first to break the silence. "Ashcradle has to have a paper trail even if it's not still standing. I left a program running on my computer to trace the money and hopefully uncover any hidden records."

Ty frowned thoughtfully. "Smart. If the clinic was tied to the Sochai, the money will lead us somewhere."

I nodded, my thoughts already racing ahead. "And if it doesn't?"

"We keep digging," Ciaran said, stabbing at his meal. "There has to be a paper trail somewhere."

Ty twirled his spaghetti into a perfect loop on his fork using his spoon. "Or we refocus on the missing girls. Someone in their lives knows something."

"Or," I said, "we use me as bait."

Ciaran's fork clattered to his plate. At the same time, Ty stopped chewing.

I took a sip of water. "What?"

Ciaran shot out of his chair, his hands braced on the edge of the table as he glared at me. "Are you out of your mind?"

I tried to keep my voice steady, but my heart hammered in my chest. "Think about it. If we let them take me this time, they'll lead us straight to the High Lord."

"What the fuck, Ava?" Ciaran looked about ready to smash the table in two.

I glanced at Ty for his support. "You and Ciaran can use my tracker implant to find me."

"Your fucking *what*?" Ciaran yelled.

But I ignored him, imploring Ty with my eyes.

Ty set his fork down slowly, his movements deliberate, but the tension radiating from him was palpable.

"Absolutely not," he said, his voice cold and clipped. "We're not handing you over to them."

I glared at Ty. "You let me make the choice with the vial—"

"That was different."

"—but you're taking his side on *this* now?"

"It's not about sides, Ava," Ciaran said, throwing my words back at me. "It's about you *not* being abused and murdered by a society of evil pedophilic bastards."

Ty's voice was icy. "Do you have *any* idea what they'd do to you?"

"It's not your decision to make," I snapped, the frustration bubbling over. "This is my life. My fight. They're coming after *me*. They took *my* friend. I have to do *something*."

Ciaran slammed his palm down on the table, making the plates rattle. "You're not using yourself as bait, Ava! If I have to tie you to your fucking bed so help me God ..."

His words hit me hard, sending a shudder down my spine at the memory of how he tied me down.

But I held my ground. "If we don't stop them, they'll just keep going. They'll never stop. The blood and shattered innocence of more girls will be on your hands."

Ty's jaw clenched, his icy exterior cracking as raw emotion bled into his voice. "There has to be another way. We'll find it. But using you as bait is *not* it."

"You're both so afraid of losing me," I said, my voice trembling with equal parts anger and heartbreak, "that you're not even willing to try. But we're running out of options. We need something to draw them out, and I'm the only thing we have."

"No," Ciaran said finally, his voice a quiet but unyielding promise. "Not *this*."

"Not *you*," Ty said.

Great. *This* they were agreeing on.

The silence that followed was heavy, oppressive. Ty stared at me, his lips pressed into a thin line, while Ciaran looked like he was barely restraining himself from tearing the room apart.

From the corner of the living room, Ciaran's computer pinged.

All three of us froze, our heads snapping toward the sound.

"The program," Ciaran said. "It found something."

He raced to the couch where his keyboard sat.

Ty and I fell on the couch next to him. I scooted forward to the edge of my seat as Ciaran clicked through the document that the program had sent him.

After tracing the shell corporations across several countries, we'd found the original incorporation document of Ashcradle House.

A single name blinked at the bottom of the screen: the owner of the Ashcradle House.

I stared at the all-too-familiar name, the blood draining

from my face. My heart pounded as the pieces began to fall into place, the enormity of it threatening to crush me.

"That's…" I whispered, my voice barely audible over the rush of blood in my ears.

We'd found the High Lord.

THE SHADOW

We had a name. We had a target for my knives. But these two wanted to keep "planning."

"Killing him solves the problem," I said again, my voice sharper than I intended as I paced the length of the living room, my fists clenched at my sides. "We take the High Lord out, and it's over. Done."

Ava sat at the table, her hands flat against the wood, steady in a way that only fueled my frustration.

She shook her head, her jaw tightening with that infuriating resolve of hers. "You're wrong. Killing him won't stop the Sochai. They'll just crown a new High Lord. The rot goes deeper than one man, Ciaran."

Her words sliced through me because I knew, deep down, she was right. But admitting that felt like surrendering. Like losing.

"So what? We let him keep breathing while we attempt to… infiltrate?" The word tasted bitter on my tongue. "Men like Dr. Vale spent years—*years*—doing the Sochai's dirty work without being let into the inner circle."

Before Ava could respond, Ty emerged from his bedroom carrying an ornate wooden chest I hadn't seen in years.

My stomach twisted at the sight of it. It had rested at the foot of my father's bed.

He set it on the table with deliberate care and opened the lid.

"Why the hell did you bring that here?" I snapped, more to cut through my own unease than anything else.

Ty's expression was maddeningly calm, like he was impervious to the chaos around him. "I took these from Blackthorn. From the professor's secret laboratory."

He opened the chest and began to unload the contents across the table.

Leather-bound journals with the Sochai's crest embossed on the front, a case of clinking vials—that made my stomach turn—and a small carved wooden box.

"His journals and his… things." His voice was quiet, focused, like he wasn't talking about the remnants of the man who had destroyed all three of our lives.

"What are you looking for?" Ava asked him, her tone soft but curious.

Ty didn't answer immediately, flipping through the brittle pages. "I thought I remembered reading something…"

I turned back to Ava, my anger reigniting. "You think infiltrating them will work? You think either one of us are going to able to walk into their lair and play pretend without them figuring it out?"

Her eyes locked on mine, steady and unwavering. "I'm asking you to think bigger, Ciaran. Killing the High Lord might feel good for five minutes, but it won't end this. We need to destroy the Sochai entirely."

Her words hit like a blow, and I hated the way they made me feel. Powerless. Out of control.

I lashed out, not at her, but at the world she was describing. "And what happens when they see through us? When they realize we're trying to take them down? They'll kill you, Ava. Is that big enough for you?"

Ava's voice cut through the air. "I'm not afraid of them."

The icy determination in her tone sent a shiver down my spine, so eerily like Ty's that it made my chest tighten.

I forced myself to look away, unable to bear the sight of how much of my brother had seeped into her—how deeply he'd shaped her, changed her.

And I hated it. Hated him. Hated that part of me feared she was better for it.

I reached into an open box and plucked out a gold signet ring. The weight of it settled heavily in my palm.

The crest of the Sochai, snakes in a Celtic knot, was etched into the gold like a brand. Memories surfaced—unwelcome and sharp.

I could see my father's hand, that ring glinting on his finger as he raised it in anger. I could feel the sting of it, the hard edge cutting into my skin, leaving its mark on my cheek as clearly as it had left its imprint on my soul.

It wasn't just a ring—it was a symbol of everything he'd been, everything I hated, and everything I swore I'd never become.

"Here!" Ty said, as he flipped open a page in the diary and began to read aloud.

"Tynan, my ever-studious son, will surely follow in my foot-steps, a gifted chemist and a worthy heir to my work.

"But Ciaran... ah, Ciaran. There is a fire in him, a raw, untamed darkness that sometimes scares even me.

"Perhaps he will find his way to the highest place of all, wearing the mantle of the High Lord himself...

"One day, when they are ready, my boys will approach the High Lord with my signet ring and ask for entrance into this holy circle.

"As it was, as it has always been."

The room fell into a suffocating silence.

Ty looked up, his expression unreadable, though his fingers tightened on the edges of the diary as if to steady himself.

But me? I couldn't breathe. My father's words hit like a punch to the gut, the air stolen from my lungs by the sheer audacity of his pride in me—pride twisted into something monstrous.

Darkness? That's what he saw when he looked at me? Not a son, not a boy struggling to survive, but a vessel for his sick, twisted ambitions?

Ava let out a gasp. "Of course."

I could already see the wheels turning in her head. But I refused to go down that train of thought.

The bile rose in my throat, and I flung the ring back into the box like it burned me.

"Fuck that," I muttered, turning away. "I'm not wearing his fucking ring."

"It's not about the ring," Ava said, her voice softer now, almost coaxing. "It's about what it gets us. A way in."

She pulled something from her bag, sliding it across the

table to me. "I stole it from Ebony's mail when I ducked home to see her."

I glanced down and saw the words Darkmoor Alumni Association Fundraising Gala printed across the glossy invitation.

"Two days," Ava said, her smile dark, her eyes gleaming with determination. "The dean will be there. So will the rest of the Sochai members. It's the perfect opportunity."

My lips curled into a scowl. "You're serious."

"As a heart attack," she said.

Ty lifted his eyebrows. "So, who wants to infiltrate a secret society?"

With a smirk that dared me to argue, Ava added, "We have to get you a suit."

My diamond cuff links refracted the dim light of the chandeliers. My Valentino suit fit like a glove even if it felt like a straitjacket.

And my father's Sochai ring burned through the flesh of my finger, straight to the bone.

Ty had wanted to be the one to attend the Darkmoor alumni gala, but Ava had quickly brought up the obvious.

"First, you're supposed to be dead. Second, you have a criminal record for killing your father, a member of the secret society we're trying to infiltrate..."

It had to be me.

It was only because I loved Ava that I said yes.

Yes, because if I didn't say yes, then she'd find some

other harebrained way of infiltrating the Society. Like using herself as bait.

At least, if *I* said yes, it was *my* life at risk. *Not* hers.

I said yes because the faster we took down the Sochai, the quicker she could put all this behind her and we had a chance at being together.

At the edge of the gilded ballroom, I reached for a glass of champagne from a passing waiter and downed it in one go. For courage. The warmth spread through my veins. I reminded myself I was doing this for Ava.

The Darkmoor Alumni Gala was held in the grand ballroom of one of the oldest buildings on campus, a place steeped in history and dripping with ostentation.

The high ceilings loomed above me, their gold-plated moldings gleaming under the light of enormous crystal chandeliers. Low-seated couches, upholstered in rich, faded fabrics from centuries past, dotted the room.

I moved carefully through the crowd, my steps measured, my expression cool. I pretended I belonged among Ireland's elite—industry titans, political giants, and heirs to fortunes older than the Republic itself.

These were people cloaked in untouchable power, their wealth and influence spanning not just the country but much of Europe.

Among the shifting tides of laughter and clinking glasses, I spotted them—the known members of the Sochai. Their whiskey glasses reflected the chandelier's glow, their cigars smoldering as they leaned in close to share secrets only the most privileged would ever hear. Predators dressed as gentlemen.

But no matter how carefully I scanned the room, my

pulse ticking faster with each passing moment, I couldn't find who I was looking for.

I passed by the double doors of a smaller side room, a drawing room, velvet green armchairs illuminated beneath a chandelier and a golden harp in a solitary corner.

Gauzy white drapes billowed into the room from a stone terrace and the foggy night. It was empty. But the sound of voices outside caught my attention.

My footsteps were damped by the thick carpet as I crossed the small drawing room.

As I pushed aside the curtains and stepped into the frigid, still air, I noticed a female figure disappearing down the stairs to the garden.

There, leaning against the stone balustrade, was the man I'd been looking for.

An Tiarna Ard.

The High Lord.

Steeling my nerves, I swiped my sweaty palms against my suit pants as I went to stand beside Dean McCarthy as if merely admiring the view.

There was little view, of course. The torches lining the edge of the building did little to cut through the mist which swallowed the gardens.

The weight of his attention pressed on me, subtle but unmistakable, as if he were dissecting me from the corner of his eye.

"You look familiar," he said, his tone veering from casual to suspicious.

It was my opening, but I forced myself not to rush.

I stood still, holding on to a carefully cultivated air of entitlement and quiet confidence. This wasn't just a conversation; it was a performance. I gambled on arrogance over deference, knowing the High Lord wouldn't respect someone that was too quick to simper before him.

The silence stretched until the dean exhaled in mock boredom. "Well, it's getting cold," he muttered, pushing away from the stone railing.

I chose that exact moment to speak, my tone unhurried as I continued gazing out into the darkness. "Ciaran Donahue."

The dean froze mid-step, his back stiffening. Slowly, he turned his head toward me.

"You knew my father," I said, finally meeting his gaze.

His eyes flickered, his composure slipping for the briefest moment. Then he relaxed, settling back into his position with a faint smile tugging at his lips.

So far, so good.

I forced myself to relax, leaning slightly against the stone railing as if I belonged there. But the ease I projected was a lie. Every second in this man's presence felt like a knife pressed to my throat.

The dean brushed an invisible speck of lint from his lapel. "Pity about your father."

It was a test. I couldn't falter.

"My brother was an ungrateful brat," I said, my voice dropping to a snarl. "I wish I'd been the one to kill him."

The dean clicked his tongue in disapproval. "He's family."

"My *father* was family," I snapped.

The dean's shrug was as dismissive as it was deliberate, his indifference setting my teeth on edge. He was holding his cards close, but I had to force him to show his hand.

I gripped the stone railing, my father's signet ring scraping against the surface.

A cold chill ran down my spine as I looked at the curl of snakes in that crest, but I couldn't afford weakness now.

I turned the ring slowly on my finger, the weight of it feeling heavier than ever. "I've recently felt... a desire to reconnect with my beloved father's legacy."

The dean tilted his head back, staring at the sky as if bored by the conversation. But his voice betrayed his interest. "Our roots are important."

I swallowed my revulsion and forced out the words. "He was a great man."

"Hmm." A noncommittal response.

My throat tightened. "I want to be a great man like him."

The dean shifted his gaze down to me, his sharp eyes dissecting every nuance of my face.

"In any particular way?" he asked softly. "Your father was a brilliant scientist... a generous philanthropist... an involved member of his alma mater's alumni society... a loving father of *three* beautiful, beautiful children."

I knew he was watching for the smallest flinch, the tiniest crack in my armor. My nails bit into the stone railing as I fought to keep my expression neutral.

"In which way do you mean, Mr. Donahue?" he pressed, his tone almost kind.

I couldn't say it. The words burned in my throat, too vile to voice. To claim a legacy tied to the Sochai—to the things they'd done to Ava—was unthinkable.

But Ava's face flashed in my mind, her fiery determination that I'd admired and feared in equal measure. This was for her. It had to be.

"I want to join the Sochai," I said at last, my voice cold and steady despite the storm inside me.

The dean's brows furrowed slightly. "I'm afraid I don't know what that is."

He moved to step away, and panic surged in my chest. Shit.

"I'm demanding an invitation to join as is my birthright," I said firmly, my voice cutting through the misty night.

The dean paused mid-step, then slowly turned back to face me.

"Really?" His voice was laced with mockery. "And you think I can grant you such an invitation? What makes you think you deserve to be part of this... Sochai, if it did so happen to exist?"

I leaned closer, keeping my voice low. "Before he died, my father showed me... everything. In an effort to groom me. He let me... spend time with my sweet, sweet sister."

The dean's gaze never wavered from mine as if we were locked in a battle of wills.

I forced myself to finish. "He taught me that my world has no limits. What I desire is mine. I shall not be excluded from the Sochai any longer."

A long silence hung between us before the dean chuckled, the sound dark and predatory.

"As it was..." He paused, a weighted pause. Like... Like he was waiting for me to answer.

Panic swirled in my chest. I didn't know the response he wanted, but I had to say something.

The dean's disappointed expression made my stomach drop.

The dean was about to leave. Disappear. Slip between

the curtains and escape. I couldn't lose this chance, couldn't let Ava throw herself into danger.

Then, like a whisper from the shadows, Ty's voice echoed in my mind—his words from the professor's diary.

"One day, when they are ready, my boys will approach the High Lord with my signet ring and ask for entrance into this holy circle.

"As it was, as it has always been."

I ripped the ring from my finger and hurled it onto the stone terrace. It skittered across the cold, unforgiving floor, each metallic clatter pounding in my chest like an iron fist, before coming to a stop in front of the dean's polished black shoes.

I spoke loud and clear. "As it has always been."

The dean turned slowly, his face twisting into a cruel smile. His gaze flicked from the ring lying on the stones to meet my eyes, assessing me like a predator sizing up prey.

He tilted his head and stroked his weak chin, his voice as smooth as venom. "I always thought it would be your brother who came to us."

My jaw tightened, but I forced myself not to flinch, not to look away.

The fog curled around us like smoke, thickening with the silence as his unspoken will pressed against me, heavy and suffocating.

After an excruciating pause, the dean bent down, his thin fingers curling around the ring.

I forced myself to stay still as he straightened and walked to me, holding the ring up in the firelight.

Then, with a deliberate slowness, he extended it toward me. Not to hand it back—but to put it on for me.

My stomach churned, but I swallowed down the bile. Forcing my hand forward, I held out my finger, every fiber of my being screaming against the submission.

The cold, unyielding metal slid onto my skin, its weight nauseating.

His grip lingered as he tilted my hand, angling the ring until the flames reflected in the gleaming band and I fought the urge to yank my hand away.

His thumb rubbed over it, almost fondly, like it belonged to him more than to me. "You'll have to pass the initiation."

My heart pounded in my chest, but I kept my expression neutral, my voice steady. "I'm ready."

The dean's lips curved in a faint, twisted smile. "You have twenty-four hours…"

Twenty-four hours for what? To do what? The tension clawed at me, but I couldn't push. Not now. Not when I was this close.

Without another word, he leaned in, brushing a cold kiss against each of my cheeks and it left a trail of ice in its wake.

Then he was gone, disappearing into the mist like a phantom.

I was left reeling.

I had no idea what he meant by his parting words—a riddle—echoing in my mind.

"Chase the raven with the Gardener's gift, across the dark moors to where the winter sun stands still."

AVA

The tension in our dorm apartment was suffocating. Ciaran paced the living room like a restless predator, his agitation palpable. His boots scuffed against the floorboards, back and forth, back and forth, until I thought I might scream just to make it stop.

I didn't blame him—not really.

We had twenty-four hours to decipher the High Lord's riddle, twenty-four hours to prove he was worthy of initiation.

Twenty-four hours or our chance to infiltrate the Sochai was gone.

And we were running out of time.

"What do they want from me?" Ciaran growled, his voice cracking under the weight of his frustration. "What kind of sick test is this?"

I clenched my hands into fists, my nails digging into my palms as I tried to steady myself.

"What did the riddle say again?" I asked, trying to sound calm, as if my own heart wasn't hammering in my chest.

He stopped pacing, his eyes locking on mine like a life-line. Then, with a deep breath, he recited it.

"Chase the raven with the Gardener's gift, across the dark moors to where the winter sun stands still."

The words sent a chill skittering down my spine. They were cryptic, almost poetic, but the meaning eluded me.

"Twenty-four hours," Ty muttered from the couch, his voice low and measured. "If we don't figure this out, they'll—"

He cut himself off, shaking his head, but I knew what he meant.

The Sochai didn't forgive failure.

"They'll kill me," Ciaran finished bluntly, his fists clenching at his sides. "Or worse."

The thought of what "worse" might mean sent nausea roiling through my stomach, but I pushed it down.

"It's another test," I said, trying to inject some steadiness into my voice. "They want to see if you're really one of them —if your father groomed you well enough to understand their twisted codes."

"Then let's start where our father left off," Ty said, standing with a quiet determination that contrasted sharply with Ciaran's fraying edges.

He returned with the chest of journals and notes we'd salvaged from the professor's secret lab, dumping them onto the table.

I stared at the messy pile, dread curling in my chest. Those journals held horrors, memories I'd tried desperately to lock away.

Ciaran must have seen the hesitation in my eyes as I reached for the closest journal because he caught my hand.

"You don't have to read them. Ty and I can handle it. But," he added softly, the edge in his voice gone for the moment, "it's your choice."

For a moment, his vulnerability softened the edges of my fear. A flicker of something new in his tone made my chest tighten—was he changing, for me?

I offered him a small, reassuring smile. "I can do it. I can help."

His grip on my hand tightened briefly before he let go, a small gesture of trust that made my chest ache.

I perched on the edge of the couch, a thick journal in my lap, while Ty sat cross-legged on the floor, flipping methodically through another.

Across from us, Ciaran paced, a journal in his hand, though it was clear he wasn't reading a single word.

Ciaran's agitation radiated off him like heat. His fist clenched and unclenched around the fragile binding, his knuckles whitening as his jaw tightened.

Every few seconds, he'd exhale sharply, mutter a curse under his breath, and toss a glance our way, as if expecting us to have figured it all out already.

"Anything?" he snapped, breaking the silence.

"Not yet." Ty didn't even look up, his tone maddeningly calm as he skimmed through page after page.

Ciaran growled, slamming his book shut. "We're wasting time. What if it's simpler than all this? 'Chase the raven'—maybe it means we just need to kill a raven or something."

Ty finally looked up, his expression as dry as his tone. "That's too literal and it's not how riddles work, Ciaran."

The tension crackled between them, sharp and dangerous.

Ciaran's shoulders tensed, his fists tightening as if he was one step away from throwing the journal. "You don't know that. You're not the only one with ideas here."

"And you're not the only one who cares," Ty shot back, his voice still quiet but carrying an edge.

"Stop." My voice cut through the rising heat. "We don't have time for this. Just… focus, okay? Every second we waste arguing is a second closer to them winning."

Ciaran grumbled something under his breath but sat down, flipping the journal open again, though his hands shook as he turned the pages.

I returned to the journal in my lap.

The professor's handwriting was neat, precise, almost clinical, which somehow made the words more horrifying. He wrote about his experiments with an almost childlike excitement, detailing the effects of his latest creations like a proud artist discussing his masterpiece.

At the edge of my consciousness, Ty began muttering in Irish. But one word made my ears prick. "…grianstad…"

Its meaning buzzed in my mind like static.

"What did you just say?" I asked, my focus shifting to him.

Ty blinked, his gaze sharpening as he looked at me. "Grianstad. It means 'sun stands still' in Irish."

"But it also means solstice," I said, the word unlocking a memory. My heart gave a small leap as a connection began to form. "Wait. During orientation, didn't Lisa say something about the winter solstice?"

Ty nodded. "Yeah, she wouldn't stop talking about Darkmoor's history. I remember her saying something about a building on campus aligned with the winter solstice."

A lightbulb flickered on in my brain.

"Darkmoor is actually a really cool old place." Lisa's voice carried as she followed Ty down the hall. "We even have a legit passagetomb on the grounds aligned with the winter solstice or winter grianstad, *if you're up on your Irish."*

I stood up so quickly that my chair clattered to the floor behind me. I began frantically searching through the mess of papers we'd accumulated at the end of the dining room table. I found what I was looking for at the very bottom. Forgotten from weeks and weeks ago, the Darkmoor new student orientation welcome packet that Lisa had brought for Ciaran and Ty at the very start of term.

I slammed it on the table between them, opened to a page.

Among other pictures of various interesting or historical spots around campus was a photo of an ancient stone passagetomb, a grassy mound rising up out of the forest, the stone entrance partially hidden by thick vines of morning glory.

Any other spot like this, on any other college campus would be ripe for late-night hookups, Adderall drug deals, and beer bottle smashing. But no one went there. I don't remember ever being told it was off-limits. But we all seemed to know to stay away.

I pointed to the passagetomb, the very one I'd run past when they had chased me through Darkmoor forest.

"The passagetomb," I said, my voice rising with excitement.

Ty's eyes lit up, and for a moment, the tension in the room seemed to lift.

"Right," he said. *"Across the dark moors to where the winter sun stands still*—it has to mean the Darkmoor passagetomb."

I turned to Ciaran, the first spark of hope igniting in my chest. "That's it. That's the place."

Ciaran let out a frustrated breath, raking a hand through his hair. "Great. So we've got a location. Now what? I'm supposed to chase a raven to the tomb? What the hell does that even mean?"

The mood shifted instantly, the fragile hope I'd felt slipping through my fingers. My stomach twisted, but I clenched my jaw and forced myself to stay steady.

"Okay," I said gently, keeping my voice calm despite the icy dread crawling up my spine. "That's progress. We've deciphered one part."

Ciaran let out a bitter laugh, sharp and jagged as broken glass. "Yeah, one part down. Fifty fucked-up million to go."

"We just have to keep going."

I sat back down and forced myself to focus on the text in front of me, my fingers trembling as I smoothed over the delicate journal paper.

My stomach twisted as I read about the professor's first trials—on his *wife*.

Mona.

Ty and Ciaran's mother.

He wrote about her suffering with cold detachment, as if she were no more than a lab rat, a tool for his genius. Like she wasn't the mother of his children. Like she wasn't even fucking human.

My vision blurred with fury. How dare he?

I slammed the journal shut, bile rising in my throat.

The sound echoed in the loft, making Ty and Ciaran glance up.

I stared at the closed cover, willing the nausea away. But I couldn't stop. I couldn't let this break me.

Ciaran's gaze softened, and for a moment, he looked like he might reach for me.

But I shook my head and reopened the journal, forcing myself to keep reading, to keep going, even as my hands shook.

Ciaran's voice cut through my haze.

"The Gardener," he muttered, his voice low, almost like he was speaking to himself. His brow furrowed as he tapped the journal in his lap, then his eyes widened with sudden realization. "Oh my God. Of course."

I straightened, my heart thudding as I focused on him. "You figured it out? The Gardener?"

He nodded, his jaw tightening. "Yeah. The Gardener was the Sochai code name for… *our father*."

The words hung in the air, suffocating and vile. His knuckles turned white as he gripped the journal, the paper crumpling under his fingers.

With a frustrated shove, he hurled the journal across the table, the pages splaying open as it landed.

He was already on his feet, pacing like a caged animal, his hands flexing at his sides.

I exhaled slowly, refusing to let his agitation shake me as I kept reading.

The pages blurred when I reached a section describing his introduction to the inner circle of the Sochai. He wrote with twisted reverence about their "gift," a "blessing" that had reignited his work.

My heart stuttered when I realized what he meant. The "gift" wasn't a thing—it was a person.

I swallowed hard, my grip tightening on the edges of the journal. "He… he called me his 'gift.'"

Ty's head snapped up and Ciaran stopped pacing, both of them looking at me in horror.

"The Gardener's 'gift,'" I said, "…is *me*."

Ciaran's brows furrowed deeply, his fists clenching at his sides. "What the fuck are you talking about, Ava?"

Ty's voice was calm but sharp, the edge of unease betraying his usual composure.

"She's right," he said, his fingers running over the line in the journal he was holding. "Our father called her his gift. It's in here. Multiple times. Fuck, why didn't I make the connection before?"

Ciaran looked like he'd been struck. His face contorted with fury, a storm brewing in his eyes.

"That sick bastard…" His voice cracked, and he slammed his fist into the wall, the sound reverberating through the loft.

I couldn't look at either of them. My hands shook as I closed the journal in front of me, but it wasn't enough to block out the words burned into my mind.

My foster father's *gift*. His muse. His *fucking property*.

"I'm part of it," I said again, more firmly this time, though my voice wavered under the weight of the truth. I forced myself to meet Ciaran's gaze, his anger bleeding into a flicker of anguish that tore at my chest. "This riddle—this initiation—I'm part of it somehow."

"It's not happening." Ciaran cut me off, his voice a growl. He crossed the room in two strides and stood over me, his shadow falling across the journal I'd shut. "I'm not letting them use you for whatever twisted game they've planned."

Ty exhaled sharply, dragging a hand down his face. "This changes things. If Ava's part of the initiation—"

"It's not up to you," I said, my voice firmer than I felt, meeting his glare head-on. "If this is the only way to bring them down, then we do it."

Ciaran's eyes burned into mine, his hands flexing at his sides like he was trying to keep from shaking me. "I'm not risking you."

Ty's voice broke through the charged silence. "We don't have a choice, Ciaran. This isn't just about you or me or Ava —it's about taking down the Sochai, all of them."

Ciaran whirled on him, his fury redirected. "You don't get to decide that, *brother*. You're not the one they want to use."

"And neither are you," Ty shot back. "But if we want to win this, we need to play their game."

Their voices rose, but I tuned them out, my focus narrowing to the words in the journal still clutched in my hand. *The Gardener's gift.* The weight of what it meant settled over me, heavy and suffocating.

Whatever this riddle led to, whatever the initiation demanded—I was at the center of it.

That left the last section undeciphered.

Chasing the raven.

The journals were dense with madness, but as I turned another yellowed page, a single word struck me like a slap. *Chasing.*

My breath hitched, and my fingers froze mid-turn. The professor had used that term repeatedly, always in connection with… with me. My throat tightened as I scanned the page, the realization crawling over me like a thousand spiders.

He hadn't meant chasing in the traditional sense. It was his twisted code for administering a potion.

My stomach churned as the memories crept closer, clawing at the edges of my mind—nights where my body wasn't my own, where the world slipped into a haze, where waking up meant discovering another bruise, another betrayal.

I slammed the journal shut, the sound breaking through the suffocating silence in the loft.

"What is it?" Ciaran asked sharply, his agitation immediately redirected to me.

"It's…" My voice cracked, and I swallowed hard, gripping the edges of the journal until my knuckles whitened. "The word 'chasing'—it means administering a potion."

I glanced between Ciaran and Ty, my eyes burning. "That's what the professor called it. *Chasing.*"

Ty's jaw tightened, but he nodded, as if it all made too much sense.

Ciaran, however, looked like he might explode, his fists curling at his sides.

"Administering what?" Ty asked, his tone careful, measured.

"The Raven," I whispered, the words feeling foreign and jagged on my tongue. "I've read it before—"

In his "recipe" book.

The recipes he'd derived by experimenting on their mother.

My stomach roiled at the thought. That book had been

the pinnacle of his depravity. None of us had dared touch it since we pulled it from the secret lab.

But now… now I had to.

My hands trembled as I reached for it, partially buried under the pile of journals.

I hesitated again before flipping it open, each creak of the binding feeling like an accusation.

The pages smelled faintly of mildew and chemicals, an eerie testament to its contents.

My breath quickened as I leafed through the entries, each coded potion more sinister than the last.

And then, finally, there it was—*The Raven.*

My hands shook as I read the ingredients, the twisted scrawls detailing its effects.

"The riddle," I said, my vision blurring, my voice cracking. "The initiation. It's clear now…"

Ciaran's voice cut through the fog. "What? What does it mean?"

I forced myself to speak despite the tightness in my throat.

"Ciaran has to bring *me* to the passagetomb tonight—*unconscious.*"

"No fucking way," Ciaran snarled, slamming his fist on the table. "I'm not drugging you and dragging you to some goddamn tomb like—like a sacrifice."

"You have to," I said, my voice steady despite the turmoil swirling inside me. "It's the only way."

"For once," Ty said, from across the table, "I agree with him. It's reckless, Ava. It's too dangerous."

Ciaran paced the room like a predator caught in a trap, his arms crossed tightly over his chest. Each step he took radiated barely restrained fury, his movements sharp, precise, and entirely focused on me.

Ty sat stiff and silent, his usual calm tinged with visible tension. His knuckles were white as he gripped the edge of the table, his body angled toward me, protective but no less stern.

Their eyes burned into me, both of them waiting for me to say something, to refute them, to justify the plan I hadn't even fully voiced yet.

But my tongue felt heavy, glued to the roof of my mouth as I stared at the scattered journals on the table before me.

The room was thick with tension, shadows from the lamp stretching across their faces. My silence only amplified it, the air between us humming like a live wire ready to snap.

My stomach churned at the thought of what I was about to ask them to do, the risks I'd have to take, the lives we'd all be gambling. The stakes towered over me like mountains.

If I went through with this, if I let Ciaran carry me into their lair, he'd pass their initiation, but I'd be risking my life —and Ciaran's too.

One wrong move, if they got even an inkling of our true plan, and the Sochai would kill us both without hesitation.

I could enter that passagetomb and never come out. This could be part of the High Lord's plan, to capture me once and for all.

My mind reeled with possibilities, each one more terrifying than the last.

But if I refused, if I walked away… we might not get another shot at taking them down. It could take months, years, to find another crack in their twisted fortress, if ever.

There would be no justice for Liath. The Sochai would keep taking girls, keep abusing them, keep killing them when they were unwanted, and no one would stop them.

Their secrets would remain hidden, their power unchallenged.

And me? They'd hunt me down and kill me, just as they had so many others. They'd gotten so close—too close—too many times before. It was only a matter of time.

I tried to steady my breathing, but the weight of the choice pressed down on me like a physical force.

I thought of Liath, her bright smile and quick wit stolen too soon. I thought of Mona Donahue, who had suffered so cruelly at their hands, and Mr. Buckley, who had simply been in the wrong place at the wrong time and had died to protect me.

All of them—gone. Because of the Sochai.

I tried walking away once. And I couldn't do it. I couldn't do it now, either.

A flicker of resolve flared in my chest, burning through the fear. No more running. No more hiding.

It was time to attack the Sochai head-on.

I lifted my head, meeting their stares with a fire I couldn't allow myself to extinguish.

"We have to stop them," I said calmly, willing the steadiness in my voice to drown out the pounding of my heart. "And this is our best chance."

Ciaran's pacing stopped abruptly. He turned to me, his frustration snapping like a live wire. "Are you hearing yourself, Ava? You're talking about walking into their lair unconscious! What if they don't let you leave?"

"You claim me as your 'daughter' through their 'inheritance' rule. Members aren't to touch another member's 'daughter' unless their owner decrees."

The room fell into a stunned silence as they both stared at me.

I reached for one of the journals on the table and snatched it up, waving it toward him. "It's part of their disgusting manifesto."

My hand trembled as I held the journal, the weight of its twisted knowledge bearing down on me.

Ciaran's face twisted with outrage, his fists clenching at his sides.

Ty, sitting stiffly across the table, recoiled like he'd been slapped.

"Those sick bastards," he muttered, his voice low and seething.

I dropped the journal onto the table like it burned, the revulsion curling in my stomach making it impossible to hold on to any longer.

"We use their strict rules against them," I said, my voice quieter but no less resolute.

Ty exhaled a sharp, bitter sigh. "Fuck."

Ciaran rounded on him, his fury now directed at his brother. "Are you actually entertaining this madness?"

Ty's jaw tightened as he straightened in his chair, his voice calmer but taut with tension. "I don't like it either, Ci. But maybe with some precautions—with you 'claiming' her, with me nearby as backup…"

Ciaran stepped closer, his eyes blazing. "Easy for you to say. You're not the one who has to carry her into their den—unconscious—like a lamb to the slaughter."

Ty's expression darkened, his calm veneer cracking.

"Then *I'll* do it," he said, his voice cool and cutting. "I'll pretend to be you."

Ciaran barked out a laugh, sharp and humorless. "Please. You couldn't pass as me even on your best day."

Ty leaned forward, his gaze steady and unflinching. "What? Like playing an impulsive hothead is hard?"

He smirked slightly, his tone turning teasing as he

glanced at me. "Please, I've fooled even Ava before. Haven't I, *rabbit*?"

He winked at me, and for a moment, his face shifted—animated in a way that was eerily reminiscent of Ciaran.

My breath hitched as I shivered, memories of Scáth stalking me in the shadows flooding back. How many times had I assumed it was Ciaran chasing me, stalking me, fucking me… when it could have been Ty?

Ciaran noticed my reaction immediately. His eyes narrowed, and he turned on me, his voice low and dangerous. "What is he talking about?"

Ty leaned back, folding his arms across his chest.

"We don't need you, Ci," he said with quiet finality. "Ava and I can do this on our own. *If* she chooses to go through with it."

Ciaran's voice cracked as he fell to his knees before me, clasping my hands in his like a prayer, his dark eyes brimming with an emotion I wasn't sure I could bear to face.

"Please, Ava. Don't do this. We'll find another way. I can't—" His voice broke, then steadied into something raw and desperate. "I can't drug you like this. What if something goes wrong? What if something goes wrong and you're just lying there un-fucking-conscious?"

My chest ached at the way his voice wavered, but I couldn't afford to let my emotions show. Not now. I had to find a way to convince him to take a chance on this. On me.

He searched my face, looking for a crack, a glimmer of hesitation.

But I couldn't give him that.

My expression remained calm, unreadable, even as my heart broke under the weight of what I was about to do.

"What if…" I said slowly, "what if I'm not actually drugged?"

Ciaran froze, his brow furrowing in confusion. "What are you talking about?"

I glanced at Ty, and understanding flickered in his eyes, a small shift that spoke volumes. His gaze softened, though his knuckles remained white where he gripped the edge of the table.

"She's pretended before," Ty said, his voice measured. "Played the part. And succeeded."

Heat flushed through me as the memory surfaced—how I had faked being paralyzed to escape Ty. He'd touched me, licked me, brought me to orgasm, and I hadn't made a sound, hadn't moved an inch.

I'd fooled the man who lived to study my body. If I could fool him…

A flicker of resolve ignited in my chest. I could do it again. I had to.

Ciaran's head snapped toward Ty, his eyes blazing with frustration and betrayal.

"Don't fucking encourage her," he snarled, venom lacing every word.

Ty's expression hardened. "I'm not encouraging her. I'm being realistic. If she's going to do this—and we both know she will—then she has to do it in a way that gives her some control."

Ciaran barked out a humorless laugh, his voice rising. "She won't be able to last two minutes without giving herself away."

I took a deep breath, steadying myself, and looked directly at Ciaran. "I can do it."

Ciaran shook his head, his voice laced with bitterness. "You think you can fool them? These people are predators, Ava. They'll see through it. They'll see through *you*."

I straightened, meeting his fiery gaze with a calm I didn't quite feel. "Then I'll prove it. I'll lie down right here, and you can do whatever you want to me. I won't move a muscle."

His eyes widened, shock breaking through the anger etched into his features.

"You're serious?" he asked, his voice disbelieving.

My heart pounded in my chest, but I kept my expression unreadable. "If I flinch, if I cry, if I so much as twitch, the plan is off. But if I pass your test, we go through with it."

Ciaran hesitated, his jaw tight as he warred with himself. Finally, he crossed his arms over his chest, his voice cutting. "Fine. But when you fail, this plan dies here."

Ty remained silent, his gaze flickering between us like he was caught in the crossfire.

The weight of what I'd just proposed hung heavy in the room, but I didn't give myself time to second-guess it.

Without a word, I turned to the table where journals and notes lay scattered across its surface, a chaotic reminder of the horrors we'd already uncovered. I swept a few aside, making space for myself, and climbed onto the table with deliberate calm.

The wood was cold beneath me, grounding me as I stretched out across the surface. I closed my eyes, forcing my breathing to slow.

Inhale, exhale.

I let my body go limp, my muscles relaxing one by one until I felt weightless.

With my eyes closed, all my other senses heightened.

The musty scent of old leather and ink filled my nose, mingling with the faint spice of Ciaran's cologne and Ty's musk.

Every sound seemed amplified—the rasp of Ciaran's uneven breaths, the brush of clothes as Ty picked himself up off the floor and walked around me, the distant hum of the loft's floor lamp.

The hard edge of a journal pressed into my shoulder, and a cold draft brushed over my skin, raising goosebumps I fought to ignore.

I kept my face slack, my breathing steady, pushing down the adrenaline surging through my veins.

"Well?" Ty's voice broke the silence, expectant and sharp.

"Well, what?" Ciaran snapped back, his frustration bubbling over.

"This isn't much of a test, is it?" Ty replied. "*Do* something to her."

"Do what?" Ciaran's tone was wary, his voice tight with suspicion.

Ty hummed thoughtfully under his breath, and I felt the faint brush of his thigh against my arm as he leaned closer.

"Whatever you'd like to do to her," he murmured, his words a slow, deliberate taunt.

Anticipation began to hum under my skin, the tension unbearable.

"What… What would you do to her?" Ciaran's voice faltered, low and raw.

I could almost imagine the wicked hint of a grin that played like a passing shadow over Ty's face.

"Would you like me to *show* you?" Ty asked, his tone dangerously soft, as if daring his brother to say no.

Before Ciaran could answer—or maybe he just nodded —Ty ripped my top open, the cool air making my nipples harden instantly.

He ran his rough palms over my breasts and I lay there like a doll as pleasure surged through me.

It had been weeks now since my twisted therapy with Ty in Blackthorn. But the dark sensation of not being in control of my body had never left. It lurked in my subconscious.

I clung to it, a wicked thrill rushing through me at the thought of being helpless and laid out on this table for my two dark lovers.

Ty rolled my hard nipple between his thumb and forefinger, and the desire to moan was so strong that it made my chest tight to the point of pain.

But I clutched on to that darkness deep within me, cold and slick as oil. And I kept silent.

Ty slapped my breast hard enough to leave a mark, but I didn't even flinch.

"Don't hurt her!" Ciaran yelled.

Ty's chuckle under his breath made shivers go down my spine. "Hurt? Hardly. She can handle more pain than you realize, dear brother. Go on… try it."

I couldn't see my Scáth from behind my closed lids. All I could use to judge his state of mind was his ragged breathing and the lusty strain in his voice as he said, "This is *wrong*."

And yet, despite how wrong it was, Ciaran also began to

touch me, hesitant at first, his fingers brushing down one arm, from my shoulder to my hand.

Then he kneeled down beside me, his hot breath against my hand as he sucked my fingers one at a time into his mouth.

Shivers broke out over my skin, but I did not move.

Ty, I was sure it was Ty, continued to cup my breast, rubbing his thumb over my nipple. "Come on, Ci. You can do better than that."

As Ty's daring taunt thickened the air, his wet mouth closed over my nipple and sucked.

Pleasure coursed through me and heat rushed between my legs. Inside my head, I cried out and arched my back. But outwardly, I kept still.

Footsteps moved around the table.

The anticipation of what Ciaran would do next made my clit throb against my wet panties.

Ciaran's hand trailed up my legs, then growing bolder as he reached my thighs. Delicious frissons skittered across my skin as he pushed my skirt up to my waist.

I felt him grip my panties, then tug them down along the length of my legs. The cool air kissed my exposed skin, and I fought the urge to shiver.

"She's wet," Ciaran murmured, his voice thick with a mixture of awe and desire.

Ty hummed in agreement around my nipple. "She always is. Aren't you, hummingbird?"

As Ty continued to tease my nipple with his tongue, I remained motionless.

Even as Ty's fingers ghosted over my lips, tracing the shape of my mouth, his touch featherlight, teasing, as if daring me to part my lips and take him in.

Ciaran's fingers dipped between my thighs, and I felt a jolt of electricity shoot through me as he brushed against my clit.

I remained perfectly still, though every nerve in my body screamed for more. His touch was tentative at first, exploring.

"God, she's soaked," Ciaran breathed, his voice husky with desire.

I felt Ty shift beside me, his mouth leaving my breast. "She likes this. Being helpless. Being at our mercy."

Ciaran's fingers grew bolder, circling my clit with more pressure.

I focused on keeping my breathing steady, on not letting my hips buck up into his touch.

"How far should we take this?" Ciaran asked, his voice strained.

Ty's laugh was dark and rich. "As far as you want, brother. She can't stop us without losing, can she?"

The implication in his words sent a thrill through me, a mixture of fear and arousal that threatened to shatter my composure. I clung to that darkness within me, using it as an anchor to keep myself still.

Ciaran's fingers slipped lower, teasing at my entrance before I felt the blunt pressure of his finger pushing inside me, slow and deliberate.

My inner muscles clenched around him, but I managed to keep the rest of my body still.

"Fuck," Ciaran breathed. "So tight."

Ty's hand cupped my face, his thumb brushing over my lower lip.

"You should feel her mouth," he said, his voice low and seductive. "It's even better."

I felt Ciaran's finger withdraw, only to be replaced by two. He began to thrust them in and out, his movements growing more confident.

The pleasure built inside me, a relentless tide threatening to overwhelm my control.

"Look at her," Ty murmured. "Not a single twitch. Our little Ava has become quite the actress."

Ciaran's fingers curled inside me, finding that spot that made stars explode behind my eyelids.

I fought to keep my face impassive, to not let my breath hitch.

"I don't believe it," Ciaran said, his voice tight with a mixture of awe and frustration. "She can't possibly…"

"Oh, but she can," Ty replied, his voice dripping with dark satisfaction. "And she will. For as long as we want her to."

Ty's fingers traced my lips again, more insistently this time. "Open up, hummingbird."

Ty parted my lips with his fingers and slipped them inside.

"Good girl," Ty purred, pressing his fingers against my tongue.

Ciaran's fingers continued their relentless assault, curling and stroking inside me.

The pleasure was building to an almost unbearable level, and I focused all my willpower on staying still, on not giving myself away.

Ty's fingers pushed deeper into my mouth, almost to the point of gagging me. "I think she's ready for more, don't you?"

Ty's fingers withdrew from my mouth, leaving me feeling empty for a moment.

I heard the rustle of fabric, the soft hiss of a zipper being lowered.

My heart raced in anticipation, but I kept my breathing steady, my face impassive, and I relaxed the back of my throat, my mouth filling with saliva in anticipation of him.

I felt the smooth, warm head of his cock press against my lips. Slowly, deliberately, he pushed forward, sliding into my mouth.

The familiar taste of him flooded my senses—salty, musky, uniquely Ty. He didn't stop until he hit the back of my throat, filling me completely.

"Fuck," he groaned, his voice strained. "So perfect."

Ciaran's fingers stilled inside me, as if he was transfixed by the sight of his brother's cock disappearing into my mouth.

For a moment, the room was silent save for Ty's ragged breathing and the obscene wet sounds as he slowly thrust in and out between my lips.

Then I felt Ciaran shift, his fingers withdrawing from my slick heat. The loss made me ache, but I remained motionless, committed to my role.

I heard him lean over the table, felt his breath hot against my inner thigh. My heart raced, anticipation coiling tight in my belly.

When his tongue finally touched me, it was like a jolt of electricity. He started tentatively, with light, teasing licks that barely grazed my sensitive flesh. Each swipe of his tongue sent shivers through me that I fought desperately to suppress. I wanted to arch into his mouth, to beg for more, but I remained still as a statue.

Ciaran grew bolder, his tongue delving deeper, circling my clit with increasing pressure.

Ty's fingers tangled in my hair, gripping tightly as he thrust deeper. "That's it, hummingbird. Take my whole cock like a good girl."

I relaxed my throat further, allowing him to push in until my nose was pressed against his pelvis. The lack of air made my head spin, adding to the overwhelming sensations coursing through my body.

Ciaran's tongue was relentless, lapping at my folds, circling my clit with maddening precision, his moans vibrating against my clit. His hands gripped my hips, fingers digging into my flesh as he pulled me closer to his hungry mouth.

"Come on, Ava," Ciaran growled against me. "Move. Moan. Scream for me."

My skin was on fire and my pulse was so fast that sweat broke out across my brow.

I refused to give in. I would win.

But the dual sensations of his mouth on me and Ty's cock sliding in and out of my throat were almost too much to bear.

It was becoming too much of a temptation to just throw

it all away—fuck the Sochai, the meeting with the High Lord, the chance to take down those evil fuckers.

Writhing on the floor with Ty and Ciaran all night, screaming so loud our neighbors had to call the cops, kept sounding better and better.

It was what my body wanted.

It was what my soul wanted, too.

I could feel my orgasm building, a tidal wave of pleasure threatening to crash over me. Every nerve ending in my body was on fire, screaming for release.

Even as I urged it on, part of me feared the oncoming wave. It would be my ultimate test of will. Could I remain still as the two men I loved brought me to orgasm?

Just as I teetered on the edge of bliss, Ciaran pulled away. The abrupt loss of contact left me aching, my inner muscles clenching around nothing.

I wanted to whimper, to beg him to continue, but I remained silent and still, clinging to my resolve with every ounce of willpower I possessed.

"No," Ciaran growled, his voice raw with desire and frustration. "You won't be able to hold back when I *fuck* you."

He was furious at the thought that I would win. He was determined to break me.

Ty chuckled darkly, still buried deep in my throat. "Then fuck her and make it good. But my money is on her."

I heard the rustle of fabric, the clink of a belt buckle being undone.

I felt Ciaran position himself between my legs, the blunt head of his cock pressing against my entrance so much thicker than two fingers.

My body tensed involuntarily, anticipation coiling tight in my core. But I forced myself to relax, to remain pliant and unresponsive.

With a low growl, Ciaran thrust into me. The sudden fullness, the delicious stretch, nearly undid me.

In my head, I screamed and arched my back so I could take him deeper. But I held on to that darkness within me, letting it consume me, using it to stay still.

"Fuck," Ciaran hissed through gritted teeth. "So tight. So wet."

He started to move, his thrusts slow and deep at first, then building in speed and intensity. Each stroke sent waves of pleasure crashing through me, threatening to shatter my control.

I focused on my breathing, on the weight of Ty's cock in my mouth, using it as an anchor to keep myself grounded.

Ciaran's pace increased, his hips snapping against mine with growing urgency, the sound of skin slapping against skin filling the room, punctuated by ragged breaths and low groans.

Ty's hand tightened in my hair as he thrust deeper, his cock hitting the back of my throat with each movement.

"That's it," he panted. "Take us both."

The sensations of being filled from both ends were over-whelming. Every nerve in my body sang with pleasure, my core tightening as my orgasm built relentlessly. I was a live wire, crackling with electricity, teetering on the edge of explosion.

Ciaran's rhythm faltered, his movements becoming desperate and erratic as he slammed into me.

"Scream, damn you," he yelled, his anger palpable, his

voice strained with need. "Moan, writhe, flinch, something, *anything.*"

I remained motionless, even as Ciaran's desperate pleas sent a thrill through me.

Ty chuckled darkly, the vibrations reverberating through his cock and into my throat. "She won't break, brother. Our little hummingbird is stronger than you think."

Ciaran growled as he pounded into me like he hated me, each thrust threatening to shatter my resolve.

His cock hit that perfect spot deep inside me, again and again, stoking the fire that burned white-hot in my core.

Ty's grip on my hair tightened as he thrust deeper into my throat, his breathing ragged and uneven. The taste of him, salty and musky, filled my senses. The slight ache in my jaw, the pressure against the back of my throat, the fullness of him—it all added to the overwhelming sensations coursing through me.

The pleasure was excruciating, building to a fever pitch that threatened to consume me entirely. Every fiber of my being screamed for release, but I held on, clinging to that dark, slick core of control within me.

Ciaran's movements became frenzied, desperate. His fingers dug into my hips with bruising force as he slammed into me, each thrust a punishing blow meant to break my resolve. The table creaked beneath us, the scattered papers rustling with each violent motion.

"No," he groaned, his voice tight with frustration and awe. "How is she not moving?"

His anger was a living thing that filled the room with

crackling energy. I could feel the heat radiating from his body, the tension in his muscles as he came with a shudder.

His breath came in ragged gasps, hot against my skin as he leaned over me, his chest pressing against mine.

Ty chuckled as he pulled his cock from me. "Accept it, brother. She's won."

Ciaran pulled out in defeat, and I heard the smash of something against the wall, a glass perhaps. He stomped across the living room and his door slammed shut with a crash.

"But the game's not over yet," Ty whispered against my ear.

A dark thrill went through my body.

His mouth crashed onto mine as he lowered himself between my legs and pushed his cock into my pussy, filling me again.

The sudden fullness made my inner walls clench around him, needy and desperate from being denied an orgasm. His hands gripped my thighs, fingers digging into my flesh as he pulled my legs up and apart.

The new angle allowed him to sink even deeper, his cock hitting spots that made sparks explode behind my closed eyelids. Pleasure radiated through my body, building the pressure.

Ty's breath was hot against my neck as he nipped and sucked at the sensitive skin there.

"Good girl, hummingbird," he murmured, his voice a low, dangerous growl. "Take your reward. Take it all."

He hooked my legs over his shoulders, bending me nearly in half as he drove into me. The new angle allowed him to hit that perfect spot deep inside me with every stroke.

My nerves sang with electricity, every touch amplified to an almost unbearable degree.

I drowned in the sensations—the stretch and fullness of him inside me, the slight burn in my thighs as he held me, the tickle of his breath against my ear as he whispered filthy encouragements.

The scent of sex and sweat filled the air, mingling with the musty smell of old books and the faint metallic tang of the antique table beneath me.

Ty's fingers dug into my flesh, sure to leave marks that I'd feel for days. The thought sent a thrill through me, knowing I'd carry the evidence of this moment on my skin.

His thrusts grew more erratic, his breathing ragged against my neck. I could feel him swelling inside me, on the edge of his own release.

"Come for *me*, hummingbird," he growled, his voice thick with desire. "This pussy is *mine*."

My inner muscles clenched around him involuntarily, my body responding to his command even as I fought to remain outwardly still.

Ty's hand slipped between us, his fingers finding my clit with unerring precision. He circled it roughly, the added stimulation pushing me over the edge.

It was my undoing. The dam broke, and pleasure flooded through me in an overwhelming rush.

My inner walls clamped down on Ty's cock as wave after wave of ecstasy crashed over me.

I couldn't stop it. A cry tore out of my mouth and my

back arched as the most intense orgasm of my life rocked through me, shattering me into pieces.

Ty groaned, burying himself deep inside me as he followed me over the edge. I felt the hot pulse of his release filling me as his hips jerked against mine.

Ty chuckled as he pressed kisses along my jaw. "Don't worry, I won't tell him. You'd already won anyway."

His words should have soothed me, but guilt twisted sharp and heavy in my chest.

I should tell Ciaran the truth—that Ty and I hadn't stopped after he left.

That, technically, I'd lost because Ty had made me come, harder than I'd ever come, and I couldn't hold my cries back.

But I could *never* admit that to Ciaran. It would destroy him.

And Liath and the missing girls were counting on me. They needed me to take down the Sochai, to get them justice. I couldn't let anything jeopardize that—not even this.

The euphoria ebbed, replaced by the cold clarity of reality. The weight of what lay ahead bore down like a suffocating fog.

I was entering the Sochai's lair with Ciaran for his initiation, playing the part of the drugged, helpless girl.

And I had no idea what horrors were waiting for us.

THE WARDEN

The surveillance van we'd parked behind the ruins of Ashcradle House was goddamn claustrophobic. I'd only been in the back for ten minutes and yet I couldn't fucking breathe.

I wanted to burst out the door, to sink my bare feet into the grass and suck in fresh air, but I was supposed to be paying attention to Ciaran as he went through all the listening equipment I was in charge of while he went in with Ava.

Ciaran looked over his shoulder at me from his place at the computer, which he'd installed in the back of the van along with a shit ton of other technical equipment.

"So does that make sense?" he asked.

He stood to make room for me to take his seat.

I did, but I would have rather been strapped down to an electric chair. I couldn't remember the last time I'd lost so much control of myself. Panic rose in me like a flood and there was nothing I could seem to do about it.

All the tricks I'd learned during my time in prison—my

breathing, my repetitive tapping, my mental disassociation —were proving useless.

I had never been enthusiastic about this plan—Ava's plan —but I had wanted to support her. But now, when I was actually faced with letting her go, with letting go of the sight of her as she descended into the passagetomb, with giving up control, I wasn't sure I could go through with it.

Ciaran frowned. "Are you alright?"

I glanced over toward the front of the van where Ava sat hunched over a laptop in the passenger seat. I could just see her small, delicate fingers moving over the keyboard. What if I never touched them to my lips ever again?

Get ahold of yourself!

It wasn't fucking working.

Gesturing wildly to the panel of instruments, I said, "I'll just fuck all this up."

I tried to push the chair back to escape, but Ciaran set his boot behind me to lock me in place.

The sound of my own teeth gritting against each other set me on edge. Evidence of my breakdown. *Fuck.*

"I should go in as you. You should man all this shit," I said, shoving back again with the same result.

In a cold, unrelenting voice stolen from me, Ciaran said, "You'll manage just fine."

He knew I wanted to be the one to go with Ava.

Did he feel the same as me? That it was torture to leave her side for what could be the last time?

"We both know I could pass as you," I said.

"What about your tats?" my brother asked.

"If I cover them up—"

"Too much of a risk," Ciaran said, his only kindness

being to withhold the words *and you know it.* "We have no idea what we'll be walking into. A security check being the least of our worries. The lift of your sleeve and there would be a bullet between your eyes regardless of how much they look like mine. And Ava…"

Ciaran's silence allowed the implications to hang like a guillotine over my head.

My shoulders slumped and I rubbed my eyes. I suddenly felt so tired, like it'd been five long years since I slept properly.

"You okay?" Ciaran asked, an unusual softness in his tone. I heard him speak to Ava that way. But never to me.

A nostalgia for our childhood days stirred a mix of pain and sweetness in my heart.

I nodded. "Grand."

Ciaran removed his boot from behind my chair, both of us knowing that I would remain in place.

My place.

There in the van.

Watching. Helpless. No control on whatever might happen in that fucking tomb.

I rested my elbows on the desk and dragged my fingers through my hair.

"It's meant for me to do this now," Ciaran said softly. "As it was meant for me *then.*"

I raised my head and found Ciaran watching Ava at the front of the van.

It was the only thing I had left to hold on to—that my brother, as much as I hated him for it, loved her as much as I did.

He would die for her.

I just didn't want him to.

Maybe it was because I felt like Ava had always been *mine* to protect. Maybe because I was older, by four minutes, but it counted, at least in my head, and I wanted to protect *him,* too.

After a tired sigh, Ciaran met my pained gaze. "It should have been *me* who went to prison."

Even in the dark of the van with its sickish green glow from the array of computer screens, I could see that this was a wound Ciaran carried with him. All his erratic emotions and wild impulses blurred the edges of a deep, deep cut.

I only understood how he felt because it was *my* turn to stay behind. My turn to have the sacrifice stolen from me.

I couldn't reach out to physically touch Ciaran. That was too far across a burned bridge. But I knew I had to speak now or risk never getting to tell him.

"I would do it again if I had to," I said in little more than a whisper.

"But—"

"You are my *brother,*" I said, my voice firm, admitting far more than my words would allow me. "Then, now, and always."

You are my brother.

And I love you.

Have always loved you.

Even after the woman we both love tears us apart, I will always love you.

The only sign that Ciaran heard me—really heard me— was a quiver in his chin.

He gazed down at his hands which he rubbed against one another.

"It was never a choice," I said as if it could end the conversation.

As if that could bury the hatchet. Could alleviate the guilt he felt for letting me take the fall.

Apparently not.

"And now, neither is mine," Ciaran said, his words heavy and full of a meaning I couldn't quite grasp.

I would. Much later, I would understand what he meant to do if it came to it.

But not in that moment.

Ciaran winced as he rubbed his face, the muscles along his arms strained, his gaze distant.

Torturing himself, I realized.

So we were identical twins it seemed. Even after all that had come between us.

My heart ached in a way it hadn't for longer than I could remember as I watched him.

Say something, a part of me whispered, a younger me from the days before a black car door opened on a gravel drive and a beautiful girl with raven hair and startling round eyes emerged.

Release him from his debt to you. He is your brother.

But the words we'd left unsaid piled high like a wall between us. I couldn't find the right words to cast over the crumbling bricks.

In the end, it was Ciaran who broke our fragile silence.

"I'll find a way to repay you." My brother's eyes held a storm of terror and determination as he lifted them to mine. "I must," he said with emotion enough to make me look away in shame.

The answer was there on the tip of my tongue. What he could do to rectify the years of imprisonment I endured in his stead.

All I had to do was say it.

Let me have Ava.

But I knew in my heart that it wasn't up to Ciaran just as it wasn't up to me.

In the end, Ava would have to decide.

The tension was back between my brother and me as both of our gazes instinctively moved toward the object of our shared desire.

Ava was oblivious to our mutually beating hearts, the unspoken war neither of us could command. She lifted her slender fingers to tuck a strand of dark fallen hair back behind her ear, completely unaware of her intoxicating beauty as she worked, lips pursed in concentration.

She was drafting an article revealing all the sordid details we'd discovered about the Sochai.

Once she was finished, it would be sent to Lisa with instructions for what to do with it should things end badly and none of us made it through the night alive.

We were in the precarious position of not knowing what our enemy knew.

We thought we had the upper hand, that our ruse would be convincing, but we were dealing with a shadow group and all three of us understood that we might have only stumbled upon the tip of the iceberg.

I looked up to study Ciaran's face as he continued to watch Ava type against her drawn-in knees, crumpled in the seat like the normal student he wished she could be, stressed about tests and papers instead of secret societies and missing girls.

He and I imagined vastly different things for the girl who changed our fates forever. But they were two sides of the same coin—wanting the best for Ava.

"*She* survives this," I said.

A demand.

A promise.

He did not flinch nor hesitate with his response. He nodded. "No matter what."

We were both silent, the meaning of our words heavy. The agony of what we were about to do was shared between us, a brotherly burden.

I wondered what—or *who*—we'd have to sacrifice in order to keep that promise.

I chewed my lip as the phone rang, the night mist dampening the leaves beneath my pacing feet.

This was my last phone call.

In and out of the glare of the van's headlights I moved, certain that my every step was watched by either Ciaran or Ty, eyes hidden behind the black of the windshield as they made their final preparations.

I cradled my arm against my stomach for warmth as I started to panic. She wouldn't pick up. I wouldn't get to hear her voice one last time before—

She picked up to my relief.

Ebony's voice came on over the phone. "…don't care how, just get it done. Hello, Ava?"

"Ma?"

She sucked in a breath. Then for a moment there was silence.

"Ava, what's wrong?"

I hadn't meant to frighten her. But knowing that this

could very well be the last time I spoke with her, the word I'd never used with her just came out.

Ma.

It was a name most Irish girls had uttered more times than they could count. They'd whined it, shouted it, giggled it, rolled their eyes with it.

It was a name I'd always longed to call Ebony, but I never did because I felt I hadn't yet earned the right to be her daughter.

It took being on the verge of oblivion to say 'fuck it.' I deserved a mother's love just as much as anyone else, no matter what had happened in my past.

But I forgot that Ebony would read my use of 'Ma' out of the blue as a sign that something terrible had happened.

"No, no, everything is fine," I said, probably a little too rushed. "I just—I was just thinking about you is all."

Ebony was a smart woman and I hadn't been that convincing. Surely she sensed something wasn't right.

But perhaps she also sensed that this wasn't the time to push.

"Oh. Alright." After a moment, she added, "I think about you, too, Ava. More than you know… and certainly more than I say."

I turned my back to the van to hide the start of tears in my eyes. I worried they would interpret them as signs of second-guessing.

I was more determined than ever to bring these fuckers down. I felt like I was stronger than I had ever been.

But I was sure that even the strongest woman in the world could be brought to her knees by her mother's simplest affections.

I knew what I was saying. I knew it would worry her. I knew it was a step forward neither of us had ever taken. I knew Ebony would not sleep that night for fear of just why I said it. But I couldn't stop myself. I had to speak.

"I love you," I said even as my throat constricted with emotion.

I'd never told her before.

But I did.

I loved her.

Underneath her reserved exterior and brusque attention was a woman who had opened her home to a young orphan.

She was the only mother I could ever remember having.

I covered my mouth so Ebony wouldn't hear my strangled sob. Tears ran hot down my cheeks.

I thought we'd have so much more time to break through each of our reasons for withholding ourselves from the other.

I always imagined a future where we'd meet up for mimosas in the city and stay up late cuddled next to one another in her bed with a pint of chocolate chip ice cream between us.

I'd pushed it off too late and now I might never have it.

I regretted all the missed opportunities which I'd let slip through my fingers like water. I hadn't expected this phone call to hurt this much and I struggled to keep breathing.

"Oh…" Ebony's voice cracked. "I… I love you, too, Ava."

If this was the last moment between us, I hoped Ebony could find comfort in it. I knew it would be difficult for her if things did not go as Ciaran, Ty, and I intended.

Either I would go missing and she would never know what happened to me…

Or the article I sent to Lisa just in case would catch like wildfire and she would know more of the nightmares I'd experienced than she could ever possibly forget.

As I hung up, Ty stepped to my side, silent, his presence heavy with unspoken tension. I held out my phone for him to take—I couldn't take it with me where I was going.

He took it and in return he held out a small sharp hairpin blade.

"If anyone *dares* to touch you," he said, the violence sharp in his voice, "give them hell."

His jaw tightened, his hesitation stretching the moment between us. When his eyes finally met mine, they carried more than his words ever could—a quiet, lingering goodbye.

"Thank you," I murmured as I pulled my hair up.

"Here, let me." Ty's voice stopped me.

I hesitated for just a heartbeat. I didn't need him to do it; I was more than capable of securing my hair on my own.

But something in his expression—a kind of quiet reverence—made me turn.

His fingers brushed the nape of my neck as he gathered my hair, his touch both gentle and deliberate.

My eyes fluttered shut at the shivers running down my spine as he twisted and pinned it into place.

The blade slid softly into the bun, and then I felt his warm lips press against the curve of my neck. For a fleeting moment, I let myself savor the contact, the way it steadied my heartbeat and softened the edges of my fear.

Ty turned me around gently, his hands warm against my shoulders, his eyes filled with love and... pride.

I love you for believing in me, I wanted to tell him. *I love you for seeing the strength in me before even I did.*

But before I could speak, he slipped a ring onto my finger—a delicate band with a ruby stone that gleamed like blood.

"Another gift? Ty…"

I still had his engagement ring burning a hole in a drawer of my dorm room.

For a moment, his fingers lingered on my hand, turning it slightly so the light caught the gem.

"I only ever wanted you to wear diamonds," he said softly, wistful. "But…"

With a flick of his thumb, the ruby shifted aside, revealing a tiny, sharp pin beneath it.

My breath caught as he continued. "It's dosed with the deadliest poison from one of the professor's vials. A mixture of wolfsbane, oleander, and Belladonna, which he called The Dark Queen."

I stared at the lethal mechanism, the weight of the ring suddenly unbearable.

Ty pressed the stone back into place, his expression unreadable. "They'll be incapacitated within ten seconds and dead in thirty. But it's for one use only. One attacker. So choose wisely."

I touched the cool band of the ring, letting its significance sink in. My voice came out low, almost detached as I vowed, "It's for the High Lord…"

The words escaped before I could stop them. "Or if I'm taken alive… *me.*"

"No." Ty's sharp tone snapped my gaze to his. His

expression darkened with horror, his hands tightening on my arms. "You can't— Ava, don't even think it."

"I know more than anyone how depraved they are," I said, my voice rising. "I'd rather die than let them—than go through that again."

"If this goes wrong—if *anything* goes wrong—" Ty said, his voice firm and unyielding, his grip tightening on my arms, "Ciaran and I will do whatever it takes to make sure you survive."

"Don't *you* dare talk like that," I snapped, cutting him off before he could say more.

The idea of him and Ciaran plotting behind my back, deciding that their lives were expendable to save mine, sent a jolt of fear and fury through me.

I couldn't bear it. The thought of losing one of them was excruciating, but losing *both*? The dread clawed at my chest, threatening to crush me whole.

But Ty wasn't finished. He leaned in closer, his voice dropping into a low, commanding tone. "I'm serious, Ava. I'll be nearby just in case. But if it all goes to shit, you *run*. Run and don't look back. *Promise me.*"

I shook my head, resolute, even as my chest ached with the weight of the moment. The thought of leaving either Ty or Ciaran behind was unbearable. The idea that this could be goodbye? I couldn't accept it.

"I'm not running," I said, my voice firm despite the lump in my throat. "We do this together or not at all."

Ty's lips twitched into a faint, sad smile that didn't reach his eyes. "Stubborn girl. It's part of why I fell in love with you—"

He hesitated, lifting his hand to brush a stray strand of

hair from my face, his fingers lingering at my jawline, his touch warm and achingly gentle. His gaze softened, but I caught the flicker of fear behind it, the vulnerability he tried so hard to hide.

"Why I keep falling in love with you," he said, his voice faltering. The words hung heavy in the air, a truth too raw for either of us to fully bear. "Ava, if this is the last time that—"

I pressed my lips to his to silence him, to stop him from saying something that might shatter me completely.

He kissed me back with a desperation that stole my breath, his hands sliding to crush me to him like he could hold me there forever.

It wasn't just a kiss—it was everything we hadn't said, everything we couldn't.

It was love and grief and fear swirling together; it was hello and I love you and goodbye, and I clung to him like he was my anchor in the storm.

My hands gripped his shirt, pulling him closer, as if holding him tighter might keep him safe.

I lost myself in the feel of his mouth, his tongue, his hands claiming me, letting it drown out the fear, the uncertainty.

For a moment, the world beyond us ceased to exist. There was only Ty, and the way he kissed me like it was both the first and the last time he ever would.

"I love you more," he whispered against my mouth.

"This isn't the end, Mhaor," I said softly, though the words were as much for me as they were for him. "Don't you dare say goodbye to me."

Ty let out a shaky breath, resting his forehead against

mine. For a heartbeat, we stayed like that, the space between us filled with unspoken promises.

"Then don't give me a reason to, Ava," he murmured, his voice low, steadying.

I heard Ciaran's footsteps approaching, the weight of each step an unwelcome reminder of what lay ahead.

Reluctantly, I pulled back from Ty, though my hands lingered on his chest for a moment longer.

"I love you," I mouthed to him.

Resolve hardened in my chest as I thought of Liath, the missing girls, and all the lives the Sochai had destroyed. I couldn't let them win.

Ciaran's shadow fell over me as he stood at my side.

"It's time," he said, his voice rough. His eyes lingered on my face, betraying more than he probably wanted me to see —worry, pain, and something far deeper that made my chest ache.

Ty pulled back, his mask of calm precision slipping into place so effortlessly that it almost hurt to watch.

I envied the ease with which he could hide his emotions. I rubbed my thumb over the ruby stone on my ring, its sharp edges grounding me as I glanced between the two of them.

"We'll all make it out of this," I murmured, mostly to myself. My resolve solidified as I looked at the two men I couldn't bear to lose.

"Together," I said, my voice firm as steel. "Or not at all."

The forest was quiet in a way that made every sound sharper, louder. Ciaran's boots crunched on the brittle twigs and fallen leaves, each step like a gunshot against the stillness.

The cold bit at my skin despite the warmth of his chest radiating against my side. My head rested in the crook of his neck, his scent—something clean, woodsy—mingling with the damp, earthy air around us.

I let myself imagine, just for a moment, that he was carrying me to my bed, not toward the dark unknown.

"It's not too late to stop this," Ciaran whispered, his voice cracking slightly. "Just say the word, Ava, and I'll turn around. We don't have to do this."

I forced myself not to respond, to resist the tug of his desperation, keeping my breathing steady, my body limp in his arms. Every fiber of me screamed to reassure him, to tell him I wasn't afraid—but I couldn't.

If I gave in now, his resolve might crumble, and we couldn't afford that. Not with what was at stake.

He adjusted his grip on me, pulling me closer like he could shield me from the world if only he held me tight enough.

His voice dropped lower, edged with raw pain. "I've spent these last few years protecting you. Every single thing I've done has been to keep you safe. And now, you're making me hand you over to them. How could you do this to me? This is *killing* me, Ava."

The guilt hit like a sucker punch, sharp and twisting.

My chest tightened, and I wanted to scream that this wasn't about him, about us—this was bigger than either of us could even begin to grasp.

But I stayed silent, my lips parted just enough to mimic the slackness of unconsciousness, and let his words hang in the air, unanswered.

If this was killing him, then what would the rest of the night do to us both?

Ciaran's steps faltered, his voice softening, shifting from desperation to something quieter, almost hopeful. "Fine. We can run. You, me... *and* Ty. We'll figure it out. We can... share you."

The absurdity of his suggestion drew a small, involuntary laugh from me despite the tension.

"Don't lie," I whispered into his ear. "You couldn't share your schoolbooks with Ty. There's no way you'd share me."

Ciaran's breath caught, a faint hitch audible in the stillness. His grip on me tightened, as though holding me closer would make his words truer.

"If it meant you were safe," he murmured, his voice a fierce, quiet promise, "I'd do *anything*."

My heart twisted painfully at the sincerity in his tone. Images of Ciaran and Ty swearing to sacrifice everything for me flashed through my mind. Their vow to protect me —at any cost.

The rage bubbled up from deep within, fierce and unrelenting.

I couldn't stop myself this time, my whisper turning into a hiss against his ear. "No. You don't get to die for me."

Ciaran froze mid-step, the forest swallowing the sound of his halted motion. For a moment, the only thing I could hear was the steady thrum of his heartbeat against my side.

His arms tightened around me protectively, his grip

almost painful. When he finally spoke, his voice was soft but unyielding, carrying a weight I couldn't deny.

"You don't get to decide how I feel, Ava. I love you, and I *would* die for you."

His words hung between us, heavy and unshakable.

I wanted to scream, to argue, but I couldn't. Not now. Not when we were this close to the tomb, this close to stepping into the lion's den.

Through the slit in my eyelids, the trees parted like curtains, revealing the passagetomb ahead.

It rose from the earth like a relic of an ancient and terrible Celtic god, its moss-covered mound seeming to breathe in the silver light of the moon. Morning glories twined up its sides, their haunting purple blooms almost ghostly in the dark.

It seemed to pulse with a silent life of its own, beckoning us closer with an air of malevolent patience, as if it were waiting to swallow us whole.

The entrance loomed before us, a stone face interrupted only by a faint outline of a door in the ancient rock.

Ciaran slowed, then stopped. His grip around me tightened, his fingers pressing into my side as though grounding himself. The tension in his body radiated into mine, and I could feel the unspoken war raging inside him.

He glanced down, his face shadowed but his eyes searching, almost pleading, his voice softer than I'd ever heard it. "This is it."

I didn't respond, didn't dare. I kept my breathing steady and my body limp, even as my pulse thundered in my ears. My resolve was iron, but the weight of the moment pressed heavily on my chest.

Ciaran's head dipped lower, his breath warm against my skin. His lips found mine in a kiss so soft, so achingly final, that it felt like it might shatter me.

Panic twisted in my chest, the overwhelming urge to respond almost breaking through my resolve. But I didn't move, didn't give in.

The kiss ended too soon, leaving my lips cold.

He pulled back, his breath hitching, shaky and raw. His forehead brushed against mine, and for a second, the world seemed to pause, suspended in the silence between us.

"I love you too, Scáth," I whispered, the words barely a breath, but I knew he heard them.

Ciaran straightened, his shoulders stiff with determination as he balanced me in his arms as he pressed his father's signet ring into a small depression carved into the stone wall.

The sound that followed was deep and ancient, the groaning of mechanisms long dormant. Stone shifted against stone, grinding and echoing in the clearing, as the entrance slowly revealed itself—a spiraling staircase descending into darkness.

A blast of icy, stale air washed over me, carrying with it the scent of damp earth and decay. The oppressive weight of the tomb pressed down on me, even from here.

Standing at the threshold, Ciaran tightened his hold on me, his voice dropping to a whisper. "Last chance, Ava…"

His voice cracked slightly, the plea in it cutting through the cold air.

But I didn't respond, my silence more resolute than any argument I could make. I couldn't afford to waver now.

Ciaran took a step forward, crossing the threshold into

the tomb. The cold air enveloped us immediately, seeping through my clothes and sinking into my bones.

The staircase spiraled down, the shadows growing darker and heavier with each step. The walls seemed to press closer, the damp stone radiating an oppressive chill.

I kept my body slack in Ciaran's arms, my breathing even.

Even as we descended farther into the jaws of a beast.

THE SHADOW

The stone steps spiraled downward into darkness, the air growing colder and damper with every step I took. Ava lay motionless in my arms, her head resting against my shoulder.

I tightened my grip on her as the faint flicker of torchlight greeted me at the bottom of the staircase, casting long, twisting shadows on the stone walls.

The passage opened into a cavernous circular room. Fire torches lined the walls, their flames guttering in the draft, illuminating the space in an eerie glow.

The dean stood at the edge of the room, cloaked in a dark-brown robe, the fabric catching the firelight like oil on water. A gold rope belt twisted around his waist and knotted in a Celtic knot before falling into ropes along his thigh, ending in two golden snake heads.

His smug expression twisted my stomach, but what unnerved me more was the four hooded guards flanking him, their faces hidden in shadows.

Three of the guards casually clutched rifles, their fingers resting a little too comfortably near the trigger.

The fourth, the smaller build of the four, stood empty-handed, his posture relaxed but watchful.

They wore the same kind of robes, except their belts were bronze instead of gold. The gold must mean the High Lord. Or maybe the inner circle.

I eyed the guards. They were all too slim to be the police commissioner.

One of them could be Cormac Senior. But... I couldn't imagine that silver-spooned elitist dirtying his hands with guns and blood.

I clocked them all, silently cursing the knives concealed on me—Arya, Dundee, and Jack. Useful in close combat, maybe, but they were nothing against the firepower in this room.

Guns were illegal in Ireland, the rare exceptions being antique shotguns used by the wealthy for archaic pheasant hunts, ancient rifles clung to by stubborn old farmers, and the occasional smuggled pistol.

Yet the weapons these guards carried gleamed with precision, unscarred by age or misuse. It spoke volumes about the Sochai's reach—powerful connections and friends utterly devoid of scruples.

"Bravo, son." The dean's voice was oily, dripping with false warmth. "Welcome."

I forced myself to smirk, masking the unease threatening to choke me. "Not much of a warm welcome. I thought the other members would be here to greet the son of one of their own."

The dean chuckled, the sound echoing off the walls.

"Patience, Mr. Donahue. Besides, you've not passed your initiation yet."

I froze, my muscles tensing instinctively. My grip on Ava tightened ever so slightly, grounding myself—and maybe her too. "I thought deciphering your damn riddle was the initiation."

"No, my dear boy." The dean's eyes gleamed with something predatory, and his gaze flicked to Ava. "The pretty little gift you're carrying *is* your initiation."

The guards stepped forward, their movement subtle but deliberate, as if ready to wrest her from my arms.

My heart thundered, and for a split second, I thought I felt Ava's breath hitch against my neck. I squeezed her closer, a silent promise, *Not a chance in hell.*

"*'What the father possesses, his heirs shall claim,'*" I quoted from the Sochai manifesto as written in my father's journals. I met the dean's gaze, letting steel edge my voice. "I am my father's heir and I claim her as *my* daughter. No one touches her but me."

The dean's smile faltered. His jaw tightened briefly, irritation flashing across his face before he smothered it with feigned amusement.

"What a clever little heir our dearly departed Gardener raised," he said, his voice a mix of mockery and spite. "We don't need to touch her for you to initiate… but *you* do."

He clapped his hands, the sound sharp and deliberate.

The unarmed guard stepped forward, grabbing a crimson cloth that covered something at the center of the room. With a dramatic flourish, he pulled it away, revealing a stone altar beneath before he stepped back.

The dean gestured toward the altar, his hand lingering

on a camera mounted on a tripod nearby. How had I not seen it before?

The lens was fixed squarely on the altar, a sickening testament to whatever twisted ritual they had planned.

A dark apprehension poisoned my blood and I clutched Ava even closer. Every cell in my body screamed at me to *run*.

"There's no need to be shy," the dean drawled, adjusting the camera with deliberate precision. "No one will see the recording outside of the Sochai, unless…" His smile sharpened, wolfish. "…you need reminding of your loyalties."

"I don't understand," I said, though dread had already begun to creep into my veins.

"It's simple," he said. "You lay her down on the altar and fuck her."

The implications short-circuited my brain and I almost broke character.

"That's rape," I blurted out.

The dean smiled. "*Exactly*."

Bile rose in the back of my throat. Was this their initiation? Did every entry into their twisted society happen through this sick act? To rape a drugged girl in front of their camera, the evidence tucked away to keep everyone in line?

If the dean really thought I was going to fuck Ava as he watched, he could add senile to the list of sadistic and perverted.

The only way I would expose even another inch of Ava's thigh would be if I gouged out the eyes of every man here first.

The dean settled onto a low cushioned bench that

curved around the room, his critical gaze slicing through me. He tilted his head just slightly, the smallest movement, but it carried the weight of a predator sizing up its prey.

I was unraveling. I knew I was risking the mission, but I couldn't—God, I fucking couldn't.

My chest felt like it might collapse under the pressure. My skin burned, my heart pounded like a drum in my ears, and my legs betrayed me, frozen in place. Gray flecks swarmed at the edges of my vision.

The dean shifted his legs, uncrossing and recrossing them with practiced ease. He brushed some invisible speck from his knee, his posture casual, but his voice was razor-sharp. "If this is a problem—"

"It's not." The words ripped out of me before I could stop them, harsh and unsteady. I dragged in a breath, forcing air into my lungs, commanding my body to comply.

I hated him.

He didn't just destroy good things—he savored its destruction.

And I knew, as clearly as I knew my own heartbeat, that he wouldn't stop.

Not until someone stopped him.

Not until we stopped him.

And if I had to pretend to rape Ava for their cameras, for their sick perverted eyes, I had to do it.

With a hint of entitlement in my voice to cover up my faux pas, I said, "I've just never had to perform in front of a camera and a room of wrinkly old men before."

The dean narrowed his eyes. "Trust me, son. If you can't stomach this, then you certainly *don't* belong with us."

With an equal measure of pain and acceptance in my

heart, I stepped toward the altar and lay Ava down on it, her lower legs dangling off the end.

I laid my sweaty palms flat on either side of Ava's thighs and its cold shocked me because all I felt was churning heat inside.

I studied Ava's body for any sign, a flinch, a whimper, a wince—that she didn't want me to go through with it.

But there was nothing.

My darling Ava was stronger than I was. Braver than I was. Able to endure more than I ever could.

If I loved her, I had to honor her sacrifice. Her choice.

Okay then. I would do it. I would defile Ava before these monsters, but it would kill me. It would fucking end my soul.

As I slid my hand onto Ava's thigh, the beep of the camera beginning its recording drilled a hole through my ear straight into my brain.

I almost faltered.

This act with Ava was a precious thing.

Not to be soiled in their memories, recorded as blackmail.

I pulled my hand away and dragged it through my hair to hide how terribly it was shaking.

I could do this. I could pretend to do this.

I reached for her skirt and pushed it up her thighs, just enough but not enough so they could see her panties and the spot meant just for me.

I stepped up close and unzipped my pants. Fuck, how was I supposed to get hard with them watching.

"Strip her," the dean said.

I spun, my open fly forgotten. "What?"

The dean tilted his head, an evil smirk on his face. "Take her clothes off. All of them. We need to *see* what you're doing to her."

A dozen different scenarios of attacking the High Lord ran through my mind, but each ended with my body riddled with bullet holes and Ava left helpless against five armed psychopaths.

For a moment, I hated, truly hated my brother for putting the woman he claimed to love in this position.

And for a moment, I hated Ava too, for not running when we could have.

"Unless," the dean added, "you aren't serious about becoming one of us."

My hands fisted into painful knots by my sides, and I had to force my fingers apart. I forced a shrug even as hatred swirled in my blood.

"If that's what it'll take," I said.

It felt like there was a hand around my neck. My own.

The dean smiled, then replied, "It is…"

I turned back to Ava, unmoving, but she would have heard everything. I scanned her soft features for any hint for me to stop, for any trace of fear or resistance.

She didn't move, didn't flinch. Her breathing remained steady, a silent consent to keep going.

I sent her a wordless apology as I began to lift the hem of Ava's top.

From the corner of my eye, I noticed the dean's crossed legs tightening. The sick fuck. I was going to enjoy killing him the most.

I pulled the top over Ava's head and gently laid her back

down. Her head rolled to the side like she was asleep, so beautiful, so innocent.

The dean made a sound at the reveal of Ava's naked chest. "Beautiful."

I had to close my eyes for several long seconds as blood rushed in my ears. I saw nothing but red, even behind my eyelids.

When this was over, I was going to carve his eyeballs out of his sockets and make him eat them. I was going to rip his testicles from his wrinkly old ball sack and shove them where his eyeballs had been.

I forced myself to keep going, bolstered by my violent promises when this was all over. If... we got through this.

I slid off her shoes and dropped them to the ground. They echoed through the cavernous space.

I wanted to kiss her toes, to whisper to her that I was sorry. But I refrained.

I unzipped her skirt and pulled that off her hips and down her legs, bowing my head to her as if in prayer.

I tried to focus on the loveliness of Ava's smooth skin, the flames casting a flickering warm glow over her curves. I tried to pretend that it was just her and me. And that we were playing some sort of dark game.

But I could feel their eyes burning into me.

My fingers curled into the edges of her panties, the only clothing left, and I paused.

Fuck. Could I really do it? Could I expose her to them?

"Don't stop now," the dean said with a husky chuckle. "It's just getting good."

My fingers trembled as they curled around the delicate

lace of Ava's panties. The soft fabric felt like sandpaper against my skin, every nerve ending raw and exposed.

I closed my eyes, drawing a deep breath that tasted of damp stone and smoke from the flickering torches.

With agonizing slowness, I began to slide the underwear down Ava's legs. The lace caught on the curve of her ass, and I had to force myself not to be gentle, not to caress her skin as I normally would.

Instead, I tugged roughly, feeling the fabric give way.

As I pulled the panties past her knees, I risked a glance at Ava's face.

Her eyes remained closed, her expression peaceful, betraying nothing of the violation happening to her unconscious form. A strand of her dark hair had fallen across her cheek, and it took every ounce of willpower not to brush it away.

Once I tugged them off her toes, I pocketed her panties, because I would fucking die rather than any of these assholes getting their dirty little hands on them.

My stomach churned as I heard a soft intake of breath from one of the guards.

Ava lay completely exposed now, vulnerable and beautiful on the cold stone altar. I pulled her hips to the edge and positioned myself between her legs, shielding as much of her body from view as I could with my own.

It made me sick that I was already hard. Throbbing almost painfully. Leaking against the front of my black pants. I wanted to have to struggle to be aroused by this fucked-up charade.

But my body betrayed me. My cock knew only lust and

desire when it came to Ava. It only saw her naked and laid out for me.

I wet two fingers with my mouth before I reached down between Ava's legs. I didn't care if meant arousing the High Lord's suspicions. I wouldn't force my way in.

"A gentleman," the dean snickered from his place on the bench like it was an insult.

"A cunt isn't worth fucking if it isn't wet," I shot back.

But her pussy lips were already slick as I ran my fingers along her folds.

A jolt of surprise shot through me, quickly followed by a small wave of relief. At least there was a part of my dark little rabbit that would enjoy being fucked.

As I readied her with two fingers, stretching her, I silently promised to make it good for her.

Or at least, as easy as possible to bear.

"Well?" the dean's impatient voice cut through the silence. "We're waiting, Mr. Donahue."

I gritted my teeth, forcing myself to maintain the facade. "Patience, Dean," I spat his words back at him, infusing my voice with a bravado I didn't feel.

My hands shook as I undid my belt, letting my pants fall open, hyper-aware of the eyes boring into my back.

I took a deep breath, steeling myself for what I had to do. With one hand, I guided myself to Ava's entrance, the head of my cock brushing against her folds. I closed my eyes, trying to block out the reality of our audience, focusing only on the softness of Ava's skin beneath my fingers.

Slowly, I pushed into her, feeling her body yield to me.

A low groan escaped my lips as I buried myself deep

within her, the sensation so overwhelming that for a second I forgot about the guns and the video camera and the High Lord's soft panting.

There, inside of her, was home.

I began to move, establishing a steady rhythm. The sound of skin on skin echoed in the cavernous room, punctuated by my ragged breathing.

I kept my eyes fixed on Ava's face, searching for any sign of discomfort or awareness, but she remained still and peaceful.

The dean said something, no doubt crude and ugly, but I ignored it, pushing his voice away into the distance.

It was just Ava and me.

Back in her bedroom at the loft. Candlelight soft on her naked skin. This was just a kinky game she wanted to play.

It took everything I had not to moan a praising, 'Good girl,' when Ava's pussy tightened around my throbbing cock without warning.

But then fear coursed through the pleasure humming in my veins. Oh shit.

She was going to come.

God help us both if she couldn't stay quiet.

AVA

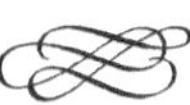

Lying on the altar, I forced my limbs to remain slack as Ciaran's clammy, shaking hands began to undress me.

Each layer he removed left more of my bare skin pressed against the icy, unyielding stone, but instead of cooling me, a strange heat churned in my core, burning brighter with every second.

I could feel their eyes on me, a prickling weight crawling over my exposed skin.

The sense of vulnerability was suffocating, yet beneath it simmered a darker thrill—electric, dangerous, and impossible to ignore.

My body betrayed me, a skittering ripple of sensation racing over my flesh as if it could sense the peril in the air.

I focused on my breathing, keeping it slow and even, inhaling the damp, earthy scent, tinged with smoke.

But the silence wasn't still. It pressed in on me like ghostly hands all over my body, broken only by the faint crackle of the fire torches on the walls, the red glow flickering across my lids.

Boots scuffed against the stone floor, heavy and deliberate. Each step sent a faint vibration through the altar, a reminder of how exposed I was, how close they were, predators circling their prey, and my nipples hardened as an unwanted ache grew inside me.

Despite loathing every part of their sick initiation ritual —hating being trapped in this nightmare, hating the way they were forcing Scáth to corrupt something sacred between us into something vile—a dark thrill surged through me, unbidden and unwelcome.

I grew wet and achy at the anticipation of Ciaran fucking me while I lay "asleep" while strangers watched.

He tugged off my skirt and I was left almost naked. But Ciaran's fingers paused on the hem of my panties.

"Don't stop now," the dean said, his dark laugh cutting through the darkness behind my lids. "It's just getting good."

I willed Ciaran to be strong. We could get through this together.

If I could look into his eyes for just a moment, I could reassure him that I was alright. That *we* would be alright.

But it was impossible. If I moved even an inch, opened my eyes for just a moment, we'd be caught. He would have to trust I was strong enough.

Ciaran tugged down my panties and the feeling of exposure was like nothing I'd ever felt.

My hair dragged behind me when Ciaran slid me toward the edge of the altar, and I felt him stand between my thighs as if he was trying to shield me.

The heat from his thighs burned me even through his pants and I felt his cock brush against me.

Fuck. He was hard. He was ready. A rush of need went through me.

"A gentleman," the dean laughed cruelly.

"A cunt isn't worth fucking if it isn't wet," Ciaran snapped back as he stroked two fingers against my pussy lips, his fingers sliding through my wetness, my dark shame.

I wanted him. Even in this forced and twisted situation, I wanted him.

He let out a soft gasp. A surprise at my welcome.

Shame threatened to overcome me but I shoved it down. No. I would never *ever* apologize for how he made my body feel. Or how my body reacted.

The body was the most primal part of me. It knew no morals, no judgment, no law. It only knew pleasure and pain, need and want, my sexual instincts the most natural thing in the world.

No matter how twisted this initiation was, nothing Scáth did to me could ever feel wrong.

But I could feel him fighting with himself as he pushed two fingers in to stretch me, to ready me for the size of his cock.

I could feel his torment in his jagged breath, how his hand shook as he positioned his cock at my entrance and hesitated.

My body flushed with need, ached to grab him and pull him deep inside me.

But I remained still, waiting, wanting, aching.

Finally, he pushed inside me. For a moment of bliss, the

surrounding tomb faded away and I was taken back to all the times he'd fucked me, filling me so deeply.

There was no High Lord. There was no Sochai. There was no altar, no watching guards or video recording.

I got so lost in the pleasure of him that I almost let a filthy groan escape my lips. But I caught myself.

Ciaran began to take long, steady thrusts as I remained limp beneath him.

My breasts shook with every thrust, my nipples bloomed to hardened peaks, and my bare feet swung from the edge of the table.

I knew Ty was listening to the wet sounds of me getting fucked through the listening device hidden in the necklace, Ciaran's groans echoing in the tomb.

I imagined him watching just like he did at the doorway, his hand on his cock. Imagined him leaning over me to suck my nipples the way he did as his brother fucked me on the table.

The image was so powerful, I felt the ghost of his mouth on my breasts, felt his cock filling my mouth, and I nearly gave myself up with an uncontrollable rock of my hips as I begged for more.

I hadn't considered how risky it would be to lose myself so completely in this little show.

But as my orgasm came barreling toward me, fear lashed me.

Oh God.

I hadn't been able to keep myself silent when I came during my 'test.' I hadn't been able to stop the groan from slipping from my lips or the way my hips had twitched up, to milk every last wave of pleasure from Ty's cock.

What if I couldn't stay still now?

We'd be caught. Tortured. Killed.

I tried to stop it, tried to push down the surge of pleasure, tried to pull myself back from the edge.

But it was no use.

My pussy clenched around Ciaran's cock as he thrust into me. There was no way he didn't sense my impending climax, his rhythm faltering for just a moment.

Then he redoubled his efforts, thrusting harder and faster, his fingers digging into my hips. I knew what he was doing—trying to mask my inevitable reaction with his own.

The pressure built inside me, a tidal wave I couldn't hold back. Just as I was about to shatter, Ciaran let out a guttural groan, loud enough to echo off the stone walls.

His hips jerked erratically against me as he came, and in that moment of chaos, my orgasm crashed over me.

I bit my tongue so hard I tasted blood, desperately fighting to keep my body still as waves of pleasure threatened to overwhelm me.

My inner muscles clenched around Ciaran's cock, milking him, and I prayed the pulsing would be mistaken for his own climax. Prayed that my involuntary twitches would get lost in the rough way Ciaran spasmed against me.

Then Ciaran collapsed on top of me, his arms shaking on either side of me as he kept from crushing me.

For a moment, the only sound I could hear was his ragged breathing and my heart pounding so loudly I was sure everyone could hear it. It filled the silence like a war drum, beating out the fear I tried desperately to suppress.

Sweat slicked my skin, cooling as it mingled with the cold air of the tomb.

Every instinct screamed to move, to reassure him, to break the sick tension in the air, but I fought to keep my face slack, my limbs loose, my body convincingly limp. The effort was excruciating.

Then the beep of the video recording being shut off pierced the silence like a blade. It was a splash of cold water dragging me back to reality.

I'd almost forgotten where I was—forgotten that this wasn't just Ciaran and me. For one desperate, deluded moment, I'd let myself believe the room was empty but for us, and that our pleasure wasn't being watched, dissected, and judged.

Ciaran made this sound in my ear—a low, guttural noise, raw and unfiltered. It wasn't just pain; it was agony, shame, and the unbearable weight of what they were forcing him to do.

My heart ached in ways I couldn't describe.

He shook against me, his breath hot and uneven on my shoulder, and it took everything in me not to wrap my arms around him, not to shatter the illusion. I wanted to whisper that I was fine, that there was nothing wrong with him, nothing broken, that I wasn't hurt.

But I couldn't.

Instead, I focused on my breathing, forcing it to stay slow, steady. My heart hammered anyway.

Ciaran withdrew from me, his cum trickling down my thighs making me feel exposed, vulnerable, and utterly filthy. But beneath it all, a flicker of triumph burned. I'd done it. I'd come without moving, without screaming.

Anticipation flooded me, a sickening wave of hope and

dread all tangled together. Did we do it? Had we fooled them? Or was the next second going to be my last?

The dean's slow clap echoed through the chamber, deliberate and mocking, and my chest constricted. He was pleased, the sadistic bastard.

His voice followed, cruel and cutting. "Well done, son. Your father would be so proud."

A chill ran through me. The words were poison, laced with malice, and I wanted to scream at the injustice of them.

Ciaran was everything his father wasn't. Every fiber of my being knew this.

Beneath his shadowed layers lay a core of goodness, a stark contrast to his father's heart, rotten to its very core.

Ciaran was strong, driven by a relentless fight for what was right, even when his path was paved with blood. His father had been weak, hiding behind power and control, wielding cruelty as a means to an end to satisfy his twisted selfish desires.

But I feared, in the horrible silence that followed, that Ciaran didn't know it. Not truly.

What if he saw himself as his father's reflection? A monster wearing his face? What if he believed the dean's vile words? The thought gutted me, leaving a void of helplessness in its wake. What would Ciaran allow to happen to himself if he believed that? What would he become?

My chest tightened, panic rising. I couldn't lose him—not to them, not to himself, not to this. I wouldn't.

My body may have been still, a facade of unconsciousness, but my heart screamed the truth. I couldn't let them corrupt him.

"Hope you enjoyed the show," came Ciaran's bitter response.

I felt a cloth swipe over my inner thighs, the tender motion at odds with the bitterness in his tone.

My heart clenched, a war of emotions waging inside me. What was he using as a rag? His shirt? His pride?

"Now, if you'll please come with me," the dean said smoothly, his voice a sinister calm that made my blood run cold. "It's time to get fitted for your robe, Mr. Donahue."

The grating screech of stone against stone filled the chamber, signaling the opening of another door. The sound was as much a warning as it was an invitation, and my heart leaped into my throat.

Two equally overwhelming thoughts flashed through my mind.

We did it. We fooled them.

And, God, Scáth, please don't leave me here alone.

Ciaran's hesitation was a physical thing, his hand lingering on my thigh for a beat too long.

I fought the primal urge to reach out, to clutch his wrist, to beg him not to go. But I couldn't. Not if we were going to survive this nightmare.

"Now, Mr. Donahue," the dean's voice cut through the moment, sharp and commanding. There was no room for defiance.

Ciaran's hand slipped off my thigh, and I heard his footsteps moving away, each step feeling like a blow. He was leaving me behind.

My chest tightened, panic clawing at the edges of my resolve.

"Give that to me," I heard him mutter to someone.

And then, suddenly, his footsteps returned and before I could process it, he draped a cloth over my exposed body, the weight of it feeling both protective and crushing.

"*Nobody* touches her," his voice echoed through the chamber, a fierce command. "Or I'll tear their fucking arm off and beat them to death with it."

For a moment, everything was still; even the tomb seemed to hold its breath.

I could almost feel the fingers sliding onto the triggers.

Then the dean laughed, breaking the tension like snapping bone. "Mr. Donahue, please. We're not savages. No one's going to touch your property."

His property.

Rage flared hot and fast in my chest, so potent it almost forced me to break character.

God, I couldn't wait to burn their fucking sick, misogynistic society to the ground.

The heavy door groaned as it creaked shut behind them, the sound echoing like a death knell. And then, silence.

But I wasn't alone.

The air in the chamber shifted, tense and charged, and I caught the faintest shuffle of movement. Someone was still here. Someone was getting closer.

I stopped breathing, straining every nerve to listen.

My skin prickled with the undeniable sensation of being watched, of eyes raking over me, assessing, judging. My pulse pounded, deafening in my ears, and I prayed they couldn't see it hammering at the base of my throat.

The sheet was ripped away from me so violently it was as if the room itself exhaled in shock. My body jolted instinctively, but I swallowed the scream that clawed its way up my throat.

A presence loomed above me, heavy and oppressive. Fear slammed into me, twisting my insides into knots.

No. Oh God, no.

Ciaran's words meant nothing now. His decree that no one touch me was worthless against whatever monster the dean had left behind.

I could feel the heat of his breath against my skin, hear the low rasp of his breathing as he leaned closer.

My mind spiraled, wild with terror, as I imagined what was about to happen.

What if there's more than one? What if they all—

Time warped, stretching into a cruel mockery of itself. Seconds felt like hours as my mind fought to reconcile my rising panic with the cold logic of survival.

Could I keep pretending I was unconscious if they decided to violate me? Could I endure this charade at the cost of my soul?

No. Fury surged like wildfire in my veins, burning away the paralysis of fear.

I wouldn't let them take another piece of me. I wouldn't lie there, motionless, while they shred my body to pieces.

I'd rather die fighting than let the Sochai steal any more of my soul from me.

But the figure above me didn't move. There was no grab, no violence. Just… stillness. It unnerved me even more.

What the fuck are you waiting for?

His sharp inhale cut through the suffocating silence, and then—*whoosh*—a rush of air swept over my face.

My lashes flickered.

No.

No, no, no.

The reflex was instantaneous and damning. I'd managed to stay silent, to stay still, through all of it. But a reflex I couldn't control had betrayed me. This had been their final test and I failed.

My only choice now was to fight.

Before I could reach for the blade in my hair, a feminine sigh sent goosebumps down my spine.

"You can stop pretending, Ava, darling."

AVA

My eyes opened in horror, locking on the shadowy face of the smaller guard standing over me.

A pale delicate hand emerged from the dark folds of the robe and threw back the hood, revealing *her* all-too-familiar face and pale eyes the color of *Hydrangea macrophylla*.

"Ebony?" My voice cracked, the word barely audible. "What are you doing here?"

The stone beneath me, which had moments before been warm and slick with my sweat, felt like ice again, stealing the heat from my body.

My muscles protested as I pushed myself up on trembling arms, but my mind raced faster than my body could keep up.

The heavy stone door that Ciaran must have disappeared behind had been shut tight, and the only sound now was my own rapid breathing.

The other guards and their guns were gone.

We were alone.

Was she here to help? My chest tightened. Was she investigating them too? Trying to infiltrate the Sochai to take them down from the inside?

"Why did you have to be such a stubborn girl, Ava?" Her voice cut through the silence like the edge of a blade, sharp and filled with something dark I couldn't name.

I flinched. "What—what are you talking about?"

"I did *everything* I could to keep you away from this," Ebony said, her pale eyes blazing. "From remembering. From meddling. From serving your goddamn head to them on a goddamn platter, Ava!"

Her words hit me like a slap, each one heavier than the last.

My heart pounded as I stared at her, the woman who had been the only mother I'd ever known. The woman who had taken me in, fed me, clothed me, loved me in her own way.

"No," I whispered, shaking my head, trying to make sense of her words. "No, you can't be part of the Sochai."

I choked on the realization, my mind spinning in circles, desperate to find a reason—any reason—that explained why she was here.

They got to her. Of course, they did. The Sochai had found her and broken her. Tortured her. Manipulated her. She'd been brainwashed, coerced into this.

She tried to help me as much as she could, in her own way, but she was being controlled by them somehow…

As I stared into her face, a flicker of something from my darkest memories took hold. It clawed at the edges of my mind, dragging me back to that room, that sterile, white hell of my forced abortion.

That voice that had seemed so familiar. *His voice.*

"You dare second-guess my command? You are my fucking heir. You will do as I say. Now... take care of it."

My breathing quickened as it clicked into place. The voice I had heard during my abortion—the one giving calm, authoritative commands—the voice that had haunted my dreams wasn't just familiar. It was *him.*

Ebony's father.

My mind reeled. Her father had been the monster behind all of this, the architect of so much pain. My stomach churned with the realization. But another thought came, sharp and desperate.

Ebony had been forced into this by him. Of course she had.

"Get dressed." Ebony's voice was clipped as she tossed my top and skirt at me.

The fabric hit my chest and slid to the floor, my shaking hands barely managing to catch them in time.

I fumbled to tug the pieces back on, my movements clumsy and frantic. The chill of the tomb still seeped into my bones, and my feet were bare, my shoes lost somewhere on the uneven floor.

"Now get out of here before they return," Ebony hissed, her eyes darting to the door where the guards had disappeared. Her urgency felt raw, genuine, and for a moment, hope sparked in me.

Whatever they had on her, she'd been trying to protect me all along. She was still trying to protect me.

"No," I whispered, my voice hoarse but urgent, my resolve stronger than the terror coursing through me. "They'll kill him if we don't get him out too."

Ebony's scowl deepened, her face twisting into a mask of irritation. "This is your last chance, Ava. Otherwise, I won't be able to help you anymore."

"No." My voice wavered, but my words were firm. "I'm not leaving without Ciaran."

"Stubborn girl," she muttered, her voice a blade of frustration.

"Ebony," I croaked, my voice breaking. "What did they do to you? Did they threaten you? Please—"

Her laugh stopped me. Cold and humorless, it echoed in the chamber. "Threaten me?"

She stepped closer, her delicate features twisting with something dark, something foreign. "Do you really think I'm some poor victim, Ava?"

I froze as her words sank in.

"I wasn't dragged into this. I wasn't forced." She leaned in, her breath cold against my skin. "This is my birthright."

Her words struck me like a physical blow, stealing the air from my lungs. Birthright. The word reverberated in my mind, loud and damning.

My stomach dropped as realization crashed over me like a tidal wave. "You..."

She tilted her head, her lips curling into a slow, cruel smile. "*I* am the High Lord."

"No." The word tore from my throat as I scrambled back, the edges of the altar digging into my back. "No, it can't—it can't be you."

But it was. The High Lord wasn't some faceless monster. It wasn't an untouchable evil lurking in the shadows.

It was Ebony.

It all clicked into place, each revelation like a slap to

my face, the numbness in my limbs burning away, replaced with a quickening of my pulse, a thunder in my ears.

Ebony was on the Board of the Darkmoor Alumni.

I remembered her standing in the photo she kept on her desk, the line of steely-faced men, her smile a beacon of charm in a sea of indifference. The only one with bare ankles beneath her sharp black pencil skirt.

She was the only woman on that board.

And for that, we'd ignored her. I'd ignored her.

She was the one who had insisted—*insisted*—I see Dr. Vale with his gaslighting and memory suppressors.

Her phone hadn't been bugged when I called her from Mr. Buckley's farmhouse. *She* had the call traced. *She'd sent those men after me.*

She was the only one, apart from Lisa and the twins, who had known where my new dorm room was the day I moved in.

And she was the one who had told the dean that Earl Grey was my favorite tea. That I'd supposedly gone sailing around Greece and Croatia. She was the one who had fed them details about me.

She had betrayed me.

The betrayal hit me harder than I thought possible, like a blade cutting through flesh and bone.

My heart lodged in my throat as my mind flashed back to just hours ago, to the moment I'd called her *Ma* for the first time, to the way I'd whispered, *I love you.*

And my heart broke for the loss of *everything* she had been to me—my protector, my guardian, my *mother* in every way that mattered.

My knees buckled, and I clutched the edge of the altar to steady myself, even as my mind screamed for escape.

"Did you ever love me?" The words slipped out before I could stop them, fragile and trembling in the thick silence.

Her gaze softened, her voice dropping so low it barely carried across the cold chamber.

"I did love you, Ava," she murmured, almost wistful. "I *mourned* you when I thought they'd killed you."

My breath hitched as the pieces began to slot together.

She hadn't been upset about some *stupid surgery* when I'd returned from Paris. She'd been upset because she thought the man sent for me had killed me.

Ebony hesitated, her shoulders shifting as if the weight of memory pressed down on her.

"You were just a girl when you came across my table. When my father forced me to..." Her voice cracked, the pain in it so raw it sliced through the haze of my fury.

The memory hit me like a physical blow, the images bright and vivid behind my eyes.

The surgical light glaring above me.

Her father's deep voice.

And her pale-blue eyes, staring down at me over the surgical mask. *Her eyes.*

It was Ebony. She was the doctor. She was the one who'd performed my abortion.

My body shuddered with revulsion, and I fought to hold myself together.

"And when Adam died mere weeks later," she continued, her voice turning steadier, colder, "I begged my father to let me have you, to keep you from falling into another one of their dirty hands."

I wanted to scream, to rage at her, to demand *why* she would do any of this. Instead, I managed, "Then why become High Lord?"

Her face hardened, her chin lifting as though she were justifying herself to a cruel and unforgiving judge.

"You have no idea the work I'm doing," she said, her voice sharp with conviction. "I'm *cleaning up the Sochai.*"

Her posture straightened, a twisted kind of pride swelling in her tone, even as her quivering chin betrayed the weight of her delusion.

"My father let it rot, let it become a cesspool—a respectable guise for pedophiles and perverts. But I'm going to bring it into this century. The Sochai, with all its power and riches, will become a force for good instead of evil."

I stared into her pale-blue eyes, eyes I had once trusted, once turned to for love and protection.

Now all I could see was the glint of madness in them, so sharp and bright it was undeniable. She believed what she was saying. She truly believed she was *saving* the Sochai.

I couldn't stop the tremor that ran through me. This woman—my mother in all but blood—wasn't just part of the monster. She *was* the monster.

And worse, she thought she was the hero.

"Liath, Sarah, Keela..." My voice cracked, the names catching in my throat as I stared at her pale, detached face. "Why are you killing the 'daughters' off? One by one?"

I swallowed hard, my chest tight with the unspoken question lingering in the air. *And me?*

Would she kill me too? Her only daughter?

"The lesser of two evils," she said, her tone unnervingly even. Her words landed like a slap, their cold detachment sucking the air from my lungs. "The Society can do much good in this world—I wouldn't expect you to understand even a fraction of its power, Ava—but it would all be ruined if our… unsavory past were to come to light."

"'Unsavory'?" I repeated, my voice sharp and brittle as glass.

It wasn't a word for their atrocities, for the lives they destroyed, for the utter destruction of innocence.

Ebony offered no further response. Her expression was locked into a perfect mask of indifference. The color drained from her cheeks, leaving behind a pale, marble facade.

Gone was the flicker of emotion I'd seen earlier—the pain, the pride, the madness. Her eyes, once alive with conviction, were now dull and lifeless.

There was no trace of humanity left. She looked like a statue carved from the cold stone walls around us.

And I understood why. If she let herself *feel*, it would all come crashing down. If she allowed even a moment of reflection, she would see the warped wreckage of her beliefs, the mountain of sins she'd committed in the name of good.

Her soul was a house of cards. One gust of truth, and it would collapse. She couldn't afford to pause. Couldn't afford to look back.

As I stared at the woman before me, I knew what I had to do.

My fingers brushed against the ruby ring, the poisoned stone a deadly promise, ready to end this nightmare with a flick of my wrist.

But I couldn't.

My chest tightened, my resolve fracturing beneath the weight of heartbreak.

She wasn't the High Lord in this moment. She was still *Ebony.* Still the woman who had taken me in, who had saved me from the clutches of yet another Sochai 'father.'

The woman I had once believed loved me like a daughter.

Instead, I reached up and slipped the blade from my hair, its sharp edge gleaming in the torchlight.

My grip tightened as I pointed it toward her. "You're not going to get away with this."

Ebony's expression didn't flicker, her voice resonating with the cold authority of the High Lord. "I thought you'd understand, Ava."

Her hand disappeared into the folds of her robe. The metallic glint of a gun caught the corner of my vision, and instinct took over.

I moved faster than I thought possible, my training with Ty snapping into place.

Using a disarming technique he'd drilled into me a hundred times, I grabbed her wrist, twisted it sharply, and sent the gun clattering to the floor.

I spun her, yanked her against me, and pressed my blade against her neck before she could react, the sharp edge biting into her pale skin. "Where's Ciaran?"

Ebony didn't flinch, even with the blade at her throat. Her lips curled into a faint, chilling smile. "Yes, it's about time they joined us."

They?

She snapped her fingers, the sharp, jarring sound echoing through the chamber.

The screech of stone against stone followed, reverberating through the air like a scream, the noise grating against my senses like nails on a chalkboard.

Ciaran stumbled forward through the doorway, his expression wild and desperate as one of two hooded guards jabbed a gun between his shoulder blades.

His eyes locked on mine for a fleeting, tortured moment before we both turned at the sound of footsteps coming from the stairs at the entrance.

A shadow emerged, pushing through the gloom, his hands raised in surrender.

My breath hitched when the light caught his face, his familiar expression taut with restrained fury.

Ty.

Ty's face was stone, a mask of defiance even as a gun pressed into his back, forcing him forward as two more guards piled in after him.

My chest clenched at the sight of him—*Ty,* who was supposed to be our backup, our failsafe if anything went wrong.

And it had gone so, so wrong.

A wave of terror surged up my spine, freezing my limbs and threatening to drown me. The obvious truth became unavoidable with every passing second.

There was no cavalry storming in to save the day. We were alone—Ciaran, Ty, and me. Caught in the Sochai's claws.

We had been outplayed.

The dean wasn't the High Lord. Of course, he wasn't. If Ciaran had truly been groomed by his father, he would have known that. We had tipped them off when Ciaran had made his request to join the Sochai to the dean.

This had been a trap from the start, and we had walked straight into it, blind.

"You bitch," Ciaran snarled, his voice sharp with rage and betrayal, his glare locked on Ebony. "She's your daughter."

A guard stepped forward and slammed the butt of his rifle into Ciaran's cheek.

The crack of bone echoed through the chamber like a gunshot, and my scream tore from my throat, raw and desperate.

"Don't!" I cried, my voice breaking as Ciaran staggered but didn't fall.

Blood streamed down his face, painting his skin with crimson streaks, but he still stared at Ebony, defiant and furious.

His chest heaved, and his eyes burned with a hatred that frightened me. Ciaran was going to get himself killed.

They were both going to get killed. And me? They'd make sure I wished I was dead before the end.

The sight of Ciaran's blood snapped me out of my spiraling thoughts. I needed to act.

There was no fighting our way out of this, not with these guards, these guns. My only weapon was the part of Ebony I had once believed in—the part that had raised me, even if it was a lie.

"Please, Ebony… *Ma*." The word tasted bitter, almost choking me as it left my mouth. "I know you don't want to do this."

Her gaze flickered, the faintest shadow of doubt crossing her face.

I latched on to it like a lifeline, even though my own words felt hollow.

The truth was, I didn't know this woman. The mother I'd called just hours ago, the one I had told I loved for the first time, wasn't here. She was gone—if she had ever existed at all.

"Just let us go," I said breathlessly, my words spilling out faster than I could think them. My lungs burned as I forced myself to hold her gaze, to find the humanity I prayed was still there. "We'll leave. We'll go far away. The three of us. We'll never set foot in Ireland again."

I paused, gasping for air, my chest tight with fear. If I stopped, if I gave her a moment to consider, she might give the order.

Ty and Ciaran might be executed right here, right now. Or worse, one of them might do something reckless, something that would get them killed.

"The Sochai will be safe," I promised, my voice cracking. "Your secrets will stay buried. You can keep your plans, build your new society. Just let us go."

It felt like dying. The words left my mouth, but they left a part of my soul behind with them.

This was a retreat, a surrender of everything I had fought for. Justice for Liath, for those missing girls, for myself.

I was choosing Ciaran and Ty over those girls. Over justice. I was letting the world burn—for them.

And while it felt like dying, I knew there was no other choice I would ever make.

Quietly, I said, "I know you never wanted to kill me."

Ebony's gaze softened, just barely, and for a moment she looked more human than the monster I had come to fear. Her voice, when it came, was quiet, carrying a weight of regret that almost broke me. "Let's not talk about what I wanted."

We stared at each other across the dim tomb, the air between us thick with unspoken words and shattered dreams.

The silence was oppressive, broken only by the faint drip of water from the stone walls in one damp corner. Each drop echoed, an ominous reminder that time was running out.

I hated her. I hated what she'd become, what she'd done.

But as I looked into those pale eyes, I couldn't deny the trace of sympathy clawing at my heart. She was twisted, corrupted by her own pain, but for a time, she had been something else to me. I had loved her.

I couldn't reconcile that love with the revulsion churning in my gut, and it tore me apart.

We had both imagined a bright future with the other, one where she was my mother and I was her daughter. That dream, fragile as it had been, had shattered tonight.

It was gone, along with the last shred of hope I'd held for us.

And yet the ghost of it lingered, tugging at the edges of my resolve.

The glimmer of emotion in Ebony's eyes was gone as quickly as it had appeared. She dragged her hands roughly over her face, wiping away the tears before they could fall. When she looked at me again, the cold, unyielding darkness had returned, a shield of ice encasing her heart.

"I'll make you a deal," she said, her voice sharp and

detached, as if the moment of vulnerability had never existed. "I'll let you leave…"

My heart stuttered with hope.

"You… and *one* of them."

The ground beneath me felt like it was falling away. I barely registered the words, their weight too much to bear.

One of them.

It was a choice no human being could make. And yet she demanded it of me, her voice calm and indifferent, as if she were asking me to pick out a loaf of bread.

"What?" I whispered, the word barely audible, as though saying it louder would make it more real.

Ebony smiled, soft and venomous, like a snake coiling for a strike. She tilted her head, her pale eyes cold and calculating. "You heard me, darling."

I turned my gaze to Ciaran, his cheek bloodied and his jaw tight with rage, then to Ty, whose calm facade cracked under the weight of realization.

Both of them looked at me, their expressions a heart-breaking mixture of defiance and desperation.

I couldn't choose.

How could I choose?

For one to live, to carry my heart with them, while the other was left behind, condemned to the Sochai's twisted clutches. To Ebony's clutches. The thought tore through me, ripping me apart at the seams.

My chin quivered, and I shook my head, more to myself than anyone else.

"I can't," I whispered, my voice breaking. "I can't do this."

"You will," she said, her voice smooth and unyielding. "While it would be nice to trust you when you say you'll leave Ireland and never again interfere with the Sochai, I can't take that risk. A good mother must always be wise, mustn't she?"

The mockery in her tone was a dagger to the chest, twisting with every word.

I couldn't breathe. My vision blurred, and my hands trembled as I fought the overwhelming panic threatening to consume me.

She continued, her voice so calm it was almost clinical. "To protect myself and my organization, you may take one brother and flee. The other will stay here with me, as assurance that you'll keep your word."

The room spun. Ebony's words sounded distant, like they were coming from underwater. I couldn't process them. Couldn't comprehend the cruelty of what she was asking.

I must have looked horrified, but she didn't care. I wasn't her daughter anymore. I was just another adversary to be outmaneuvered.

Her tone hardened, final and unyielding. "It's really quite simple. One… or the other. *Choose.*"

"I can't," I croaked, my voice breaking into pieces.

Ebony's eyes narrowed, and she shrugged again, as though my refusal meant nothing to her. "Then I kill them both. And you."

The guards moved in unison, raising their weapons with a cold precision that made my blood run ice-cold. Two barrels pointed at Ciaran's head, two at Ty's, and two more… at me.

My body froze, every muscle locking in place. My mind

screamed at me to do something, *anything*, but I was paralyzed, my breaths coming in shallow gasps.

Ebony stepped forward, and I flinched, but I didn't pull away when she took my hands in hers. She lifted them to her lips, kissing the backs with an obscene tenderness, her touch as cold as her heart.

"Well, my darling," she said, her voice dripping with false affection. "What will it be? Or rather… *who* will it be?"

Disbelief, panic, and utter grief collided within me, a storm raging in my chest, tearing through every shred of composure I had left. It clawed at my insides, twisting and writhing, leaving me raw and exposed.

"You must decide *now*," she said softly, her voice carrying the finality of a guillotine.

The sound of weapons cocking echoed in the tomb, loud and brutal, like the snapping of bones.

The room spun. My knees threatened to give out.

"I can't," I whispered again, my voice barely audible over the pounding of my heart.

"You will." Ebony's lips twisted into a mockery of a smile. "Or *I* will decide for you."

Ebony grabbed my jaw tightly and I yelped when her long, pointed nails pierced my skin. She roughly shook me as I choked on her Chanel No. 5.

"Don't embarrass me, Ava," she snarled. "No daughter of mine will take the easy way out. You've made your bed, now lie in it with whichever brother fucks you best."

"Get your hands off her," Ty shouted, lunging forward, earning him a hard crack of a gun butt to the back of the head.

He lurched as they yanked him back and when his hand came away from his head, there was blood.

Ty's eyes met mine and for once, feeling blazed in them, a reflection of my own—fear, conflict, pain, and utter hopelessness.

"This one, then?" Ebony laughed as she pointed my chin toward Ciaran. "Fast on the keyboard, fast on the clit? Does his rage excite you, Ava? Or will it consume you like it's consumed him? Will you two fizzle out just as fast?"

Ciaran's eyes burned like embers beneath ash, a tempest

of restrained emotions threatening to break free. For once, he wasn't the fiery storm I was used to, all fury and heat laid bare.

Instead, there was a quiet, agonizing depth to his gaze, a raw vulnerability that he wouldn't dare voice but couldn't entirely hide.

I felt the weight of his silent plea pressing into me, heavier than the air in the tomb.

Pick me. Love me. Save me.

I tried to wrench my chin away from Ebony's claw, but she held me like iron. The more I struggled, the deeper she sank her nails.

"Or this one?" Ebony asked, jerking my attention toward Ty. "Did prison carve the soul out of him, or did he lose it willingly? Are his broken pieces enough to satisfy you for the rest of your life?"

This time, Ty's mask cracked. His anguish shone through, raw and unguarded, his eyes blazing with a storm of emotions he couldn't contain—pain, love, and a resignation so deep it nearly brought me to my knees.

I love you. Forget me. Let me go.

"Please," I begged, my voice raw and broken, sobs strangling my words. "I can't choose. Please, Ebony, don't make me."

Tears poured freely, scalding my cheeks, blurring my vision. Ebony hated weakness—especially mine—but I couldn't stop the flood. It was like the anguish was being ripped from my chest in waves, each one more violent than the last.

"Pathetic," Ebony muttered, her voice sharp enough to cut. Her hand shot out, shoving me back so hard that I slammed into the altar's unyielding stone, pain lancing through my spine, stealing my breath.

"You bitch!" Ciaran roared, his voice a weapon hurled across the room, every syllable drenched in fury and desperation.

Ty fought against the guards holding him back, his teeth bared in a snarl, his body straining as if sheer force of will might be enough to break their grip.

"Take me instead!" The words burst from me before I could think them through. "I'll stay with you. Let them go. Please—just let them both go!"

Ebony laughed, the sound cold and hollow, echoing off the tomb walls like the cruelest mockery. Her pale eyes gleamed with something as dark and unfeeling as her voice.

"Do you think I'm stupid, Ava? They'll come back for you. But once one has you all to himself, there's no way in hell they'll risk coming back for the other."

She turned her gaze to Ciaran first, her icy scrutiny peeling back his anger like layers of armor.

His features contorted in a snarl of hatred, the slightest flicker of anguish breaking through.

Then she shifted her attention to Ty, who met her stare with quiet defiance, his emotions raw and bleeding for all to see.

Her certainty solidified like steel, her posture straightening with cruel resolve. Ebony looked back at me, trembling and crumpled on the altar, my face streaked with tears.

I hated that she could see me like this—weak, broken—but I had no strength left. Her impossible choice had bled me dry.

"No, you cannot stay," she said, her voice devoid of mercy. "Choose now. I'm growing tired of this game."

The guards stepped closer to Ty and Ciaran. The sight of gun muzzles pressing against their skulls made bile rise in my throat.

I hid my face in my hands as my body racked with sobs, and I screamed, the sound primal, ripped from the depths of my soul, a cacophony of fear, grief, and helpless rage.

Nothing had prepared me for this. Nothing could have.

The tears came harder, hotter, until they blurred into a haze of despair.

The weight of the decision—of *their* lives—crushed me, suffocating every ounce of reason I had left. I braced myself for the inevitable crack of gunfire, for the end to come.

"I love you both," I choked out between sobs.

I couldn't bear to look at them. I couldn't let their faces—marked with anger, fear, and love—be my last memory of them. So I closed my eyes and went elsewhere.

I went to the Darkmoor library in the moonlight, to Paris bathed in the soft glow of dawn.

I retreated to the safety of my childhood bathtub and to my bed where Ty had held me, whispering promises he couldn't keep.

I let myself drown in the fragments of a life that had already slipped through my fingers.

I held on to those moments, desperate and fleeting, as the seconds ticked down, knowing that whatever came next would shatter me completely.

Ebony sighed, the sound almost bored. "Enough of this. Guards—"

"I'll stay."

The words hit like a thunderclap.

My hands fell away from my face, and my eyes flew open to see Ty staring down Ebony, his expression as calm and resolved as I'd ever seen it.

Ebony's lips curved into a mocking smile, first directed at me and then toward Ty, as though his offer was an expected gift she was pleased to receive.

"No." Ciaran's voice cut through the air, sharp and unyielding.

Ebony paused, her attention flicking between the twins, and to my horror, she chuckled. "Well, this just got interesting."

"No one is staying," I said, my tears momentarily dried by a surge of desperation. I stood, trembling but firm. "Ebony, let all of us go or kill us all. No one is getting left behind."

But Ebony didn't so much as glance in my direction. She smirked, her arched eyebrow a silent taunt.

Neither Ciaran nor Ty acknowledged me either. Their gazes locked on each other, a silent war waging between them.

Ciaran's voice, tight with emotion, shattered the silence. "You did your time. You've made your sacrifice. It's *my* turn."

"No," I whispered, my head shaking instinctively as the words clawed out of me. "No, no, no."

But I was invisible.

"Please," Ciaran said, his eyes never leaving Ty's. "I have to do this."

"No!" I screamed, the sound raw and echoing off the damp, unfeeling walls of the tomb.

Neither of them flinched.

Ciaran and Ty seemed trapped in a world of their own, a space where only they existed, where only their history mattered.

Ty's voice cracked as he whispered, "Ci, I can't let you—"

"Remember what we promised each other," Ciaran said, his words a quiet plea, heavy with meaning I couldn't grasp.

Ty's eyes widened, the pain in them deepening, a silent argument spilling between them without a single word spoken aloud.

I looked between their faces, frantic, desperate, trying to unravel the cryptic exchange.

Their expressions were mirrors of anguish, love, and resignation.

"What are you talking about? What is he talking about?" My voice was a thin thread, shaking with fear.

But neither of them answered.

I didn't exist in this moment. It was theirs.

And whatever they had promised each other, I could feel the weight of it looming over all of us like the edge of a cliff I was about to be pushed off.

"Let me make this right, Ty." Ciaran forced a faint smile, though his voice carried the kind of resignation that made my stomach churn. "I owe you this."

Ty looked like he might argue back.

But then his lip stopped trembling, the fire in his eyes extinguished as stone hardened over his face, his mouth, his jaw, his very soul locked tight behind a cold and unfeeling mask.

He nodded, his voice hollow and resigned. "Okay."

"No!" The word ripped from me, raw and jagged, as my legs moved on instinct.

I barely made it two steps before a guard grabbed me from behind, his grip like iron bands locking me in place. I writhed and kicked, but his hold didn't falter.

Ebony barely spared me a glance as she raised a finger at me to shush, a patronizing gesture that cut through me like a blade.

Her attention snapped back to the twins. "We have an agreement, then?"

"Yes," Ciaran said immediately, his voice steady even as I saw his knuckles whiten at his sides.

I held my breath, clinging to the hope that Ty would refuse. That he wouldn't let this happen.

But Ty didn't meet my eyes. He kept his gaze locked on Ciaran, as if the rest of the room had ceased to exist.

"Ty," Ciaran urged, his voice dropping, low and imploring.

Ty finally broke, his voice quiet and firm. "Deal."

The word echoed in my mind, shattering everything inside me.

I stared at them both, my vision swimming with tears, unable to comprehend the betrayal I felt—by them, by the world, by the very air around us.

When Ebony clapped her hands together, the sharp sound snapped through the chamber, but I didn't flinch. I was too numb, too stunned to react.

"Wonderful," Ebony cooed, her voice dripping with satisfaction.

She turned to Ty, her expression as gleeful as a predator's. "You have twenty-four hours to leave Ireland with

Ava. And you will *never* return. Otherwise—and please don't test me—I will kill your brother. Slowly and painfully. Understood?"

Ty inhaled deeply, his chest rising and falling as if to steady himself, and then said, "Yes."

No.

This wasn't real. It couldn't be real.

Ebony waved her hand dismissively, and the guard holding me released me. My arms dropped to my sides, limp and useless, as Ty approached me.

His face was devoid of emotion, a blank mask that made him seem almost inhuman. He reached for me, his hands steady as if this wasn't tearing him apart as much as it was me.

"No," I sobbed, shaking my head as I swatted at him like a cornered animal. My tears blurred my vision, but I could still see the shadows of the guard's weapons poised and ready to end everything.

"Go, Ava," Ciaran said, his voice cracking as I saw the agony he tried so desperately to hide. His jaw was clenched so tightly I thought it might shatter, his lips pressed into a thin line.

His eyes—those brilliant blue eyes that had always burned with intensity—were dim now, veiled by a pain so raw it stole the air from my lungs.

He was crumbling, and I could see it, the cracks in his armor spreading with every breath he forced himself to take. I knew the weight of this moment was too much for anyone to carry, even him.

For all his attempts to stand strong, he couldn't stop the truth from bleeding through—the unbearable grief of a choice he'd made to save me, to save his brother, the sacrifice he believed he had to make.

Because behind it all, there was love. Not just for me. But for his brother. A love so fierce it broke me all over again.

"Take care of her for me," he said to Ty, his voice cracking.

"Ciaran!" I cried, his name catching in my throat.

Ty managed to get a grip on my upper arms, his hands like iron, and even though I clawed savagely at the backs of his fingers, digging my nails into his skin until I felt the warmth of his blood, he didn't flinch.

He pulled me into his arms as if I weighed nothing at all, his grip unrelenting, his arm locked around my waist as he hoisted me over his shoulder like I was baggage.

Tears blurred my vision, mixing with strands of my damp hair plastered to my face.

"Ty, let me go!" I screamed, my voice raw with desperation as I punched and kicked out, but he only grunted and shifted my weight.

"Ciaran!"

I saw him—my Scáth—just as Ty turned toward the passagetomb.

Ciaran's jaw tightened, and his head dipped, turning away as if hiding the agony he couldn't keep contained, his hand flexing uselessly at his side. He wouldn't even look at me, and that hurt more than anything. It was as though he'd already resigned himself to his fate.

The jagged doorway of the tomb loomed closer. Each step Ty took brought me farther from Ciaran, farther from the brother he'd sworn to protect, and I lost myself in my panic. I kicked harder, screaming his name with everything I had left, but Ty's grip didn't falter.

"Stop it, Ava," Ty muttered, his voice hollow, like he couldn't even bear to hear the sound of his own words.

"No!" I thrashed, clawed, and shoved against his back, but it was like hitting stone. I begged him, cursed him, accused him of cruelty, of heartlessness.

"I'll never forgive you, Ty! Let me go! I *hate* you!" My voice broke on the word, a sob tearing from my chest.

Ty flinched under me, his step faltering for the first time. The smallest crack in his resolve.

And it shattered me. I knew, deep down, that he wasn't heartless. He was just as broken by this as I was.

I knew my words hurt him, cut him as deeply as a blade.

But I had no other weapon, no other way to fight back, so I wielded my grief and rage against him, hoping— praying—it would be enough to stop him.

But Ty was stronger, his grip like a vise as he carried me through the doorway and up the slick stone stairs, one determined step at a time. Each one echoed in my ears like a death knell.

With every step, Ciaran's figure grew smaller, swallowed by the dark of the tomb.

"Scáth!" I screamed, my voice breaking as I reached for my shadow, who was already vanishing from me.

Ty kept climbing, his pace steady despite my struggling.

My fists pounded uselessly against his back as my world narrowed to the doorway—the one that would seal my fate. The one that would leave Ciaran behind.

My heart shattered when he appeared one last time in the fading light of the tomb, guards holding him back.

"Ava!" His scream echoed in the passage, raw and filled with every ounce of love and anguish he felt. "I love you!"

Something inside me broke at those words. A fury I hadn't known I possessed burned through me, blinding in its intensity.

No. I wouldn't let this happen. I couldn't. I would not condemn another brother to prison, to pain, because of me.

Before I could think, I drove my knee into Ty's stomach with all the force I could muster.

He grunted in pain, faltering as the air rushed from his lungs. His grip loosened, just enough for me to slip free.

I hit the stairs hard, the jagged edges biting into my skin, but I scrambled to my feet before Ty could recover.

"Don't shoot her!" Ebony's voice rang out, sharp and panicked, as the guards lifted their weapons toward me.

I didn't care.

All I saw was Ciaran, his bloodshot eyes locking on mine, his expression a mix of anguish and love so profound it felt like it would break me.

I lunged for him, my hands outstretched—

And then came the pain, sharp and blinding, as something struck the back of my skull.

Before I even hit the ground, darkness consumed me.

THE WARDEN

The Darkmoor forest loomed around me, its shadows twisting under the cold light of the moon. Each step felt heavier than the last, each step away from my brother a bitter reminder of what had been lost—and what couldn't be undone.

Ava's limp body, fragile and so damn still, pressed against my chest. Her head lolled against my shoulder, and her hair brushed my jaw, a cruel echo of the countless times I'd held her this close.

It should have felt like freedom—escaping that suffocating tomb—but all I felt was the weight of what waited for us. For her. For me.

The ache in my chest hollowed me out, leaving only the shell of a man still moving forward because I had no choice.

Ava was still in danger. Every moment we lingered was another moment that Ebony could change her mind and come for her.

Ava wouldn't truly be safe until we left Ireland.

I glanced down at Ava's face, pale against the darkness,

her lashes fanned out across her cheeks. She looked so delicate, almost peaceful in a way that made my chest tighten.

A part of me wanted her to stay unconscious, to never wake up and realize the truth of what I had done.

Of who I had left behind *for her*.

Of the sacrifice that had been made, one I couldn't undo no matter how much it ripped me apart.

Her soft groan broke the stillness, and my heart kicked against my ribs.

Ava shifted in my hold, her fingers twitching before pressing weakly against my chest.

My grip instinctively tightened, bracing myself for the storm I knew was coming.

"Shh," I murmured, my voice low and raw. "Ava, please, stay still. That guard hit you hard. You might have a concussion."

Her eyes fluttered open, and for a moment, there was only confusion as she stared at my face. But then her body jerked in my arms.

"Ciaran!" she screamed, her voice splintering with desperation as she pushed against my chest, her fists weak but frantic. "We have to go back for him!"

I said nothing. I just held her tighter, feeling her fists batter against my own shattered heart.

"Put me down!" she screamed again, thrashing harder. "We can't leave him!"

Her words were arrows of guilt aimed at my fractured soul. But I forced myself to stay steady, to keep walking.

"Stop, Ava." My voice came out rough, thick with the emotion I tried and failed to keep buried. "Don't make his sacrifice mean nothing."

She froze for a heartbeat, her chest heaving against mine as she stared up at me. Her wide, tear-filled eyes searched mine, disbelief etched into every line of her face. I could see the moment her grief twisted, sharp and venomous, into anger.

"*His* sacrifice?" she spat, her voice cracking. "You left him, Ty! *You* sacrificed him!"

Her accusation hung in the air, freezing me mid-step.

My chest felt hollow, my heart beating too fast and too hard against my ribs as the forest seemed to close in, every shadow pressing down on me as if the trees themselves condemned me.

She thrashed harder, her nails raking against my arms. "Let me go!"

I didn't loosen my grip, but her grief had turned her into something feral, wild.

Somehow, she slipped free, tumbling out of my hold and staggering toward the tomb.

My pulse spiked as I saw her take off, her silhouette barely visible in the dim moonlight.

"No," I muttered, my voice hoarse, and I gave chase.

My legs moved on instinct, my boots crunching against the frost-covered ground as I closed the distance between us in seconds.

She didn't make it far—I caught her by the arm and spun her toward me, holding her tight despite her thrashing.

"Let me go!" she sobbed, pounding her fists weakly against my chest. "I have to go back for him."

Her strength was nothing compared to my grip, but her despair was a force I couldn't fight.

"Would you trade him for me?" The words escaped me, quiet and raw, a vulnerability I hadn't meant to show.

Ava froze, her lips parting as if the question had shocked her into silence. For a second, I thought she wouldn't answer, that her anger would dissipate into the cold night air.

But then her grief surged forward, and she screamed.

"*Yes*! I wish it had been *you*."

Her words tore through me. It echoed in the stillness, a sound that seemed to linger in the trees, in my chest, in my mind.

My arms didn't loosen, but something inside me broke.

Her screams dissolved into sobs, her body collapsing against mine like a rag doll. The weight of her grief pinned me down, her words reverberating in my skull.

She would trade me.

I had believed we were meant to be, that maybe, just maybe, she would realize that she loved me the way I loved her.

But now, her words filled me with doubt.

Maybe Ava didn't belong with me.

Maybe she belonged with him.

The brother I'd left behind.

The brother I had sacrificed.

As the dawn was peeking through my dorm bedroom, I threw the last of my essentials into the backpack—a change of clothes, wallet, the fake passport tucked into a side pocket.

The zipper caught for a second before sliding shut, and the sound seemed deafening in the suffocating silence of the dorm.

My hands were steady, my movements deliberate, but my mind was chaos, still reeling from Ava's angry admission.

"Would you trade him for me?"

"Yes."

No. Stop it. First, I had to get Ava out of here. Far away. Where she was safe.

Then I could strategize what to do about Ciaran.

I shouldered the bag, the weight of it nothing compared to the weight crushing my chest, and strode to her room.

The door was ajar, a sliver of light spilling into the hall. I shoved it open, my voice ready to bark out an order to hurry—but the words stuck in my throat.

She wasn't there.

"Ava?" I called, though I already knew she wouldn't answer.

My gaze swept the room, desperate for a sign she'd been packing, preparing. Instead, it was pristine, untouched, as if she hadn't even considered leaving.

My eyes landed on the single photo on her bedside table, framed in simple black. I stepped closer, the ache in my chest sharpening like a blade as I took it in.

Ciaran. Asleep in some hotel bed, his face soft with an unguarded peace I'd almost forgotten he was capable of. Behind him, the Eiffel Tower loomed through a window in the background, blurred but unmistakable.

I thought of all the photos I had of her—on my mantle,

tucked into books, locked in the drawer of my nightstand back at Blackthorn.

Every snapshot I'd stolen, moments where she looked alive and happy, or even sad and distant. I had collected her like treasures, each one a reminder of why I couldn't stop loving her.

But this?

She only had one. And it was *him*.

I set the photo down, the glass smudged with the faint outline of my thumb, and turned toward the hallway.

My heart was pounding, each beat a dull thud against my ribs as I walked to Ciaran's door, slightly ajar.

I pushed it open, slower this time, bracing myself for what I might find.

The first thing that hit me was the scent. Faint but unmistakable: Ciaran. The woodsy undertone of his cologne lingered in the air, mixing with the stale, hollow atmosphere of a room left empty too soon.

And then I saw her.

Ava was curled up on Ciaran's bed, her shoulders shaking as silent sobs racked her body. Her face was buried in his pillow, her fingers clutching it like it was the only thing tethering her to the earth.

She didn't hear me—or maybe she didn't care.

I stepped back, the door creaking slightly as it moved against my hand. My chest tightened, a vise squeezing every ounce of air from my lungs.

I sagged against the wall outside his room, pressing the heel of my hand to my forehead as the weight of it all crushed me.

"You've always belonged to me," I had told her, *"and I will prove it to you."*

And I hadn't listened when she replied. *"Maybe if I had fallen for you first, things would be different. But... it's always been him."*

She loved *him.*

She always had.

I clenched my fists as the memories hit me, cruel and relentless. Every moment that had given me hope now felt like a taunt, a mockery of my feelings.

Memories flooded my mind, unbidden and cruel in their clarity.

I saw her in the Blackthorn kitchen, sitting on the counter with that sly little smirk.

I saw her hand lingering on mine as she bandaged my bloodied knuckles, her touch light but her concern heavy.

I saw the look in her eyes when I gave her the engagement ring I'd secretly bought her.

Foolish.

Each memory felt like a dagger, driving deeper into the raw wound of my heart. Those moments—moments I had clung to, that had given me hope—now felt like silly dreams.

And yet I couldn't hate her for it. I couldn't even hate him. Ciaran. My brother, who had somehow stolen her heart even as I bled for her.

My legs gave out, and I slid down the wall, my back scraping against the plaster. The numbness came first, spreading like frost through my veins, followed by the burn of helpless anger.

A hollow, bitter laugh escaped me, too quiet for anyone to hear.

I had thought I could win her. That I just had to show her.

But the truth stared me in the face, as undeniable as the girl I loved sobbing on *his* bed.

I had already lost.

I don't know how long I sat there, my head in my hands, listening to the muffled sound of her grief. But when I finally looked up, the answer was clear, as sharp and cold as the edge of a knife.

I knew what I had to do.

The heaviness lifted—not entirely, but enough for me to move, to stand. I pushed off the wall, my legs unsteady but determined, and turned toward Ava.

I loved her enough to let her go.

Even if it killed me.

AVA

The car ride to the airport was a blur, the silence which hung between Ty and me thick and oppressive.

I leaned my head against the passenger seat window, the cold glass pressing into my temple, soothing the ache that throbbed in time with my pulse.

My chest was hollow, emptied of all the screaming, crying, and pleading that had consumed me. There was nothing left but the numb weight of exhaustion.

I barely noticed the turns Ty made or the hum of the tires on the road.

When the car slowed, gravel crunching under the wheels, I blinked and glanced out the window, expecting lines of cars, concrete terminal buildings, and planes taking off overhead.

But this wasn't the airport.

The sea glimmered in the distance, framed by towering pines that swayed gently in the salty breeze.

I frowned, my thoughts sluggish, trying to piece together where we were.

Ty put the car in park and got out without a word.

He opened the passenger door and offered his hand, and I stared up at him, too drained to ask why we had stopped.

"I wanted you to see it before I go," he said, his voice calm but edged with something I couldn't place.

I blinked at him, his words barely registering, and turned toward the house in front of us, a quaint two-story with a wraparound porch.

For a moment, it felt like déjà vu. The scent of the pine trees mingled with the faint sweetness of strawberries from a large patch in the front garden, and I paused mid-step.

"Have you brought me here before?" I asked, my voice hoarse and unfamiliar to my own ears.

Ty shook his head, his expression unreadable. "It was actually you who brought me here."

The words didn't make sense. My brow furrowed as I stared at him, waiting for an explanation, but he just gestured toward the house.

"Go on," he said softly. "See if I got it right."

I hesitated but moved forward, the gravel crunching beneath my shoes as I approached the porch.

The wind shifted, carrying the tang of saltwater and the faintest memory of a conversation I couldn't quite grasp.

My hand trailed along the smooth wood of the porch railing as I stepped onto it, and something in me faltered.

"This is... where we would drink tea," I whispered without thinking, the words spilling out before I could catch them.

A chill ran down my spine as the familiarity solidified. I turned to Ty, my heart beginning to race.

He said nothing, just nodded for me to continue.

I pushed the door open.

Inside, the light was golden and soft, filtering through blue curtains that swayed in the breeze. The smell of the sea mingled with pine and the faintest trace of fresh paint.

I stepped inside, and my breath hitched as I took in the details—the light and airy rooms overlooking the sea, the antique writing desk beside the sunny window, the large comfortable bed piled high with pillows.

My eyes burned as I wandered deeper into the house, the lump in my throat growing heavier with each step.

It was perfect.

"I had it built for you," Ty said quietly, his voice steady. "I hope I got it right."

I turned to look at him, my chest tightening.

He stood beside me, close but not quite touching, his eyes watching me carefully.

He'd done this for me. Every detail was thought out, intentional, and *right.*

I cupped Ty's cheek, guiding his hesitant lips toward mine. His resistance was slight, but it was there, a wall of guilt and doubt I was determined to shatter.

The kiss started soft, a gentle test, as if to confirm he hadn't drifted too far away from me. That we hadn't lost each other completely.

My heart ached when I remembered the hateful things I'd screamed at him in the forest. The cruel accusations, the raw anger that had cut him like a blade.

I would have to apologize, to tell him I hadn't meant it—but not now.

Now, I just wanted to be with him. To be with the man who had built this house for me, who knew me better than anyone.

Even if we had to leave soon. Even if this moment was all we'd ever have.

I pulled back just enough to lift my sweater over my head, my movements quick and determined.

Ty froze, his eyes searching mine, conflicted and anguished.

"Don't stop," I whispered to Ty, my voice cracking as my fingers yanked at his jacket, a surge of defiance coursing through me, one that burned away the grief and left only raw, aching need.

"Loving each other doesn't mean we love him any less," I said. My voice was barely audible, but it was enough.

His gaze held mine for a beat, the anguish in his eyes deepening before something broke. His lips crashed into mine, the kiss fierce and desperate, filled with everything we couldn't say aloud.

Our tongues twisted together as his hands found my waist, pulling me against him like he couldn't bear even the smallest distance between us.

As we stripped each other, his touch was fire and comfort, a balm for the wounds we carried but could never heal. And in this moment, there was no room for guilt or doubt, only us.

I lunged at him, naked and desperate to feel him inside me.

Ty chuckled as he lifted me into his arms, and I wrapped

my legs around his waist. "I have one more room to show you."

I made a frustrated noise, but I let him carry me into the room next door, the only room I hadn't seen.

The library.

It was so large it spanned from front to back, filled with books on shelves like driftwood.

I froze against Ty, my heart pounding in my ears, as he lowered me to a soft couch the color of sea glass.

I glanced around the room as he pushed his pants down into a pile beside the couch before lowering himself between my legs.

Over his shoulder, sunlight poured through tall windows overlooking the sea, illuminating shelves the exact color of driftwood.

This wasn't just my house. This was *my dream house.*

The realization hit me like a tidal wave, knocking the breath from my lungs as fragments of a long-ago conversation resurfaced.

I'd described this exact room. The big library filled with light, with a view of the sea. The shelves like driftwood. The couches like sea glass.

But not to Ciaran.

My heart twisted violently in my chest. I hadn't told Ciaran.

It was Ty.

Ty had been the one who had saved me from that party. He'd sat me on the counter and fed me strawberries.

I'd told Ty about my dream house, about what would become *our* dream house.

The earth tilted beneath me as the weight of the realization settled in my bones. All this time, I had thought it was Ciaran whom I had fallen for first.

But it was Ty.

It had always been Ty.

"You…" I started, but the words got caught in my throat.

He thrust into me, cutting me off, igniting a fire that spread through my entire body.

Nothing else existed in that moment except for him, filling me, consuming me, claiming me.

"Fuck, you're so tight," Ty groaned, his voice low and gravelly. "You fit me so perfectly."

His movements were hard and rough and desperate, each thrust more forceful than the last.

"You…" I gasped, my nails digging into his shoulders. "You remembered."

He growled, a sound that reverberated through his chest and into mine.

"I remember everything about you, Ava," he said, his voice breaking just enough to send a fresh wave of emotion crashing over me, even as his hands gripped my hips, fingers pressing into my flesh hard enough to leave marks.

I welcomed the pain, craved it even, as it grounded me in this moment.

"And I will remember *this.*"

Before I could ask what he meant, Ty snatched something from the side of the couch and stuffed it in my mouth.

I smelled my own arousal on my lace panties and groaned.

There was another scent which I couldn't place, but it was familiar.

Ty sealed his hand over my mouth and nose and fucked me roughly, on the edge of brutally.

My head went light, the afternoon sunlight blazing into twinkling sunbeams as I moaned desperately against my panties, feeling the pressure building.

I was already so close.

Ty's pace quickened, his hips snapping against mine with an urgency that bordered on desperation.

The couch creaked beneath us, the sound mingling with our heavy breaths and cries, the faint sound of waves crashing against the cliffs just audible through the thick glass windows.

I wrapped my legs tighter around him, pulling him closer, deeper, as I came hard.

My body convulsed around him as waves of ecstasy crashed over me, my muffled cries barely escaping past Ty's hand and the panties in my mouth.

Ty shuddered against me as he came as well.

But even as I rode out my orgasm, stars exploding behind my eyelids, a realization hit me just as hard.

The second scent, the one that seemed so familiar…

Ty had laced my panties with a drug.

His hand fell away from my mouth and I spat my panties out.

But it was too late. The drug was already working its way through my body, making my thoughts heavy.

"Ty?" My voice wavered, weak and hoarse as I tilted my head to meet his eyes. "W-why did you d-drug m…"

His face softened, but his eyes—God, his eyes were distant, full of something final.

His hand moved to cradle my cheek, holding me as

though I were something precious, fragile. "Even if I'm not the one you love, I'd give my life to protect your happiness."

A cold, sharp fear twisted in my stomach. I tried to push myself upright, but my arms refused to cooperate. "W-what—?"

I blinked furiously, fighting the encroaching darkness.

What was happening?

Oh God, was he going back for Ciaran on his own?

No. *NO*.

"I'm sorry," he murmured, his breath warm against my temple. "For everything."

A gasp escaped me, panic surging through my chest, wild and desperate when I realized he was saying goodbye.

My body betrayed me, collapsing in his arms. "T-ty, d-don't—"

"I love you more," he whispered. "And when I say 'I love you more,' I don't just mean I love you more than he loves you or more than you love me—which I do. What I mean is… I love you *more* than any time, space, or distance that could ever separate us. I love you more than any flaws you think you have, more than any broken pieces or darkness in your heart. What I mean is… I love you more than I love myself. I love you more than *everything*."

My lips trembled, trying to form the words that burned inside me.

I needed him to know. I needed him to hear me.

But my body wouldn't obey. My lips wouldn't move, my voice trapped in the heavy fog.

The room narrowed to a single point, to his pale-blue eyes, blackness swallowing the edges of my vision.

"*Slán leat, mo ghrá,*" he murmured, his breath ghosting over my skin.

Farewell, my love.

My heart screamed as everything else slipped away.

No. I love you *more. Mhaor, I choose—*

But then there was only blackness.

AVA

The first thing I noticed when I woke was the couch beneath me, unfamiliar and wrong.

The cushion was too soft, the blanket draped over me carried Ty's scent.

My chest tightened as the memories came rushing back —the house, his admission, the panties he'd drugged and shoved into my mouth as he fucked me.

The library which had before been aglow in a bath of hazy golden light was deadly still in a dusky purple.

"Ty," I rasped, my throat dry, the name barely audible even to myself.

I sat up too fast, the room spinning as the blood rushed to my head. My heart pounded as I tried to steady myself, clutching the edge of the couch.

Déjà vu slammed through me as I glanced down and found myself wearing a silky crimson robe and knew he'd dressed me after I'd passed out.

I winced as I reached around to the sore spot on the back of my neck and froze when my fingers came away red.

My gaze was drawn to the small implant sitting on the side table, sticky with dried blood.

The finality of it slammed into me.

Then the last thing he said whispered in my brain —*Farewell, my love.*

"No." My voice cracked as panic clawed its way up my throat. "No, no, no."

I scrambled to my feet, calling his name louder now. "Ty? Where are you?"

The house was silent, too still, as though it was holding its breath. My eyes darted toward the staircase, then the front door, my chest heaving with the weight of unspoken dread.

Then, through the suffocating silence, I heard it—the crunch of gravel. My head snapped toward the sound.

The beam of headlights swept through a window like that of a lighthouse in a storm.

A car. My pulse stuttered. He was here. He'd come back.

"Ty!" I yelled, my voice cracking with desperation as I stumbled toward the front door.

My bare feet skidded across the hardwood, and I grabbed the frame for balance before fumbling with the handle and yanking the door open.

The cold air hit me like a slap as I hurried down the porch steps, the gravel drive biting into my soles.

The car pulled up, the headlights cutting through the shadows of the surrounding pines.

The driver's door opened, and I froze, hope surging like a tidal wave.

"Ty?" I called, my voice trembling as I took a hesitant step forward.

But it wasn't Ty who stumbled out of the car.

It was Ciaran.

A flood of emotions hit me all at once—relief, disappointment, elation, and fear. They tangled in my chest, paralyzing me for a beat until he took a shaky step forward and faltered, collapsing to one knee.

"Ciaran!" I yelled, the fear taking over as I sprinted toward him.

When I reached him, I grabbed his elbows to help him stand, but my hands came away slick and warm. My stomach turned as I stared at my palms, streaked with blood.

"God," I whispered, horrified as my eyes lifted to his face.

His features were a mess of cuts and bruises. Blood poured from deep gashes along his cheek and temple, his left eye swollen nearly shut, only a sliver of blue peeking through. His breaths were shallow, rasping, and his arm clutched his ribs protectively.

"Ciaran…" My voice cracked as I tried to steady him, my arms wrapping tightly around him as his body shuddered. "What happened? Where's Ty?"

At the sound of Ty's name, a broken sound escaped Ciaran—a mix of a sob and a groan. His head hung between his shoulders, and his arm trembled as he barely supported his weight.

"I'm sorry, Ava," he rasped, his voice weak but filled with anguish. "I begged him not to do it."

His words sent an icy lance of dread straight to my heart. My chest tightened as the truth threatened to crush me.

"What did he do?" My voice wavered, frantic.

Ciaran tried to push himself upright, but his strength gave out.

I tightened my hold on him, lowering us both to the ground as the sea breeze howled around us, battering us with cold.

"But you know Ty..." Ciaran whispered hoarsely, his bloodied fingers clutching the silk of my robe. "*Stubborn*."

His words slammed into me, but my mind refused to accept their meaning.

"No," I whispered, shaking my head in denial. My voice cracked, rising in desperation. "Why? Why would he do that?"

Why did he do it? Why would he leave after fighting so fiercely to stay by my side? How could he possibly think I'd be better off without him, that I could live without him?

Ciaran's body shivered against mine, his breath coming in weak, shallow gasps. "He said... 'She'll need your expertise now more than ever.'"

I gripped his shoulders, shaking him lightly despite the injuries I knew he had. "What does that mean, Ciaran? Where is Ty?"

My voice rose to a scream, the rawness scraping my throat, when the shrill ring of a phone cut through the storm of my emotions.

Ciaran fumbled weakly for the source of the sound, and I reached into his jacket, my shaking hands pulling out the device.

The screen glowed with *Unknown Number*.

My breath caught, and I jabbed at the screen, barely able to hold the phone to my ear.

"Ty?" I croaked. "Is that you?"

His voice came through the line, rough and heartbreakingly steady. "I only have a few minutes, hummingbird. Please, listen carefully."

The tears started without me realizing. I tasted salt on my lips, felt my chest quaking, but all I could do was cry. "Why?"

"It was the hardest thing I've ever done," Ty said softly. "But if it means you get to fly free, I'd lock myself away for a thousand lifetimes."

"Ty, no. What did you do?"

"I thought I was your warden. But I was *your* prisoner all along," he said, his voice strained but resolute. "I know you chose Ciaran. But it's okay. Do you hear me?"

"No," I sobbed, shaking my head even though he couldn't see me.

"You belong with him, Ava. And you *need* him now more than ever."

My chest felt like it was splitting open. Deep down, I knew he was trying to tell me something, but the overwhelming tide of emotion drowned out any clarity.

"Heartwarming," Ebony's cold voice sneered in the background. "But that's enough."

There was a scuffle, Ty's voice growing distant as he shouted, "From every cell, from every shadow…" The line jolted with static, and his voice came again, farther away, raw and broken. "…for as long as I breathe and for whatever comes after, I'll love you more."

The dam inside me shattered.

"I love you more, too," I sobbed, the words pouring out uncontrollably. "I've always loved you! I choose you, Ty."

But the call went dead.

I stared at the phone, my breath catching in my throat.

"No, no, no!" I screamed, my voice echoing into the night.

The weight of his absence hit me like a physical blow, shattering me from the inside out. My knees buckled, and I crumpled to the ground, unable to hold myself upright beneath the crushing grief.

The phone slipped from my trembling fingers, clattering away, forgotten. A guttural scream tore from my chest, raw and primal, as if releasing it could somehow fill the unbearable void he'd left behind.

I couldn't breathe.

My sobs racked my entire body, jagged and unrelenting, each one cutting deeper. Tears blurred my vision, but it didn't matter—everything around me had dissolved into chaos.

He was gone.

He'd misunderstood the cruelty of my grief, mistaking my desperate accusations for truth. *I wish it had been you.*

And in doing so, he'd condemned himself. The man who fought for me, who knew me better than I knew myself, believed he wasn't enough.

But it had always been *him*. I'd been blind, stumbling in the shadows, and he'd seen it all along. He'd waited, hoped, and finally sacrificed himself—for me.

For what? To give me to Ciaran, because he thought that's what I wanted most? Because he thought I didn't love him back?

But I did. God, I did. It had always been him, and now... he was gone. He'd given himself up so I could be with the one I loved most, never realizing that it had been him all along.

The realization ripped through me, hollowing me out.

My hands clawed desperately at the gravel beneath me, seeking some anchor in a world that had suddenly become unrecognizable.

And yet nothing grounded me. Nothing could.

Through the haze of despair, I felt it—Ciaran's gaze.

It burned into me, filled with his own anguish and helplessness.

When I turned, his face—too fucking familiar, a reminder of everything I had lost—was pale, his eyes wide and filled with something unreadable.

He'd heard everything.

The realization tore through me like a jagged blade. The brother I had chosen would never hear my confession.

But Ciaran had.

EBONY

I swirled the twenty-five-year-old Macallan in my glass, watching the amber liquid catch the flickering firelight, its color shifting like molten gold. This was supposed to be the whiskey of victors. A taste for the triumphant.

Yet as the smoke curled on my tongue, I couldn't decide if I actually enjoyed it or if I had spent years convincing myself I did.

Colleagues always assumed it was my favorite. A bottle every Christmas, without fail. A glass ready and waiting at every meeting, a silent toast to my victories, my lineage, my power.

But sitting now in my father's worn leather chair in his study, the same one I'd once stood beside as a child watching him sip from the very same cut-crystal glass, I wasn't even sure if I liked the taste.

I swallowed the burn, wincing as it scorched its way down my throat, and forced myself to think it was pleasant.

Delicious, even. A pleasure far greater than the power plays cloaked in intimacy that always left me hollow.

This, I told myself, was my victory drink. The sweet sting of conquest.

The Sochai was mine, firmly and unquestionably. No more whispers of dissent, no more grumbling fathers, angry over my ordered loss of their daughters.

Ciaran Donahue had inadvertently strengthened my grip by silencing them for me. Their depravities had died with them, and now, the society was free to evolve.

My era had begun.

The filth my father allowed to fester would be cleaned away, burned like the rot it was. I would rebuild the Sochai into something powerful, untouchable. I would steer it into a future no longer mired in the unspeakable crimes of the past.

Guilt crept in, unbidden and sharp, like the edge of a scalpel I hadn't seen coming.

No. *No.* I slammed the door shut on it, but it slipped through the cracks anyway, a shadow I couldn't escape.

I'd done what I'd done for a reason. For a *good* reason! Why couldn't that be enough now? Why wasn't it enough to silence the echoes of their screams in my head, the way their frightened eyes would haunt me in my sleep?

The Sochai had become an evil thing. A rotten tooth, blackened to the root. A diseased lung, festering with every breath.

There was no cutting around the infection, no delicate excision that would save it. Even my surgeon's hands—the steadiest, most precise in the country—weren't capable of that kind of miracle.

No one's hands were. The rot was too deep. The nastiness that had taken root required death.

Only from the ashes could something clean, something pure rise up. That was the truth I'd clung to, the truth I still held on to like a lifeline in this sea of whiskey and regret.

Those girls—those *innocent girls*—they couldn't remain. Not when they'd started to remember.

They were a case of sepsis waiting to happen, poised to infect everything I was trying to salvage. Keeping them alive would have tainted the waters I was working so desperately to clean. *They had to go.*

I made the decision because it was the only decision.

And yet, no matter how many times I told myself that, the weight of it pressed down on me like a lead apron. Their blood clung to my soul, an unrelenting stain I would carry to my grave.

A surgeon didn't weep over the leg she amputated, even when the patient survived and went on to change the world. She didn't cry for what was lost when the sacrifice ensured a future.

So why couldn't I? Why couldn't I stop feeling this hollow ache, this gnawing grief that tore at the edges of my resolve?

The empty glass trembled in my hand as I reached for the bottle, my fingers unsteady.

The Macallan spilled, sloshing onto my father's oriental rug, soaking into the dark velvet robe I'd wrapped around myself like armor.

The robe that had concealed the weakness in my legs as I tore the sheet off Ava after watching that boy fuck her.

The robe I had clutched tightly around me as I contemplated the unthinkable—murdering my own daughter to save myself.

But I hadn't. I had let her go.

As the fire crackled and my victory settled in my chest, I felt an ache I hadn't anticipated.

I would never see Ava again.

The girl I saved. The girl I loved, though I could barely say it, barely admit it even to myself. The girl I tried so desperately to protect—from them, from herself, from *me*.

I tipped back the glass again, but the burn this time was hollow.

My mind flickered back to that day in the hospital room, to her youthful dark eyes locking on mine, wide with confusion and terror.

I hadn't seen her as anything more than an order then. Another test of my loyalty to my father. Another step toward my heirship that I was too afraid to refuse.

But when I was forced to rip her baby from her, it changed me—something maternal, buried deep inside me, sparked to life.

I swore that day I would fix this. Fix her. Fix everything.

And when her foster father died and she was left to fend for herself, I saw it as a sign. I took her in. I saved her because it was the only way I could save myself.

And now, I had lost her.

She had been my last connection to my humanity. Physical proof that I was still *good* underneath.

See, another human cared for me, perhaps even loved me.

The ache grew heavier as I poured another drink. The

weight of it pressed on my chest, and for a moment, I couldn't breathe.

My hand shook as I gripped the glass, the fine crystal threatening to shatter under the pressure. I stared into the fire, willing it to burn away this unbearable grief.

"Hello, Mother."

I froze, the glass slipping from my fingers and hitting the rug with a dull thud.

I turned toward the doorway, and there she stood.

Ava.

Her dark eyes, so achingly familiar, met mine with a cold fury that stopped my heart.

I blinked, certain the whiskey was playing tricks on me. Certain the grief had twisted itself into cruel hallucinations.

She looked so real.

Like all those times she came to lean against the intricate white molding with her schoolbag slung over one shoulder and a heel crossed over the other.

All those times I made her wait for my attention, my love.

I could feel those long seconds as I sat there, staring at the doorway, willing my cruel hallucination to stop haunting me.

But she didn't vanish. She didn't waver.

She stepped forward, the firelight catching her sharp cheekbones, her defiance carved into every inch of her face.

"Did you miss me?" she asked, her voice cutting through the silence like a blade.

And just like that, the weight on my chest shifted. Triumph curdled into something darker, something I couldn't yet name.

Ava had returned.

But she hadn't come home.

"Stupid girl," I hissed. "Now I have to *kill* you."

AVA

The firelight danced on the walls of the study, casting long shadows over Ebony's figure slumped in her father's leather chair, the faint tang of spilled liquor clinging to the air, mingling with the crackle of the hearth.

Her eyes lifted to meet mine as I stepped into the room, disbelief flickering across her face as though I'd walked out of her deepest guilt, a specter come to haunt her.

Then, like a mask snapping into place, the High Lord emerged, and her lips curled into a sneer.

"You stupid girl," she spat, her voice sharp as glass. "Now I have to *kill* you. I gave you twenty-four hours to leave."

"I'm not leaving." My voice was calm, controlled—a blade honed to perfection.

"You think I'm bluffing?" Her eyes narrowed, venom pooling in her voice. "I will kill you and everyone you love."

Her hand moved quickly, slipping into the folds of her robe, and I tensed, half expecting a weapon. But instead, she pulled out her phone, the movement quick and precise, and dialed.

Pressing the phone to her ear, she barked the command with the cold authority of a queen. "Kill Tynan Donahue. Now. And make it hurt."

I stood unmoving, watching her, waiting. Waiting for her to realize what we had just done.

Her brows furrowed, confusion flickering across her face as muffled voices filled her ear.

"What do you mean, it's all over?" she snapped, her voice rising with every word. She pressed the phone tighter against her ear, leaning forward in her chair, her tone spiraling from anger to desperation.

"I demand to—put on—no, I—I'll have you shot for—" Her voice faltered, and her face twisted with fury and disbelief. "I am your High Lord!"

The title hung in the air, brittle and meaningless. It didn't matter anymore, and for the first time, Ebony seemed to realize it. Her hand, still clutching the phone, trembled, and the firelight caught the faint sheen of sweat forming on her brow.

Her eyes snapped to mine, fury flashing across her face. "What did you do?"

"Ty figured it out, actually," I said, my tone maddeningly casual, as though we were discussing the weather.

Her face reddened, blotches of anger blooming on her pale cheeks. "Figured out what?"

I smiled faintly, letting the silence stretch before I answered. "He figured out that the camera in the tomb was digital. Which means you had to store your little initiation blackmail films somewhere virtual."

I went on. "Ty isn't great with computers. He would tell you as much, if you ever see him again. But he knows someone who happens to be excellent with them."

"No," Ebony scoffed. "My servers are impenetrable."

Ciaran stepped to my side and into the light, his expression sharp, mocking.

"I barely broke a sweat hacking in." he said lazily, as if he were discussing breaking into a child's toy box.

Ebony's mask cracked. Her lips parted, her breath coming in shallow gasps. "No. You're bluffing."

"What better way to blackmail all your members to stay in line than to record their twisted initiation. Sickening, but clever," I said, my voice calm as ever. "But you know what else it makes?"

I picked up the remote from the edge of her father's mahogany desk, its surface still damp with spilled whiskey, and pointed it at the sleek television mounted on the far wall.

"Great evidence," I said as I switched it on.

The screen lit up with a familiar news anchor, her voice calm but firm as she delivered the story of the decade.

"A secret society, known as the Sochai, has been exposed for decades of illegal activities, including blackmail, assault, and corruption at the highest levels of society."

The anchor's voice faded as the faces of high-ranking members flashed on the screen—the dean, Cormac Foley Senior, the police commissioner—one after another, their names and titles displayed like a grotesque gallery of shame.

Ebony let out a choke, and her grip on the phone faltered, her knuckles blanching as she stared at the screen.

For a moment, the weight of what she was seeing seemed to crush her.

But then she rallied, her lips twisting into a defiant sneer.

"Impressive," she said, her voice shaking with a false bravado. "But you don't have anything on *me*. I certainly never raped anyone as part of my initiation."

I met her gaze evenly, my tone calm, almost conversational. "You think so?"

Her sneer faltered, her composure cracking as her cell phone chimed with an incoming message. The sound cut through the tension like a knife, her eyes darting to the glowing screen as unease flickered across her face.

"You should open that," I said, my voice calm but edged with steel.

I folded my arms, grounding myself as I watched her wrestling with the hesitation that gripped her. Each breath I took felt deliberate, steady, in stark contrast to the erratic rise and fall of her chest.

Her pale finger, tipped with a bloodred nail, hovered above the screen as the firelight glinted off its polished surface.

Seconds stretched into an eternity, my steady heartbeats filling the silence.

Then, with a sudden, jerky movement, she stabbed at the screen, opening the video file.

The sounds of Ebony's pleasure filled the room.

I'd seen the video and so the sudden crack of a whip did not surprise me.

But Ebony's cry of pain and demand for more was something I would be happy to not hear a third time.

The video Ciaran had uncovered was the dean's own guarantee against the new High Lord.

Judging by the way Ebony's face completely drained of blood as she watched it, she hadn't known about the dean secretly filming them. Not that she could have done anything about it even if she had known.

She'd been in a room that was half boudoir, half torture chamber, bound and hanging from a complex contraption on the ceiling.

The dean wasn't even undressed as he circled her and teased her naked body with the tail of the whip. The more she begged for it, the less he gave her.

His voice was tinny from the small cell phone speaker and it only reached me all the way across the room faintly, but it didn't matter, because I remembered it word for word.

"Why doesn't Daddy do this for you anymore?" he asked.

Even without the video in front of me, I could still see him circling the ropes, Ebony snagged within them, her welted body writhing for the sting of the whip.

I didn't even blink when I heard Ebony's response. "Because I killed him."

The crack of the whip was nothing compared to the volume of Ebony's cries of pleasure.

"Tell me again," he hissed. "*Who* killed the High Lord?"

Ebony's response was near euphoric, the high-pitched cry of a woman on the edge of orgasm.

"Me, me, *me!*" she screamed, each answer punctuated by another brutal strike of the whip.

Ebony cut off the prolonged noise of her orgasm by turning off the phone.

Ebony's breath caught audibly, her earlier composure shattered. She was white as a sheet.

"No," she whispered, shaking her head as if she could will the truth away. "You... you couldn't... you wouldn't send this to anyone, would you?"

I didn't answer right away.

My mind wandered—to another recording. One I hadn't shown her.

To a shadowed altar where her father stood during *his* initiation.

And to a naked girl lying pale and still on the cold stone altar.

A girl with pale eyes the color of *Hydrangea macrophylla*.

The saddest thing of all was that Ebony had been a victim once, just like me.

And yet she had chosen to perpetuate the very system that had shattered her.

Instead of breaking the chains, she had tightened them around others, condemning victims who were as powerless as she had once been. She had taken the cruelty she'd suffered and wielded it like a weapon, carving out her own twisted sense of control.

There was no redemption for her. No undoing the horrors she had inflicted, no path to absolve the blood on her hands. The weight of that truth pressed down on my chest like a stone, heavy and unrelenting.

But for a fleeting moment—just one—I glimpsed her as she must have been before it all. A frightened little girl trapped in her own nightmare, crushed beneath the weight of her father's sins.

Hers, too, had been an innocent life, but no one had

come to save her. No pair of dark, possessive brothers with eyes as blue as the ocean had torn her from the darkness.

No one had fought for her.

I tried to block it out, but the ache rose in my chest regardless. Against my will, I pitied this woman who had hurt me so deeply. I saw the shadow of the person she could have been if someone had just reached her in time.

And worse—God, so much worse—I saw who *I* could have been if my life had taken just one different turn.

It hurt. It fucking hurt.

My throat tightened, but I forced the pity back down and lifted my chin.

"We'll give you a head start…" I said. "You have twenty-four hours to leave Ireland."

She blinked, stunned. "What?"

"Twenty-four hours," I repeated, my voice hollow, my resolve absolute. One final mercy for the innocent girl she had been. "And then we come for you."

Ciaran stepped closer, his hand a steadying weight on my shoulder. I didn't glance at him, but his touch anchored me, gave me strength I wasn't sure I possessed anymore.

I stared Ebony down, watching her unravel before me.

And for the first time, I felt a flicker of power in the ashes of everything she'd taken from me.

"And when we catch you," I said, the words coming out like ice, "you're dead."

THE SHADOW

The dawn filtering through Darkmoor forest felt jarring, too bright for the weight of the moment. My every step was slower than hers, my body aching from more than just my injuries.

Ava glanced back at me again, concern flickering in her eyes, but I shook my head with a faint smile. She didn't need to worry.

She thought my lagging pace was because of my swollen eye or the sharp pain in my ribs, but that wasn't it. Not entirely.

I was holding back on purpose. I needed these few moments to watch her—to memorize the way she moved through the forest, her fingertips brushing moss on ancient trees, her face lifting toward the lace of branches and the sky beyond.

She looked so young, so light, so free. And I wanted to keep that image of her, to burn it into my memory before everything changed.

I stayed just behind her, letting the dewy leaves brush

against me, grounding me in the moment. The birdsong rising in the distance felt like a cruel serenade.

Eventually, she reached the edge of the grove near the passagetomb entrance, her figure bathed in light as her fingertips left the last tree. She took a few steps into the clearing before she noticed my absence.

When she turned back, silhouetted by the sun, I almost forgot how to breathe.

She was radiant—stronger than I'd ever seen her. And somehow, I knew the frightened girl who had walked into Blackthorn all those years ago was gone. She stood in the light, fearless, her future ahead of her.

I could almost see the childlike shadow of her past lingering in the woods beside me, and I knew it would stay with me, not her.

She didn't need it anymore. She didn't need me.

"Ciaran?" Ava called, her voice gentle but questioning. "Are you alright?"

I couldn't speak at first, my chest tightening with emotions I didn't dare name.

When she moved to come back to me, I finally found my voice. "I'm fine, rabbit."

But even as the words left my mouth, I felt a tremor run through me.

Ava stepped closer, peering into the shadows where I stood.

"You're trembling," she said, concern deepening.

When she reached for me, I instinctively stepped back, leaning heavily against the nearest tree.

She rushed forward, her hands on me, and I closed my eyes against the warmth of her touch.

It was too much—too much to hold her when I knew I had to let her go.

"Let me help you," she urged, trying to slip an arm under my shoulder. "It's not far now."

I pushed her away, not trusting myself to stay steady if she kept touching me.

"Goodbyes are never easy, are they?" I managed, forcing a faint smile.

"What? No." Ava's head shook violently, tears welling in her eyes. "*No.*"

Her refusal felt like a dagger, but I couldn't falter now. When she leaned into me, resting her ear against my chest, I gripped the back of her sweater tightly, grounding myself in her presence one last time.

"I know you've chosen Ty," I whispered, the words tasting like ash.

She shook her head, but I held her close, not allowing her to meet my gaze.

"You've chosen him," I repeated, quieter this time, as if saying it aloud would finally make me believe it.

I rested my bruised and bloodied cheek against the crown of her head, breathing in the faint, familiar scent of jasmine shampoo. The fragrance was bittersweet—a tether to the love I couldn't keep, and the goodbye I wasn't ready to say.

But that wasn't the only reason I held her this way. I couldn't bear to meet her gaze. Those gentle, heartbroken eyes would undo me, strip away the last fragments of resolve holding me together.

"Say it," I murmured, my voice barely louder than the rustle of the leaves around us.

Her voice came, muffled and hesitant against my jacket. "Do I really have to?"

I closed my eyes, swallowing the lump in my throat. I didn't want to hurt her any more than I already had. This wasn't some cruel test, some twisted punishment to satisfy the darker corners of my soul. It wasn't even about me clinging to pain like a lifeline.

I just needed to know. To hear it. To understand that it wasn't a moment of confusion or desperation clouding her mind. That it was real, undeniable, and *final*.

I didn't answer her, but my silence spoke volumes.

It was the same language we'd always shared. When midnight shadows stretched between us, words had always been secondary. Our silences—they had spoken first.

And now, in this moment, my silence was a plea. A surrender. A final request for the truth.

Her breath hitched as she finally said the words. "I've chosen Ty."

A part of me shattered, but another part of me was strangely numb, as though my heart had prepared for this all along.

I nodded, holding her for a moment longer before gently pushing her away.

She didn't resist this time, wrapping her arms around herself as she stepped back.

For a moment, we stood in silence, the sunlight creeping farther into the grove.

When I finally spoke, my voice was quiet. "I wonder if there's a world where I could've been enough for you."

"Ciaran—"

"I know there isn't," I said, shaking my head. "But it's nice to think about, isn't it?"

Her gaze searched mine, and I saw the pain mirrored there.

"You gave yourself up to Ebony," she whispered.

I nodded. "Too little, too late, eh?"

She tried to protest, but I cut her off.

"It's okay. I understand. I always have." My voice cracked as I added, "You were his. You always were."

Her tears fell freely now, and I felt my own building behind my bruised eyes.

"It's time for you to go," I said softly, nodding toward the passagetomb entrance over her shoulder.

Ava's breath caught.

"Wait." Her voice wavered, brittle as the morning breeze. "Wait, this isn't goodbye, is it? Not like a real goodbye."

I forced a smile, but it was a weak, unconvincing thing, and I could see her fear deepen.

Fidgeting with the hem of my jacket—still stiff with dried blood—I replied, "It's just something people say. We can say it, too."

"But…" She bit into her lower lip, her eyes darting across my face as though trying to read my thoughts. "Where will you go?"

The breeze stirred the surrounding trees, their rustling a quiet whisper against the weight of her question. It felt cruel almost, how the sunlight warmed the earth, promising renewal while everything between us cracked and crumbled.

I steeled myself, drawing a hard line with my mouth. "I know the name of every single rotten one of them. Most would have fled before the authorities caught up to them. Their victims deserve… justice."

My words were calm, deliberate, but I saw her flinch as if I'd raised my voice.

Her wide, searching eyes darted between mine, her brow furrowed. She was looking for the man she had known—the man who would never survive what lay ahead.

Ava's voice dropped to a whisper. "You're going after the Sochai."

I didn't respond. I didn't have to.

The silence stretched between us, heavy and suffocating, as she wrapped her arms tightly around herself, shivering. "That's a long, dark road to take, Ciaran."

I laughed bitterly, the sound sharp and jagged.

"To take?" I repeated, my voice cracking with something between anger and resignation. "I've never left it. I've been walking this dark path since the day Adam Donahue dragged a beautiful little girl into the shadows of Blackthorn Hall."

My fists clenched at the memory. I didn't say the rest—that I hoped this journey would finally end it. That I wanted, needed, to sever myself from the darkness that bound me. To burn it all to the ground, every last piece of my father's legacy.

Ava's voice softened. "And after?"

Her question hit me like a punch to the chest.

She was looking at me with those wide, hopeful eyes, so much like the frightened girl I'd fallen in love with. It was almost enough to make me lie. To spin a sweet, comforting fiction.

But I couldn't. Ty had rubbed off on me more than I cared to admit.

"If I were a stronger man…" I hesitated, my gentle smile faltering as I stared at the ground. "I'd come back."

"No," Ava began, her voice rising with protest, but I raised a hand to stop her.

"It would be too painful, Ava. Being around you two together… happy. It would be like burning up beside the sun." The bitterness in my voice was unintentional, but I couldn't take it back.

Her lips parted, but whatever words she might have offered, she kept to herself. Compassion flickered in her tear-filled eyes, a mercy I didn't deserve.

Raising my gaze, I forced myself to look directly at her. "But I will always be watching."

A tear wobbled on her chin, glinting like crystal in the morning sun.

"My shadow. My Scáth," she whispered, her voice a broken thread of sound.

"I love you," I said, the words agony to speak, but I couldn't leave her without saying them.

Of all the daggers I had plunged into myself—this was the one that twisted deepest.

And I'll always love you—from the shadows. These were the words I felt, the truth I held in my chest, but I left them unsaid.

Ava was too overcome with emotion to reply, her mouth opening and closing as if every word failed her.

"It's okay," I murmured.

I knew what it felt like to be choked by the inadequacy

of language. To find words incapable of carrying the weight of love, of sorrow, of goodbye.

If I'd found the right words sooner… perhaps. But no. I couldn't drown in what-ifs. Not yet. Not until she was gone.

"Promise me," I said, my voice steady even as my heart cracked. "Promise me you'll look after him for me."

"Right," she said, laughing weakly through her tears but failing to hide the emotion in her voice.

We shared a quiet moment then, a rare and precious understanding passing between us without the need for words.

"I promise," she whispered at last.

I nodded, more to myself than her. It was time to let go. Time to set her free and walk into the darkness that awaited me.

"Go," I said, nodding toward the tomb, my voice barely above a whisper.

Ava hesitated, glancing back at me with wide, tear-filled eyes.

She took a step closer instead, pressing up onto her tiptoes to kiss me one last time. Her lips were soft, cool against my bruised mouth, like a balm and a blade all at once.

When she stepped back, her hands clutched desperately at her chest, and I clenched my fists behind my back to keep from reaching for her.

"I love you, Ciaran," she said, her voice breaking.

I closed my eyes, unable to speak.

Instead, I mouthed the only words I could. *I know.*

And then she turned and walked away, leaving me in the shadows as she stepped into the light.

If I cared more about preserving what little was left of my heart, I would have turned away too. Spared myself the agony of watching her disappear, step by step, into a world where I could no longer follow.

But I was selfish. I stole one last moment, one last image of her, burning it into my memory with the kind of desperation of a man who knows he's losing everything.

I stood rooted there, dying a little more with every footfall, with every sway of her dark hair in the sunlight.

Searing it into my mind, the way the morning kissed her skin, the lightness of her steps, the way her shoulders squared as she hurried toward Ty, toward her future.

This was the vision that would haunt me, the one that would rise unbidden every night when sleep refused to come. The memory I would clutch to my chest like a lifeline and a curse.

And even though she was walking away, leaving me to the shadows, I knew she meant it.

She loved me, but she *belonged* to Ty.

TY

The Sochai guards thought they were breaking me. When they shoved my face against the cold iron bars, when their fists cracked against my ribs, when my blood slicked the damp stone floor beneath me—they thought they were inflicting pain.

But how could they know that physical pain was like a fading bruise?

Because the worst agony I'd ever endured had already hollowed me out.

I had lost her. Ava.

I had lost the love of *my* life. Because I wasn't *hers*.

I lay on the dirty cot in the corner of the cell, cradling my side where the worst of the bruising was, the moldy dampness of the walls pressing in.

A trickle of water from somewhere above kept time with the throb of my battered body.

My thoughts returned to her, as they always did. Not to her absence, but to the life she now had—happy and free.

That thought was my mantra. The thing that kept me alive for one more second. One more breath.

I told myself I could bear this.

My brother had borne it before me. He'd accepted this dark, damp fate, and now so would I.

It felt right somehow, sitting here where he had, staring at the same jagged cracks in the ceiling.

I remembered his resignation, his voice raw as he called my name while being dragged away. I'd replayed that moment so many times that my throat tightened every time.

This is your place, Ty. You were meant to be caged so they could go free.

If my message was received and if Ciaran was able to find what I suspected he might, I could be released from this cell.

But knowing that Ava had chosen Ciaran, it made little to no difference to me.

No matter where I was, no matter how free, if I wasn't with Ava, I would remain in prison.

No bars or walls could trap me worse than the knowledge that she had chosen him.

I lay back on the ragged cot, letting my swollen eye drift shut. My body ached, but it was nothing compared to the numbness spreading in my chest.

I reached for the only relief I could find—memories of her.

The images flickered through my mind like a cruel slideshow.

Her smile illuminated by the blue light of the fridge, her silvery shoes swinging as she sat on the counter.

The gentle sway of her hair as the summer breeze carried in the scent of mint through the kitchen window.

The way her lips curved around a giggle as water from the glass in her hand teetered dangerously near the edge.

I could still hear her voice, soft and slurred from too much alcohol that night.

"Strawberries," she'd said dreamily, plucking one from the bowl I offered her. "I want a strawberry patch."

I'd fed her strawberries.

And she'd told me her dream life. Our dream life. Or at least at the time I thought it was.

The country house by the sea surrounded by a pine forest. The wraparound porch. The strawberry patch. The light and airy rooms with blue drapes. The antique writing desk beside a sunny window. A peaked ceiling in our bedroom. Her library filled with shelves like driftwood and couches the color of sea glass.

For years, I'd held on to that moment as if it were gospel. I'd built her a life in my mind, in stone, in reality. I'd built her a house by the sea, a dream life that would cradle her every want, every need.

And now, that house would stand empty, haunted by the ghost of a man she never truly loved.

A sharp creak of metal jolted me from my thoughts. The heavy door to the cellblock groaned open, and the sound of footsteps echoed against the stone corridor.

I didn't move. I didn't need to. It was the guards, here to take their pound of flesh. They could take whatever they wanted. I had nothing left to give.

But then the steps slowed.

They were lighter than a guard's. Deliberate. Hesitant. My heart gave a single, sharp jolt.

The lock of my cell rattled.

My pulse quickened despite myself, though I kept my face pressed to the wall. I refused to hope. Refused to let myself believe.

Then I smelled jasmine.

My chest seized, and I bit down hard on the inside of my cheek to stop the sound that wanted to rip free. It wasn't possible. It couldn't be.

Do not believe. Do not hope.

A hand gripped my shoulder, warm and soft, and I jerked as if burned. I turned slowly, not trusting my eyes or the dim light. And then I saw her.

Ava.

The bulb above cast shadows on her face, but the trembling of her chin and the sheen of tears in her eyes were unmistakable.

"Are you real?" My voice cracked, a hoarse whisper.

Her tears fell faster. She reached out, cupping my cheek, her touch featherlight against the swelling there.

"Ty," she breathed, and my name was a prayer on her lips. "We did it. It's over. The Sochai, they're finished, thanks to you."

I couldn't speak. I couldn't breathe. My chest ached with the force of it—of her, here, against every rational thought.

Then she leaned in and kissed me. Her lips brushed mine, hesitant, desperate, grounding me in a way that made the room spin. I should have pulled away. I should have told her to leave, to go back to the man she'd chosen. But I couldn't.

When she pulled back, her forehead rested against mine.

Her voice broke as she whispered, "Mhaor, I've come to free you."

The moment Ava and I stepped outside the tomb, the weight of everything that had happened seemed to rush over me all at once.

The dawn was breaking, casting the forest in a pale, ghostly light, and yet it all felt muted compared to the woman standing beside me.

Her hand brushed against mine, hesitant but deliberate. I turned to her, ready to ask if she was alright, but the look in her eyes stopped me. It wasn't the weariness I expected, or even the lingering fear. There was something softer there. Something I hadn't dared let myself hope to see.

"I have one last gift for you," she said, her voice quiet but steady.

A gift? My heart clenched painfully in my chest.

After everything, she was still thinking of me. Of giving *me* something. Didn't she know that the only thing I'd ever wanted was *her*?

She reached into her pocket, her movements slow, deliberate, as if she were carrying something fragile.

When she pulled her hand free, the sun caught on it, the large diamond glittering like the first star of evening.

The engagement ring I bought her.

My knees nearly buckled as I remembered what I told her. *Return it if you want me to propose to you for real.*

My heart thudded against my ribs as I searched her face for an answer, any clue as to what this meant.

"W-what does this mean?" I asked, my voice hoarse, barely above a whisper, not daring to hope.

Her lips quirked into the faintest of smiles, and she stepped closer, holding the ring between us.

"It means," she began, her voice soft but steady, "that I have a story to tell you."

I didn't move, didn't breathe, terrified of breaking whatever spell had brought us here, to this impossible moment.

My entire body felt locked in place, every muscle coiled with tension, as if the wrong movement could shatter everything.

Ava's fingers traced the edge of the ring, and the way her eyes lingered on it made me ache.

"Many years ago," she said, her lips curving into a faint, almost wistful smile, "I fell in love with a boy. A boy who came to rescue me when I needed him most."

My breath hitched, and I wanted to speak, but the words lodged in my throat.

"I told him about my dream house," she continued, her voice thick with emotion. "About the big library with a view of the sea, driftwood shelves, sea-glass couches. A strawberry patch out back. I told him *everything*. And that night, I fell in love with him."

I closed my eyes, remembering that night like it had just happened. Her thighs on either side of my waist as I stood before her, legs dangling from the kitchen island, her voice filling the air as she painted a picture of a life so vivid I could almost taste it, her lips brushing my fingers as she bit the strawberries I offered her.

Ava's voice broke through my memory. "And for years, I thought that boy was his brother."

I opened my eyes to find her staring up at me, tears glistening on her lashes. "But all this time, it was you."

My breath left me in a rush, and I fought to keep myself steady.

She reached out, taking my hand and pressing the ring into my palm. "I choose *you*."

I couldn't stop it.

My knees gave out, and I sank to the ground in front of her, clutching the ring like a lifeline. I tipped my head back, looking up at her like she was the sun itself, blinding and impossible and everything I'd ever wanted.

"I vowed my life to protecting you," I said, my voice shaking. "But, my little hummingbird, it turns out you don't need protecting. You never did. So, please…"

I swallowed hard as I clutched at her hands and offered her this ring. "Let me vow my life instead to holding you close when you can't sleep and chasing away your nightmares before they find you. To challenging you when you're too stubborn to see sense, but always trusting you to know your own strength. To making you laugh, even when you're angry with me. To remembering how you take your coffee and to building every dream you didn't know you had. Marry me."

For a moment, Ava was still, her expression unreadable again, and my heart stopped. Had I said too much? Was it too soon?

And then she laughed, a soft, breathy sound that stole the tension from the air.

"Silly, Mhaor," she said, her lips curving into a smile that lit up the world.

Her nickname for me struck me, and my heart stuttered in my chest. I stared at her, caught between hope and disbelief.

"I've always been yours," she said, her smile widening, her tears spilling freely now. "*Yes.*"

The world spun, and I surged to my feet, slipping the ring onto her finger before pulling her into my arms.

My heart felt like it was going to burst, an overwhelming surge of joy and disbelief crashing over me like a tidal wave.

As I kissed her, laughter escaped me—deep, raw, and unrestrained. God, when was the last time I'd laughed like this? It felt foreign, almost startling, but so damn right. Like something buried deep inside me had finally clawed its way to the surface after years of suffocating silence.

Her fingers curled into my hair, her breath warm and steady against my skin. I closed my eyes, letting the moment anchor itself deep inside me.

Ava had freed me—*truly* freed me.

AVA

Afew weeks later, out on our country estate, with the smell of the salt and pines in the air, the officiant pronounced us husband and wife just as the sky was turning golden.

"I love you more," Ty whispered as he leaned down and kissed me.

His lips moving against mine, soft but firm, our first kiss as husband and wife, it felt like the entire world stilled for that moment.

My heart raced, my breath hitched, and for a moment, it felt as though the sheer magnitude of my love might consume me entirely, leaving nothing but the unrelenting ache of feeling something so vast, so infinite.

When we finally pulled apart, his expression was a beautiful storm of emotion. Pride, love, disbelief—it was all there, etched into the lines of his handsome face.

And his blue eyes—those eyes I'd fallen in love with before I even realized they were *his*—were glistening.

Something had changed in Ty the moment I chose him,

something I never expected. The mask he so often wore, that cold, calculating exterior that had kept him alive all these years, began to crumble.

Slowly, the Ty beneath—the one who loved deeply, fiercely, possessively, who built me a home with my every youthful wish, who cherished me with every fiber of his being—was emerging.

Lisa sniffled audibly behind me, breaking the moment.

I turned to see her dabbing at her eyes with the hem of her peach bridesmaid dress.

"Don't start, bish," I whispered with a laugh, but my own voice wavered.

Lisa's tears turned into a sob, and she lightly punched my shoulder. "You heartless bish!"

We both burst into tears—happy, uncontrollable tears.

Only one shadow marred the perfection of the day as I glanced over Ty's shoulder to where no one stood.

The ache in my heart was sudden and sharp, but before it could overwhelm me, a whisper of leather and spice brushed past on the breeze.

I looked toward the edge of the pines and thought, for just a moment, I saw a figure—tall and shadowy—standing among the trees.

That night, I woke with a start, my skin prickling as though I were being watched.

My heart skipped a beat, the stillness of our bedroom in the house Ty built for me pressing down on me like a heavy blanket.

Ty wasn't beside me. The empty space in the bed, the faint warmth still lingering where he had been, made the feeling worse.

"Mhaor?" I called softly, my voice cutting through the silence as I slipped out of bed.

The cool air kissed my skin, raising goosebumps against the thin slip I wore. The shadows of the room felt too heavy, too alive, and as I turned, my breath caught.

Red writing streaked across the mirror. The words were sharp, deliberate.

"Ready or not..."

My stomach twisted, a mix of dread and anticipation curling low in my belly.

Before I could process, a crash shattered the silence.

I jumped, my heart slamming into my ribs as my head whipped toward the sound.

It came from downstairs.

I rushed out of the bedroom, feet padding quickly over the cold wooden floor.

I gripped the banister tightly as I crept down the stairs, my fingers brushing against the worn wood as I strained to hear anything—any sound, any movement.

But the house was silent. Too silent.

My pulse thundered in my ears as I reached the base of the stairs, the faint creak of the back door swinging open and slamming against the frame sending a chill down my spine.

The door swayed on its hinges, the night breeze pushing it back and forth. I swallowed hard, forcing myself to move toward it, to close it.

My eyes flicked around the living room as I passed, the

furniture sitting in eerie stillness, their silhouettes strange and unfamiliar in the dim light. The clock on the mantel ticked faintly, each second stretching longer than it should.

Every instinct screamed at me to turn around, to go back upstairs and lock myself in the bedroom. But I couldn't. The unease gnawed at me, demanding answers, driving me forward.

Just as I reached for the door handle, I heard it.

A voice behind me, low and taunting.

"Run..."

I froze for a split second, every nerve in my body on high alert.

And then I ran.

The cool night air hit me as I burst through the door and into the yard, making my nipples harden. My bare feet pounded against the damp earth, and I cast a quick glance over my shoulder.

He was coming for me.

My warden and my stalker, his tall broad frame cloaked in shadow, the glint of moonlight catching the half skeleton mask covering his face.

His icy eyes locked on mine, and the dark thrill in them mirrored the surge of adrenaline coursing through me.

My fear and excitement tangled together in a dizzying rush. I sprinted toward the pine forest, my breath coming fast and sharp, heat rushing into my core.

The tall trees loomed ahead, their silhouettes stark against the night sky, a haven and a trap all at once.

The sound of his footfalls grew louder behind me, each one steady and deliberate, like a predator toying with its prey.

I pushed myself harder, the pounding of my heart urging me forward, a manic giggle trapped in my chest.

The forest enveloped me, the air smelling like pine and damp earth. The ground was uneven, twigs snapping beneath my feet as I darted between the trees.

But no matter how fast I ran, he was faster.

I felt his presence just behind me, the air shifting as he closed the gap. The thrill of the chase still hummed in my veins, but now it was mixed with need—dark and dangerous, intoxicating, and impossible to deny.

And then—impact.

Ty tackled me to the ground, his weight pinning me as we tumbled through the underbrush.

He pinned me to the ground underneath him and a gasp tore from my lips, and for a moment, all I could hear was the pounding of my heart and the rough sound of his breathing.

He loomed over me, his intense eyes over the skeleton mask crinkling with dark hunger as he wrapped his hand around my throat and squeezed, stopping me from screaming for help.

Even if I could scream, Ty purchased so much land around our house that no one would hear me anyway.

I was here alone with him and helpless.

He used his knees to kick out my legs, exposing me for him, my slip riding up around my waist.

As I struggled for air, clawing at his hand, he calmly unzipped his black pants with his free hand and pulled out his hard, thick cock.

Only then did he loosen his grip on my throat.

I sucked in air.

He tore my panties off me and stuffed them into my mouth.

He thrust his cock into me, splitting me open, my scream cut off by his hand clamping down over my mouth, my tongue coated in my musky wetness from my panties.

He fucked me as I thrashed underneath him, hips bucking for more as I tried to fight him off, leaves and sticks scraping my back and bare ass.

Because our childhood pastime had become our favorite fucked-up game.

Dots sparkled in front of my eyes as I fought for air, as my orgasm crashed over me. He let out a feral growl as he slammed into me, filling me with his cum.

And with the promise of our future babies. I didn't have my implant in anymore, after all.

I sagged into the dirt, chest heaving as his hand slipped from my mouth, pulling my panties out, and he rested his forehead on mine.

"I love you more, hummingbird," he whispered from behind his mask.

"I love you, mhaor," I whispered back.

AVA

A few months later...

I woke to the sense of being watched.

My eyes adjusted to the soft light of the moon filtering through the gauzy curtains.

Beside me, Ty lay sprawled, his arm slung possessively across my waist even in sleep. His face was peaceful, and my heart thrilled at the sight of him, the word "husband" reverberating in my chest like a melody.

My gaze drifted to the balcony doors where one of them was ajar, and the breeze carried the unmistakable scent of the sea, mingled with the faintest trace of something else.

Some*one* I knew all too well.

I slipped from the bed, careful not to wake Ty, and padded barefoot across the room. Pushing through the fluttering curtains, I stepped out into the cool night air.

There, by the latticed ivy, he stood. My shadow.

I didn't know whether to run to him, curse him for coming, or beg for forgiveness I didn't deserve.

He stepped forward, and the moonlight revealed his face. His expression, so full of conflict and pain, twisted something deep inside me. His torment mirrored my own.

My breath hitched, and the chill in the air seeped into my skin.

Ciaran must have seen it as a shiver because he whispered, "It's cold. I shouldn't have brought you out here."

"Scáth," I whispered, reaching out to him, my hand hovering in the space between us.

He stepped back, retreating into the shadows with a sad smile that tore through me like a knife.

"I just wanted to make sure you were happy," he said, his voice low, almost lost in the crashing waves below.

The truth clawed at my throat. I was happy—terribly, painfully happy.

And the weight of that truth, that I had chosen happiness at the cost of his, was almost too much to bear.

But I couldn't lie to him.

"I am," I admitted, my voice breaking.

Tears blurred my vision, and I didn't see him move. Suddenly, he was there, his lips brushing my cheek, so soft it was almost a memory.

When I blinked, he was gone.

I spun, searching the misty corners of the balcony, the potted plants Ty and I had tended together, the dark lattice leading to the strawberry patch below. There was no trace of him.

I leaned over the railing, desperate to catch a glimpse of his retreating figure, but the garden was empty, the shadows empty of the one I could never hold. Only the wind remained, carrying the echoes of his presence.

As I gripped the railing, something fluttered in my hand. A piece of paper, so light I hadn't even realized it was there.

It could only have come from Ciaran, but I hadn't felt a thing.

But what message could he possibly have for me?

Ciaran's path to hunt down every last member of the Sochai was shrouded in blood and darkness.

He had chosen it, embraced it, and it terrified me to think of what cruel or heart-wrenching truth he might leave behind.

My heart thudded painfully against my ribs, each beat reverberating with dread. What if his words were meant to sever the last thread between us? Or worse, what if they carried a truth so unbearable it would break me completely?

The note in my hand felt impossibly heavy, like it held the weight of every secret, every sacrifice he had ever made.

My fingers trembled as I held it, the edges whispering against my skin in the cool breeze. I hesitated, fear locking my chest tight.

For a brief, fleeting moment, I wanted to crumple it up and throw it into the sea—to let it drift away with the mist and take with it whatever pain it contained.

But I couldn't. This was Ciaran. Whatever he had to say, I had to face it.

With a deep breath, I unfolded it slowly, as though it might detonate in my hands. The faint creases gave way, revealing the words inside.

They were written in tight, looping letters.

Three words. Just three.

And they stopped my heart cold.

Then the weight of them—the *meaning*—stole the breath from my lungs and sent my heart into a wild, erratic rhythm.

484

Liath is alive.

EPILOGUE 1

Several years later...

Our beautiful baby girl was born with her father's eyes and her mother's strength. Her tiny face was a perfect blend of us, her mother's mouth and chin, her father's inquisitive gaze.

She came into this world through love—messy, tangled, imperfect love—and when I held her against my chest for the first time, her velvety skin warm and new, I understood with unshakable certainty that love didn't compete for space in your heart, nor did it push aside what was already there. It didn't carve out its own hollow to fill.

Love *grew*.

Ty's palm rested on her impossibly tiny head, his touch so gentle it made my heart ache.

"She's perfect," he whispered, his voice rough with emotion.

"She's ours," I replied, barely able to speak through the lump in my throat.

We named her Ciara, a name that carried the weight of all the love, loss, and redemption that had brought her here.

That night, Ty climbed into the narrow hospital bed with me, his arms wrapping around me as if holding me was the only thing keeping him steady.

I leaned into his warmth, our daughter sleeping peacefully in her bassinet beside us. Her tiny breaths were the sweetest sound I'd ever heard, a soothing melody in the quiet room.

Exhaustion claimed me, happiness too overwhelming to keep my eyes open, though I fought to steal one last glance at her before sleep pulled me under.

When I woke, the faint gray light of dawn seeped through the blinds, and a soft, sweet fragrance filled the air. It was familiar, so achingly familiar that for a moment, I thought I might still be dreaming.

My gaze dropped to the bedside table, and there it was: a single Belladonna lily, its pale-pink petals as soft and velvety as my daughter's skin.

Tears pricked my eyes as my chest tightened with an all-too-familiar ache.

Scáth.

I brushed a finger over the delicate bloom, my heart caught in a strange, bittersweet tangle of emotions.

I imagined him here in the quiet hours of the night, standing in the shadows, seeing what could never be his. How hard it must have been to witness Ty holding me in the way he had once dreamed, to see a baby that wasn't his.

My happiness would always carry this shadow. A corner

of my heart, dark and quiet, would always ache for the man whose only crime had been not being loved first.

And for that, I let a tear slip from my eyes—not just for him but with him.

The Belladonna lily was his message.

A silent declaration that he loved me still, loved every part of me, including the tiny life now entwined with ours. I lifted the flower to my nose, breathing in its sweet but deadly fragrance, and held it close as if it were him.

Carefully, I slipped from Ty's embrace, his warmth still lingering on my skin, and I crossed the room to Ciara's bassinet, my heart swelling at the sight of her.

The sunlight creeping through the blinds painted her tiny face in soft gold. She was so small, so perfect.

I traced a finger over her feathery hair, as dark as midnight, as dark as her father's, and I prayed it would stay that way.

She stirred slightly as I reached to lift her, her tiny fist uncurling just enough for me to notice something new on her wrist. My breath hitched.

A bracelet.

Its chain was impossibly fine, as delicate as spun silk, glinting faintly in the muted morning light. From it dangled a single charm—a rabbit.

I twisted it gently, letting it catch the soft rays filtering through the blinds. It was simple in its beauty, but the weight it carried was immeasurable.

A promise. A silent vow.

My shadow would protect my daughter with the same unyielding fierceness that he'd once protected me.

He would watch over her, unseen but ever-present, as he had always done for me.

The thought filled my heart with a bittersweet ache—a comfort wrapped in longing.

"You'll never be alone, little one," I whispered to Ciara, my voice thick with emotion. "Never."

I rocked her until the sun rose fully, casting its golden glow over everything—the flowers, the hospital room, and the bracelet on her tiny wrist. And in that light, I felt the weight of all my love, my sorrow, and my gratitude.

Ciaran might have been gone, but he would never truly leave us. Not while his love lingered in every shadow, in every whispered breeze, and now, in the tiny charm that would forever remind me of the boy who loved me in his own, unforgettable way.

As I swayed gently in the dim light, rocking my daughter and listening to her soft, even breaths, I couldn't help but imagine her running through the meadow outside our home, her laughter carrying over the sound of the sea.

I would watch her from the window at my writing desk, smiling as she darted away from her father chasing her among the wildflowers, free and joyful.

And, perhaps, from time to time... I'd see a shadow among the trees.

AVA

EPILOGUE 2

Many, many years later...

The ache of time had settled in my bones long before Ty's final days arrived, but nothing could have prepared me for the way it would feel to lose him.

Everything about the world felt muted. The beeping of the machines faded into a dull hum; the nurses' chatter outside the door was muffled and unimportant; even the recorded piano music—*Ava's Lullaby*—was just a faint melody that couldn't reach me.

All I could hear was the silence between us. A silence filled with the knowledge of what was coming.

His hand, fragile and cold, slipped out from beneath the pale-blue blanket. I hadn't realized he was awake until his fingers brushed mine, pulling me from my thoughts.

I forced a smile, weak and tired, as I raised his hand to my lips and kissed it.

His faded tattoos blurred against his wrinkled skin, a stark reminder of the years he'd sacrificed for me and of the life we'd built together.

If only I could go back. Do it all over again, from the very beginning. I wouldn't change a thing.

I just wanted *more*.

"I don't know what I'm going to do without you," I whispered, pressing my lips against his hand, holding it to my cheek as if I could anchor him here. "Mhaor, I don't want to be free."

He smiled faintly, his eyes distant, already halfway gone. His pinky traced the trembling line of my lips.

"Don't cry," he murmured. "I have one last gift for you."

My brow furrowed, confused. My eyes darted to the bedside table, searching for something—a box, a flower, a note—but there was nothing.

When I turned back to him, Ty wasn't looking at me anymore. His gaze fixed just over my shoulder, his smile softening into something deeper, something I hadn't seen in years.

Then a voice—so familiar even as age had roughened it —spoke from behind me. "Hello, brother. Did you miss me?"

My breath hitched. My heart thundered in my chest as I gripped Ty's hand tighter.

No.

It couldn't be true.

"Take care of her for me," Ty whispered to him, his voice so light, it felt like it was carried away with the rising dawn.

I froze, unable to turn, unable to look. The silence behind me grew heavy, like the weight of a sunrise waiting to break over the horizon.

He was there. I could feel it in the shift of the air, the quiet heat at my back.

My shadow had returned.

Tears filled my eyes as Ty's smile turned back to me, his strength fading fast. He brushed a strand of my gray-streaked hair behind my ear, his touch achingly tender.

I shook my head, words caught in my throat. Nothing I could say would be enough. Nothing could capture what he meant to me, what he'd always meant.

His hand slipped from my cheek, and I caught it, holding it against my chest as if I could keep him tethered to this world.

"It's *my* turn to watch over you from the shadows," Ty said, his voice barely more than a breath.

My sob escaped before I could stop it, raw and broken.

"I love you *more*, hummingbird."

And then he was gone.

I held his hand to my chest as his spirit slipped away, collapsing into myself as grief tore through me. I was lost, a ship adrift in an endless sea, the anchor of his presence gone.

Until warm, rough hands pulled me from my seat.

I turned, blinded by tears, and collapsed into his arms.

Ciaran held me tightly, his embrace steady and unyielding as I clung to him with all I had left.

Though the pain of Ty's loss was overwhelming, a fragile thread of hope flickered in the depths of my heart.

He was here.

And after all this time, now by my side.
My shadow had finally come home.

My dearest readers,
Thank you so much for coming with me on this journey.
Ava, Ty and Ciaran ripped my heart out with their story. I
know some of you might hate that they couldn't both be
with her—and trust me, I *tried* to force a why choose ending
—but my boys are stubborn. It was always *all or nothing*
with Ava.

*But wait, Sienna! What happened with Ty in prison with Eamon?
How did he escape? And WTH happened to Liath???*

Don't worry. The story isn't over…

**Grab your copy of an exclusive novella, Keeping Pretty:
subscribepage.io/keepingpretty**

Keeping Pretty

My secrets will destroy us

My nightmares are getting worse. And the secret I'm hiding
from Ava is eating me alive.
But my beautiful, stubborn wife won't let it go—even when
I punish her for it.
She's digging into my past. Into Skellig Mór prison.
Into *him*.

Eamon.

The man I owe my life to. The man I've tried to bury in the shadows of my soul.

And I fear when she finds out the truth, it will end us.

BOOKS BY SIENNA BLAKE

LOVELY BROKEN DOLL

Hunting Pretty

Catching Pretty

Claiming Pretty

Keeping Pretty ~ *(newsletter exclusive)*

DUBLIN INK

Dublin Ink

Dirty Ink

Dark Ink

Devilish Ink

IRISH KISS

Irish Kiss

Professor's Kiss

Fighter's Kiss

The Irish Lottery

My Brother's Girl

Player's Kiss

My Secret Irish Baby

ALL HER MEN

Three Irish Brothers

My Irish Kings

Royally Screwed

Cassidy Brothers

DARK ROMEO UNIVERSE

Dark Romeo (standalone)

Bound by Lies (#1)

Bound Forever (#2)

A GOOD WIFE

Beautiful Revenge

Mr. Blackwell's Bride

BILLIONAIRES DOWN UNDER

(with Sarah Willows)

To Have & To Hoax

The Paw-fect Mix-up

Riding His Longboard

Maid For You

I Do (Hate You)

Man Toy (Newsletter Exclusive)

Paper Dolls (standalone)

ABOUT SIENNA

USA Today bestseller Sienna Blake writes angsty and dark romance reads. When she's not busy writing about morally grey villains and the strong women who bring them to their knees, she spends her time reading or binge-watching mafia shows, hanging off aerial silks, or adding to her personal reverse harem of Irish men.

9 780645 494082